AS THOUGH SHE
WERE SLEEPING

Also by Elias Khoury in English translation

The Little Mountain (1977)
The Gates of the City (1981)
White Masks (1981)
The Journey of Little Gandhi (1989)
The Kingdom of Strangers (1993)
Gate of the Sun (1998)
Yalo (MacLehose Press, 2009)

Elias Khoury

AS THOUGH SHE WERE SLEEPING

Translated from the Arabic by
Humphrey Davies

MACLEHOSE PRESS
QUERCUS·LONDON

The events, characters, places and names in this novel are creatures of the imagination. Should any resemblance be found between the novel's characters and real persons, or between the places and events of the novel and real places and events, such resemblance is purely coincidental, a product of the workings of the imagination, and devoid of intent.

First published in Great Britain in 2011 by
MacLehose Press
an imprint of Quercus
21 Bloomsbury Square
London WC1A 2NS

First published in Arabic as *Ka annabâ nâ ima* by Dâr-al-Adâb, Beirut, 2007
Copyright © Elias Khoury, 2007

English translation copyright © 2011 by Humphrey Davies

A CIP catalogue record for this book is available
from the British Library

ISBN (HB) 978 0 85705 051 9
ISBN (TPB) 978 0 85705 052 6

10 9 8 7 6 5 4 3 2 1

Designed and typeset in Perpetua by Libanus Press, Marlborough
Printed and bound in Great Britain by Clays Ltd, St Ives plc

Translator's Note

Resonances and continuities between members of the Holy Family and characters in the novel have persuaded me to use the Arabic forms of the names of the former in this translation. Thus the names familiar to English readers as Mary, Joseph and Jesus are rendered here as Maryam, Youssef and Eesa. Other biblical personages, however, have been given their English names, to spare the reader having to puzzle out, for example, that "the Old Hawa'" is "the Old Eve".

The reader may find it useful to know that the Church of Our Lady of the Fright (Kanisat Sayyidat al-Rajfa) in Nazareth is so named because Mary felt afraid there when the congregation tried to throw the young Jesus off a precipice after he had preached in a synagogue (Luke 4:29). The church, which was built by Franciscans in 1882 and is now in ruins, commands a panorama of the area.

Glossary

abaya	Kind of cloak
al Ahrar	Name of a newspaper (*The Liberals*)
alif	The first letter of the Arabic alphabet
dar	Large room forming the primary unit of traditional houses
dhikr	Ceremony performed by Sufis in which the name of God is repeated rhythmically in order to induce a sense of His presence
firman	Decree issued by the Ottoman sultan
hajj, hajjeh	"Pilgrim": honorific form of address and reference used for men/women who have performed the pilgrimage to Mecca (if Muslims) or Jerusalem (if Christians)
kaf	The twenty-second letter of the Arabic alphabet
khawaja	Honorific used for men of a certain social status
kibbeh arnabiyyeh	*Kibbeh* (patties or croquettes of chopped meat mixed with bulgur or rice) with citrus sauce (to which lamb shanks and chickpeas are sometimes added); it does not contain rabbit (*arnab*)
kibbeh nayyeh	Raw chopped lamb or beef mixed with fine bulgur and spices
labaneh	Strained yoghurt
leewan	Enclosed portico attached to the *dar*
mashiach	Messiah (Hebrew)
naskh	A widely used form of Arabic script

Death is a long sleep from which there is no waking,
Sleep a short death on which resurrection follows quick.
— Abu al Ala al Maarri

The maiden is not dead, but sleepeth.
— Luke 8:52

THE FIRST NIGHT

Meelya's lids parted to reveal eyes veiled in drowsiness. Then she decided to close them again and continue with her dream. She saw a small white candle, its pale flame flickering in the fog. Mansour was carrying the candle and walking ahead of the taxi, the air buffeting his long coat, but she couldn't make out her husband's features. Reaching for the glass of water that was usually on the bedside table, she didn't find it. She was thirsty, the dryness splintering against her tongue and the back of her throat. She pulled her arm from beneath her head on the pillow to stop the tingling running along it to her neck, turned over onto her back and reached for the glass of water, but didn't find the table. Shaking herself, she found that she was sitting up. She leant back, resting her head against the wooden edge of the headboard. Where had it gone, the white wall against which she used to lean her head, feeling the cracked paint flaking beneath her long hair and becoming entangled in it? As she crossed her arms over her chest, they touched her naked breasts. She was overcome by fear, and a chill crept into her thighs. When she reached towards them to still their trembling, her palm touched their nakedness. She moved it upwards, to the base of her belly, and felt cold blood congealing there.

"This is marriage," she said in a low voice, closing her eyes again.

In her mind's eye Meelya retained an image of Dahr el Baydar in the form of a silhouette. She could see her husband, Mansour Hourani, carrying a small candle, walking ahead of the car in his black bridegroom's suit and wearing the long olive-green coat. The young woman sat in the back seat in her white bridal outfit, cloaked in darkness, looking at the driver's bald head, which glittered with dandruff. On reaching the city of Nazareth in Galilee, she would tell her husband that his image had imprinted itself upon her eyes in the form of a black ghost tottering in front of the car, whose headlights could not pierce the thick fog covering the heights of Dahr el Baydar on that freezing night.

At 3.00 in the afternoon on Saturday, 12 January, 1946, Meelya and Mansour were married at the Church of the Angel Mikhail, Reverend Boulos Saba officiating. When the ceremony was over, the bride and groom stood at the church door surrounded by members of Meelya's family to receive felicitations. Tears poured from Meelya's eyes and she couldn't see the well-wishers; the tears leapt from her eyes as if they were flying, before coming to land on her white cheeks. Mansour, his thin lips stretched into a broad smile revealing small white teeth, paid no attention to his bride's weeping until he heard her mother scolding her: "Shame on you, Meelya, you'd think it was a funeral. It's a wedding." But when the last guests had left, carrying their silver boxes of sugar-coated almonds, and only family members remained in the courtyard, the mother went over to her daughter and clasped her to her chest, and the two women were convulsed with weeping. Finally, the mother pushed her daughter away, saying, "That's enough, daughter, before you break my heart. You leave the crying to me. You have to be happy." The bride smiled, choking back her tears, and the mother wept again, only finally to break into a ululation of joy. Meelya's brothers surrounded the couple. The bride watched her brother Moussa's pupils shrink to pinpoints and sensed danger there. Without thinking, she raised her hand to shield her husband's face and protect him from her brother's gaze.

Meelya opened her eyes and saw only darkness. She decided to continue with the strange dream, feeling secure despite her fear. The dreams had returned at last. In them, Meelya would see herself as a seven-year-old girl, dark-complexioned and with short, curly hair, running among people and seeing everything; when she got up in the morning, she would tell as much as she wished of them, and everyone would regard her with fear and amazement because her dreams were like prophecies that always came true. Here, though, in this strange bed and in the midst of the darkness piled above her eyes, she dreamt of herself as a 24-year-old lying naked on a bed that was not her bed, her head resting on a pillow that was not her pillow.

Meelya opened her eyes to organize her dream. When she went back to sleep, all she could see were two eyes opened onto the darkness.

She opened her eyes and saw her eyes and was frightened.

The man leant back against the trunk of the china-bark tree and told her that the whites of her eyes were suffused with a pale blue, lending them a touch of the divine. He said her white skin, her long neck, her honey-coloured eyes and her chestnut hair falling over her shoulders had made him come from his distant city to marry her. He said that he loved her.

Where had he said those things?

And why, when she awoke from this dream, did the dream remain, so that all she saw were two eyes opened onto the darkness?

3

Meelya decided to get up and fetch a glass of water. She saw her white nakedness reflected in the mirrors of her eyes, so she shut them and decided to ask the man sleeping beside her on the bed, his back to her, to come back to the car because she was afraid for him. She shut her eyes and saw herself sliding into the white cloud. She saw a woman lying naked, a car window misted with breath and a man walking ahead of the car carrying a flickering candle as though, in his black suit and olive-green coat, he were burning up the fog. She forgot her thirst.

Silence, a naked woman, a car moving with extreme slowness through the fog, a driver bent over the steering wheel trying to make out the road through glass covered with white spots, and a man engulfed in white fog walking ahead of the car, a white candle in his hand.

The candle goes out, or so it seems to her. The man halts in the middle of the road and opens his coat, as though trying to shelter the candle to relight it. His back bends like a bow and his coat flaps in the wind, but the man remains where he is, unmoving. The driver's breath rises. He opens the car window, sticks his head out and shouts something inaudible.

Meelya is cold, and a fierce pain pierces her belly. She tries to cover her body, wrapping the brown coat around herself and clasping her arms across her chest. She hears her teeth chattering. Covering herself with the coat and the darkness, she thinks that the candle is useless. She decides to get out of the car and tell the man that the headlamps cannot possibly pierce the fog, so what good is a candle? She will tell him to come back to the car, but she doesn't dare to get out because she is naked and cold.

Who put the bed in the car? And why was she naked?

She usually wears a long blue nightdress and doesn't take off her bra. She first decided not to remove her bra when saw her grandmother's long, flabby breasts; afraid that her own breasts would end up hanging down to her belly, she decided to keep

4

them strapped up all the time, even when sleeping. Now, though, she has neither nightdress nor bra. The driver's breath rises, his chest rests against the steering wheel, and his eyes are fixed on the windscreen. Meelya is afraid. The man, whom she glimpses through the fog, is receding as though in flight. His coat has opened in the wind and seems to be flapping away over the valley on its own.

In the dream, Meelya saw herself as white, and couldn't understand where this whiteness had come from. The body she wore by day was not hers but a reflection in people's eyes. Her mother had wanted a plump white daughter, so Meelya's body had become plump and white for her mother's sake. By night, though, her body is her own; she is seven, with a brown complexion, slim figure, wide eyes that fill her face, curly black hair and a small, fine nose that appears to have been pencilled in beneath the long, thin eyebrows. She wears shorts and runs barefoot. Her eyes have borrowed green pupils to replace the honey-coloured ones that people see by day, and her pupils swim in a whiteness suffused with a pale, barely detectable blue.

Meelya loves the night and runs through its narrow streets. She throws herself onto her bed and opens her eyes, and night traces itself about her eyelids. When the darkness is complete, she closes them and goes to her dreams. In the morning, she doesn't wipe the dreams from her eyes; she leaves them as circles drawn in invisible ink so she can return to them when-ever she wishes. It is enough for her to close her eyes for the voices to be silenced and the lights extinguished. Then she goes to where she sees all and uncovers secrets.

Meelya tells no-one that she hides her dreams deep down under the darkness. She digs in the darkness and puts her dreams there. When she wishes to, she goes to the pit, takes out the dreams she wants and dreams them over again.

This dream had come out of nowhere. In the pit where she

stores her dreams there is no such Meelya. Meelya of the night is not Meelya of the day. Where, then, did these images of the day come from? Was it because she was married? Was that what marriage was?

Meelya feels as though she's suffocating, and shivers. The night has become a well and she is at its bottom. The bald driver's breath rises and wraps itself around her neck. He seems to be moaning with pain. She tries to ask him what's wrong, but her voice has disappeared. She tries to raise her head from the pillow, but her head has grown heavy. Suddenly, the driver gets out of the car. He disappears and Mansour disappears and the naked woman is alone on the bed, fog encircling her, snow falling around her. She tries to raise her left foot, which has gone stiff with cold, but she can't. She feels that she is falling out of the bed. A terrible pain strikes her between her thighs, a knife stabs her. Blood. She screams. She wants to scream that the driver is raping her, but her voice has disappeared and her mouth has filled with cotton wool.

Meelya is alone in the darkness and the cold. She decides to open her eyes and leave this dream and sees a white face with white eyebrows. She reaches towards it and feathers stick to the ends of her fingers. She screams, begging him to release her, but he doesn't hear her. She tries to say that she wants to go home, that she doesn't want to get married any more, but she doesn't say anything. The face with the eyebrows hovers above the car, above the valley and above the two men. It recedes and the feathers fall from it – white feathers like the little snowflakes falling before the car's pale headlamps.

Meelya had said that she didn't want to spend the honeymoon in Chtaura. Snow was falling over Dahr el Baydar, and it was cold. She said there was no need for the Hotel Massabki or for a honeymoon: "We can stay in Beirut for a couple of days with my family and then go on to Nazareth."

6

Her mother said it was the middle of winter and that no-one honeymooned there in the middle of winter: "Come back and do the honeymoon in the summer."

Sister Milaneh said it would be better not to go to Chtaura in this cold weather though there was no danger: "It would just be a stupid adventure, one best postponed."

Mansour insisted. "I'm not having any of that," he said. He wanted to go to Chtaura for the honeymoon because you couldn't have a wedding and a honeymoon without the Hotel Massabki.

Moussa knit his eyebrows and told his sister it wasn't a problem: "The man wants Chtaura, so why not? Go there with him."

She got into the American car and sat in the back seat in her long white bridal gown next to Mansour, the ululations deafening her to the voice of her mother bent over at the window, whispering prayers and women's advice. Moussa came over to the car, tossed her two coats – his own olive-green one and his mother's brown one – and looked deeply into Meelya's eyes. Turning to Mansour, he said, "Congratulations, bride-groom," and went away.

The car moved through a silence penetrated only by the slooshing of the Beirut rain, which is like ropes. Meelya closed her eyes, then opened them to Mansour kissing her neck. Pushing him away, she said, "Later, not now," and went back to sleep. The car glided along the mountainous curves that lead to Chtaura. She slept, resting against the door, opening her eyes on hearing Mansour ordering the driver to keep going. The car had stopped in an all-enveloping white fog, so she closed her eyes, but Mansour's raised voice made her open them again.

The driver said he couldn't keep going because he couldn't see the road.

Mansour opened the rear door and leapt out onto the

highway. In a couple of steps he was in front of the car. Turning, he signalled to the driver to follow and took a few more steps, walking as though the ice were slippery. When the car failed to move, he returned to the back seat, put on Moussa's olive-green coat and told the driver that he would walk ahead and the car should follow.

Meelya thought he'd disappeared because for a few seconds she hadn't been able to see him. The cold wind had buffeted her face and the falling snowflakes had spread themselves over the endless fog. Meelya lost sight of her husband, but then saw him again through the windscreen, looking like a ghost clambering up the wind.

"Excuse me for saying this, Ma'am," the driver said, "but the groom's insane. What's he doing?"

Meelya, shivering with cold and fear, didn't answer.

"Tell me what he's doing," the driver said again.

"Drive after him," Meelya said in a strangled voice.

"And the bride's barmy too! What a mess!" the driver said, pressing his foot on the accelerator, causing the car to slide forward over the ice.

She saw Mansour carrying an unlit candle in his right hand and walking, while the driver bent forward towards the windscreen and drove extremely slowly behind the olive-green wind-puffed coat.

The driver turned around to look at Meelya, who saw his black pupils like dead coals. She was transfixed by his eyes and frightened by his hoarse voice. She asked him to keep his eyes on the road and a tight hold on the steering wheel because the car was skidding, but he kept looking at her while the car continued its slow slide and he maintained his incomprehensible flow of words.

"What are you saying?" screamed Meelya.

"Who on earth goes on honeymoon in Chtaura in midwinter?

8

Your husband's an idiot," the driver said, his words emerging slowly and in fragments. Staring into the darkness in front of her, Meelya discovered that what she had thought were the driver's pupils were indentations in the back of his bald head, which was covered with what looked like spots of oil and gave off a stench of putrefaction. The blush of confusion faded from her cheeks, the cold returned to her bones, and her teeth started chattering. She pressed her lips together and closed her eyes.

Meelya doesn't know what the driver said, but remembers that he spoke at length, with much cursing. He kept opening the car door so that he could see, the falling snow making a whispering sound and the cold air slapping the face of the bride where she sat in the corner of the back seat.

Meelya decided to arise from her dream and speak with the man whom another dream had chosen as a husband. She opened her eyes, rubbed her cheeks with her palms and found herself in the car. Mansour wasn't by her side; he was walking in the distance amid the fierce winds, while the driver trained his pupils on her.

"Please don't go to sleep!" the driver said.

Meelya looked at him, her eyes as wide as they could be, saw his red pupils moving on the back of his head, and cried, "O Virgin, O Mother of Light, O Mother of God, save thy servants!" before falling once more into sleep.

Meelya didn't see what happened next, didn't hear the driver say, "A miracle!" or notice how her husband turned around and stood at the side of the road waiting for the car.

At the instant of Meelya's scream, visibility returned, rays of light pierced the fog, and the snow stopped falling. The driver stopped the car to wait for Mansour to get in and turned around to look at the woman who had wrought this miracle with her voice. Meelya's eyes were closed, however, the dreams forming rings around her lids. The driver said, "It's a miracle!" She mumbled where she sat, rubbed her eyes with her palms and smiled. That was when Mansour opened the car door and got in beside the driver.

"God, it's cold!" Mansour said.

"How am I supposed to get back to Beirut?" the driver asked as the car glided downhill towards the plain of the Bekaa.

"The fog was just on Dahr el Baydar," Mansour said. "Now it's fine."

"And where am I supposed to sleep?" the driver asked.

"I was afraid I was going to be blown away. I *was* blown away!" Mansour said, turning towards where his wife sat in a heap on the back seat, covered by a quivering brown coat.

"The bride," the driver said.

"What about the bride?" Mansour asked.

"She screamed, 'O Virgin, for thy name's sake!' and the fog went away and the snow stopped. The bride performed a miracle," the driver said.

"Meelya," said Mansour, and started sneezing, after which his body was gripped by a fit of shivering, his teeth started chattering, and he began making sounds like sighs that came from deep within him.

"Rub your hands together," the driver said.

Mansour sneezed and moaned as though he were about to faint, and shivered and shook without stopping.

"It's nothing," the driver said. "You'll just have to grin and bear it. It was your idea to keep going. Pull yourself together."

Mansour tried to pull himself together, but his strength failed him. The muscles in his chest, his arms and his thighs went into spasms, and he felt as though he might suffocate. The driver yelled at Meelya to look to her husband because his face had turned blue and he could no longer speak.

Meelya moved restlessly where she sat, reached over and

touched Mansour's hair. "Be calm, my dear. Soon we'll be at the hotel and get warm."

The man calmed down, his breathing became regular, and he managed to say to his wife, "Don't be afraid. I'm strong, and I'm better now." Then he started sneezing over and over again and asked for a handkerchief. The driver offered him his, but Mansour waved it away. His wife handed him the white handkerchief full of holes that she had inherited from her grandmother and left untouched in her bridal chest all those years, waiting for her wedding day. He took it, buried his face in it, and started blowing and hawking and spitting.

Meelya doesn't know how they reached the hotel. She only remembers that fog, fierce winds and snow had beset them on the heights of Dahr el Baydar, that she'd seen her husband get out of the car and walk, and that the fog had swallowed him up. She remembers too how, at the entrance to the village of Sofar, the driver had pleaded with him, saying he couldn't cross over to Chtaura in this snowy weather, and how Mansour had insisted on continuing the journey no matter what. She remembers that the driver had looked to her for help, but when she'd started to speak Mansour's eyes had fastened on her lips and made them close. She'd seen his thick black moustache trembling above his upper lip, imagined him with a red tarboush on his head and fallen in love with him.

In the midst of the winds that set upon the car and the driver's appeals and laments that he couldn't continue the journey came the love that Meelya had been waiting to feel for so long. Love fell into her heart and she felt a pain behind her ribs, as though her heart itself had dropped. She wanted to gasp with fear, but didn't dare to. She said nothing, thinking to herself that this was love. In the beginning she had felt no emotion towards this man whom she'd seen standing beneath the palm tree in the garden next to her house. Leaning out of the window, she had seen him standing there motionless and looking into her eyes, trying to wrest a smile from her lips. His own smile had never faded and he didn't lower his gaze until she'd disappeared, flushed with confusion.

"What does that strange man want?" she had asked her mother.

Meelya knew nothing about the man and was in no state to love him. His hair was always shiny, as though covered in oil; the white hairs around his temples indicated that he had begun the descent into old age. She didn't see in him the image of a long-awaited lover, but rather of a father searching for his lost daughter, and when she accepted him as her husband she didn't tell anyone the real reason.

She told Moussa she'd accepted because her future husband looked like him.

She told her mother she was tired of waiting and wanted to get married.

She told Sister Milaneh she was leaving to escape the suffocating atmosphere that had taken over the house since one of her other brothers, Saleem, had departed for Aleppo and her mother's illnesses had burgeoned.

The first time she spoke to him, she told him he was old.

"Me?"

She pointed to the white hairs at his temples.

"My hair turned white when I was twenty. Do you know what white hair means? It means we're lions. The only animal whose hair turns white is the lion." He said he was thirty-seven and intended to get married before he was forty. "The first age of prophecy passed and I didn't get married. I'm not going to let the second one slip by or it'll be too late."

Although Meelya didn't understand what he meant, she smiled. Taking heart, the man said that he loved and wanted her, and asked if she loved him.

"How can I love you when I don't know you?"

"I love you and I don't know you," he said. "I feel you within me. Do you feel me?"

She nodded, not to say yes, but because she didn't know. Mansour interpreted her nod as assent.

"So it's possible?" he asked.

Looking into the distance, she closed her eyes.

It was only at the Hotel Massabki in Chtaura that Meelya had understood what Mansour had meant by the two ages of prophecy. On the second night he had tried to take her.

"No, I'm tired," she'd said, turning her back to him and going to sleep. He left her to swim in her deep breathing. Then, moving stealthily behind her, he began to play with her body, turned her over, climbed on top of her and had sex with her. That night Meelya became aware that she was wet and the sheets were wet, and the cold made her shudder. She wanted to get up and go to the bathroom, but felt that her knees wouldn't support her, so she closed her eyes and tried to go back to sleep.

"Get up! Get up! Who sleeps at a time like this?"

Opening her eyes, she rested her head against the wall and beheld his naked torso, a cigarette between his lips, his shining eyes.

"Have you seen how beautiful you look? Look in the mirror. Love makes a woman more beautiful."

Closing her eyes, she heard him talking about his "ages". The Age of Christ, he said, had passed him by, but he wasn't going to let the Age of the Prophet Muhammad get away as well.

Meelya didn't understand, but she didn't ask. She could feel a burning sensation down below and wanted something to drink, but was embarrassed to get out of bed because of her wet nightdress.

"Christ was crucified when he was thirty-three, and Muhammad's prophethood was revealed when he was forty.

13

Either a man becomes a man at one of these two ages or it's all over for him. The first age is gone, but in the second I found you."

"The driver was right," Meelya whispered. "You're mad."

Love came to Meelya in the car. She closed her eyes and searched for her Uncle Mitri's tarboush to put on Mansour's head and found it in the pit where she kept her dreams.

She sees Mansour wearing her uncle's white silk coat and jaunty red tarboush and chasing her with a thin bamboo cane. The rod strokes Meelya's brown feet and the man wearing the coat is screaming that she must eat the *labaneh* bridegroom. Meelya hops about in her shorts beneath the whipping of the cane, her feet on fire. The rod withdraws and the girl is sitting on the ground, gobbling a sandwich of *labaneh* and olive oil. She tastes white onions and mint. Meelya eats, but the sandwich gets no smaller. Turning to her Uncle Mitri, she invites him to share the food with her. The man approaches and devours the sandwich at one go. Meelya snatches the rod from the man's hand and runs. The man runs after her. Meelya is in a garden full of green plants. She leaps over puddles, the man's voice pleading with her to stop and give him back his cane. She falls to the ground and her uncle is on top of her, panting. She opens her eyes, the uncle is erased, the tarboush disappears, and she finds herself in the car in the midst of the fog.

The uncle disappeared, leaving the ghost of a smile on the woman's lips, a jaunty red tarboush on the head of a man whom she'd decided to love, and a woman, to whom she surrendered, lying on the back seat of an American taxi, sinking into a dark dream from which she didn't wake until they reached the hotel.

She didn't see Mansour's darkened face, in which the blue of the cold had blended with the brown of his skin, until they arrived at the hotel a little before midnight. Mansour shook her by the wrist and she heard a voice saying, "Come on. We're here." Like someone coming out of a swoon, she awoke asking,

"What? Where?" Then she remembered that she was a bride on her honeymoon. The car door opened and Mansour stood waiting for her, holding their suitcase. When he pointed to the door of the hotel, she set off beside him, then turned back and saw the driver's bald patch. He was bent over the steering wheel, his hands slack, as though he were sleeping.

"What about the driver?" she asked.

"We'll see to him right away," Mansour said.

He led her to a wooden door. Mansour had to knock for a long time before Georges Massabki, the owner, opened it wearing white pyjamas and a brown *abaya*. *Khawaja* Georges regarded them with his small eyes, an astonished expression on his face, as though unable to believe that two such strange beings could have descended upon him at that hour of the night just to taste the honey of marriage.

"You're the bridal couple," the hotel's owner said, muffling behind the sleeve of his *abaya* his cough, which swallowed up half his words.

Mansour nodded, then turned to the waiting car.

"Welcome, welcome. I thought you wouldn't come in all this cold and snow. Please come in, please come in. The room will be ready in a few minutes." Leaving them standing at the door, *Khawaja* Georges called out, "Wadeea! Wadeea! The bride and groom have arrived." Then, rubbing his hands together in front of the stove and talking, as it seemed, to himself, he said, "What a night! Where are you, Wadeea? Light the stove in the bridal couple's room and then come in here. You know, Mr . . ."

Turning to Mansour, *Khawaja* Georges found he'd disappeared. But Meelya was standing in front of him, her brown coat partly covering her white wedding gown, her eyes wide and sleepy and her cheeks starting to glow.

"What is your name, my dear bride?"

Meelya looked to one side as though seeking the person to

whom the hotel owner had spoken, raised her hand to her chest and asked if his question was directed at her.

"Who else would I be asking? Aren't you the bride?" asked Georges Massabki, overwhelmed by a coughing fit that forced him to bend over. Sitting down on a sofa, he gestured to the bride to sit next to him, but Meelya remained standing, waiting for Mansour to return. She didn't know why, but she was suddenly struck by the thought that Mansour was going to run away. She could see him sitting in the taxi next to the driver, asking him to drive him back to Beirut.

"What am I to do?" Meelya asked in a faint voice.

"Come and sit next to me," Georges Massabki said. "Wadeea will be along in a moment and you can go up to your room."

Meelya put her hands over her eyes and heard Mansour asking the hotel owner for an extra room.

They were four in the spacious hotel lobby, whose most prominent feature was a small black table behind which was a rack of room keys. Meelya noticed that the rack was full and deduced that the hotel was empty. Three sofas covered in velvety red cloth formed a semicircle around the stove. A Persian carpet, predominantly red in colour and bearing images of tame animals, took up most of the floor, and there were photographs hung haphazardly on the opposite wall. The three visitors stood in the lobby while Mr Massabki remained seated. He called out a second time for Wadeea, then stood up and started to climb the stone staircase leading to the rooms on the first floor.

The heat put out by the metal stove began to steal into the bodies of the men and woman who stood waiting for Wadeea. Going over to one of the photographs on the wall, Mansour gestured to his wife, saying, "Come and look at Faisal. This is King Faisal I." Going slowly over to where her husband was standing, Meelya saw a gilded frame within which men wearing tarboushes formed a circle around a short man with a pallid, oval face who gazed unseeingly into the distance.

"That's Faisal," said Mansour, pointing to the thin man.

"Did he honeymoon in Chtaura too?" the driver asked sarcastically.

"What would you know about anything?" Mansour asked. "When he comes, we'll name the boy Faisal," he continued, looking into his wife's eyes. "What do you think?"

At first she didn't answer, as she'd been expecting Mansour to name his first-born son Shukri, after his father. Then she said, "I have no idea."

"And what do *you* think?" Mansour asked the driver, who after rubbing his hands in front of the stove had put them in his trouser pockets as though trying to tuck away the heat.

"Damn, it's cold. Good for you, Mr Groom."

The driver looked at Meelya standing next to her husband beneath the photo of the King of Syria whom the French army had driven out of Damascus and for whom the British had established another kingdom in Iraq. "Good for your husband, Mrs Bride," he said, and threw himself down onto one of the sofas.

The hotel owner appeared with two short women at his side, the first white, apparently half blind and in her sixties, the second golden-skinned and in her thirties, despite which the two of them were as alike as twins.

"Wadeea, take the bride and groom to Room 10," said *Khawaja* Georges.

The two women, moving as one, approached the driver. "Come along then. Follow me, Mr Groom," said Wadeea 1, while the eyes of Wadeea 2 widened in astonishment and she asked, "Which of you is the groom?"

"This one, this one," Wadeea 1 said, pointing to the half-sleeping driver, who was sitting on the sofa.

"Me. I'm the groom," Mansour said.

"Sorry, sir, I thought he was the groom because they always look like that, ugly and old and bald, and they take the loveliest girls up to the rooms. Ah me, what we poor women have to put up with!" Wadeea 1 said.

"Shush now, Wadeea," the hotel owner said, yawning.

"He's the groom. I knew it," golden-skinned Wadeea 2 said. She took Mansour by the arm.

"What about me?" the driver asked.

"Who are you?" Wadeea 1 asked.

"I'm Hanna Araman," he replied.

"Charmed, I'm sure," Wadeea 1 said. "But who does that make you?"

"It makes him the driver who brought us here, and we have to find a place for him to sleep," Mansour said.

Wadeea 1 looked at Wadeea 2 and then at *Khawaja* Georges, who was muttering, "Room 6. Light the stove in Room 6." Then he turned to the bride and groom and bade them good night. Bending over the stove, he put out the fire and went along to his room at the end of the lobby. The other three caught up with the women, who took them up a long staircase that brought them to two facing rooms.

Wadeea 2 opened the door of the first room and gestured to the couple, while Wadeea 1 stood with the driver at the door of Room 6, whispering with him.

Entering the spacious room, Meelya found a large bed, and a mirror that took up most of the opposite wall. A square table in the middle of the room was covered with an orange tablecloth on which had been placed a bottle of champagne, two large rounds of floppy bread and a dish of white cheese. The bathroom was to the left of the bed, and the stove, which was by the table, had been lit. Mansour locked the door and Meelya heard the driver and Wadeea 1 whispering and guffawing loudly.

Meelya doesn't remember clearly what took place in the room. She watched Mansour take off his coat and hang it behind the door. She watched him go over to the table and work on the champagne bottle and pop the cork, the white foam over-flowing as he poured it into the glasses. He gave his bride a glass and raised his.

"To your health, bride!"

Meelya took a sip and swallowed the white bubbles brimming on the liquid's surface. Feeling slightly nauseous, she put the glass down on the table and said she wanted a cup of hot tea. Mansour didn't seem to hear her. He ate a mouthful of cheese and prepared one for his bride. She pushed his hand away and said she wasn't hungry, so he ate it himself and gulped down the champage he'd poured for her. Then he poured another glass, and his eyes started to glaze over as if he were thinking strange thoughts. Smiling, Meelya remembered what her mother had said about the foolishness that possesses men on their wedding nights.

The man took her by the hand and led her over to the bed. She felt her throat go dry. This was the long-awaited moment and she had to be brave.

They sat on the end of the bed. Mansour rested his head on her neck and kissed it. A slight shudder ran through the bride's body and she wanted to lie down. Falling back a bit, she imagined herself flying in Mansour's arms. Now he would pick her up and fly with her before putting her down again on the bed and taking her.

Meelya fell back onto the bed and waited. The kisses on her neck ceased and the man started to shake. She wanted to hold him to her to make it easier for him, but he jumped up and started taking off his clothes. This was the last thing Meelya had expected – that the groom would stand in the middle of the room and start taking off his clothes and throwing them on the floor. His face had receded, as though he'd put on a mask, and the hair on his shoulders and chest was like a thick black skin.

"Now he'll launch his attack and conquer me," thought Meelya, and a strange feeling took hold of her, as though she were standing at a high lookout point waiting for someone to push her over the edge and was resigned to the waiting. She closed her eyes to the image of the terrifying fall and of the two hands that would throw her onto the bed and pull off her dress before ripping at her underclothes.

The wait continued, and she was overcome by drowsiness. As she supported her head with her wrist, a light, fitful sleep stole over her. The fog on the road gathered in her eyes. Shaking herself, she opened them, but instead of seeing Mansour standing naked in the middle of the room, she found that the man had disappeared. She saw his rumpled clothes on the floor and remembered the sight of him struggling out of them – the trousers mixed up with the shoes, the shirt wrapped around his neck, the socks sticking to his feet. Also, she recalled his thick black moustache trembling above his lips, and her waiting smile returned to her. Then she heard a kind of low moaning and realized that it was coming from the bathroom. The moaning grew in volume, accompanied by sounds of retching and gagging. Instead of going to the bathroom, though, to see what had happened to her husband, she lay down on the bed and, without taking off her dress, covered herself with the quilt.

"What kind of a honeymoon is this?" she asked loudly, thinking that the bridegroom, seated on the lavatory, would hear her. When he didn't reply, she felt afraid, and the man who had been swallowed up by the fog on the summit of Dahr el Baydar appeared before her, shaking, running towards the car making sounds like barks enveloped in moans, then opening the car door and sitting down next to the driver, trembling and gasping. She got up and went over to the stove, where she saw that the fire had died down, put some logs into it and waited for the flames to rise again. Then she went over to the bathroom door and called out to Mansour. He didn't reply. She knocked several times, but all she could hear was a faint moaning that seemed to come from far away. Becoming warm, she decided to take off her dress. Bending over the suitcase, she took out her long blue nightdress and put it on. She heard the man calling to her. Going back to the bathroom door, she called out, "Open up, Mansour. It's Meelya." The voice that answered fell almost to a whisper.

Did he call "Meelya" or "Mother"?

"Open the door, please."

"Keep your voice down or the driver will hear," the man said hoarsely.

"Do you want us to get a doctor?"

"Be quiet. Please be quiet."

The words stopped and the man's moaning turned strange. Meelya was certain that he was dying and sank to the floor. She found herself kneeling and knocking. She grasped the doorknob as though to pull herself up by it and heard Mansour calling for his mother in a whisper. Hearing him gagging and retching, she begged him to open up. She remained on her knees for a long time, feeling alone and impotent.

"I'm going downstairs to ask the owner to get the doctor."

"Keep your voice down or the driver will hear and make fun of us."

Mansour's voice seemed to come from deep inside a well as he told his wife not to leave the room, that nothing was wrong.

"You get into bed and I'll join you."

She doesn't know how she got to her feet or how she lay down on the bed and covered herself with the quilt and slept.

Why is she naked now?

And what is this shudder running through her?

Meelya decided to open her eyes because she had felt the presence of death, and death comes only in the shape of a long dream that never ends. "Death is a dream," she had said to her brother Moussa. "Come and see your grandmother, how she dreams." The grandmother was stretched out on her bed in the midst of the white sheets, the women seated around her, and there was a faint sound of weeping. No-one dared to lament over Malakeh Shalhoub when she closed her eyes and passed away: their grandmother hadn't approved of weeping for the dead. "The dead are not dead! No-one is to weep!" Malakeh had yelled at them when her daughter had died. When darkness fell that day, people heard her husband Nakhleh bellowing like an ox with its throat cut, and rumours ran through the quarter that the man had died, two weeks after his daughter Salma, from holding back the tears his wife had forbidden him to weep.

Meelya didn't tell her brother Moussa that she'd seen her aunt in the dream. Moussa was three and couldn't understand things like that.

On the eve of her aunt's death, Meelya had opened her eyes to her mother's howling and decided to go back into her dream and save her mother's sister. Her young aunt, only twenty, remained sunk in sleep, however, and refused to open her eyes. The dream was mysterious, and Meelya only understood its meaning years later, when she began menstruating and dreamt that she was flying.

By the time Meelya told her grandmother her dream, everything was over. Holding back her tears, her grandmother asked the child to tell all, and it was then that Meelya learnt to speak of the mysterious things that she saw in the night. Her cheeks flushed, her tongue protruding through the gap where her milk teeth had fallen out, burring her 'r's as she spoke, she said that she had seen her Aunt Salma fall into the pool in the garden and flail about amid the little red fishes, crying for help. Meelya had held out a rope to her and Salma had taken hold of it and tried to climb out, but the rope had slipped from Meelya's hands. The aunt had been stretched out on the ground, which was covered with green grass. Meelya had gone over to her and tried to wake her, but then she'd heard her grandmother say, "Do not wake her. Leave her. She is dreaming." Meelya had woken up shaking with fear; then, after she'd gone back to sleep, she'd heard her mother scream, so she'd got out of bed in terror, understanding that her Aunt Salma had died.

Meelya hadn't told the truth. She'd lied because she was afraid of telling the rest of her dream. She was afraid to say she'd entered her aunt's dream and dreamt it. Who would believe that anyone could enter another person's dream? Meelya couldn't take in what had happened and only under-stood what it meant to enter another person's dream at the moment of her own death, when she saw what no-one else had seen, and revealed her secret only to the child that came out of her belly.

Meelya had lain down next to her aunt on the green grass, where a white cloud covered her aunt's closed eyes. She had seen herself entering the cloud and her aunt flying over a cavernous valley. She had heard the heartbeats of the flying woman and beheld the fear in her eyes. Salma was wearing her wedding dress, and a long white veil flapped behind her. Suddenly, the veil fell into the pool and the rain came down like ropes. Meelya tried to catch up with Salma, but couldn't. She ran, tripped over her own feet and fell. Blood gushed from her right knee. She looked up and saw Salma disappearing into the distance and turning into a white spot. Then Meelya heard her mother crying, opened her eyes and saw Saada mourning in the corner. She discovered that death had come and understood that it was a long dream, just as her grand-mother had said, and that she, seven years old, had been able to slip into the dream of death and taste its watery flavour.

Salma's death came as no surprise. The girl had refused all offers of marriage while waiting for Ibraheem Hananiya, who had gone to Brazil promising to return rich and marry her. She had caught yellow fever, which at the time still dragged itself through the streets of Beirut. Everyone had known that Salma was going to die. Malakeh had bought a white wedding gown in which to dress her daughter on her bier; Meelya heard something of this from her mother, who had contributed part of the cost of the dress. At the same time, though, things had got mixed up in the girl's mind. She had heard her mother saying that the time for Salma's wedding was close and seen her grandmother, who had come to visit them one morning, weeping for her lost daughter's youth. She didn't understand what it all meant, though, until she saw him in her dream; and when her tongue told the tale, which slipped out through the gap in her teeth, and she recounted to her grandmother how she'd seen what no-one else had seen, she was frightened by her grandmother's response: "Don't say such things, girl. Only the dead see the dreams of the dead." Her grandmother drew the sign of the cross on her forehead and prayed to God to protect her: "May the Cross of the Greeks protect you, my child!"

And in the dream, she saw him.

Meelya told her grandmother and her mother that she'd seen Ibraheem Hananiya walking behind Salma's coffin. A short, round man wearing a long green coat, his head bent forward as though his little neck were too weak to hold it up. She said he was wearing brown-and-white shoes and walked like someone stumbling and finding no-one to steady him. She said he was alone and she'd spoken to him. Or rather, he'd spoken to her. He'd come over to her and said that no-one recognized him. He'd said that he'd changed a lot while in Brazil: "I didn't used to be short like this, but I got fat, and being fat makes a man shorter. Maybe that's why no-one recognizes me." He smiled, showing yellow teeth, and asked her if she was Salma.

"Salma's dead, and it's nothing to do with me."

"I know, I know," he said. "But you are Salma, aren't you?"

When she tried to reply, her tongue stuck in the gap between her teeth. She felt she couldn't form the words properly and that what was coming out of her mouth was no more than incomprehensible mumbling. She started crying.

She wanted to ask him why he hadn't come back from Brazil before Salma had died, wanted to know if he'd got rich like all the other Lebanese who migrated to that far-off land, wanted to say that her aunt had died because of him, but she couldn't. She felt the words disintegrating before they could form, and that she was being suffocated and couldn't speak.

The image of Ibraheem engraved itself on her memory as her first man. She had felt she loved him and had understood from the tears in his eyes that he'd lost everything when he had returned to Beirut only to find the woman for whom he'd returned in the throes of death.

This was what she would have told Mansour, if she could have. Mansour talked all the time and left no space for the silent words that hid themselves among the contours of his white bride's face. And when he did try to listen to her, Meelya was unable to speak and would scream with pain. She would scream for her mother, who wouldn't come and save her from her long dream.

When she told her grandmother and her mother of her encounter with Ibraheem Hananiya, her mother told her to be quiet: "Enough talk, my girl. We're too busy to keep listening to your dreams."

"Ibraheem Hananiya was in Beirut?" her grandmother said to

her mother, holding back her tears. "The bastard was here and he never came to see us? He waited until she died before doing us the honour of paying a visit?"

"What's wrong with you, Mother? You believe Meelya's dreams? What's got into you?"

"Yes, yes. He'd got short and round and he had no voice – but why didn't he come and see the girl before she died? That wasn't right," the grandmother went on.

"The whole family's mad," the mother said.

"You're the mad one. Meelya saw the man, and I saw him too."

"What do you mean, you saw him, Mother? The man's in Brazil. It was his brother who came and said Ibraheem was very upset but wouldn't be able to come to Lebanon."

"No, no. He was here, and he didn't come and see the girl, and he broke both our hearts."

Ibraheem had told her he was afraid of dying. "Aren't you Salma?" he'd asked.

"No, I'm Meelya."

Starting to weep, he'd said he didn't dare visit his fiancée on her deathbed.

"That's enough now, my girl," Saada had said.

Meelya looked fearfully at her mother and stopped talking. She left the *leewan* attached to the house and went out into the garden, where she stuck the hose onto the end of the tap set over the pool, turned it on and watered the trees.

Moussa had been seven when he'd stood holding his sister's hand at their dead grandmother's bedside. The boy didn't understand the meaning of death or of his grandmother's journeying in her dreams. He'd heard the moaning of the women around the bed where the white woman lay covered with a white sheet, and his eyelashes had filled with something that looked like water. He didn't weep or sigh. He stood waiting for his sister to brush his lashes with her fingertips and bend over and kiss his eyes. Whenever she thought he was afraid, Meelya would brush Moussa's lashes and kiss his eyes, bringing the boy back to himself and releasing him from his night-time fears. Moussa feared the creatures of the night and its trees. Meelya had told him that the trees of night filled the empty space left after the sun went down and that dreams built their nests in the branches. The boy was afraid of the night and its nests. When he awoke in the dark, his naked feet would march to his sister's bed and Meelya would move over a little without opening her eyes. The boy would curl up next to his sister, who would reach out her hand and brush his lids with her fingertips and kiss his eyes, and Moussa would fall into a deep sleep.

Moussa, now twenty, came and told his sister that Mansour Hourani wanted to marry her. The young man stood before his sister, who was sitting on the end of the bed, head bowed over a stocking she was darning. Before he spoke, she saw that his eyes were wet with tears. He spoke of Mansour and she said nothing. Putting the stocking, bulging with the wooden darning egg, down on the bed, she stood up. She reached out and brushed his lids with her fingertips. Then she bent over, kissed his eyes and tasted the tears. She saw him as a little boy again, his eyes full of fear and his lower lip quivering, and said, as she kissed his eyes, that she would agree to whatever he wanted.

"Isn't this what you want?" she asked him.

The boy had grown tall and become a man. He knitted his brows, looked down at his sister with eyelids lowered, and said, "Yes."

"As you wish then," she said.

He didn't ask about her relationship with the man and didn't mention that when he'd asked for her hand Mansour had said she'd already agreed and declared her love for him, which had made Moussa feel betrayed, though he didn't use that word when he asked his sister what she thought.

"So you love him?" he asked.

She looked at him as though she didn't understand what he meant. Then she smiled and said she'd agreed because Mansour looked like him.

"He's just like you, you know," she said.

"Like me?" he responded, with distaste.

"You're handsomer than he is, but he looks like you. He could be your brother."

Moussa frowned and muttered something about the wiles of women.

"What did you say? I didn't hear," Meelya said.

"Congratulations, Sister."

Meelya felt that day as though she'd been set the task of discovering life anew, or as though she'd just been born, or as though she'd been bending over her little brother's lashes and then straightened up only to find herself standing in front of a young man who was a full twenty years old and on whose head a few grey hairs already gleamed – as though she'd lived her whole life as one does a dream. She put her hands over her eyes, then stretched out her arms in an effort to grasp the meaning of what had emerged from her brother's lips.

He had said that she would be travelling to Nazareth immediately after the wedding.

"As you wish," said Meelya, bowing her head so that her glance broke on the tiles veined with flowers outlined in black.

Moussa said the photographer would come the following day. "If you want to go on being here with us, I'll hang your picture on the wall."

The photo would remain hung on the white wall of the *leewan*. Moussa, who inherited the house from his mother, left the photo where it was, as though it had become part of the wall. Printed on a large piece of white paper and framed in black wood, it reveals Meelya's features, her long hair, her honey-coloured, almond-shaped eyes, her long neck, her thin cheeks and her narrow eyebrows, which meet above her nose – a half-length portrait by the photographer Sharif Fakhouri, who had inserted his head into a wooden box covered with a black cloth and made Meelya stand in front of the white wall for two whole hours so that he could choose her best pose. The picture made Meelya look as though she was starting out of the white wall, a white woman with black contours to her face and a gleam of light coming from her eyes.

Moussa was convinced that there was something strange about the photo. Everything was outlined in black curves except for the pupils, which appeared to be drawn in green.

Moussa brought the picture home three days before the wedding. Banging in a nail, he hung it on the wall. Then he took three steps back and called to his sister. Meelya hurried to the *leewan* to find Moussa in front of the picture, his eyes filled with surprise.

"Do you see it?" he asked.

"Thank you, thank you. It's lovely," she answered.

"Do you see the eyes? Do you see the colour? It looks as though there's something green inside the black. Do you see?"

The girl looked at her picture, was taken aback and felt tears in her eyes. The tears filled them, the picture broke up into little pieces within a vast watery field, and she feared that her guardian angel had deserted her. How had the photographer from Zahleh managed to capture the secret of her green eyes? Her eyes were green only in her dreams, in which Meelya became young and brown-skinned and had short black curly hair. How had the photographer managed to discover her secret? Had her eyes given her away? Was that why she no longer saw dreams, and why, from the moment she'd agreed to marry, her sleep had become a kind of plunging into a deep, dark pit?

Meelya had begun to fear sleep. She would lie on her bed, open her eyes, try to resist the drowsiness and, when sleep started to steal in through the tips of her toes, shake it off. Nonetheless, sleep would wrap itself around her, stealing up from behind, abducting her and carrying her off into its darkness. Her nights witnessed her body's tremors. Her thigh would twitch as though it had been struck, and she would feel as though she were falling; then she would shudder and go limp, and try to put together the right story for sleeping. But the story would escape, and darkness would envelop her.

Meelya had lost the way to the pit where she hid her dreams and only understood why when the photograph revealed the secret of her eyes.

Moussa stood before his sister, perplexed. Why did Meelya hate the beautiful picture he'd hung on the wall?

"Stand in front of it and look. It's like your mirror-image," he said.

Meelya contemplated the photograph and saw how the imprint of the green shadows had been caught within the black ink. Averting her face, she left the *leewan*. Moussa stood in front of the photo and felt it was speaking to him and that he could now consent to his sister's marriage. Meelya would never go to Nazareth with Mansour; she would stay here on the wall and he would never have to yearn for her.

Turning, he found that his sister had gone. He caught up with her in the garden, sitting on the wooden swing that hung from a branch of the huge fig tree. Seeing that his sister was shaking with tears, he didn't go up to her. Instead, he went back to the *leewan* and sat down on the sofa facing the picture.

Meelya didn't tell Mansour that she had wept bitter tears as she sat on the swing; she'd felt the tears on her lips, savoured their taste and discovered that tears don't taste the way they're supposed to. Tears are salty, but when we describe their taste we say they're bitter. Meelya drank her salty tears and savoured the bitter taste that came to her from a dream she hadn't dreamt. She thought that the colour of that bitterness was green, like the two small pupils that had disappeared from the screen of her dreams.

Meelya came into this world at noon on Monday, 2 July, 1923, on a white iron bedstead next to the white wall where Moussa would one day hang his sister's picture. It was a hot, humid day and Beirut's leaden sun was flaying the streets with cords of fire. The yellow sheets that Nadra Salloum the midwife had hung over the windows of the *leewan* burned with the light that pierced them, turning the room into a fiery yellow cube. Saada lay on the bed moaning with the pains of labour. Nadra, short, dark-skinned, full-bodied and round-faced, a cigarette stuck to her lips, scolded the woman whose upper body was stretched across the bed and whose face was covered in sweat that spotted her white shift with liquid coloured yellow by the sun's glare.

"Snap out of it, sister. It's not your first time and there's no need to yell," Nadra said, standing there, arms folded, chewing on the burning butt of her cigarette and waiting for the new baby.

Saada was having her sixth child. Three boys had survived – her first son, Saleem, her fourth, Niqoula, and her sixth, Abdallah. Two had died – her second-born, who hadn't been given a name but had become known as the blue boy because he'd been born with the umbilical cord wound around his neck and had strangled in the colour blue, and the third, Naseeb, who'd become jaundiced at one week and who lived on in the family's memory as Yellow Naseeb.

Saada lay on the bed awaiting her fourth son, whom she had

decided to call Moussa. After her first two births, her deliveries had become easy, the children seemingly just sliding out of her womb. Feeling the first pangs of labour, she would sit in the birthing chair in front of Nadra, wreathed in steam from the pot of boiling water on the floor of the *leewan*. She would feel the slipping, be overcome by a sensation like giddiness and slide along with the small being exiting her guts. Nadra would pull the child out, lift it up by its feet and slap its bottom to make it cry. If she saw a willy between its thighs, she'd let out a long ululation, and Youssef would know that another boy had been added to his family.

On that sweltering July morning, with the temperature at 34 degrees centigrade, Saada was stretched out on the bed, pounded by pain. Her cries grew louder and the yellow spread over her face and hands. Saada hadn't seen the birthing chair and she didn't ask where it was. Usually, when the waters broke and labour began, Youssef would go running to Nadra's house, where the midwife would open the door in welcome, saying she could see a boy in Youssef's face. Interlocking circles of thick smoke would pour from the house. Youssef would hear the coughing of Nadra's husband Moallem Camille and the racket made by his friends, who filled the place with the bubbling of their water pipes and the din of their card games. Rather than watch them play, however, and as a way of proclaiming his objection to gambling, he would hurry to the back of the house, pick up the birthing chair and leave. Nadra would follow, cigarette in mouth.

That day, however, there had been no smoke when the door had opened, no sounds of water pipes or card players' racket. Moallem Camille wasn't there, and Nadra was in the kitchen making lunch. Bending down to pick up the chair, he couldn't find it. He stood there silently, not knowing what to do, till Nadra tugged on his arm and told him to follow her.

"The chair got broken," she said. "From now on, we're going to deliver like Europeans."

He didn't ask what "delivering like Europeans" meant. He followed behind her as they climbed the long flight of stairs that connected Abu Arbeed Street, where Nadra lived, with Zaroub el Taweel Street, where his wife was waiting. Following Nadra's instructions, Saada lay down on the bed, but the midwife told her off, saying, "Lie down crosswise and raise your legs. I have to be able to work."

Saada changed her position, her body wrung with pain. Saying one word, "Where's . . .", she couldn't finish her sentence because she'd started to convulse with agony.

"No chair," said Nadra. "Today we're going to deliver like *moderne* people. Pull your legs up onto the bed and grip hard."

Saada started to cry.

Nadra washed her hands with soap and water, went over to Saada and told her not to be afraid.

Saada, writhing on her bed, didn't hear what Nadra said. She needed air. She'd push and the air would be choked off inside her lungs. She'd open her mouth in a cry for oxygen and feel Nadra's hand holding a little towel with which she dabbed at the sweat on Saada's forehead and neck.

"Snap out of it, Saada."

But the child refused to begin its journey into the world. Nadra knelt between the thighs of the woman stretched out on the bed, reached in to feel the head, which was in the right position, and tried to grip it, but couldn't.

"Push! Push!"

"Air! Please, air! I can't breathe," Saada said, shaking. A violent spasm overwhelmed her and her teeth started chattering.

"Please! I'm going to die."

"Don't worry. Nothing's going to happen to you," Nadra yelled.

Saada closed her eyes and heard nothing more. The ringing

in her ears grew louder and she surrendered herself to the spasms that convulsed every part of her body. The midwife hurried out and fetched a small pot of cold water, applying compresses to Saada's forehead. The spasms grew weaker and the pregnant woman appeared to recover her ability to breathe.

"Now he's going to come down," said Nadra, "and when you feel the contraction, push. We're going to give one push and, God willing, it'll be over."

The midwife knelt, the sweat spreading over her short blue dress, and she started to feel that she was suffocating too. She wanted to swear – "Screw this lousy job and everything that goes with it" – but controlled herself and yelled, "Push!" Saada pushed with every ounce of strength she possessed. "Keep pushing!" yelled the midwife. But Saada's body had suddenly gone limp.

The spasms returned to the body of the pregnant woman on the bed and the midwife couldn't think what to do. As she stood there waiting, she noticed a strange colour: Saada was swimming in green. Green was creeping over her cheeks and eyes, and everything around her was fading into the background as green spots spread over her face, hands, thighs and feet. In all her long career, Nadra had never seen such a colour. When she'd entered the room and told Youssef to hang sheets over the two windows that looked out over the Rahhal family's garden next door, she'd felt as though fire was leaping out of the yellow.

"What kind of a colour is that? Change those sheets."

But Youssef didn't budge.

"That's all we have," he said.

"Out!" she had ordered him. "Get out!"

"It was like we were in an oven," Nadra told Sister Milaneh as she said goodbye to her at the door.

"Take that cigarette out of your mouth," the nun said as she left, raising her hands as though calling on the world to witness that she was the one who'd performed the delivery.

The yellow had spread through the place like an all-consuming fire. Then came the green, a light green that gradually changed until it became a dark green and spread in circles over the pregnant woman's hands and feet. Her limbs went limp, her tears mingled with the sweat dripping from her forehead, and she turned into a moaning mass. Nadra couldn't believe her eyes. She bent over Saada's face, wiped away the sweat and tears with a little white towel, and saw the napkin change colour with the sweat, which had turned yellow.

Nadra grew frightened and her heart skipped a beat. "My heart skipped a beat, *Ma Sœur*. What was I to do?" The nun calmly contemplated the scene; then she issued her orders and it was all over.

In the presence of that creeping green spreading its putrid gaps over everything, Nadra was convinced that there was nothing more she could do. Her only thought was to open the door to the *leewan* and escape that hell.

Once she told Meelya that she had been so frightened by Saada's colour that she'd been on the verge of running away and leaving the girl in her mother's belly.

"You mean I'd still be in my mother's tummy?" asked the little girl.

"No, dearie, that's not what I meant, but it's what the words say."

Meelya nodded as though she understood, but she didn't. A long while later she discovered that words say the opposite of what they mean. When that other man left her for unknown reasons, she understood that words have no meaning and that people talk to fill the spaces that separate them from others, to fill their souls with the sound of words.

Meelya dreamt fragments of her birth but refused to hide

35

that dream in her pit of night. She would see the yellow spreading, shake herself and, on hearing a scream explode inside her, open her eyes and find herself rising from the bed and going to sleep next to her brother Moussa.

Nadra had opened the door, dust motes rising into the air. A tall, thin man had approached from the doorway and whispered, "Tell me what's happening." Nadra asked him to hurry to the house of Dr Kareem Naqfour and bring him right away: "The woman's sick and needs a doctor immediately."

"What's the matter?" Youssef asked.

Nadra reached out her hand to close his mouth and he tasted a mixture of blood, sweat and faeces. He leant against the door to disguise his nausea and dizziness.

"Why are you standing there like an idiot?" the midwife yelled. "Go and get the doctor!"

The man ran to the doctor's house. He knocked at the door, but no-one opened, and he was bewildered. The taste of blood clung to his lips, dizziness enveloped him, and he felt a sense of loss. Loss fell on him from all sides and his feet refused to carry him. He sat on the steps of the house waiting for the doctor, then remembered that his wife was dying and that he had to do something. Pulling himself up, he started running beneath the burning sun to the Convent of the Angel Mikhail. He had no idea why he was going to the convent. He didn't like "*Hajjeh*" Milaneh and hated the spell she'd cast over his wife. He'd cursed her dozens of times and threatened that he'd leave the house if his wife didn't comply with his demands for sex. But Saada had said no – "*Hajjeh* Milaneh told me it's wrong when you're fasting". He had waited fifty days for the fast to end and Christ to rise so that he could make love to his wife. He took her on Easter morning, but she'd felt like a dry stick and he'd got no pleasure from it. The springs that had watered him when he slept with her before were gone.

His water had gushed out but his thirst hadn't been quenched, and that unsatisfied thirst had stayed with him for the rest of his life. Saada's initiation into the rites conducted by the eccentric nun had destroyed his sex life. He started seeing shame in his wife's eyes every time he went to her. She would no longer allow him to touch her breasts and would squirm every time his mouth came close to hers. Sleeping with her became an excuse just to finish and leave, while she'd hurry to the bathroom and wash herself as though to remove the traces of sin.

"It's all the nun's fault. She's a devil, not a saint," he once told his wife when, after practising that wooden sex, he'd felt pain in his member. "I hate her and don't ever want to see her ugly face again. Listen to me carefully. *Hajjeh* Milaneh is forbidden to come to this house."

But Saada turned a deaf ear to Youssef. She would visit the convent daily, bring the nun back to the house to anoint the children with holy oil, and entreat God to forgive her husband his sinful lack of love for the saintly sister.

For some reason he couldn't understand, then, Youssef found himself at the great iron door in the middle of the convent wall, his hand knocking and his voice crying, "Open up, please, *Hajjeh* Milaneh!"

The nun opened the door and came out, saying, "It'll be Saada and her daughter. Follow me back to the house."

Surprise tied Youssef's tongue. He wanted to say that he only fathered boys, but instead found himself walking behind her, sheltering in the large moving shadow she cast on the ground. The sun burned down on the unpaved road that ran between the Convent of the Angel Mikhail and his house, and the smell of cracked earth filled the air. Youssef panted as he walked, sweat pouring down his back, his clothes sticking to his body. The nun was tall, with broad shoulders and a huge rump, and she preceded him at a half run, her long black habit flapping.

Youssef moved in that huge shadow that lay aslant the unpaved road, breaking crookedly over the stones. Climbing the rise to the Shabboua family's garden and coming down to the olive orchard, he felt as though the air he breathed was burning his chest.

Youssef felt the presence of death and feared for Saada. He told himself that he would agree to whatever she wanted, that he'd stop having sex with her if that was her wish, so long as she didn't die.

He walked in the shadow of the nun, seized by the fear of death, and found himself mumbling the prayer his wife repeated every day: "O Lord, how are they increased that trouble me! Many are they that rise up against me. Many there be which say of my soul, There is no help for it in God. But thou, O Lord, art a shield for me; my glory, and the lifter up of mine head."

"What are you saying?" the nun asked.

"Nothing, nothing," Youssef replied, watching her shadow as it tottered ahead of him, her huge body squarely facing the sun, and imagining the old man's features outlined on her face – the thick eyebrows, bulging, half-closed eyes, broad forehead, thin lips, huge nose and swarthy olive skin – a face dominated by that huge nose with three hairs like a cock's comb in the middle and a thin violet moustache that looked as if it had been drawn with an indelible pencil.

Youssef had told his wife that the nun wasn't a woman but a man in disguise, and had said that he hated her – her size was out of keeping with her holiness. Saints, male and female, were usually distinguished by their thinness, the body melting away so the spirit could shine through, but this woman's huge body was killing off her thin spirit, making her into something more like a man with a woman's voice.

In the July heat, though, Youssef forgot about all that and thought only of death. He found himself walking in the black shadow like a small boy following his mother and clinging to her shade.

When the nun reached the house she turned and signalled with her eyebrows to Youssef that he should enter first. Youssef ran up the five stone steps and crossed the garden with the chinaberry tree. Opening the door to the house, he gestured to her to enter. The nun hurried to the *leewan* and went into the yellow room, her shadow spreading over everything. She didn't give Nadra a chance to curse as she usually did, and the midwife swallowed her bad language ("Where's the doctor, that bloo. . . ?") in midstream, the words swallowed up in the darkness of the nun's habit before they could pass her lips. The large room, bathed in the yellow of the sheets draped over the windows, lost its colour, as if the sun had been extinguished. As the black flowing from the nun's habit covered it, Saada's shaking body grew calm.

"Her colour! Please, *Hajjeh*, the women's turned green and I don't know what to do. We have to get a doctor."

"What do we need a doctor for?"

"Alright, but her colour!"

"What green?" the nun asked. "I don't see any green."

The green disappeared from Saada's body and was replaced by a pale blue that faded quickly, leaving her her own shining white, a milky white like white velvet that cloaked her body and absorbed the light into its folds. This was the colour that Meelya would inherit and that was to be the symbol of her special beauty, which so enchanted Mansour that it compelled him to come from the land of Galilee to let his eyes drink of the white that blazed from the body of his Beirut beloved.

"There isn't any blue and there isn't any green," the nun said. "The woman's body was exhausted and now everything's alright."

Saada grew quiet and stopped shaking. Youssef saw tears unlike any he'd seen before: Saada's tears rolled down and

39

spilled onto her nightdress and onto her exposed lower body. Youssef stared wide-eyed at the place that till then he'd known only as a dark spot to be fondled in search of the pleasure that God has granted humankind. Then he heard Nadra's voice ordering him out of the room.

"Let him stay!" the nun said in her high-pitched nasal voice. "Let him stay so he can see how a woman suffers!"

Youssef had turned to leave when the nun's voice nailed him to the spot: "Don't you move an inch! Stay here!"

The nun ordered Nadra to get down so she could pull the baby out.

"Come on now, Saada, my daughter, my sweetheart," the nun said. "Just one push and it'll be over."

"Push," Nadra said in a low voice. She knelt on the floor and reached for the small head waiting to descend.

The room drowned in silence, as though Saada had surrendered to sleep. Her face relaxed and whiteness swept over her. Youssef saw his wife's face expanding in the whiteness, bathed by the sweat spreading over it.

Nadra cupped her hands to receive the child and it fell into them from the womb. She hugged the child to her chest, forgetting in her amazement and excitement to take hold of its feet and turn it upside down.

"Hold it up!" the nun screamed.

The midwife got up heavily and held the child up by its feet. After she'd cut the umbilical cord and before she could strike the child on its bottom, a trill of joy escaped her lips.

Saada told her daughter that she hadn't cried when she was born, as every other child did: "Nadra forgot to hit you on your bottom so the holy nun held you up. No-one cries in the hands of a saint."

Youssef had a different view: "The nun hit her on her bottom and the girl never stopped crying, but you don't hear a thing, woman. When the nun's here, I don't know, it's like you've been hypnotized."

The nun took hold of Meelya, who was all wet with blood, and held her up as though sticking her to the wall. "Congratulations. Meelya has arrived," she said, and ordered the midwife to wash her in salt water.

"Why salt?" Nadra asked. "We don't wash with salt."

"Water and salt," the nun replied.

Turning to Youssef, she asked him to fetch a bottle of olive oil. Nadra washed Meelya in water and salt and then the nun wiped her with the oil, swathed her in a white cloth and held her over the bed as though sticking her to the chalky white wall.

"Congratulations. Meelya has arrived. May God raise her, guard her and keep her from harm," the nun said. Placing the child at her mother's breast, she left. Youssef ran after her and kissed her hands in thanks, the taste of salt and oil imprinting itself on his lips. Then he bent over Saada and kissed her forehead.

"Meelya has arrived," Saada said, looking at the wall, where she saw an image adhering to the white lime at the spot where the nun's hands had held the child.

"What kind of a name is Meelya?" Youssef asked. "No. I want to call her Helena."

"Her name is Meelya; she was born with it. Didn't you see what the nun did and how she said her name? So there you are," Saada answered.

Twenty-four years from that day, Saada would stand, dumbstruck, in front of the picture that Moussa had hung on the *leewan* wall at the very place where the nun had held up Meelya's salt-water-and-olive-oil-washed body. The mother would tell her son that she'd seen the very same picture the day her daughter was born, and Moussa would look at her with troubled eyes, knitting his brows to make her stop talking.

Saada would tell no-one else the story until a year later, when the picture was all that was left to her of her daughter.

"When the nun held her up, the girl turned into a picture. This is the picture. I saw it. I saw it when Meelya was born and I read beneath it the words that are written there now: *Rather, she sleepeth*. I saw everything then just as it is now. God, why didn't I understand? Everything was drawn in black and the nun kept muttering the words written beneath the picture."

The picture that Moussa hung in the *leewan* stayed in its place and was taken down only when he decided to demolish the old house so that he could put up a new building in its place. When she made the journey to Galilee, Meelya carried with her, waking and sleeping, the image of her home, which was in fact two joined houses with a large garden. She told Mansour that she had brought the scent of the house with her and could smell it every morning. Standing on a rise that looked out over the slope leading down to the Convent of the Angel Mikhail, it was protected from swarming summer gnats by chinaberry trees whose green leaves, with their penetrating scent, repelled every sort of insect.

The house, originally half a house, had only been made complete when Youssef had married. The original structure, bought by Saleem Shaheen, his father, had consisted of a large *dar* separated from the *leewan* by arches and glass windows, plus a small, dark kitchen and a bathroom at the end of the corridor that led from the kitchen to the garden. The garden was shaded by a large fig tree with three trunks on which Moussa and Meelya hung the oblong wooden swing that took them flying up to the sky.

To please Saada, Youssef had added a bedroom, a dining room and another bathroom, turning it into two interconnecting units. The large old part was built of yellow sandstone, the new one of concrete. The roof of the old part was made of wood covered with earth and a shallow layer of white lime, the roof of the new of cement. The house thus became two houses side by side: a house in which the breeze played in summer and which was warm in winter, and a house which was hot in summer and cold in winter. The four boys lived in the new, concrete, room, while Meelya lived with her parents in the *leewan* until her father died, at which point it became the place where she lived with her mother. This geographical division occurred following the death of her grandmother, for originally Haseeba had lived in the *leewan* along with all the children. After she died, Saada decided to change the whole look of the place, gave the boys the concrete room and moved with her husband into the spacious *leewan*. No-one, however, could find a solution to the problem of Meelya. Her mother suggested the girl sleep in the *leewan* with her parents, but Moussa insisted that Meelya stay with him on a small sofa in the boys' room. So Meelya found herself with nowhere. She would have preferred to put her bedding on the floor in the dining room, but in practice was left with no place of her own, and had to sleep either on the sofa in the one area or on an iron bed that her mother had put up in the other. Thus did she carry her dreams from place to place, living out a nightly homelessness, the problem being resolved only when her father died and she took over his bed.

Meelya was nine years old when Youssef died. Niqoula and Abdallah took control of their father's shop while the eldest son, Saleem, continued his law studies at the French-language Université Saint-Joseph and little Moussa stayed at the Mar Elias School in Teena.

Meelya saw her birth dream three days after her father died. The nine-year-old had been struck speechless when she saw Youssef laid out in death and heard the women's cries and mysterious utterances.

"The Best Beloved is come!" one of the women screamed.

43

The girl saw herself standing in the midst of the throngs of black-draped women waving their white handkerchiefs over the corpse of the man laid out on the bed in the *leewan*. Meelya gathered that she was the Best Beloved, but she didn't know what best beloveds were supposed to do when their man died. Her legs buckled and she found herself on the floor. She dreamt this dream times without number – legs buckling, a little girl falling, then the nun coming and hanging her on the wall. She saw herself wrapped in white cloth, two hands lifting her up high, then herself falling.

Meelya couldn't get close enough to look into her father's closed eyes; she never got there because she fell and tasted burning inside her. The same taste returned when she found herself moving closer to the man sleeping beside her. She wanted to get to him so she could cover his trembling body with the quilt and pat him on the shoulder and tell him not to be afraid, but instead she fell. She opened her eyes to drive away the dream and saw the light stealing through the cracks around the yellow curtain covering the window. She looked over. Mansour was sleeping on his back, his mouth slightly open, snoring loudly. Reassured, she smiled and decided to go back to sleep.

In the morning, Meelya got up, dressed and sat on the end of the bed, waiting. She looked at her husband and saw that Mansour had become a half circle, his knees bent, his head resting on his right hand. He was breathing deeply and every now and then would let out a sigh that came from the depths of the world of sleep. He looked to her like a young child. She bent over him but then drew back and went out into the hotel's small garden.

"You wanted to kiss me," Mansour said.

"No. I wanted to cover you up."

"So why won't you let me?"

44

"Take your hand away. I want to sleep."

"But I want to make love to you."

"Please don't say that. I'm sleepy."

Mansour couldn't understand why his wife always went to sleep in such a hurry. As soon as she laid her head on the pillow, she'd doze off and an expression of deep relaxation would print itself on her face. Then he got used to taking her while she was asleep. When he heard her breathing grow louder and sensed that she had entered her nightly world, he would move in close and start caressing her, going higher and higher, and then enter her. Her half-opened lips would moan, but she wouldn't open her eyes. She would be like someone dreaming, everything about her floating, and Mansour would float on top of her as though, when he entered her water, he too was swimming in the dream.

"Yesterday I made love to you," he said.

"What?"

"You don't remember?"

"Please don't say such things!"

Mansour stood at the threshold of his house getting ready to leave for work, a cup of Turkish coffee, made in the Ottoman way, in his hand. He took a final sip, placed the cup on the table, looked into Meelya's honey-coloured eyes outlined in the colours of light, and asked her what she had seen in her dream.

"Go back and dream your dream again," he said. "I want you to be awake today. Take a nap before I come home, dream another dream, and it'll all go fine tonight too."

Mansour thought Meelya was terrified by the events in Palestine, though Nazareth was far from the disturbances erupting throughout the country and the uprisings against British occupation and Jewish immigration. She never talked to him about politics, and he, despite his modest political interests, the raucous arguments with his friends at the café and his fear that

45

all of Palestine might be lost, only discussed the subject with his wife in general terms and in passing. It never occurred to him that the woman, preoccupied with her private experience of pregnancy and of the city of Nazareth, might not care about these events or be aware of their significance. The dream that had brought her there and persuaded her to marry Mansour repeated itself every night, while at the same time the feeling that even the city in which the Lord Christ had lived nineteen hundred years before was in flux made her aware of the transience of all things. So she would set off in search of sleep and of the life she lived within a world encircled by the walls of night.

When he asked her to dream her dream over again, she smiled at her husband and said, "At your service." He said he loved her dream, even though she hadn't told it to him, because she'd been kind to him in the night. "You were like sugar melting in the mouth," he said. Meelya remembered nothing, or so she claimed. Each night she'd dream, redraw her image in the mirrors of the darkness as a seven-year-old girl with short black hair and wide green eyes, rediscover her feeling that the night's spell could last into the day, and continue with her dreams after she woke, intertwining the reality happening around her with their reality – all of which alarmed her husband. In the end, however, Mikhail Muawwad, the Syrian priest who ministered to the flock at Our Lady of the Fright, explained to him that his wife's visions were symptomatic of pregnancy and there was no call for alarm. Meelya would emerge from the life of the night as soon as she had borne her first child.

Meelya left the hotel room and went out into the sunshine of the small garden. Patches of snow like white islands amid the grey of the trees. A blast of cold wind. A sun mingling with the clouds scattered in the sky. She washed her dream in the light and the wind and walked in the garden, sensing that her womb was rounding out. Everything inside her was round and hot. She sat on the edge of the small pond in the centre of the garden, reached towards the cold water, and the heat in her fingers was extinguished, the thrill from the water running up to her shoulders before descending into her breasts, and the pain of the milk coming. She saw the milk coming out of her breasts as drops forming circular threads, and her tears flowed, falling onto her large breasts, and the milk mixed with the tears.

Meelya had been four when Hanneh had come to work as a maid in their house. Hanneh hadn't stayed long, however. Sister Milaneh came with a piece of cotton wool dipped in holy oil for Saada and stayed three days and nights with her in the *leewan* until she recovered. At least they said that the mother had recovered, but she hadn't. "She's become another woman," Youssef said to the nun. Her eyes like arrows, the nun cleared her throat and declared, "Shame on you, Moallem Youssef!" Shame inscribed itself above the greying man's head like a halo for all his children to see, and that word, like a ring sticking to his hair, was erased only at the moment of his death. When his sons bent over their father's brow and kissed it, Meelya saw how the ring was erased and the man left to sleep in peace on his final journey towards his brother in the craft.

"Ah, your craft, the craft of Christ!" Saada wailed, weeping as they lifted the dead man into the coffin.

"Shame on such words!" the nun said.

"But he was a carpenter and Christ was a carpenter," Saada said.

"Shame on such words! Christ loved fish and he was a fisherman," the nun said.

"But he was a carpenter too," Saada said. "God forgive you, Youssef, for leaving me like this. Greet my father for me."

Meelya didn't see her father's last dream. She had lied to

everyone when she said she'd seen him in a dream carrying his carpenter's tools, a beautiful bearded youth at his side, the two of them fading into a black cloud that veiled the daylight. When she went to kiss him, she fell. The nun helped her up and took her out of the room.

"Shame on you, Moallem Youssef!" the nun said as she announced Saada's recovery from her strange illness.

No-one knew the nature of the mother's affliction. She nearly lost the ability to walk; upon rising in the morning, she would feel dizzy the instant her feet touched the ground and be unable to stand. She'd utter a piercing "Ah!" filled with pain, and one of her sons would hurry over and help her up from the bed. Thereafter she'd move about by leaning on the wall. Upon entering the kitchen she'd start vomiting and collapse once more. It was because of this illness that Hanneh came, though she didn't stay long; thanks to the nun's miracle, Saada recovered somewhat and they no longer needed a maid. But all the same Saada remained sick. True, she was able to get out of bed without help, but she started neglecting the housework and little Meelya took on all the chores – cooking, washing and cleaning the house.

By the time the mother's illness had become part of the family story, it was recalled as having started after the father's death, or as having been caused by it. Youssef died when Meelya was nine, but Hanneh came when she was four. Meelya's transformation into sole mistress of the house took place after her father's death, however. Families make up their stories and then believe them. Meelya lived the story that her mother's illness had occurred after Youssef's death and believed it. Hanneh only seeped through the cracks of her memory at the moment when she found herself alone beneath a sun whose rays were obscured by a white haze of cloud. She reached towards the pond to extinguish the burning in her fingers and saw Hanneh uncover her breasts beneath the olive tree and knead them, weeping as she did so, her milk spurting. Hanneh was short and round, her face broad and white, her eyes sunken beneath bushy eyebrows, her lips thick. She sat down beneath the olive tree, tucked her breasts back inside her ample black dress and then noticed Meelya close by, her eyes filled with bewilderment. Hanneh gestured to her to come closer. The girl approached on stumbling feet and heard Hanneh say, her voice choked with tears, that she longed for her son.

The little girl didn't understand much of the disjointed story told to her by the servant, who came from the distant village of Jage, near Jbeil, but she felt the blood leap to her cheeks and ran as fast as she could into the house. Now, her hand in the water, a puzzled smile played on her lips as she tried to recapture the memory of the woman. She remembered that Hanneh had told her of a boy who'd died at the age of just three days, of a husband who'd disappeared from the village and of milk-filled breasts.

Meelya heard Hanneh's voice seemingly coming from a hidden place within her and saying, "My breasts hurt," and sensed a slight catch in the woman's voice as she asked Meelya if she would like to taste the milk.

No, it hadn't been like that. Had Hanneh really asked her that? She didn't know, but she had become aware that her mouth was watering, and an obscure fear had driven her to run away. Did she taste the milk? Why had its sugary taste remained on her tongue so that whenever she waited for Najeeb she'd feel the same taste rising from her breasts to her lips?

Meelya didn't dare go out into the garden any more with Hanneh standing there beneath the olive tree, her back turned to the old house, her breasts bared, the milk falling onto the grass.

What was Hanneh's story, and why did the nun drive her from the house?

The ghost of the woman with the large breasts started appearing again and again in Meelya's dreams, with Youssef's brown face in the background greedily watching the spurting milk. Had he? She doesn't know. What she does know is that Hanneh left her village and came to Beirut and worked as a maid in their house, and that her only child had died three days after he'd been born.

Hanneh had told her of a blonde child who'd lived for three days before its hair, which resembled the down of a bird, had turned hard as thorns and she'd realized it was dead.

But why had the nun driven her out of the house?

Was it because Meelya had told about the breasts? And had she been the only one who had seen the woman as she suffered the pain of the bursting milk?

Here, at the edge of the pond at the Hotel Massabki, Meelya felt the woman's milk and the pain in her breasts. Greyness invaded the sky; she closed her eyes and remembered.

She was alone, she felt a great heat, and she was hovering, naked, above her garden at home. Darkness, but not total darkness. How had she forgotten that disjointed dream amid the thronging dreams of the first night after her wedding?

Young Meelya stands naked before the pond in the garden of the old Beirut house. The olive tree is there, and the snow, falling white and scattering itself across the surface of the water, and she feels heat, and almost suffocates.

Her short orange dress falls as though a hand has undone a long zipper running from her neck down her back. The same hand reaches for her underclothes and snatches them off. The little girl beholds herself naked in the centre of the pond, the snow falling hot upon her as she gathers it to her chest. She feels thirsty and starts devouring bits of snow. She eats the snow and swims, she eats and her thirst isn't quenched, she swims and doesn't get cold; a dream without end, thirst without end, sleep without end, snow without end, and water; everything swimming in water, and little Meelya swimming and eating and sleeping, and the snow covering her and the heat radiating from inside her.

Meelya withdrew her hand from the water, the thrill spread from her breasts to her belly, and she saw the face of her father, Youssef. His eyes are half closed and he moves in and out of focus as she tries to say something, but her voice won't leave her throat. Hanneh had told her breasts, swollen with milk, the story of how her husband had divorced her and snatched the child from her hands. So the child didn't die, it was kidnapped. Why had Hanneh said that its hair had turned hard as thorns? Did its father kill it?

"What does it mean, she divorced him?" Meelya asked her mother.

"Don't say that word. We don't have divorce. Divorce is a sin."

Hanneh disappeared, her story disappeared with her, and Meelya never told anyone what had happened. Moussa was little; he was the only one she could talk to, and by the time he grew up the story had entered into darkness and oblivion.

After her husband died, Meelya's mother contracted the chronic illness that caused her to spend most of her time at the Convent of the Angel Mikhail, surrounded by prayers, icons and nuns. By the time she was a grandmother she too had become a saint, or something like one, preparing cotton wool dipped in oil which she would give to sick family members, none of whom could ever claim he wasn't cured because no-one would have believed him. All the family, young and old, believed in Saada's miraculous powers, which she derived from her special relationship with the nun of the huge body and high, screeching voice.

Meelya became aware of the water, and Chtaura's morning

cold began to steal into her limbs, so she decided to go back to the room. She entered the hotel lobby, where breakfast was laid out, and saw the driver sitting at the table alone, wolfing down fried eggs, *labaneh* and cheese. When he saw her come in, he rubbed his hands, looked at her out of the corner of his eye and smiled. She could see words hovering on his lips as though he wanted to say something, but he went on chewing his food, his mouth maintaining its mocking twist. Meelya tiptoed up the stone staircase and opened the door to the room; its curtains were still drawn and it remained plunged in darkness. Smelling a strange scent, like that of the pond in the dream, and feeling sleepy, she took off her clothes, put on her nightdress and crawled into bed next to Mansour, who was wrapped up in the quilt, hugging his knees to his chest in a half circle. Laying her face near his closed eyes, she felt tenderness as well as a slight pain running from her shoulders down to her lower back.

Meelya would never say it was love. Here in the bed, and there in the car, she had felt something obscure whose name she discovered only in Nazareth. She used the word *love* only once, and that was after returning home from the church, her belly swollen and her clothing filled with the smell of incense. Mansour was in the garden smoking a cigarette and inhaling the scent of dust awakened by rain. Turning to her, he said, "You know, Meelya, you're going to give birth at Christmas, at the end of December."

She was in her fifth month and the rains of early April were intoxicating her with their smell. She knew exactly when her baby would be born, and at what hour, but when Mansour said the word *Christmas*, she felt a spasm in her belly, as though the foetus had moved, saw a white cloud around her husband's eyes, remembered them closed that morning at the Hotel Massabki and said that she loved him.

"If you love me, why won't you let me sleep with you?"

She placed her finger on his lips to silence him. Why did he have to talk like that, use that expression? She had told him a thousand times that she didn't like such talk, that sex existed for the procreation of children and that she was pregnant, thanks be to God.

Mansour started to speak, and silence enveloped her. She was like someone drawing a veil of soundlessness over her face, tiptoeing around the house, tidying, preparing food, waiting for her husband. She never questioned him, and he could be as late as he liked, come home whenever he wished and be sure that his wife would neither complain nor ask.

He talked to her about love and about how he had been bewitched by her beauty the moment he had set eyes on her, and she smiled and lowered her eyelashes. He told her a lot before telling her that marriage made him thirsty.

"Me too. I'm always thirsty," she said.

He didn't tell her that the cause of his thirst was her silence and that he had to fill in the gaps created by the absence of her words, nor did he ask her why she pretended to be asleep when he had sex with her; he knew that the pleasure of it made her writhe and that her moans were not those of pain or refusal. That low moan that emerged from her tightly closed lips set his skin on fire and transformed him into a swimmer in a sea. He would wait for the dark, close his eyes onto the colours of his desire and set off, caught on a gentle wave that would raise him up, wrapped in a hot wind calling on him to persevere. In an instant, he would reach a point where he felt everything within him coming to a head and want more – but the woman with the closed eyes would close her thighs and cough, turning away and leaving him to cup his member in his hand and go to the bathroom.

That moan of hers, coloured by her dreams, took him back to the first moment of his love, and he'd forget that he hadn't been able to sleep with her properly in Room 10 at the small hotel. There he'd felt that all his faculties had betrayed him and that, what with the long walk through the fog, the snow flurries swirling in the raging storm, his fear that he'd be blown away and fall into the valley, and his awareness of the role he had to play as a man, he was on the verge of dying. There, in the midst of the fog, his manliness had walked ahead of him, confident of itself, and he had staggered along behind it, on the point of falling, his eyes watering. He had wanted to close his eyes to stop the cold from burning them and had looked back at her, but all he had seen was the ghost of the car, creeping along like a tortoise. When the driver got out at the top of Dahr el Baydar saying that he could go no further and was going to take them back to Beirut, Mansour had screamed at him that he'd take over the driving himself and started back to the car, but the driver had run ahead of him and taken his seat at the wheel, gesturing to Mansour that he'd follow.

"Everything's fine," Mansour had said, his words lost in the raging wind, but everything wasn't fine. The road was full of danger. He slid many times, the car skidding behind him, and when the fog cleared, Mansour had returned to the car only to find Meelya asleep, wrapped in her mother's coat, her body shaken by intermittent spasms. He'd tried to talk to her, wanting to recite a poem – he had prepared many lines of old Arabic poetry to recite to this woman as he drank champagne in the hotel room before gathering her into his arms – but all he could think of were two verses:

"Ah you mountains of Lebanon, how shall I cross you
    In winter when your very summer is a winter too?
Your snows have obscured the tracks I follow,
    Their whiteness so white they now seem black in hue."

The woman had opened her eyes and then closed them again, seemingly not hearing, or not understanding what she heard, and making Mansour feel like a fool. He'd been saving the poetry as a surprise for his wife. He'd decided to start her off with some ancient love poetry; he'd tell her that he, in his way, was a poet too, because he'd memorized hundreds of lines, preparing a banquet of poems for his wedding night. He had imagined himself in the hotel room drinking and rolling out a carpet of words in front of this woman who had stolen his heart and forced him to devote his days to journeying between Nazareth and Beirut.

Mansour hadn't known that that first fleeting encounter in the garden would turn his life upside down and transform him into a permanent traveller. He'd seen a white girl, her hair tied in a ponytail, bending over to water a bed of basil, and had lost his heart. He had come to Beirut to buy cloth for the shop he'd opened in Nazareth. Following a disagreement with his brother Ameen over the running of the Jaffa metalworking shop the two of them had inherited from their father, he'd decided to become an independent trader and start over again in a new place.

"The plan is to make some money and return to Jaffa," he told his wife when they arrived at their home in Nazareth.

Meelya bowed her head and said she would prefer Bethlehem.

"What's in Bethlehem?" he asked her.

Not replying, she saw the golden halo flickering between her eyelashes. She had told no-one of her dream. What was she supposed to say? That she'd accepted him as a husband because of the dream, and that she had found herself here because she'd heard a voice telling her, "Go unto Nazareth"? Things were mixed up in Meelya's head: the woman whom she'd seen in the dream had been carrying a baby; she'd given the baby to Meelya and vanished into her long blue dress. Meelya watches as the blue forms waves and fills the valley. The woman leaves the baby – a brown-skinned boy-child with closed eyes, swathed in what looks like a shroud, a halo of light above his small head – in the arms of the little girl. Blue light settles on the knees of the seven-year-old, who is sitting in front of a cairn of stones close to the edge of the valley. Behind her is an old abandoned building, like an ancient church, built of white stone. The woman appears out of nowhere, then vanishes, leaving her robe undulating behind her, covering the valley. Meelya stands up to try to grasp the edge of the robe and feels she's falling. Gathering the child to her chest, she moves back, trips on a rock, and, as she begins to fall, opens her eyes and takes a deep breath. The oil lamp in front of the wooden icon case hanging in the corner of the *leewan* is on the point of going out. The wick is burning blue and the blue woman, having left Meelya's eyes, is entering the case, the brown colour of which appears halfway between red and gold. Meelya closes her eyes, but the blue woman returns and places the child on her knees, then vanishes once more into her blue robe. The robe covers the valley. Meelya approaches the edge of the valley, reaching out to catch the end of the blue robe. She feels afraid, pulls back and falls.

The following morning Moussa came and told her about the suitor and mentioned Bethlehem, so she bowed her head in consent. Then he said, "No, I'm wrong. He's from Nazareth, not Bethlehem," and she bowed her head again and said yes.

Had she heard the names of both cities in her dream? Had the blue woman told her the city's name? Meelya can't remember hearing voices, but when she smiled at her husband after he asked her, "What's in Bethlehem?", she felt the names of both cities rise from the depths of her dream and couldn't answer his question.

Had she really told the man from Nazareth that she loved him?

Through Mansour's eyes she sees herself bending over the bed of basil, intoxicated by the scents of dust, water and perfume rising from it. The man, seeing her from the back, decided not to leave Beirut without her.

"When I see you, I feel thirsty," he'd said.

"What thinketh the moon of the moon?" he'd said.

"I stand here to guard the scent of the basil," he'd said.

She'd heard him, turned around, seen a face like her brother Moussa's, and felt an intoxication that came from the blending of the basil with his words. The man's words took on a scent like that of basil, and the crunch of his footfall in the next garden sent a shudder down her spine. But she spoke with him properly only once. The first rains of autumn were watering the earth and Meelya was standing in her long dark-blue dress and white blouse watching the trees become bare, when she'd heard a voice rising from among them saying, "You are she."

"I'm what?" she'd asked.

"You know what I'm talking about," it said.

"Me?"

"I love you," it said.

"Why?" she asked.

"I love you and want you."

"Me?"

Then she had "gathered her whiteness about her" and gone into the house. That was how Mansour would describe it later. He'd say that she'd "gathered her whiteness about her" and gone in. That she'd bowed her head and said yes.

Disappearing into the old house, she had felt his eyes planted like nails between her shoulder blades, and her neck hurt. And when Moussa said reproachfully that she must have got to know the man and fallen in love without telling him, she couldn't think of anything to say, so she reached behind her to pull out the nails and said yes.

Mansour was sleeping and Meelya was trying to sleep; she closed her eyes and felt a trembling beneath her left foot. She was falling against the ladder, and Moussa was telling her not to be afraid.

A tall wooden ladder, a beach and a sea. Everything is coloured light blue. Meelya is climbing the ladder, Sister Milaneh is standing at the bottom and shaking it. Meelya is above and the ladder is shaking beneath her and she's holding onto it and trying to keep on climbing. She looks down, sees the waves and the foam, and suddenly falls against the ladder like an acrobat performing exercises. Her head goes down first, she stretches herself out against the ladder as though lying down on it, and then starts doing somersaults. She falls quickly, but the ladder has no end. The nun comes out of the photograph and Moussa reaches out to catch them both. Moussa falls into the water and the sea swallows him up. Meelya stands on a rock in the midst of the waves, her shorts messy with seaweed and her eyes stinging from the salt. She looks for her brother among the waves but can't see him. A hand reaches out and casts her into the vast ocean and she feels she is drowning and starts choking. Then she opens her eyes, licks the salt from her lips and sees only darkness.

Meelya sat on the edge of the bed and placed her hand on her chest to still her hurrying heartbeat, which pounded in every part of her – in her neck, in her temples, in the soles of her feet. Everything within her was trembling violently.

Why this fear? What is she afraid of?

The shadow of a smile drew itself on the woman's darkness-enshrouded lips as she remembered this old dream, which had abandoned her three years earlier when she had met Najeeb Karam for the first time and felt that this young man would wipe the dreams from her eyes and force her into real life. But Najeeb had disappeared, taking the dream of the ladder and the sea with him, and here she was, sitting on the end of the bed in Room 10 at the Hotel Massabki in Chtaura, asking questions and knowing the answers and being afraid.

"I fell in my dream and my foot still hurts," Meelya told her mother, who screamed, "Stop telling your grandmother's fibs. You're a big girl now and you have to find someone to marry."

The white woman's body shuddered and she got up, bent over, picked up her long nightdress, put it on, sat on the end of the bed and once more heard the rasping voice of her mother as it used to emerge, saturated with nargillah tobacco, from the depths of her throat. The same voice would accompany Meelya to Nazareth and be the last she heard before seeing the youth seated beneath her picture, trying to copy the Gospel verse written in small *naskh* letters inside the frame.

Why did the honeymoon room look the way it did?

The man turns away from her and she opens her eyes onto a dream that isn't like her dreams. Where had the old dream gone?

Once, Meelya had lived to the rhythm of her dreams. She would get up in the morning, wipe the dreams from her eyelids and go on with the story. She would dream that Najeeb was sitting with another girl in the garden of her house and that she was standing at a distance and watching the man reach towards the girl's hair and then bend over and place a kiss on her neck before the two of them disappeared beneath the large fig tree. Then, when he came to visit her the next day, she would refuse to sit with or talk to him, and things would only return to normal when a new dream came to wipe away the one before it.

"What was wrong yesterday?" Najeeb would ask her.

She would smile but not reply.

"I don't understand. Did something happen?"

"Ask yourself that question." Then she'd burst out laughing

and say, "It's not your fault. I had a bad dream and was in a bad mood. Forget it."

But Najeeb wouldn't understand, and when he'd insist on knowing the reason and hear her accusations of infidelity and the story of his relationship with a brown-skinned girl whose name Meelya didn't know, he'd go off in a huff.

When Najeeb disappeared from her life and went off to marry the fat woman he married, she dreamt of him at night and heard him telling her that he'd run away from her dreams: "How could any man live with a woman like you?"

"What I dreamt turned out to be true. I saw you; I had to leave you and not let you leave me. It was my fault."

She saw him standing next to the fat woman whose backside filled the garden, her brother Saleem standing next to them.

"I hate you!" she told Saleem. "Making yourself out all sensitive and saintly. Shame on you!"

She saw herself on the ladder and started turning somersaults and screaming, with Moussa standing at the bottom, reaching out and waiting for her. Then she crashed to the ground and felt as though her bones had shattered.

"Where did you go off to and leave me, Moussa? You're still upset about the money, aren't you?"

She had dreamt that Moussa had stolen the few piastres she was hiding under her mattress. She'd got up one morning, couldn't find the money and, when Moussa had come home from school, had reproached him. The boy's face turned red and he tried to deny the accusation before collapsing in front of his sister and admitting his crime. Meelya kissed his eyelashes and forgave him.

Meelya used to play a dream game with herself: when she couldn't remember a dream, she'd close her eyes and pretend she was still asleep, waiting for a dream that could take the weight of her day. Her nights would begin with her sketching out her dreams before falling asleep. Or things weren't that simple; she'd decide on the settings for her dreams, which were mostly on the beach or looking out at the valley. Even in the depths of winter she'd go to the beach, wrap herself up in the quilt, close her eyes onto the colour blue and find herself in the water.

In summer, the four brothers used to go swimming every day at Beirut's rocky beach, and sometimes she'd go with them. She'd stand on the beach and watch them swimming.

"You're a girl, and it's not decent for girls to swim," her big brother Saleem said.

"Why isn't it decent?" Meelya asked.

"Because you're a girl," Saleem answered.

"I'm not a girl," she said.

"Why? Have you got a willy?" Moussa asked.

"Shut up, idiot!" Saleem yelled. "You, stay there and watch us."

Once she ordered Moussa to take her to the beach. There was no-one else at home; her mother was at the convent "licking the icons" (as Saleem used to say, describing his mother's constant visits there), Saleem was with the Jesuit fathers, and she was at home with Moussa. She was twelve and a half. She begged him, and then she ordered him, so they went. She took off her clothes and put on the bathing trunks she'd taken from Saleem's cupboard, and she felt Moussa looking at her small breasts, which had begun to round out. Trembling and naked in the presence of the endless blue, she steadied herself before stepping into a small pool that lay like a rocky tongue within the dry land. Seeing her brother's eyes fasten on her breasts, she became aware of them. They were like two small figs drawn on her hairless chest. Meelya hadn't noticed them before and would go on trying to forget them later on, when they had grown larger and turned into two apples – acquiring that special colour of breasts where violet explodes within white – and budding pink nipples.

Mansour would discover these breasts in the dark, take them during his wife's eternal drowse and tell her that the apple was tastier than the pear.

"What are you talking about?"

"I'm talking about breasts. I prefer apple-shaped ones. There's nothing wrong with pear-shaped ones, but apples are round and fill your hand. What lovely apples you have!"

"Stop it, please!"

Having despaired of convincing her that sex was neither a sin nor indecent, he'd let her fall asleep. The problem lay in her inaccessibility, which set him on fire and made him try to take her by force, then retreat before the water that covered her face. He had come to fear her sorrow and the way she would sit at the end of the bed, dabbing at her tears with a corner of the white sheet.

She would be slow to respond, would ask him to stay away from her bed, would writhe in the bedclothes, get up, go to the bathroom, and then return and turn out the light, asking him to put it off to the next day; so he would wait until she was asleep. Her eyes would be closed, her body slack and unmoving. He would take her, her water would begin to gush, and he would drown. Then he would feel that he was no longer erect, as though, when she took him inside her, he dissolved into her world of darkness and closed eyes. Her body would vanish in his hands; he would pull out her breasts and start kissing them, absorbing their taste, a mixture of jasmine and the scent of apples, and then he'd hear her low moan and start on the sliding journey within, where he would dissolve in her water. When he was done but wanted to continue, she would cough and expel him, turning onto her side and sinking into a deep sleep.

In the morning, he would find no sign in her face of what they had done. Her white face, rounding as her pregnancy advanced, would overflow with light. Did she wait for him to fall asleep before going into the bathroom and washing, or was it that she really was asleep and didn't wash till the early morning?

Once he committed a major blunder. They were sitting in the main room of the house. Mansour was listening to the radio and Meelya was crocheting a woollen sweater for the baby on the way. He got up, went over to her, placed his hand on her left breast and bent over to kiss the blouse that covered it. When he reached inside, she shook him off.

"Let me kiss it," he said.

As he extracted the breast from the folds of the blouse and took the rosy nipple between his lips, pain traced itself on her face. Caught up in the scent of apples, Mansour heard her scream, "Stop!" The pain vanished from her face, she gulped, said, "Stop!" and stood up.

Mansour didn't dare follow her into the bedroom, where she curled up and went to sleep. That night he didn't go near her breasts. He possessed her utterly, and she was hot and soft. The next morning, she told him that it wasn't allowed: "Breasts are for the child. You have to understand." Three nights later, as he held her breasts, he heard the same moan as before and sank into the drowsiness of love, but he never again attempted to uncover them in the light, content to let their luminosity penetrate the darkness of the room and open the doors of night to him.

Hiding her breasts with her arms, Meelya threw herself into the sea, and the taste of salt engulfed her. The same taste would return to her lips that cold winter morning when she found herself in bed in the small room at the Hotel Massabki, when she licked her lips and went back to sleep. There, though, on Beirut's rocky shore, she had plunged her breasts into the salty water and stood watching Moussa as he played his games in the water, swimming under the surface until she thought he'd drowned and would never come back, then suddenly popping up somewhere else in the huge sea, waving at her but moving away.

She closed her eyes, put her head under the water, opened them onto the blue that changed to a light green mixed with grey, and realized that the sea's depths had green eyes and that the green that enveloped her nights came from the mixing of these rocks and those colours. She raised her head, a chill swept over her, and her eyes hurt. She screamed for Moussa, but Moussa was swimming far away, rowing himself with his arms, his head sunk in the waves.

When Moussa came back, he found her standing in the water, panic in her eyes. He took her hand to help her out of the sea, but she withdrew it, crossed her arms to hide her breasts and followed him. She got dressed and felt hungry. A chill seized her. The July sun shone over the water, but Meelya was shivering under her short skirt, which covered the wet swimming trunks that she hadn't dared take off. Moussa bought a pastry with thyme, divided it with his sister and wolfed down his share while she watched him and ate crumbs of hers.

That same night she had dreamt of the sheep and tasted its kisses, and her menstrual blood had come. Her mother told her that she was a woman now and would have to behave like other women. Meelya was afraid of the blood and didn't understand why the egg that had formed in her intestines had to explode in such a gory way. "Does that mean the egg is dead?" she asked her mother. "Does it mean that every month someone dies inside me?"

"That's silly talk. It's not death, it's nature," Saada said.

Meelya understood that nature was death. A sensation grew inside her that repeated itself each month as the time approached: she would move more slowly, feel as though a ball were forming inside her belly, and her nerves would suddenly become taut; she'd place her hands on her belly as though she were pregnant and wanted to prevent the foetus from falling out; and when the blood came, the little sheep would appear too, along with much pain. The fear of the egg falling out continued to haunt her until she became pregnant. In that small, distant city, though, she no longer saw the little sheep kneeling on top of her. She took to walking every day through the lanes and streets until her feet grew tired, at which point she would return to the house and sleep and dream of the blue woman who would draw close and then, having placed the child in her arms, disappear into the valley. She would hug the child to her chest, let him suck on the orange nipple and swoon, her womb contracting, copious water flowing from her guts.

She didn't tell Mansour that she was leaving the house and walking in the lanes. In the mornings, she would feel she was complete, like a circle, and she would walk. But Mansour saw her. She had sat down on a white stone overlooking a field of olives close to the Church of Our Lady of the Fright and allowed her gaze to wander over the view. Mansour had seen her by accident and followed her; he was leaving his shop to smoke his morning nargillah at Suleiman's café when he saw her shadow, like a circle gliding quickly along behind her, and recognized her. She sat down on the white stone and he hid behind the wall, neither accosting nor speaking to her, remaining where he was, holding his breath. When she stood up and began to walk back towards the house, he went to the café. In the evening, he returned home and found her sleeping as usual. He woke her and she made him his dinner, and then she went back to sleep without their having exchanged a word.

The following morning, as she was making his coffee, he went to kiss her, but she moved away. He spoke to her, but she didn't reply; in fact, she looked at him reproachfully. Mansour was sure she hadn't seen him at the church and wasn't prepared to believe the stories she told him about her dreams, convinced as he was that she pretended to be asleep so that she could have the freedom to interpret things the way she wished to. He asked what was wrong but she didn't reply. He felt as if he were suffocating. He had become used to the silence and to living with a woman who resembled a phantom, but he couldn't bear her anger or her sorrow.

"Tell me, what's the matter?"

"You know."

"No, I don't know. Tell me."

"It's nothing," she said, and went into the main room. Catching up with her, he put his hand on her shoulder. She turned to him and said, "Take your hand away, please."

"What's the matter? What have I done?"

"You were following me."

"Me?"

"Yes, you. You stood behind the wall of the church and didn't come over to me. I saw you."

"When?" he asked.

"I don't know. Maybe yesterday, maybe a few days ago."

"How did you see me?"

"I saw you through my back."

"No-one sees through their back," he said.

She looked at Mansour and saw him change into Moussa. She saw his trembling lower lip and the tears suspended in his lashes. She bent over, brushed his eyes with her fingertips and kissed them. "Don't lie to me any more. Promise me that you won't lie. Go on, say it."

"I promise," Mansour said, admitting his fault.

That day Mansour conceived a fear of this woman. He heard her call him Moussa and said nothing. Previously he had reacted violently and yelled at her to stop calling him by her brother's name: "My name's Mansour. Why do you keep chasing me with your brother's name?"

"I've no idea," she replied. "Maybe because I miss him."

"Miss him as much as you want, he's your brother. But my name is Mansour."

"Mansour," she said. "So be it. You're Mansour."

But Moussa's name wouldn't go away. Once he heard it, or thought he heard it, when she was sleeping. He was about to reach out to her when he heard the name, pulled away and tried to sleep but couldn't. Turning back to her, he took her, telling himself he was mistaken, had misheard. At the same time, though, he had sensed her great loneliness; the woman was a stranger here and he no longer knew how to talk to her. Her low voice made him feel the terror of voices, and her sleepy eyes looked only into the distance, making him feel that he could never catch up with her.

That morning, when she bent over, brushed his lashes and kissed them, Mansour felt as though he'd been transformed into a child, and he confessed that he'd seen her by accident, followed her and stood watching her as she sat on a stone in front of the church steps.

"But tell me honestly, how did you see me?"

She said she'd seen him through her back, because in her dreams she saw everything. She told him of the four directions one sees when dreaming and asked about his dreams.

He told her he didn't dream.

"I don't believe you," she said. "You just don't remember your dreams" – and went on to explain that one had to train one's memory because dreams were an extension of life: "You spend as much of your life in the dark as you do in daylight, so anyone who doesn't remember his dreams lives only half a life."

As she explained the importance of dreams in a person's

life, it was the voice of her grandmother that she heard coming from her mouth.

"I'm not like that," Mansour said. "I never dream."

"Everyone dreams," she said.

For the past three months, Meelya had been rounding out with pregnancy, drowsiness and thirst. Her breasts were becoming larger, her face more radiant.

He asked her why she went walking every day on her own and why she didn't go for a walk with him in the evenings when he came home from work instead. He asked her if she was sad because she was living far from her family.

She looked at him and didn't reply. Then she said she was introducing the boy to the city.

"What boy?" Mansour asked. "Anyway, in my heart I'm sure it's a girl. My mother says that when a pregnant woman becomes more beautiful it means she's going to have a girl, and you're becoming more and more beautiful."

"I said boy and I meant boy," she replied.

On that other day, when she'd covered her small breasts with her wrists, Meelya had discovered that she'd travelled to a distant place from which she would never return. Her naked breasts in the middle of the pool within the sea had given her away, and that night the little sheep had come to her. This dream repeated itself so often that Meelya ceased to be able to tell it. She would remember it in her waking hours as though it had really happened and see it as a monthly visitor in her sleep – a small white sheep, walking unhurriedly across a field of green grass. Meelya is asleep beneath a large fig tree. Her eyes are closed and her small brown body is curled in a half circle. The little sheep approaches, stands next to her and lays its cheek on hers. The girl turns over and lies on her back. He retreats and then gallops towards her, clambers on top of her, places his front legs on her chest and lowers his head as

68

though to crop the grass. The young sleeping girl sees only the rays of the sun. The sun shines through the wool and pours into her open eyes. The little sheep brings its mouth close to her eyes, so she closes them, afraid he'll think that her green eyes are part of the grass of the garden and devour them. She closes her eyes, feels the little sheep's tongue on her neck and smells the smell of the sun. The sun-sheep shudders and heat floods out of him. There is pain in her belly, the green grass surrounds her, her eyes are closed, and the pain extends from her eyes to her lower back. She strains her eyes in the darkness. She strains some more and awakes from her sleep. Two closed eyes, and Meelya awakes without daring to open them. The heat envelops her, the hot blood falls on her thighs. She rises, washes her thighs with cold water, puts a towel between them and goes back to sleep.

The sun-sheep, as she called it, would come, surrounded by a blue halo radiating light. It appeared in different forms, some-times galloping over her small body, which would assume the size of an infinite field, sometimes sitting on her chest and kissing her shoulders or burying its head in her neck. Always, however, she feared for her eyes. With the little sheep, contrary to what usually happened, she awoke when she closed her eyes instead of when she opened them.

The little sheep disappeared when the foetus started to form in her belly, and it didn't reappear until the end of December 1947, when Meelya would hear the doctor's voice asking her to push and she would enter her long dream. That day, the little sheep would return, and she would feel a mixture of longing and fear and forget to close and protect her eyes; instead, she tried to open them before the white wool could cover them and draw blue halos around them.

The man sleeping beside her lay sunk into his staccato breathing interspersed with nasal whistling. She wiped the traces of the foggy car journey from her eyes and tried to collect her memories.

Meelya didn't know the man. Or, she knew him only as her husband-to-be. Mansour's story of his love for her had passed her by without her noticing. When, on the night before the wedding, he had told her parts of it, she'd felt that she'd lost the only story that it would have been worth her while to live.

The night before the wedding, he had turned up un-announced. Normally, the groom disappears the day before, going with his male friends to a "farewell to bachelorhood" party, as they call the final orgy permitted the groom before he enters the cage of marriage. Mansour did not do this, however, not because he was a man of noble qualities, but because he had no friends in Beirut. Mansour turned up at the Shaheen family home on that cold December night to offer his apologies because, in view of the events in Palestine, his relatives would be unable to attend the wedding, and to express his desire that the ceremony not be postponed. Moussa sat with the unexpected guest next to his mother in the *dar* while Meelya made coffee in the kitchen. Moussa knitted his brows and the mother said nothing. Carrying the coffee tray, Meelya entered the *dar*, which was plunged in silence, and placed it on the table in front of the guest. Pouring four cups of coffee, she said, as though finishing a sentence she had begun earlier, "It doesn't matter."

"It doesn't matter," Moussa repeated.

"Then we'll go ahead," Mansour said, his voice shaking, and he stood up to leave. Yawning, the mother stood up to say goodbye. "Sit down," Meelya said. "Let the man drink his coffee," she told her mother, tugging at her arm and sitting her down again on the sofa.

Mansour sat on the edge of the sofa as though about to get up at any moment and took a sip of coffee while Meelya sat opposite him, looking at him as though waiting for him to tell her a story.

"You know . . ." Mansour said.

"I know," Meelya replied. "Things don't look good."

"That's not what I meant," Mansour said.

The silence was only interrupted when Moussa left the room. The oil lamp trembled as it cast its light. Meelya, wearing a yellow dress and resting one cheek on both hands, waited for the man to speak. Her mother slipped out of the room and silence mingled with silence.

She wanted to tell him that he too was planning to run away at the last moment, but she didn't. The shadow of a sad smile drew itself on her lips. With her hand she pushed away the ghosts of the memories that had stolen into her eyes as she sat for the first time in a semi-darkened room with this man who, in a few hours, would be her husband. She could feel his fear. How was she to tell him that she had known he would visit that evening and tell her that his relatives would not be coming from Nazareth?

"The road is blocked. The British army blocked the road three days ago," she said.

The coffee cup shook in Mansour's hand and he saw what appeared to be ghosts floating above the chinaberry trees. He didn't ask her how she'd come to know about events in Palestine or how she'd heard him say that his relatives wouldn't be able to come. He put his coffee cup on the side table bordered with Kufic inscriptions which he tried to read but could not.

"What does the writing say?" he asked.

"I've no idea. You'll have to ask Moussa. I think it's poetry. Moussa said a friend of his brought it as a gift from Damascus."

Mansour stared at the table and tried to read the words. "No," he said. "That's not poetry, it's verses from the Koran."

He rubbed his hands together against the cold. Meelya got up, put a log in the stove and then sat down again. Warmth permeated the place, words returned to Mansour's throat, and he dismissed his embarrassment with a flick of his fingers, thinking the girl had not noticed his fear. Then, taking her hand, he kissed the turquoise signet ring she was wearing, cleared his throat and said,

> *"Playfully for a signet ring I tussled with one*
> > *Like a full moon in the darkness shimm'ring.*
> *Whene'er from her smooth and pampered fingers*
> > *I tried to take that thing,*
> *She'd throw it in her mouth and then I'd say, 'See how she hides*
> > *The signet in the ring!'"*

Then he told the story of his love.

Night, and the trees lean in on each other for support as the midwinter winds wet the windows with rain. A 37-year-old man sits in the *dar* rubbing his hands preparatory to speaking. The walls are high, the ceiling is of brown wood. In the corner a brightly burning stove, four blue sofas ribbed in black, and a woman aged twenty-four radiating the colour yellow while the milky whiteness of her skin spreads itself across her long fingers. The man looks at the floor and imagines the naked white wrists. Out of the corner of his eye he follows the movement of the flame in the paraffin lamp hanging from the ceiling, and in a low voice he tells his story. No-one looking at him as he sits on the sofa, bent forward a little, would notice the small paunch protruding above his leather belt, though they would see the stooped shoulders, the eyes concealed behind thick black brows, the round brown face, the black moustache.

When Meelya saw him for the first time, she thought she was looking at her brother Moussa, which was what made her accept him as her husband, or so she would tell her brother. The truth was different, however. Mansour looked like Moussa from a distance, or in the dark, or in the dim light of a lamp, but in daylight the difference between the two men was plain to see, Moussa's features being finer and smoother. His eyebrows, it's true, were thick, but they didn't droop over his eyes or conceal the lashes that Meelya's fingertips had brushed so many times. Moussa was square-set but had an athlete's body and no sign of a paunch. His arm muscles stood out, while there was a slackness to Mansour's arms and a slight stoop to his shoulders – a stoop that no-one would have noticed at the time but that was to become the final hallmark of his life, when he would be referred to as "the man with the stoop". Moussa's face was oval, with a certain length to the jaw, and his nose was large but slightly skewed to the right, as though the bridge had been broken and a bulge had formed at the place where it went out of true. His neck was long. Mansour's face, on the other hand, was round and his nose large and proportionate to his lips. Only the thick black moustaches were astonishingly similar.

Anyone who saw the two men might have thought at first that they were brothers, but would gradually discover that Mansour was simply an inflated version of Moussa. The main points of similarity were their voices and their backsides. Moussa's voice was melodious and came from the back of his throat, like Mansour's, and his backside was so flat you'd think there was no flesh at the top of his thighs, which was what made Meelya pause when Mansour turned and left the garden: she saw that his buttocks were flat and said to herself that this man was her brother's twin.

Meelya noted the points of similarity and dissimilarity and agreed to the marriage without hesitation.

The mother said that the girl had suffered greatly and that, after two unsuccessful experiences, it was time for her to marry.

73

Moussa agreed but hesitated: "Nazareth is a long way away, sister. Where are you taking yourself off to?" But he accepted Mansour readily because the man was, as he put it, "a decent type".

Meelya heard Milaneh ordering her out of the room so that she could minister to Saada. "The Devil – I can smell the Devil," the nun said, turning towards the young girl who was holding her mother's hand and trying to calm her heated body.

The nun had entered the *leewan*, which was filled with the smell of incense. She held a small brass censer from which rose a piercing scent cloaked in white motes. The nun blocked the door with her vast body as she swung the censer, peering right and then left. Approaching the sick woman slowly, the sound of her breathing grew louder. Then she turned to Meelya and said it was the Devil.

"Get out, girl!"

Meelya looked at her with indifference and didn't respond.

Dr Naqfour had been and examined the sick woman whom he said had a chest cold, for which he had prescribed medicine. Saada, however, refused to swallow the bitter liquid. Meelya would force her mother to open her mouth and swallow it, but the patient would spit it out and then be sick.

"Don't be so hasty, *Hajjeh*. The woman's sick," Meelya said.

"I know, I know. Niqoula came and told me, which is why I'm here. But you get out. I can't work with the Devil around."

"What devil?"

"Ask yourself and your dreams and all those fiancés that run away from you. Better repent and come to the convent."

Dumbstruck, Meelya stood up and watched as the nun bent over Saada, placed a piece of cotton wool soaked in oil in her mouth and ordered her to swallow it.

"She can't swallow," Meelya said.

"Shut up, you, and get out!"

Meelya fell silent but didn't leave the room. Remaining at her mother's side, she saw how the woman swallowed the cotton wool with her eyes closed and how her body relaxed to the rhythm of the mutterings emerging from the nun's lips.

Could it be true that her dreams were the doing of the Devil?

The nun said the Devil got into women because their bodies were beautiful and complete: "God created woman complete, but she chose to be incomplete. Look at Our Lady Maryam, peace be upon her. Did she need a man to be complete? Of course not. She became complete through the Holy Ghost because she was complete from the beginning."

"But not all women are the Virgin Maryam," Meelya said.

"Have you noticed, Meelya, how ugly you're becoming?"

"Me?"

"Yes, you. Why don't you come to church, my daughter, with your mother, so we can drive the Devil out of you?"

What was she supposed to say? That she was afraid of the church? That when she found herself with the throngs of worshippers beneath the Byzantine icons, enveloped in the smell of incense, she felt afraid, as though the church were a graveyard? There people stooped over the icons of men and women who had died long years before and spoke with them, as though the distance between the living and the dead had been erased so that all were dead. Meelya feared that space that opened onto death; she would go to the church on Good Friday and weep with the others for the crucified Christ. The rest of the year, she prayed alone at home and asked God to open to her the doors of life that had been shut in her face.

No, what the nun said wasn't true. Her dreams weren't the Devil's doing. How had the nun found out about her dreams? It was Saada's fault. Since her father had died, Saada had become nothing more than a ring on the nun's finger, to play with as she wished. All the family's stories were being passed on to the nun under cover of the confessional, by which hung a strange and unprecedented tale.

Saint Milaneh wasn't content to rule over the nuns at the Convent of the Angel Mikhail; her influence extended to the priest of the convent, Father Boulos Saba, who permitted her to administer the sacrament of confession. The agreement between them was that she would confess the women and then send them to the priest for absolution, and that the priest would make his own confession to the nun. This was contrary to all the traditions of the religion, but the nun's miracles and her power to cure the sick allowed her to overstep boundaries.

Via the confessional, all the stories and secrets of the Shaheen family had become *Hajjeh* Milaneh's property. Meelya could no longer bear the nun's looks, in which she saw a mixture of pity and contempt, and understood that her experiences with Najeeb and Wadee had been revealed, her secret tossed in to join the thousands of others filling the saint's head.

Her mother grew calmer, and her body seemed to sweat as the oil spread over her nightdress.

"After I leave, rub her body with rubbing alcohol. That's it. The woman's better."

The nun made to depart, but stopped at the door and called out to Meelya in her high-pitched voice.

"Yes?" Meelya said.

The nun put her hand on the girl's shoulder, bent over and whispered in her ear, telling her not to be afraid. "The groom will come, and I see a journey, but you have to wake up and pray to God to save you from terrible sin. Forget Najeeb and that other one, whatever his name was. The groom will come soon, never fear, but what matters is that you have to forget all this business of dreams. The believer, my daughter, doesn't dream, and if he dreams, he doesn't remember, and if he remembers, he doesn't tell. Night is a journey of darkness and a preparation for death. Only prophets and saints see visions at night; the ordinary person sinks into the darkness when he sleeps, for God, great and glorious, created sleep as a preparation for death. The world of night and the world of day do not meet. God is light and Satan is darkness. You must forget your dreams, my daughter, and when you do, God will open the path before you, I'm sure."

"But, I . . ."

The nun didn't let her finish her sentence. She said that dreams were the Devil's way of trapping man into sin. "Anyway, enough. You're a liar: no-one can remember all her dreams. Every day, first thing in the morning, your mother trembles with fear as she listens to your dreams. That's why she's taken to running off to the convent. Shame on you! What fault was it of your mother's? It was your brother Saleem's fault. She had nothing to do with the Najeeb business. Stop it, Meelya. You're like a daughter to me. I pulled you from your mother's belly and held you up high so you'd be close to God. Stop it, Meelya. Stop this nonsense."

The nun left without listening to Meelya's response. The girl wanted to say it wasn't true, she didn't tell her dreams to her mother every day, and they were her own and not the promptings of Satan or they wouldn't have turned out to be true. She had told her mother her dream about Najeeb because she'd felt hard done by and humiliated and wanted her mother to know that she didn't care. The nun left Meelya standing there, stripped naked by her words, having discovered with a shock that her dreams weren't hers to own and that her mother had handed her whole story over to the nun.

Night, and the trees lean in on each other's darkness as the rain whips the roofs of the houses with its ropes. Meelya opens her eyes, wipes the dream from her lashes and finds herself in water. The ceiling of the *leewan* is leaking and a shudder runs up

77

her arms. Instead of rising, however, and taking up the carpets and placing containers beneath the holes in the ceiling through which the rain is making its way, she closes her eyes again, not having believed them the first time, and the dream returns to her just as it had been minutes before. She sees herself as a small brown girl sitting on a rocky ledge before a deep valley, behind her a white building like a church. She is alone, not knowing where, listening to the whisperings of the valley and the sounds of the wild plants. A woman, her hair covered with a blue veil and wearing a long blue robe, approaches.

The blue woman, who has appeared out of nowhere, is carrying a suckling child wrapped in a white shroud-like cloth. She places the child in front of Meelya and vanishes. Meelya is alone. She picks up a small brown boy-child, who is breathing deeply. The child's breaths begin to penetrate her neck. She raises him up to hug him to her chest, sees the large eyes that take up the greater part of his rounded face and beholds herself entering the shadows of their pupils, where she finds herself in a high place. The child looks at her and takes her into his eyes, and water encircles her on all sides. She tries to get out of the water of the eyes; she reaches out and feels that she is drowning. She opens her eyes and sees the rain falling in the *leewan* and feels a chill on her arms. She closes her eyes and immerses herself in the dark child's eyes. Meelya has never seen eyes like these before. Two large whites in whose waters swim two black pupils, a black mirror within a white mirror. The child takes her into his eyes, the young girl incapable of resisting the pull of the tears glistening around the black pupils.

When she rose in response to her mother's calls to put containers beneath the holes in the ceiling, Meelya was shaking with excitement. Cold sweat covered her breasts and thighs, and longing raged within her. Her longing was incomparable – not longing like her longing for Najeeb, or that other man called Wadee, or for the doctor who had treated her when she had broken her leg. The three men belonged to the tongue, the nose and memory – love by speech, love by scent and love postponed. This longing was the longing of the heart.

She saw him three times during one rainy night and understood that she must go to him.

The business of the Armenian doctor had drained her adolescence. The sixteen-year-old girl had broken her right leg falling off a swing hung in a fig tree and found herself facing two Armenian doctors in Burj Hammoud. Zaven Hovnanian and his brother Harut weren't real doctors, they were practitioners of "Arab bone-setting", as the popular practice passed down from father to son was called. There, in a dark house with closed windows and drawn curtains, Meelya smelled a strange smell and failed to understand her strange emotions.

Meelya felt as if she had undergone a great change. She had grasped the ropes of the swing, stretched out her long legs and risen as high as she could go, the wind tousling her chestnut hair. Then she had fallen; she can't remember how the ropes came to slip from her hands or how she found herself on the ground with a pain in her right leg. She tried to stand but couldn't. The pain rose via her shinbone to her neck. She fell again and screamed for Moussa, but Moussa didn't come and she had to force herself up and hop on her left leg till she reached the four steps from the garden to the kitchen, up which she dragged herself on her backside, resting her weight on her other leg and hands.

When the swing took her flying into the air, Meelya noticed how everything had changed. Four years had passed between the day at the sea, when she had hidden her small breasts from the boys and dreamt of the little sheep, and the day of the swing. Meelya hadn't noticed how tall her rounded body had grown and how her jaw had taken on its own shape, liberated

79

from the roundness of her face. Her legs had grown long and slender, her buttocks had filled out in a little curve, her eyes were larger, her neck longer.

On the swing, as she stretched out her legs and pulled back with her hands to make herself fly as high as she could, she became a woman. She saw her chestnut hair taking on the colour of the sun and her whiteness clashing with the thick green leaves that spread from the branches of the fig tree. The fat girl whose brothers used to make fun of her for being as round as a ball had become slender, beautifully formed, full without being fat, her eyes wide and honey-coloured, the chestnut hair flying this way and that above her head, forming undulating waves of black and red and blonde. She didn't tell the brown-skinned girl of the dreams that she had become beautiful that day, because she didn't want to abandon her. The girl of the dreams, who used to appear and disappear as she wished, was freer than the rounded girl whose breasts jutted out into the salt of the sea under the boys' greedy eyes. The girl of the dreams had thin legs and a petite, biddable body like that of an acrobat. She could claim that she was no different from the boys and could go wherever she wished, appearing and disappearing and seeing the world through eyes of mixed grey and green.

When Meelya fell from the swing, she was amazed to discover that she'd rid herself of that past image that had made her hate herself, refuse to stand in front of the mirror and feel disgust at the sight of the small spots on her cheeks.

On the swing, she saw herself looking into mirrors of water; the leaves of the trees flying around her had become watery green mirrors reflecting innumerable images of a beautiful girl who had thrown off the mantle of childhood and emerged from the night of her old body to pass into and become her new one.

Did she fall off the swing because, gazing at her new image, she'd forgotten what she was doing? Because she'd closed her eyes so as to compare the image that had been her with the image of her with white legs exposed by the swing's rise and fall? Or because she'd pushed her upper body forward in order to stop the swing before going into the house to stand in front of the mirror and gaze at herself?

Meelya had flown, and everything within her had changed. This was how she would think of herself from then on. On that swing, she would say, she had become a woman.

Her mother had told her about the sheep. Or at least, the mother knew nothing about the dream of the sheep, but she'd seen the traces of blood on her daughter's short, chubby thighs and had told her that she was now a woman and had to ready herself for marriage and motherhood. But Meelya saw herself as just a mass of flesh and bone pierced by an open wound. She saw herself confronted by her monthly wound, which would accompany her for the rest of her life, and she felt shame.

"Is it the same for my brothers?" she asked her mother.

She watched as amazement traced itself in her mother's eyes and understood that this wound was hers alone – a girl among four boys, living what Saint Milaneh called "the monthly filth". She would swell up and hear her brothers joking and calling her "The Drum" and "Fatso". Only Moussa would stick by her. When she cried in the garden after Saleem had led the others in an orgy of bullying and described her as a drum, he told her she was beautiful. He took her hand and told her not to bother about Saleem because she was the most beautiful girl in the world. She didn't believe him, but she kissed him between the eyes and smiled at him.

She would sense the blood before it came, the anger and tension rising within her and the little sheep starting its nightly visits to her dreams. Only on the final day, though, when the pain in her left side had become acute and reached down her legs, announcing the imminent exorcism of the tension devil, would he leap onto her chest.

When Meelya fell off the swing and broke her right leg, she discovered that she was no longer the rounded Meelya who had hated to look at herself in the mirror.

She sat between the two doctors, Zaven holding her right leg and massaging it with hot oil, Harut standing behind him and holding her shoulders. Zaven asked her how she had fallen and she couldn't reply. Had she dangled her legs down and pushed her upper body forward to stop the swing, then stumbled so that the swing flung her forward and she fell onto the pain? Or had she fallen off when she was high up, taking her hands off the ropes as she often did, and then found herself plunging and landing with all her weight on her right leg?

She tried to remember, but Dr Zaven's oil-filled hand drew her soul downwards, making her feel that everything in her was sliding and then picking up the pain and lifting it to where the other doctor's hands were massaging her shoulders.

Where was her mother? And where was Moussa?

She smelled that strange smell, a smell that rose all around her and enveloped the pain coming from her bones. What was the smell called? And why, whenever she remembered it, did she feel a mysterious mixture of mute desire and disgust?

They took the girl the same day to Burj Hammoud, where she experienced something she could explain to no-one but which kept her company in her dreams. It came in the form of mysterious images enveloped in the steam that rose from a pot placed beside her, and it made her feel dizzy. Only her brother Niqoula caught sight of the fear and the phantoms in his sister's eyes, so he went with her on her third and final visit to the two doctors and broke the power of the smell that had filled the girl's nostrils and which she could not get rid of. Even on her wedding night, when cold and fog wrapped themselves around the American car as it climbed the heights of Dahr el Baydar and Mansour was sitting in the front next to the driver shivering with cold, she opened the window, heard the driver yell, "Close the window!" and said, "The smell."

"Blast the smell. Close the window or we'll all die of cold," the driver said.

"It's the smell of pastrami," she said as she closed the window.

"Can you smell pastrami, Mr Groom?" the driver asked, laughing.

Meelya didn't hear her husband's reply. She saw herself struggling up the steps and screaming for her brother Moussa when she reached the kitchen door, while at the same moment her mother emerged from behind a large saucepan boiling on top of the Primus. Her mother ran towards her daughter sitting on the steps and through the kitchen darkness saw the blood oozing from her knee. She called to Moussa to run to the convent and ask the nun to come.

"Why the nun, Mother?"

Saada bent over the wound and wiped it with a handkerchief soaked in water. She felt the broken leg and Meelya screamed in pain.

"God help us," muttered her mother, drawing back and asking her daughter if she could stand up. Meelya tried to but couldn't. Skewers of pain shot from her shinbone up to her eyes. Leaning against the wall, she burst into tears and then sat down again, saying between sobs that she couldn't stand. The nun arrived carrying her metal censer. The saint bent over the girl's leg, prodded it with her short, fat fingers, said, "It's broken. Take her to the Armenians," and turned to leave.

Saada ran after her to ask for the doctor's address, then asked Moussa to help her get the girl up on her left leg. Meelya stood between her mother and her little brother, leaning on his shoulder, and they proceeded to a taxi, which took them to an isolated house in one of the lanes of Burj Hammoud. There they were met by a stocky woman, a lock of whose hair, brown shot through with grey, hung down over her face, and who asked them to wait.

In that room Meelya smelled the strange smell. She would say that she didn't grasp what was going on because she was in pain. And she would say that on her second visit to the clinic she had sensed a mysterious undulation running through her shoulders and chest. The smell was the smell of cooked spiced meat mixed with an odour that emanated from the bodies of the two men. The first man, who was tall and broad-shouldered, was seated at her feet massaging her sole with his fingers, which then climbed up to her knee, whose cap he grasped in his hand. Meelya felt the down on her upper thighs undulating, as though waking from a deep slumber during which it had been waiting for a hand that never came. The man's short brother stood behind her, holding her shoulders and asking her to breathe deeply.

When the first doctor raised his eyebrows, her mother and Moussa left the room to sit in the dimly lit reception room draped with the daylight that filtered through the slats of the closed wooden shutters. In the other room, Meelya faced four hands and strange smells, whose meaning she would understand only when she fell in love with Najeeb Karam. She had fallen in love with his words, his ringing laugh, his mockery of every-thing, and she had smelled that smell again in the garden with Najeeb when the pain attacked her in her right leg. As the evening spread its shadows, as space filled with the voices of the creatures of the night and the blind fruit bats crashed into the trees and flew in circles above the sweet acacia tree in the middle of the garden, he had moved close to her. Najeeb had been telling her jokes and she was laughing. Then he'd said that he'd talk to her brother Saleem.

"Next week," he said.

"Meaning what?" she asked.

"Meaning you'll be my fiancée and then we'll get married."

"Me marry you?"

"Of course. What's the matter? Don't you like me?"

"I do, but . . ."

"But what?"

"But maybe Saleem won't agree."

"Saleem's my friend and he'll agree for sure."

"What do you mean?"

"I mean he . . . I love you," he said, and came closer. Then he put his arms around her waist and came closer still. At that moment, when she was in Najeeb's arms, the smell arose and entered Meelya's nostrils and she felt as though her right leg had become paralysed. She leant back against the trunk of the chinaberry tree and Najeeb pressed himself against her and held her tightly. "Aay!" she whispered, but that "Aay!" didn't stop Najeeb; it made him more determined, as though something inside him had caught fire. He pulled the girl towards him and put his lips to her long white neck. Meelya found herself unable to move: the smell mixed with the pain, she felt dizzy, and the young man who had taken her in his arms started to shake as though he'd caught a fever. Then he pulled away from her and ran to the bathroom, taking his smell with him.

They were alone in the house. The mother was at the church attending evening prayer with the nuns, and her four brothers were out. Najeeb had come, she'd made him a glass of rose-water sweetened with sugar, and they'd sat in the garden. He had talked and she had listened. She had stood up to make him coffee and then he'd moved closer to her and produced that smell that brought back the pain in her leg. As soon as he'd taken her in his arms, he had started to shake, and then he'd gone running to the bathroom.

He returned to find her leaning against the huge chinaberry tree. He went to hug her again, but she averted her face and said, "We've gone far enough."

"Do you love me?" he asked.

. . .

"Do you know what us getting married means?"

. . .

"It means you have to take off your clothes and sleep next to me, and that I sleep with you."

She closed his mouth with her hand, and he took it and kissed the palm. Then he kissed the fingers one by one, sucked on them and licked them. A fire broke out inside the girl and she felt herself falling. She pulled her hand away, leant against the tree and said, her voice trembling, "Go, please. You have to go. My mother will be back from church any minute now."

"I undress you," he said. "I bathe you and I sleep with you and you become like a fish," he went on.

The evening filled with a strange smell, the breeze abruptly ceased, and the humidity cast a thick blanket of darkness and fog over the city. She felt hot and cold at the same time, and became aware of the smell of the Armenian doctors.

Her dizziness was accompanied by a slight feeling of nausea and the desire emanating from her fingers made her shoulders stiffen. Najeeb spoke and Meelya wanted to run away. He talked and talked and talked, but she wasn't listening any more. She saw herself standing in a pool of water, insects buzzing in her ears, and she wanted to get out of the viscous water that clung to her legs, but Najeeb's words kept her rooted to the spot.

He talked about the two pomegranates, and about how he would pluck every kind of fruit from her garden.

"Stop," she said, and had a vision of herself in the garden in the darkness. How had the darkness descended so quickly? The fruit bats were crashing into the trees in their blind flight, and she raised her hand to shield her head from the unseeing creatures and their excreta, which were spattered here and there on the walls. She wanted to tell him to go into the house to take shelter from the darkness, the buzzing and the bat droppings, but she was afraid of him and of herself, and of the pool full of water. She ran inside and heard him asking where she'd gone, but didn't reply. She went into the house, said goodbye to him, and then closed the door behind her.

"But I don't want to go," he said. "I'm going to wait for Saleem in the garden. You can go in if you want."

She disappeared inside and sat on the sofa, her body trembling and the bitter taste under her tongue blending with the strange smell that flowed from her broken leg. Then she closed her eyes and saw him, his smile revealing white teeth that shone in the darkness of the night. The trees were dripping water, as though washing themselves with the dew that clung to their leaves; he approached her, took her hand and guided it to his trousers, extended with desire.

"Here. Here. Put your hand here, please. See? It's like a little bird. Did you ever hold a little bird in your hand? Did you ever feel how it trembles?"

The bird trembled in her hand and she felt the water seeping through his trousers and was overcome with dizziness and fell into the pool. Strands of spider's web wrapped themselves around her chest and neck. She said she was suffocating, and the nun is there; she's carrying her censer, and the room is lit with candles. Abu Saleem Shaheen is stretched out on the bed, weeping women around him. The nun picks up the brass censer and brings it close to Meelya's face. The embers burn in the censer and the grains of incense melt. The nun blows on the embers and asks Meelya to bring her face close and blow with her: "The embers mustn't go out, my daughter; you have to keep blowing all night so that the incense covers over the death. The mortal soul must reach Our Lord wrapped in incense. Blow."

Meelya blows, the ashes fly up into her eyes, and she wipes at them with her hand, but they penetrate deep into their whiteness and everything becomes grey. The young girl stands in front of the man with the white teeth. She is holding a bird that is too large for her hand. The nun orders her to blow on the ashes. Sounds of dogs barking, and night.

Meelya shook herself awake and found herself sitting on the sofa, sweat pouring down her back. Shivering, she heard her mother saying, "The nun asked why you didn't come to evening prayers."

"Where's Saleem?" Meelya asked.

"I don't know," said her mother. "I came back and only you were here. *Hajjeh* Milaneh sent you incense. She said you have to cense yourself every day before the betrothal ceremony."

"What betrothal ceremony?"

"We were talking yesterday about Najeeb, that lawyer friend of Saleem's. He says he wants to get engaged to you. We all know he loves you and you love him."

"Me?"

"Yes, you. Don't tell me you're still moping over Wadee the baker. He's a good-for-nothing. We know what he's up to. He said he wanted your share in the house before he'd marry you."

The mother went into the *leewan*, leaving Meelya alone in the *dar*. The girl rested her chin on her hand and stared at nothing. She felt the bird convulsing in her hand, saw the two Armenian doctors and smelled the smell again. Memories of the doctors come cloaked in black, as though they were a succession of ghosts and shadows. A tall man with broad shoulders bends over her broken leg and massages it with his plump fingers. He puts his round thumb on the place where it hurts and Meelya howls with pain. Then she becomes aware of two other hands on her shoulders and a numbness at the base of her neck, and she hears the voice of the tall doctor telling her to put her other leg on the chair. She extends her leg and feels fingers creeping; pain, fingers, a smell, two men. The first man stands behind her holding her shoulders, the other man bends over her leg. The oil slides over the leg and the fingers of the man standing behind her lift her up; it's as though she were suspended between two trees and the scent of the fig leaves were mingling with her flesh. She closes her eyes, feels the pain starting to leave her calf and feels herself rising, borne on the fingers. There is a smell of mixed spices; it's as though they were cooking, or were breathing spices. A mixture of piquant scents makes her eyes tear. She is unable to wipe the tears away herself, but the fingers reach out to them and catch the falling drops; then the bending doctor hands her a hand-kerchief and she takes it and blows her nose, and the mountain of pain is lifted from her.

"My leg feels like a mountain," she had told her mother when she asked Meelya how she felt. She had repeated the phrase to the nun and to the two doctors. The nun had turned away, indicating that they should take Meelya to the clinic, and the tall doctor had smiled before telling her that they would lift the mountain off her leg.

What happened during her three visits to the clinic?

When Meelya tries to sort out her memories, she feels as though she is in a dark place. Why, then? Why on the third visit did Niqoula accompany her, scowling, and go into the room with the doctors? The red-faced doctor who was standing behind her didn't touch her, and the broad-shouldered doctor limited himself to undoing the bandage from around her leg and wiping the flesh with a handkerchief soaked in oil and essence of thyme, after which he asked her to stand up. She stood up and walked.

"My leg feels weak," she said.

"What matters is that it doesn't hurt," the doctor said.

"It doesn't," Niqoula said.

When Meelya returned to the house and stretched her leg out on the bed, Moussa sat down beside her and rubbed it with his hand and she felt his fingers making her float a little and the smell disappearing.

Meelya didn't believe the story of the two doctors as told to her by Saada. The strange smell enveloped her once more and she saw herself in the darkness. That was on her second visit, a week after the bandage had been put on her leg. She became aware of a gap in her belly and felt that her navel was sinking into water. She saw her small navel, puckered like an unopened rose, surrounded on all sides by water, and everything in her softened and became watery. The broad-shouldered doctor was massaging the leg and the short thin doctor, whose shadow stretched over her from behind, was gripping her shoulders. She let out a cry, the bending doctor smiled, gasps of pain swept through her, and she couldn't bear it any more. Feeling that she had to scream, she covered her mouth with her hand instead. "Relax," said the doctor who was bending over the leg. "Does it hurt?" he asked. She nodded and a sort of scream emerged from her lips so that instead of just saying, "Please, doctor!" she screamed it. Then she heard her mother's steps and the clamouring of her little brother Moussa. The current that had convulsed her stopped, and she saw her mother at her side.

"What, doctor?" her mother asked.

"That's it," he said as he wrapped the leg in a white bandage. "Bring her back in three weeks so we can undo the bandage. She'll be fine now."

Meelya took the words "She'll be fine now" home with her only to find herself at the centre of a whirlpool of smells and a feeling that she was leaning against two conjoined shadows who visited her in her dreams in the form of a single man with two heads. One head was bald, the other had thick hair, and they came into her bedroom and placed four hands on her shoulders and her legs, and she cried out for help, sweat dripping from every limb.

In this dream, Meelya sees herself as smaller than the hand that reaches out towards her shoulders. She finds herself in darkness, lying on dry grass close to a pool of water. There are thorns in her back and she can smell something burning far away. Suddenly, the two men appear, moving towards her and transforming themselves into one man with two heads and two necks, one long and one short, and the hands reach out towards the thin little body sleeping on the bed of grass, and there's a little pain, and indistinct voices. The two men don't speak to her. They draw close and begin rubbing her shoulders, and the pain sweeps over her, and a stifled scream comes out of her. She opens her green eyes to find herself in her bed, drowning in fear.

How can she convince her mother that the story isn't true, and that it is possible to question the word of Saint Milaneh?

"The saint doesn't lie," her mother said.

"The doctor's a good-for-nothing slimy little shit," Niqoula said.

But night tells her things she doesn't know how to put into words.

"It's the secret of life," she told Mansour when he asked her why she slept while he had sex with her.

"Why don't you answer when I speak to you?" he asked.

"Because there aren't words that say what I want to say."

That was how Meelya understood words, and they cast their spell on her only when she was listening to Mansour declaiming the lines of verse he'd memorized. He'd set a glass of arak down in front of him and then pick it up again, swirl it around and cover the sides with a milky film.

"This is real arak, thrice distilled till it's pure as teardrops. Look at the milk on the sides of the glass – like mist, like love, like milk, like tears."

Looking into his wife's eyes, he'd see that they'd veiled themselves in a delicate blue that lent colour to their whiteness.

> "Still he comes, the one who once departed,
>> For the one who's yet to come is gone."

Mansour would take a sip as though kissing the glass with his lips, and start talking:
"Do you like al Mutanabbi?

> For your eyes' ransom, all the heart has found and yet will find
>> I give.
>> For love's, all of me that lives and does not live.
> Ne'er before was I of those in whose heart love lies
>> But all must fall in love who see your eyes."

The ancient verses pour from his lips as he mixes love poems with wine poems, elegies with eulogies, and says he will call his first son Amru.

"Amru! That's not a nice name."

"No, woman, Amru it is, but the 'u' at the end isn't pronounced, it just makes the 'r' softer. It's after the poet Amru ibn Kulthoum. He was a chieftain of the Bani Taghlib, and if Islam hadn't come along the Bani Taghlib would have made short work of the Arabs. That way you'll be 'Umm Amru' and I'll be able to court you with love poems the way I should. Listen to this:

Umm Amru — may God forgive you! —
  Give me back my heart as once it was before!
Those lovely squinting eyes that look aslant
  Have slain us, leaving our dead to die in their gore."

"That's me?"

"Of course! Who else? Drink up."

He put his glass to her lips. She drank a little and felt like coughing but didn't. Instead she turned to Mansour and said to him reproachfully, "Me? Do I squint?"

"No, no, not 'squinting'. I meant 'glinting'. Glinting eyes mean beauty, meaning whiteness, meaning the most beautiful thing in the world. They're white with black at the centre, like Daad, you remember her. Ah, how I pine for Daad! You remember the poem."

"Please stop it. I don't like that kind of thing."

"She has a thing that swells to the touch,
  Hard to enter, fire throughout.
When you thrust, you feel you're thrusting into felt;
  When you pull, it won't come out.

You know what 'thing' means?"

"And we're off!" she said. "That's it. I'm going to bed."

"'Glinting' here, my darling, means whiteness and beauty."

"Yes, but all you can think of is the dirty stuff."

"When I saw you in the garden with a man beside you . . ."

"You saw me?"

"Of course I saw you. The almond blossom had made a sort of crown over your head, like a white silk shawl, and you were standing next to a man who looked like me. I came closer but couldn't make out a single word though I could see that your lips were moving all the time. I thought, 'She's a honey, a real taste of honey,' and I kept licking my lips and saying, 'Tomorrow!', and I named you Umm Amru and thought my mother would be upset because she'd want me to name the boy after my father, Shukri. I told her, 'Let it go, Mother. My brother named his eldest son Shukri.' 'So what?' she said. 'We'd have two Shukris.' See how her mind works? She didn't love my father till he was dead, but it doesn't matter. You didn't tell me, did you like my mother? She liked you a lot and said you were an angel. She said to me, 'Take my word for it, son, you've found an angel straight from Heaven.' I told her, 'But this angel's asleep all the time.' Meelya, are you listening? Why are your eyes closed? We're talking."

She had placed her hands over her eyes, feeling as though her words were buttoned up and she couldn't speak. Words were like fastened buttons on a long dress that covered her body. To get out into the world and speak its language she had to undo the buttons, but she couldn't. She saw herself confined by buttons and she saw Georges Nashif sitting in his shop and yawning, buttons cascading around him. Meelya stands there, a button in her hand, holding it out to the clerk. Georges Nashif takes the button from the girl, opens the drawer and takes out a heap of other buttons, which he puts in front of him on the counter. The shop is filled with colours and the world rains buttons. The young girl stands there alone beneath the rain of buttons and Georges Nashif laughs. Hands reach out and pick up the colours, and Meelya, beneath the hands, feels as though she's going to suffocate. She opens her eyes and discovers that the covers have slipped off her and she's shivering with cold. She covers herself, sleeps and sees the tall ladder. She falls, and her brother Niqoula carries her to the clinic of the two doctors, where the smell of spices chokes her and the hot oil gushes onto her legs. Opening her eyes once more, she listens to the snoring of her younger brother Moussa, asleep at her side.

94

Meelya hadn't known how to tell that dream or how to live with it. She had heard her mother whispering with her women neighbours about the cheek of the man, and how he insisted on flirting with all the women, and his open-handedness with the pretty ones.

Why do the buttons come along with the story of the two doctors?

She wanted to tell Mansour that words were like the buttons that hold a robe closed, and that she couldn't undo them, which is why she couldn't talk the way he wanted her to. She learned by heart the verses her husband recited, but discovered that the metres broke into pieces in her mouth and that she was like someone walking over broken glass, the words cutting her feet.

"Why don't you say something?" Mansour asked her.

There was a taste of blood under her tongue and its smell filled her nose. "What do you want me to say?" she asked. Looking down at her rounded belly, she felt that she was about to go to sleep in her chair, so she stood up.

"Are you going to go to sleep?" he asked.

"I'm sorry. Leave everything. I'll clear up tomorrow. Now I'm very sleepy."

"No. No sleep now. I stay up every night and you sleep. And then when I get close to you . . ."

She went into the bedroom, put on her long blue nightdress, lay down on the bed and closed her eyes onto buttons.

The spectre of the two Armenian doctors pursued Meelya right up to her last moments. The girl didn't know what exactly had happened, but the story engraved itself on her memory as her mother had told it, and this gave the episode special shape, both mysterious and familiar. Had things really happened that way, or had they become confused in Meelya's memory and transformed themselves into a story that issued from the mouth of the sainted nun, who cursed the doctors, saying that they'd betrayed their sacred trust and got their just deserts in prison?

Meelya wept and swore by all the saints that nothing had happened, the mother screamed and wailed, and the four brothers sat in a semicircle round Meelya and began their interrogation. Moussa was frightened and embarrassed, Saleem was grave and scowling, and Niqoula and Abdallah's faces were white as chalk.

Meelya didn't say she didn't remember anything, because she remembered everything, but she didn't know what to tell or how to tell it.

"Nothing happened," she said, and told them about the doctor who had massaged her leg and his brother who had stood behind her holding her shoulders.

"And then what?" the mother asked.

"Then nothing," she said.

How was she supposed to explain this "nothing" that took on forms she couldn't find names for because she didn't know the proper words?

"The problem is that the words aren't the right ones," she told her husband, before falling silent.

She couldn't say that she saw words simply as covers for things, and didn't understand. When she listened to people, she thought of the sounds and shapes of the words instead of grasping their meanings, as though the words were hiding them.

"Very well," he said. "Listen:

Blame not the lover for his passions,
  When your guts and his are not the same.
A man lying drenched in his tears is as one
  Lying drenched in blood, for both are slain."

Mansour asked if she liked poetry and why she didn't answer so she went to bed. She closed her eyes and saw the two doctors who'd turned into one man with two heads, and the colour white spread over everything. The whiteness enveloped the two-headed man, gasps of pain escaped from the lips of the young girl at the mercy of their hands, and pain climbed from her leg up to her spine.

When the family interrogation was over, Moussa sat down beside his sister on the sofa and took her hand without speaking. Darkness spread through the *dar*. In the pale darkness, the mother came over and sat next to her daughter, muttering. Then she ordered Moussa to leave the room and told the story.

"It was the nun's fault," Meelya said. "She's the one who sent me to the doctor."

"Don't say rude things about her, daughter. It was the nun who warned me, and if she hadn't done so, your brother wouldn't have gone and saved you."

"Saved me?"

"Of course he saved you. Better death than dishonour. It would have been a scandal."

"But, Mother, they didn't do anything. I told you what happened, and nothing happened."

"They didn't do anything because they couldn't. Thank God it's all in the open now and they're in prison. God save us, it's a sign of the last days, daughter. If I didn't have five children to care for, I'd turn my back on the world and join the convent."

"You spend all your time at the convent anyway, or most of it. I don't know what you do there. Anyway."

Then Meelya muttered to herself, "What does 'anyway' mean? It means nothing, as though I hadn't said anything to my mother and she hadn't said anything to me. I listened to the story she told me about the doctor and said 'Anyway', and let it go. Living means passing over things and not understanding and pretending that we do. Why bother to talk, then, and why should I believe what I hear?"

She raised her voice and said, "Why should I believe?" Her mother turned to her and asked her what she'd said.

"Nothing, Mother. Anyway."

When did this conversation take place?

Was it when Saada sat next to her daughter on the sofa and told her the story of the two doctors, after the family interrogation? Or after the shock that Meelya suffered on learning that Najeeb was going to marry another woman, a shock that poisoned her soul?

"It's better this way. I knew, and, anyway, if he hadn't left me, I would have left him," she said, and entered her dream once more. That day she summoned her dream in a hurry so that she could watch the birds dying in the garden.

The smell of the doctors had pursued her to this distant city, filling her nostrils. She would close her eyes and see her mother sitting beside her telling her the story in a faint voice. Saada is yellow from the colour of the curtains at the windows, and the story is a succession of intersecting images.

Meelya opened her eyes and sat on the end of the bed. Mansour was on the balcony. She felt slightly nauseous and didn't want to see the face of the man who had massaged her leg, the sweat dripping off him, his laboured breathing growing louder and louder.

The story says that her leg slid up and down under two naked hands glistening with thick black hair. The oil was as transparent as water, and the droplets of sweat that had spread over the doctor's face and neck exuded a strange smell. The other man's hand, the hand of the man standing behind her, had climbed up her neck and was crawling over her cheek.

Had that happened, or did the memory take root because her mother had told her that it had happened? What had she told her? Was it true that the two men were married, as it were, to one woman, and that the police arrested them because they were drugging their women patients and then having sex with them? Can you imagine!

The story as it had stuck in Meelya's mind was muddled. It was said that the two doctors lived in the same house with the woman. The short, stupid one wasn't a doctor but rather his tall, husky brother's assistant. It was said that the real doctor had studied medicine at the Université Saint-Joseph, specializing in bone surgery, but had refused to follow the European methods he'd learned there and resorted to traditional practices, treating his patients with olive oil and other oils he extracted from wild plants. He also refused to use plaster on fractures, which he would treat with his hands and with oil, binding them with a thick cloth, claiming this was a better method because casts made the skin mortify and go wormy. He became the most famous bone doctor in Beirut, or so Sister Milaneh believed, and no-one asked about his chronic bachelorhood or his relationship with his brother's wife until the two of them were arrested in the wake of the incident with Madame Marta, the wife of *Khawaja* Nazih Shamat.

The story goes that Madame Marta visited the clinic of the two brothers for treatment for a fractured shoulder. While there, she became aware of certain strange goings-on. The strange taste of the flower-petal infusion offered her by the doctor's wife in the waiting room aroused her suspicions. Cunningly, she succeeded in throwing the hot liquid into a flowerpot. Then she entered the small room with the penetrating odours where the doctors treated their patients. Taking her place in the chair, she feigned sleep while under their ministrations in order to make them think that the infusion had permeated her body. But when the massage began to take unusual directions, she proclaimed the scandal to all the world. Endless stories started circulating about the two doctors and their shared wife. No-one questioned the truth of Madame

Marta's accusations because she was a respectable lady and the wife of *Khawaja* Nazih Shamat, who owned a silk shop on one of the small streets off the port, not to mention the fact that he was a fine, upstanding citizen and a member of the Greek Orthodox Community Council. Her word, in other words, was not to be doubted.

Stories started to spread about the short woman named Katy and how horribly she'd been treated by her short husband, who'd forced her to have sex with his tall brother.

"Now that's what I call sin!" the nun said.

"Has the woman confirmed the story?" Niqoula asked.

"God save us!" the nun said.

Niqoula said that the brothers had fled to Damascus to escape the gossip, but Saada stuck to her version, which claimed that it was the wife who'd told on them and that Madame Marta Shamat had been called as a witness. Katy had gone to the police station and told the duty policeman that they'd married her to two men and she couldn't go on that way. Then she acted out the crime. Saada said that crimes had to be acted out and that the woman with the untidy hair had stood in front of the policeman and acted out how her husband's brother would sleep with her. She said the business took place on her husband's orders, indeed under his very eyes, and that . . . well, it was too awful to describe. Also that she'd been unable to go on that way and had wished for death, and that her husband had prevented her from having children: "The tall one stopped me, I don't know what he did, sir, but I couldn't have children, or tell whose wife I was, or who I was. They beat me too. Also they were so mean that they wouldn't even turn on the lights. I never knew such mean people. When all the patients had left the house and it became dark, they'd light a single candle and I'd feel like a blind woman – everything black, everything quaking, nothing real left." The woman acted out the colour black, closed her eyes and repeated the events of her story. They kept her at the police station because she said she was afraid to go back to the house. The policeman detained the two men on the orders of the public prosecutor, who, it was rumoured, released them following the intervention of the French high commissioner. It was rumoured too that the woman was mad and saw things, and that no-one knew the real truth.

"What happened after that?" Meelya asked.

"How should I know what happened after that? All I know is that God saved us, daughter, or who knows what, but for God's mercy, might have become of us? That Katy woman had gone to see them because she was sick and then they drugged her or something and married her and she was done for."

Saada stood up, wiped her tears away with her handkerchief and stumbled towards the kitchen. She returned with a pitcher of water, drank, and told her daughter to drink.

Katy stands before the policeman and informs on the two doctors. The woman with the untidy hair lies on the floor in the police station and acts out how the two men had sex with her. Katy is stretched out in the patients' chair; she flops about between the two men like a fish taken from the sea, opening her mouth and gasping, and falls into a stupour.

Meelya told Moussa that the story was made up. The boy, who was twelve years old, could make nothing of it. He took her hand and asked her to take him to the beach.

"Why don't you come with us to the beach any more?"

"Ask your brother Saleem. He said I couldn't go because I'm a girl."

"I want to be a girl too so I can stay at home with you and not go to school."

Meelya laughed at her brother's naïvety. "No, brother, everyone stays the way they were created. They can't become something else."

"Would you like to be a boy so you could go to the beach with us?"

"I'd like to be a boy not just because of the sea. No . . . I don't know. Anyway," she said, without saying anything, "it's the way things are."

When Moussa told her that Mansour wanted to marry her and that she would have to go and live with him in Nazareth, she saw in her brother's eyes the old, unanswerable questions: Why does the woman have to follow the man she knows not where, and why are things the way they are? Now, after what she'd been through with Najeeb and Wadee, things were even more mysterious. Wadee had taught her that being a man means wearing many masks, while Najeeb had shown her the dilemma of the man in search of a place that will take care of him. The woman, on the other hand, has to be the masks and the places and everything there is, which is to say nothing.

"It's Saleem's fault," the mother said.

"No, it's Najeeb's," Moussa said. "Najeeb's a coward. He wants someone to look after him all the time because he doesn't know how to look after himself."

"God forgive him," Meelya said, watching as the birds fell and died before her eyes. Later she would name her dream "the dream of the blind birds" and tell it to no-one.

Since that encounter in the garden when she had stood with Najeeb beneath the chinaberry tree, she'd been afraid of the blind bats that crashed into the treetops and spattered the walls with their excrement. Then came the dream of the birds, making her the first to know the truth.

She left the balcony and went to bed, leaving Mansour on his own. He had asked her why she didn't cook her favourite dish, which he too had come to love. Over there, in Palestine, among the Hourani family, whose origins lay on the Mount of the Arabs (as Mansour insisted on calling the Houran), they called it *shakiriyyeh*; in Lebanon, though, they called it "mother's-milk-and-rice".

Meelya was proud of two dishes which she said were Beirut's greatest contributions to Levantine cuisine: "mother's-milk" and *kibbeh arnabiyyeh*. When Mansour first ate *kibbeh arnabiyyeh*, he realized that he had before him a dish that called for a trained palate: the *tahineh* mixed with seven sorts of citrus, the sliced onions, the houmous almost melting in the *tahineh* that shimmered between white and brown, the *kibbeh* patties and pieces of meat – all combined to make this dish, which Meelya transformed into the great joy of her life in Nazareth, entrancing to him.

Since that moment at the Hotel Massabki in Chtaura, Mansour had failed to enter Meelya's world, walled in as it was by secrets and dreams. There, the dream had mingled with sex and the wheelings of the blind birds had blended with the scent of the chinaberry tree so that she was too confused to know how to behave. She had therefore abandoned herself to drowsiness, which took her into deep waters that lay unmoving within her depths.

Meelya had recovered her dreams and returned to herself on her journey through the fog on Dahr el Baydar. The return was at first ambiguous, the woman whom she saw in her first dream, on her wedding night, being an exact replica of herself, a 24-year-old stretched out on the whiteness of the bed and the whiteness of her skin, which wept transparency. Mansour had told her that her whiteness was as transparent as water and that she was the mirror of his life.

"Now I understand Arabic poetry and can appreciate its aesthetic," he had said, telling her that the ancient Arab poets, who had lived in the desert, had written love lyrics only to white-skinned women, as though a woman's whiteness were a window the poet's soul opened onto worlds of shade, coolness and languor: "The woman has to be white, languorous and half-asleep, so that she resembles an oasis — a woman cloaked in the mystery of half-closed eyes, who takes the man into the labyrinth of love."

"You're a poet," she told him.

"I memorize poetry, but I don't want to be a poet. My dear girl, for a native speaker of this language whose vehicle is verse that blends ecstasy with wisdom and dances with the interplay of vowelled and vowelless consonants, it's enough to recite the poetry, play with it as you wish, and become drunk on its rhythms to your heart's content. The poets, poor chaps, labour under the burden of those who went before them and have no idea how to extricate themselves from beneath the sandbags of poems already written, so they fall to their knees, or imitate, or kill themselves. Listen, my darling, listen."

That day, Mansour was saying farewell for the first time to his Beirut beloved. He was going to the capital of Galilee to finish getting the house ready and then bring his mother to Beirut for the wedding.

The mother never came because of the uprising that set Palestine ablaze, and Mansour would marry without a single member of his family being present. When the family council held that stormy night in December broke up, he turned to his beloved and talked to her of whiteness and of poetry. He wanted to recite the whole poem but could remember only the opening lines:

"*Bid Hurayra farewell — the caravan departs.*
    But can you bear to say farewell, poor man?

Do you know how al A'sha continues the ode? I swear you'd think he was talking about you, Meelya."

"About me?"

"More or less. I want you to feel the poem as though it was written about you. Listen:

Resplendent, tall and slender, her side teeth gleaming,
— a hesitant, delicately stepping doe, slowly walking,
As though her gait, moving from the tent of the women close by,
Were that of a cloud that passes, neither hurrying nor
                                                    tarrying.

You are the hesitant, delicately stepping doe, my Meelya, all white and fearful. No, not fearful — *as though* fearful. The whiteness and the long neck aren't similes, they're descriptions, but the fearful walk is a simile. White and *as though* fearful, meaning it isn't really fearful."

"What's the difference between 'as though fearful' and just ordinary fearful?" she asked.

"The difference is the poetry, the simile, meaning something that makes you think of something else, and so on."

"I don't understand," she said. "And also," she asked, "what's the difference between a simile and a description? I know what it means when you say something's white — it means it's something whose colour is white. 'White' here is a substantive, isn't it?"

"No, Meelya, my darling, it's not a substantive, it's the elative. To tell the truth, I don't really understand it either, but when I read poetry I feel I'm flying. You fly on the meaning; I mean, it's a kind of ecstasy, so how can you expect me to write poetry?"

"And the man, the poet," Meelya said. "What was his name?"

"Al A'sha," he replied. "He was half blind, which is why they called him that. It means 'night-blind'."

"Blind, and he could see the woman's beauty?"

"He saw with his heart, not with his eyes, and he was

tongue-tied in the presence of the woman, like I'm tongue-tied in yours:

> Said Hurayra, when to visit her I came,
>> Woe is you, O man, and woe is me because of you!"

Meelya didn't ask him why he didn't write poetry because she was afraid, and her fear was no simile, it was a description. She'd decided, and that was the end of the matter. Or she hadn't decided; Najeeb had decided and had gone off with her brother Saleem. The dream had told her that her fate would be written in a city far away, and she understood that she must let her whiteness flow away before this strange man of whom she knew only that he resembled her brother Moussa. Meelya saw how the brownness of the man's skin had coloured her body and taken root there, and she realized that it was up to her to divest herself of her words just as she would of her clothes. When a woman speaks, she exposes her nakedness, but when a man talks, he puts clothes on – or so she thought to herself in bed. He was dressing and she was undressing, but she couldn't find the words so decided to say nothing and not take off her clothes. Or she didn't decide; her mother had instructed her to subdue him in bed. Her mother had told her that men came in different sorts and sizes and that some of them, especially in this day and age, would ask women to take their clothes off in bed so they'd be like putty in the man's hands.

"That's what they like, and you have to do what your husband tells you."

"Did my dad do that?" Meelya asked.

"What business of yours is your dad, God rest his soul? It's wrong to speak about the dead. But no, in fact your dad didn't make me take off my clothes. He'd take off all of his, but I'd be too shy. I mean, how could I take my clothes off when the children were asleep in the same house? But it didn't make any difference to him. He used to get under the quilt, take everything off and tell me, 'Whatever you like. Stay however you like.'"

"And then?"

"You'll find out for yourself soon enough."

The mother explained to her daughter that in bed she had to hold her own pleasure in and wasn't allowed to let it peak and overflow. "It has to be inside, my daughter, because men get frightened if they hear women panting and rising with them. That's how it was with me, but I learnt. Why am I telling you all this? These are things that can't be told. There wasn't another man like your dad, God rest his soul, but I couldn't take it any more. We'd had our children and it was enough; I began to feel I couldn't take it any more. Also I smelled the smell of sin. Maybe I treated the poor man badly, I don't know."

"It was the nun's fault. She's the one who put those ideas into your head."

"Don't talk about the nun. She's a saint, God grant us her blessing."

Meelya understood things differently. She'd seen the birds and found that she couldn't speak. Najeeb had disappeared from her life and she'd lowered a black curtain over the story. Everyone whispered about it, thinking she didn't know, but she knew everything. She'd seen the truth in Najeeb's eyes when the birds had dropped dead out of the sky.

Meelya found it hard to recall the dream of the birds. She had to dive deep into the darkness to find it, and by the time she found it she could no longer talk about what had happened.

Meelya had learnt to classify her dreams, dividing them into three types.

The first was the surface dream. It came in the morning and played a role in propelling her into wakefulness. It would be a simple dream, made out of life's mundane details, and it helped the eyes remain closed when faced with the morning light. This kind of dream didn't interest Meelya, who would erase it the second she arose from sleep, ending it by opening her eyes. Then, when it had gone, she would close them again in order to go to a deeper place where she would recall her real dream, which lay hidden somewhere beneath her eyelids.

The second type was the walled-in dream. Meelya would take this type of dream with her into sleep. She would close her eyes, her head would tingle, and she'd begin to weave stories and pictures. To sleep means to lay a pillow down and place one's head on it. Meelya's pillow wasn't made of cotton or wool or feathers but of stories. She would lay her head on the long, rounded pillow which also served as a back rest, and slowly weave her dreams. She saw pictures, chose among them carefully and arranged the elements to suit her taste. Najeeb the Lawyer could become Wadee the Baker, and Wadee could become the priest of the Church of the Angel Mikhail, and the priest could be in love with Sister Milaneh, and so on.

There were things, too, that she must not forget. Thus, since her mother's illness, cooking had made its appearance within the enclosure of her dreams. She would start by mincing onions to make "mother's-milk" and suddenly Niqoula and Abdallah would burst in, the first wearing his jaunty tarboush, the second the sandals he never took off, summer or winter. The boys would talk of their visit to the house of an Assyrian magician called Dr Sheeha, who came from Iraq and was summoning men to embrace a new religion combining Islam and Christianity. Abdallah would talk about the new religion and Niqoula would make fun of him and the onion-slice "wings" would be transformed into birds, and Meelya would sink into sleep.

Meelya discovered that it wasn't these two types of dream that really mattered, but she couldn't prevent herself believing in many of them. This was the origin of her morning problem, which was that her body had to get used to moving through air instead of water. Dreaming was like water, like being a swimmer in the water of the eyes, though she didn't dare say this to anyone. These types of dream would get mixed up with one another. The beginning dream, which spread with the first stages of insensibility, would return to meet the ending dream, which was the entryway to wakefulness, the door that led to the shaking off of the waters of darkness and the emergence onto dry land. At the instant of waking, the two worlds would connect, forming one world enshrouded in mystery. With the pre-waking dream recalling elements of the dream that marked the beginning of sleep things would become so mixed up that Meelya would no longer be able to distinguish between them. And when she got out of bed she would continue with the two dreams and behave in ways many people didn't understand.

What should she say to Najeeb? Should she tell him she'd seen him in her dream embracing a fat woman beneath the chinaberry tree while the woman simpered coyly at him and spilled her firm flesh onto his chest? Najeeb had told her she was mad, and she'd believed in his innocence and decided to stop making connections between her dreams and her life. Then the dead birds had come and given everything away.

The third type of dream was the deep dream. It was there that she saw the dead birds and found out everything about that woman who had married Najeeb. In the first two types of dream, Meelya didn't see herself, she saw others; it was only in the deep dream that her own image was reflected in the mirror of night. This was the dream that didn't float to the surface, the one she had to dive deep to find. In it she would encounter the brown-skinned girl with the green eyes, the girl who ran through the alleys of night and hid her dreams in the pit of darkness. Meelya had become accustomed to not telling dreams of this sort to anyone because they didn't belong to her; they belonged to the girl who put them on and flew with them into the innermost recesses of the night before everything vanished and scattered.

The birds occupied the deep dream. There, in the midst of a forest of pines towering into the sky, Meelya saw herself. The small brown-skinned girl stands beneath a lofty pine tree whose shade covers the place. A burning sun, the taste of brass burning her lips and tongue, and suddenly she sees him. Najeeb is wearing the uniform of a French soldier and running among the trees as though trying to get away from her. She waves at him to stop, but he runs like a blind man among the tree trunks, crashing into them, and she stands, not daring to move, fear paralysing her and pressing her into the earth. The flocks of birds start filling the sky and hiding the sun. They are like sparrows, fly with a strange rapidity, crash into one another and fall. They fold their wings and fall down dead. The earth fills with death. Najeeb disappears, little Meelya stands alone beneath the sun as the clouds of darkness move towards her, and the birds die. The girl's legs refuse to move and she sees herself spreading her arms and plunging. She wants to scream to Najeeb to save her, but her voice dies in her throat and Najeeb disappears. The heart of the bird shudders and it folds its wings, but it doesn't crash to the ground. The ground splits and turns into a series of valleys disappearing into the distance, and the small birds are suspended in space.

Meelya opened her eyes and felt thirsty. She reached for the glass of water beside the bed. The glass was empty. Lifting it to her lips, she drank thirst and emptiness. She decided to get up and fetch some water but was afraid, her legs seemingly paralysed. She laid her head on the pillow and asked sleep to come. Sleep came in the form of waves of sensation and a tingling feeling, and she saw the birds again. Najeeb was standing beside her, holding her hand. Suddenly he let go and entered the tree. The trunk of the huge sycamore-fig split in two and swallowed him up, and the smell of graves filled the place. The small brown-skinned girl was barefoot, and the stones hurt the soles of her feet. The birds came, spread their wings and flew before plunging to the ground, and Meelya grew smaller and smaller until she was the size of a speck of dust.

She opened her eyes, heard the panting of her fear and understood that it was the end. Najeeb's birds had died and it was over, and when she heard the news from her mother she showed no surprise. The relief traced itself in her almond-shaped eyes and she said, "It doesn't matter." Then she ran into the kitchen to make the *kibbeh nayyeh* that the family had for lunch every Sunday.

This had happened a year before she had met Mansour. It was a difficult year because she had to chase away the birds, which had infiltrated her surface dreams from her deep ones. She started seeing the birds in the morning, and there were no trees. Before the birds could spread their wings in preparation for death, however, Meelya would open her eyes, jump out of bed and go out into the garden, where she would put her mouth to the tap by the small pool and drink and drink, wetting her chest and nightdress, this morning wetting being her way of cleansing herself of the pollution of death, the memory of the trees and the disappearance of Najeeb.

How was she to tell these things?

How was she to take off her dreams and tell the story to Mansour?

How was she to make him understand that a person had to take off his words in order to be able to take off his clothes, and that dreams couldn't be washed off with water?

The tale of Meelya and marriage has many names: an only daughter living with her widowed mother and four brothers;

the mother suffering from that mysterious, unnamed disease; the girl obliged to transform herself into the mistress of the house at the age of eleven. Saada didn't go to the doctor; the cotton wool soaked in oil that she brought from the Church of the Angel Mikhail was good enough for her. She would come home from the church, fashion the cotton wool into a kind of pill and take one after every meal. After Youssef died, Saada turned into a sort of house nun, praying every time the church bell rang, which was incessantly, since it kept pace with the nuns' prayer rituals, which occupied a good many hours of their day. She got up at 4.00 in the morning, prayed the Service of the Hours, ate her breakfast, got back into bed and put on her illness. At 11.00 in the morning, she prayed once more and, when done, sat in her room waiting for the plate of food that Meelya would prepare. After noon, she took a nap, only to return to her prayers at 5.00 in the afternoon, joining in the Sunset Prayer before eating dinner and then moving on to the Prayer before Sleep.

Her favourite ritual, though, was lunch. She'd sit in her room, the aroma of Meelya's stew wafting over her, her mouth watering, and wait. When the dish came, she'd polish it off at one go. Saada had discovered how well her daughter, who had learnt to prepare all the different dishes in record time, cooked. "If it weren't for your belly," the nun had told her, "you'd be a saint," Saada's appetite for prayer being equalled only by her craving for food. When she wasn't busy satisfying one or other of those desires, she lived with pain that migrated from one part of her body to another, settling, finally, in her feet, which became swollen and incapable of carrying her, causing her to end her life in bed, praying and eating. She died in July 1960 after devouring an entire bowl of *kibbeh arnabiyyeh* sent to her, via her young grandson Iskandar, by the wife of her son Moussa. The grandson stood staring goggle-eyed at his grandmother's appetite. "You'll kill yourself, Granny," he said, when she told him she was going to finish off the whole bowl at one sitting.

"At least I'll die on a full stomach," she replied.

Meelya knew that food would kill her mother and treated her as one might a force of nature. Her accursed illness, on the other hand, Meelya could not understand at all. She believed that her mother wasn't really ill but had first pretended to be ill and then ended up believing her own lie.

When her husband had died suddenly at the age of forty-five, Saada had felt abandoned, or so she told the nun. She also told the nun that she hated that kind of thing and couldn't stand the smell of the man, which stuck to her body when he came near her. After the weekly sex, which there was no avoiding, she'd wash herself three times, obsess over the idea that she was sinning and wish she could disappear.

"I wish, *Ma Soeur*, that I could go through the wall and disappear. That way the smell would go away too."

"You smell of bay leaves and soap," the nun replied. "What's all this nonsense, my daughter?"

"But I can still smell the smell," Saada said.

"You were created to be a nun and a virgin, Saada. If it weren't for your stomach . . . I never saw anyone love their stomach like you do."

This conversation, or one like it, had taken place two years after the man had died. Saada had been complaining to the nun about her pains and talking about the man's smell, which still hung in her nostrils. She'd mention Youssef and cry, and say he'd left her and the children to eat ashes: "Look at the poor boys! Look at what's happening to them! Working from dawn to dusk, and if the Lord hadn't granted Niqoula a bit of luck with his coffin business we'd have died of hunger. Saleem, the eldest, is enrolled with the Jesuits and says he's studying law and is going to be a lawyer. Moussa's young and still at school, and all the work is on Niqoula's and Abdallah's shoulders. I don't know what to say about Meelya. It's like she's possessed by the Devil. She learned to cook and keep house in a month. She left school but always has a book in her hand. She cleans the house, does the laundry and cooks, finishing everything in two hours flat. I used to spend all day in the kitchen and the food I made would turn out 'blah', as my late husband used to say, but she's a different kettle of fish altogether."

They were eating stuffed eggplant cooked in oil. Saada couldn't resist eating with the saint, even though she'd already had lunch at home. Maintaining a steady pace, the nun said, "This isn't proper cooking, Saada. It's just thrown together. You must stop bringing your daughter's cooking. What is this stuff anyway that tastes like you know what, God save us?"

Mansour would revive the business of the food that tasted like lovemaking. He'd finished eating dinner on the little patio of his house in Nazareth and wanted to refill his glass of arak when Meelya snatched it from his hand and rushed into the kitchen.

"Why did you do that?" he yelled after her.

"Enough drinking. Now it's time for dessert."

She returned from the kitchen bearing a bowl of *qatayif* soaked in honey. The little pancakes, fried over a gentle fire and rendered even lovelier by their golden colour, arrived borne on the scent of clarified butter of Hama and with pine nuts glistening on top. Mansour took a mouthful and said, "Wow! What makes this so tasty?" Meelya explained that she'd made the *qatayif* out of pine-nut flour mixed with sugar and rose- and orange-water. Mansour took a second piece, closed his eyes and moaned with pleasure.

"This isn't so much dessert, my darling, as love. It's as though I were sleeping with you, not eating. Unbelievable!" he said, diving into the dish and polishing it off.

"You shouldn't eat so much of it," she replied. "It's made to be savoured." She explained that she'd invented the dessert by accident. She'd been making *qatayif* and discovered that there were no walnuts or almonds in the house, so it occurred to her to stuff them with pine nuts. "Pine nuts are soft and you don't taste them right away. To appreciate the taste you have to wait. I was afraid my brothers wouldn't like it, especially Niqoula. Niqoula's a plain sort of person and he likes plain things. Moussa though – when Moussa tasted the *qatayif*, he closed his eyes and did the same as you. Then all of them liked it, especially the nun. She's a saint of the belly. I've never seen anyone eat like her. It's like her whole body is in ecstasy, you feel as though her fingers and hands are eating along with her."

The nun asked Saada to stop bringing food made by her daughter to the convent, but Saada would come bearing the provisions she'd stolen from the house hidden in a paper bag, and the nun would dive into the bowl, making the sign of the cross and chanting Byzantine hymns studded with words about the Virgin.

The Convent of the Angel Mikhail was Saada's refuge. There her bones relaxed, her pains left her, and the burdens of the body were lifted from her soul. In turn, the house quickly became Meelya's playground. Her three elder brothers treated her like a woman and imposed their masculine authority on her. Her little brother Moussa, however, regarded her as his mother. She was happy with the two roles, which made of her both a woman and a mother and transformed her into the hub of the family's life.

Two years after the father died, Meelya had found herself out of school. Youssef's death had turned the family upside down. The oldest boy, Saleem, was the only one to maintain the rhythm of his life, the reason being Niqoula and his pronouncements. Niqoula had donned his father's tarboush the day he died and had decided not to go to school but to work in the shop instead. He was seventeen and hadn't shown much sign of success academically, though he'd been getting by. Then Abdallah said, "If Niqoula's going to make a sacrifice and leave, I will too." The mother smiled and said nothing. Everyone in the family knew it had nothing to do with sacrifice, as it had already been decided that Abdallah, who was a poor student, should go and work with his father in the shop.

It had never occurred to anyone that Meelya would be obliged to leave school too and that Moussa would never go to university but have to work at the Hotel Chati in Tiberias because the shop could no longer meet all of the family's needs. Meelya had no choice. After her father's death, Saada's illness turned the house into a hell. Her right arm became paralysed, the numbness in her cheek increased, and the pain spread from her shoulders to her feet. She was like a woman in shock. Her moans – "Ah!", "Iy!", "Uw!" – resembled Arabic's "weak" letters, which Meelya came to think of as sounds of pain joining words together, thus making out of weakness a source of strength by means of which meanings could be both intensified and abbreviated. Professor Camille Samara, who had intro-duced her to the world of ancient poetry, had taught Meelya this. Samara's hair was grey, he brought his lunch to the Zahret el Ihsan School, and at noon he would spread his food out on his desk and let the classics roll off his tongue. His class was like a skiff bobbing on the sea of language. The ageing teacher saw in Meelya a future woman of letters because she was the only pupil who could memorize the old poetry and recite it back without stumbling. She would stand up and declaim the verses, swaying along with the final vowels and ascending to ecstasy, the professor having said that the final vowels were like the oars of boats and that it all came down to three sounds –

"a", "i" and "u" – which expressed, in abbreviated form, the pain of humankind ("Ah!", "Iy!", "Uw!"), formed the articulations of words and allowed them to name things.

Professor Samara was Meelya's first adventure with life after her father's death. As she clasped her exercise book filled with poems to her chest, she told Samara that she would take him with her in her heart. It was the end of the school year and the girls were saying goodbye to their teachers, holding the exercise books that showed their end-of-year marks. When she saw the tears of the ageing professor, who, as he was retiring, was bidding farewell to his students, Meelya pulled the poetry book from her brown bag and clasped it to her chest.

"It's what my children want," said the professor. "They want me to be retired, *mutaqa'id*." Drawing a slash after the "t", he read the result as though it were two separate words: *mut^a/qa'id*. "Meaning they want me to 'die!' (*mut!*) 'sitting' (*qa'id*). Can a man of letters retire? But that's what they want – they want me dead and sitting. Instead of reading out 'weak' letters they want my body to live them."

Tears flowed from his eyes and a buzz ran through the classroom. Meelya saw how the tears burned his cheeks and the letters of weakness spread over his body, clothing it in pain.

"I'm going to take you with me," she said as she bade him goodbye, unaware as she was that she'd be leaving the school and that her mother's chronic illnesses would redraw her life.

The mother's medicine was the nun, and going to the Convent of the Angel Mikhail, where secrets blended with truth. The nun summed up the whole world in one word: *secret*. The world as known to *Hajjeh* Milaneh began with the secret she had brought with her to the convent when she had arrived at the age of five. Her mother had died, so her father had placed her in the nuns' keeping because he'd decided to visit his relatives in Houran to find a new wife. "Just a few months and I'll be back," said the man whose features *Hajjeh* Milaneh had forgotten and of whom nothing remained in her memory but his hoarse voice saying, "Just a few months and I'll be back and take the child home." But he didn't come back, and his features evaporated into incense.

"Incense is the closest thing to man because it resembles the soul – air coloured thick white. That's how we are: a thick whiteness that we cover with the blackness of our clothes to show humility and mourning for our sins. Man is incense, and death returns us to the essence. God knows the sinner from the innocent by his smell. Everything is incense, my daughter."

Meelya started to fear people's souls; instead of bodies she would see massings of incense. Then she started seeing the soul in her dreams in the form of white smoke that appeared and disappeared. She started to be afraid of her mother and of the nun and her cotton-wool-and-oil treatments, in pursuit of which her mother would pick up her pain and trundle over to the church, leaving Meelya alone in the house to learn how to cook. There, the saucepan opened up suddenly before Meelya's eyes, the way Heaven opens before saints – or so she felt when she discovered that cooking was about balancing the proportions of garlic, onions, coriander and lime juice, that flavour comes from the palm of the hand, and she saw the joy on her brothers' faces. With the end of Saada's fat-free food and its replacement by Meelya's, which shimmered with count-less flavours, the atmosphere in the house changed completely, turning the daily coming together at the dinner table into a festival of pleasures. The poverty in which the Shaheen family lived never changed, but this girl, her eyes encircled by hovering words, brought to it the taste of life.

Life having forced her to leave school, Meelya entered the world of her grandmother's books. Saada said that the grandmother, who suffered from senility, had awakened one day from her stupour, called for her books, gestured at the wooden box and said it was for Meelya. "This box has been with me all my life, my daughter. Without it I wouldn't have been able to put up with things. It's for Meelya. Give it to her when she gets older and tell her, 'This is from your granny, Youssef's mother.'"

"Now that was a woman!" Meelya wanted to say to Mansour. He was telling her about his mother and brother, who lived in Jaffa and who were asking him to go back there to work in the metal shop left them by their father. Mansour told Meelya he didn't want to go back because he couldn't take the way his mother bossed him and his brother around any more and he'd made his own life in Nazareth. The man, just entering his forties, had discovered the mental and physical comfort that he sought in this unspeaking woman around whose eyes clouds of drowsiness were always ahover – a woman like the small city he had chosen as a base for his business and a home for his family.

True, the woman was odd. She started sentences and didn't finish them, her words splintering and leaping from idea to idea and from place to place before returning and coming to rest on silence, but she brought him tranquillity. His short-tempered mother, who had managed his father's affairs since his death, had made Mansour feel that work was daily retribution. His father had died when Mansour was fifteen and Ameen sixteen. Ameen, who had left school to work with his father when he was twelve, formed, with his mother, the axis around which the work turned, and they treated Mansour like an employee. The second son had thus become convinced that he would never be a partner in the business and decided to move to Nazareth, where his Aunt Warda lived. It was said that the widowed aunt wanted him as a husband for her only daughter, and it was she who had persuaded him to go to Nazareth, but the truth was that Mansour went of his own free will. He had no objection to marrying Sameeha, but she had an understanding with a young man of the Saeed family, for whose sake she'd converted to Protestantism. Deciding not to return to Jaffa, Mansour conceived the idea of opening a business selling imported fabrics for women. The Good Lord looked kindly on his endeavours and he started going to Beirut to buy stock from Souq el Tawileh, which had become, under the French Mandate, the premier market for such things. The fates arranged for him to visit the home of a friend, *Khawaja* Emile Rahhal, a merchant in the market. It would be from the garden of *Khawaja* Emile and his wife, Madame Sonia, that Mansour would catch sight of the white girl standing beneath the blossoming almond tree in early spring and fall head over heels in love. His first gift to his Beirut fiancée would be an ancient book printed in Cairo bearing the title *Passionate Lovers and their Deaths*. This went into Grandmother Umm Youssef's box, to be taken by Meelya to Nazareth along with the *Sinaksar*, which tells the stories of the saints, and *The Thousand and One Nights*.

In Nazareth, Meelya didn't open the box to read her grandmother's stories. She had no need of reading there, for everything was written on the highways and in the alleys. All she had to do to find herself was walk, thus becoming a line in a large book that she read and lived at the same time.

In Beirut, though, reading had been her way of passing the time between the kitchen and waiting for her brothers to come home. She would devour her brothers' books, solve their arithmetic problems for them and memorize the poems they had to memorize.

Living between her grandmother's box of stories and her brothers' lessons, she also became the acknowledged queen of cooks. This made her brothers fear her early marriage, which would leave them captive to their mother's food and her incurable illnesses. Things took an unexpected turn when, after a short-lived experience with Wadee the baker, Meelya found herself alone and waiting for Najeeb, who would disappear.

Meelya hadn't known why Wadee had visited them every day, smelling of flour. The baker became a part of the family's evening ritual, which began at 6.00 with the drinking of coffee prepared in the Ottoman style and exhaling the fragrance of sugar and orange-blossom water, and which reached its climax at 8.30, when Meelya would invite everyone to the table. Wadee would fidget, claiming he had to return home, and then the aroma of food wafting from the kitchen would bewitch him. Once Saleem had insisted, he would start clucking about how he was getting fat because he was eating twice every evening, once with them and once at home so as not to upset his mother.

Meelya knew she would never marry Wadee, but there he was, with his short frame and big paunch. She felt disgust at the massed flesh gathered beneath his shirt and hated the smell of flour. Meelya doesn't remember his ever speaking to her; he would sit with her brothers, having brought bread and pastries from the bakery that he'd inherited from his father and behaving as though he were one of them. Though once, when she came to think of it, he had followed her into the kitchen on the excuse that he was thirsty, and had told her that her cooking was delicious and that he was waiting for the day when she would cook just for him.

Everyone said that Wadee would marry Meelya, except for Wadee, who said nothing. After sixth months of daily visits, Saada asked him when his mother was going to honour them with a visit. Wadee's round face turned red with embarrassment. Clearing his throat, he replied that he'd let them know soon, God willing.

Then everything ended.

Meelya told Moussa that she wasn't upset with Wadee and that she'd never been able to picture herself as his wife. She told her mother that she'd been overcome by panic when she'd visited Wadee at his mother's house and Mrs Umm Wadee had taken her into the bedroom and pointed to a wide bed, made of live oak, standing in the centre of it: "That bed belonged to me and my late husband. We may have been the first wedded couple to sleep in the same bed. This will be my gift to you and Wadee when we celebrate your wedding."

"You want us to sleep in the same bed?"

When Meelya entered the room at the hotel and there was only one bed, Umm Wadee's words rang in her ears and she smelled the smell of the ancient wood. She couldn't think where to sit down. Mansour was too busy opening the champagne to notice her confusion. Meelya went to sleep alone in the bed and was only aware of her husband next to her through what she would call "the marriage dream". She heard the bathroom door open and decided to go on sleeping. Her breathing slowed and she sank into the dream – a dream without images or words, made up only of colours and of that special feeling that the world is contracting and expanding, curling up and stretching out, rising and falling. Her face expanded and broadened out, and she felt that there were eyes within her eyes too numerous to count, that she was swimming in the world of the colour blue, to which he took her. Then suddenly the dream broke up. She felt a chill on her thighs and the man pulled away. She hugged herself, the dome of heat rose from her belly and spread like circles of light, and she found herself in the car again.

Meelya had insisted on there being two beds in their bedroom, and Mansour couldn't understand why she was so insistent. Nevertheless he bought two beds, and it never occurred to him to sleep with his wife in the same one. "The wife's bed must be big enough for the first child. That's our custom," Mansour said. Bowing her head in assent, Meelya saw a blue halo trace itself above it. This was how she saw herself, head bowed in assent, and when she became pregnant and started spending much of her time among the eucalyptus trees scattered around the house, the blue halo was her constant companion. She couldn't see it in her husband's eyes, however, which confirmed that this blue that flowed from above her bent head to protect the foetus and its mother was visible to her alone.

Meelya would live nine full months in the shadow of this halo, the blueness clothing her by day and becoming by night a carpet upon which she slept and onto which her dreams could flow.

Mansour poured himself a glass and started to sway. They were sitting on the balcony of their house in Nazareth, and he was drinking and drawing circles of silence between his words as he recited poetry while Meelya yawned. She told him that his drunkenness made the music of the poetry fall into a vacuum. Though she didn't really say anything like that; maybe she wanted to say it, but in fact she said something else. She told him to stop drinking because he was drunk.

"Me, drunk?"

. . .

"You think I'm drunk on arak. Not true. Arak doesn't make me drunk."

. . .

"Which just goes to show, my darling, that drunkenness doesn't come from arak, it comes from your eyes. Your eyes make me drunk and I see a strange colour."

"You too?" she said, and bit her lower lip as though sorry she'd opened her mouth. But Mansour paid no attention to the "You too". If he had taken her up on it, she would have had to recount the story of her photograph and the green colour that Moussa had noticed.

"But someone has to know," she said as she stood before the icon of the Virgin in the Church of the Annunciation. Then, "Just him," she said. She looked down at her belly, which had started to grow round, and asked of the Mother of Light that the boy should know the secret colour of his mother's eyes.

That night, Mansour, who didn't know the secret, recited the most beautiful poetry Meelya had ever heard. It revealed to her that only the prophets knew the secret of the relationship between night and day. He spoke to her about Abu Tayyib al Mutanabbi, the only prophet to prophesy in verse. All the other prophets were either incapable or afraid of writing poetry. Until this poet – who wrote prophesy in verse and bewitched the Arabs for a thousand years, as he does to this day – came along, the prophets had written only stories and proverbs. He told her the story of how al Mutanabbi had visited Tiberias and stayed there for a while, and how he'd described the lion as no-one had done before him.

"And did he walk on water like Christ?" Meelya asked.

"No, he walked on words," Mansour replied.

"Then he wasn't a real prophet," she said.

"Why? Did all the prophets walk on water?" Mansour asked.

"I have no idea," she said.

"Listen, Meelya," Mansour said, and fell silent. He had wanted to say that words were al Mutanabbi's water and music his waves, that he mixed wisdom with rhythm so that his poetry became a door to awareness, and that the door had closed behind him when he died and no-one had been able to open it again for the last thousand years.

"If he couldn't walk on water, he wasn't a prophet," she said.

"Listen," Mansour said:

"Who has not loved this world betimes —
        Yet still we find no road to love and consummation.
Your lot, in this life, of love
        Is as that, in your dreams, of a phantom."

Meelya listened to the two verses and memorized them, but when she recited them, she would reverse the last words of the second so that they went:

"Your lot, in this life, of love
        Is as that of a phantom in your dreams."

Meelya was in her third month of pregnancy. She had become round and of a startling beauty. Mansour, though, didn't know how to tell her of his love and admiration, for when he spoke of his love she wouldn't listen but would hang her head, cloak herself in the blue halo and sink into silence. He would then resort to verse, offering her poems, and her eyes would shine and she would become a pair of listening ears and a bowed head, saying, when he had finished, that poetry was like prayer.

She sees incense above the table, as though the words have turned to incense, and the woman becomes drunk on the smell of the incense, which spreads though the place and mingles with the rhythmic words issuing from the man's lips.

She said she'd dreamt of incense. When she told him her dreams, she would pause in the middle of the story and not go on because she could see the fear in his eyes. Only this dream did she recount to him in full. It had been three months before, when Mansour had seen circles on his wife's body, and in the morning had seen the beauty of her rounded shoulders, which glided down from the neck opening into the blue nightdress. He followed her into the kitchen, where she was preparing their breakfast and coffee, and clasped her to his chest from behind, but she didn't grunt with displeasure as she usually did when he hugged her to him. His body clung to hers and desire coursed through him. He started to lift her nightdress and the whiteness exploded in his eyes, the light dazzling him. He closed his eyes, holding the woman's waist, and started to bend her over, and she bent with him, and was soft and hot and gushing with tenderness.

"Ah!" she cried, and turned around suddenly. Pushing him gently away, she said she was pregnant.

"What?"

"I dreamt that I was pregnant," she said.

He smiled and moved towards her again, but she backed away.

"I'm pregnant."

"Since when?"

"Since today."

She put the coffee pot down on the table and started to speak. She was standing in the sunlight filtering through the window, her face rounding out, her eyes widening. The man felt his legs giving way. He sat down, his eyelids drooped, and darkness swept over him.

"Granny," she said.

She told him about her grandmother Malakeh. "Granny Malakeh came and sat next to me on the bed here. I was sleeping and the bed was large. It was as though I was sleeping on water. Everything was like water and Granny was sitting beside me. She was a young woman. God, how much like my mother she looked – at first I thought she *was* my mother. 'Mother,' I said, 'what are you doing here?' But she told me, 'I'm not your mother. Your mother's in Beirut and I've come to tell you a story.' I said to her, 'Granny, is this any time for stories? Don't you see how I live here, alone, with no-one to turn to?' She said she'd come to wake me from my sleep, but before I awoke I had to receive a gift from her. She reached into her bosom, removed the small icon of the Virgin and told me, 'This must stay with you to guard you.' I took the icon but didn't know where to put it. She told me, 'Put it on your belly.' I put it on my belly and felt myself sinking. I said to her, 'Granny, I'm sinking. What should I do?' 'Take my hand,' she said, and I put out my hand but couldn't reach. I tried to scream, but my voice wouldn't come and I sank. I found myself underwater and felt I was drowning. Suddenly a woman wearing a blue headscarf came and lifted me up. I found myself on the seashore and there were many fish. Fish would raise their heads above the water, open their mouths to breath, then sink back beneath the waves. The blue woman was beside me. She was whispering to me, but I couldn't understand what she was saying. She was murmuring softly, and the only word I could make out was *Tiberias*. I understood that I was on the shore of the Sea of Tiberias. The blue woman closed her eyes and I felt I wanted to sleep and that there was nothing in this world that could wake me, and I was afraid. I remembered what Granny used to say about sleep and death, and I thought, 'This is it. You're done for, Meelya. You're going to die in the sea,' but I didn't feel as though I was drowning. I was breathing under the water and could see the colours, and the blue woman was beside me. She reached out and placed her hand on my belly, and I felt my belly begin to swell and that I was becoming round. She removed her hand. I turned and Granny was there, but she had no teeth. I used to be frightened when Granny took her false teeth out and put them in a glass of water. Her false teeth were odd. They weren't one set made of two pieces but looked as though they were four pieces, or five. It made the glass look frightening, with the water around the teeth and the teeth looking as though they were climbing the sides of the glass. 'Why have you taken your teeth out, Granny?' I asked. She said, 'Because I talk better without them.' 'No, Granny, please put your teeth back in so I can understand you.' She said she couldn't because you couldn't mess about with your teeth when you were dreaming. 'But you've been dead for a long time,' I said. She laughed. She opened her mouth and started laughing and saying things I couldn't understand. She was mumbling, and the only word I could make out was *boy*. 'What boy?' I asked. 'You'll find out later,' she said. I told her I was afraid and brought my hand close so that I could pull the false teeth out of the glass, but she smacked my hand and I started to cry. When Granny Malakeh died, I cried a lot. Everyone thought I was crying because Granny had loved me, but that's not true. Or I did cry because I loved her, but really I was crying because they hadn't put the false teeth in her mouth. I asked Mother, 'Where are the false teeth?' I ran to the kitchen. Mother followed me and said, 'Snap out of it, girl.' I didn't answer and started looking for them as though I'd gone mad. I searched under the table; I climbed up and opened the cold safe. Mother told me, 'Stop it. We threw them out.' 'Where did you throw them?' I asked. 'We threw them in the rubbish,' she said. 'Why?' I asked. 'Because it's not right," she said. 'You can't bury false teeth with the body. The dead have to return to their Lord the way they were created.' 'In the rubbish?' I screamed, and started searching in the rubbish bin, but I couldn't find them. Not then I couldn't, but yesterday, when I was sinking . . . no, maybe that was another dream. Heavens, how I've started mixing things up! I don't know why, or when, or how any longer. Anyway, what matters is that I picked up the false teeth and went over to Granny, but she'd vanished, I don't know where, and I didn't know what to do with the teeth. The women were sitting around me and crying, and then I fell, I don't know how. I was hanging on to the branches of the loquat tree with my legs dangling, eating sour green loquats, and before I knew it I was falling. My teeth broke. I put my hand over my mouth and they felt as though they were Granny's teeth, and then, I don't know – there was a lot of water, springs and tears. The women's tears started falling on the ground, I saw Granny sinking, and I started to cry. I reached out to take hold of Granny's hand, but I couldn't. I felt as though I was sinking too, and then, I don't know, everything had a blue colour and I was sleeping on the bed and the bed was like a pool and Granny was sitting beside me. She put her hand on my belly and gave me the icon and I saw the blue woman, as though she'd come out of the icon. I told her, 'Granny, that's the woman who put her hand on my belly and my belly got bigger.' She said it was a boy and we had to call him Mikhail after the convent of Sister Milaneh, so that the nun could protect me with her prayers. I told her, 'No, I'm going to call him Eesa. His name is Eesa. I'm going to call him Eesa after the Messiah, because that's what the blue woman wants.' Then I opened my eyes, got up and went to the bathroom. I washed my face, heated some water and bathed, and you were still snoring. Yesterday I tried to turn you over because you're too much, I mean your snoring's too much, but you were all curled up like at the Hotel Massabki. God, how frightened I was for you there. No, not when you were in the bathroom and wouldn't answer. That was nothing, and I understood. Then I felt – or not then but later, when I saw you sleeping and curled up like a baby in its mother's belly – then I understood that you needed a mother. No, don't misunderstand me – please don't say that. I don't want to hear that sort of thing. No, I don't know what you do and I don't want to know. Did I ask you a question? If I didn't ask, why are you answering? No, I don't want to understand; those things are only to do with you. You told me you don't want to go to Jaffa, and I don't like Jaffa. What was I saying? Yes, now I remember; I felt my belly starting to get bigger and everything in me becoming round, and I understood what the woman with the blue scarf over her hair had told me and understood that I was pregnant. I, Mr Mansour, am pregnant as of yesterday night. That's what I wanted to tell you."

Mansour was struck dumb. He could think of nothing to say. He tried to decrypt this mysterious way of talking and understand what Meelya had said. He drank his Turkish coffee slowly, his head bowed. He grew angry. Why couldn't she say things straight out? Why did the woman have to circle around the words as though she were talking in a dream and not in real life? He wanted to wake her from her long drowse and from her insistence on refusing to let him express his love. When she said she was pregnant, he interrupted her and said that he'd slept with her the night before and that it had been the most beautiful time. He said he'd seen how the female glories in bed when she receives the male and takes him to her. "That's the love that makes women pregnant," he said, a smile of triumph forming on his lips.

"What's it got to do with you?" she asked.

"What are you talking about?"

"Well, yes, maybe. I couldn't say. I don't remember."

"You don't remember?"

"How can I remember? I was asleep and dreaming the dream I just told you."

"You remember your dreams and forget what really happened?"

"Why? What really happened?"

"My oh my oh my. God give me patience. Nothing happened?" he exclaimed, boiling with anger and thinking that from then on he ought to wake her whenever he slept with her at night. He'd wake her and make her remember and put an end to this show of make-believe that had begun that first night at the hotel. True, he'd collapsed in the bathroom, but who could have stood up to the icy cold on Dahr el Baydar? Mansour had stood up to it; he hadn't been able to bear the thought of returning to Beirut with nothing to show for it and having to stay in the Shaheen family's house while they waited to go to Nazareth.

The eldest bother, Saleem, hadn't attended the wedding. When Mansour asked about him, he received an ambiguous reply from Moussa. Mansour was the only member of the Shaheen family who didn't know Saleem's story. He'd heard half of it from Moussa but hadn't understood the reason for the break. Moussa had said that Saleem had wanted to become a Catholic and join the Jesuits. He'd studied law at their university and had got a stupid bee in his bonnet. Saleem had entered the university thanks to a letter of recommendation from the monk Eugène, who had run a Sunday school in a basement belonging to a monastery of the Jesuit Fathers in the neighbourhood. The Sunday school wasn't a real school: Frère Eugène would gather the poor children together, hand out sweets, show them religious films and force them to attend Mass in Latin. Saleem was bewitched by the cinema. He took his brothers to watch a film about the agonies of Christ, but was amazed to find them falling asleep; instead of being dazzled by the light that turned into pictures, they went to sleep, except for Moussa, who was so frightened that he cried when he saw the big pictures that took up the white screen. Only Meelya was enthusiastic about the cinema, but Frère Eugène had told Saleem that Sunday school was only for boys and Meelya wasn't allowed in.

"I'm going home with you. The cinema makes me frightened. I'm going back with you," said Moussa, but Meelya told him to go in with the others and went home on her own.

Moussa said that Frère Eugène had found a "goose", meaning an easy mark, in Saleem. Mansour didn't understand the expression but pretended he did. He hated himself every time Meelya looked at him almost angrily when he asked her the meaning of an expression he didn't understand.

"Anyone would think you didn't know Arabic," she'd say.

As a result he'd had to go on behaving as though he under-stood everything she said when in fact he didn't. And when Meelya started living in Nazareth, instead of adopting the dialect of her husband and the city she continued to speak that of Beirut, whose letters are full of the tongue's flesh. The Beirutis load their words with weight from their lips and tongues, pitching all of the letters lower. Meelya was the only one to sing her letters; she kept the heavy accent, but instead of articulating the letters with her tongue and cheeks, she pronounced them with her lips, and the words came out sounding smooth.

"But you don't speak like a Beiruti," Mansour told her.

"Me?" she said, pronouncing the vowel with a swooping intonation, the way Beirutis do all their words.

He didn't ask what it meant when they said that Saleem was a "goose", and he didn't understand either why they should be so angry that he'd converted to Catholicism.

"It's all the same," Mansour told them.

Whenever he tried to discuss her son's choice of a new religion with her, the mother would snap her eyes at him and utter her famous expression: "God is Greek Orthodox."

"But we're not Greeks," Mansour wanted to tell them, relying on what a Jaffa priest had told him during the rancorous protest in Palestine against the clique from Greece that had taken control of the Greek Orthodox Church in Jerusalem. The priest had said that the word *Greek* had originally been an insult applied to them by followers of the Assyrian Church so they could claim they were agents of the Byzantine Empire: "We are Orthodox Arabs who have chosen to believe in the two natures, divine and human, of the Lord Christ, peace be upon him. As to the word *Greek*, we only adopted it because, in our naïvety, we accepted the charge that our enemies brought against us."

Mansour told Saada and her daughter what Yuhanna Azar the priest had said, but Saada started yawning while Meelya rested her chin on her hand and surrendered to her silent lethargy, so the man didn't finish the tale. Stopping in the middle, he returned to the Hotel America in the Souq el Najjarin, where he stayed on his visits to Beirut, which had become more frequent since he'd fallen in love with this woman.

Mansour said that the feeling people call "passion" had been foreign to him. It was true that he was entering his forties and had known many women, especially among the *filles de joie* of Jaffa and Beirut, and that he . . .

"Please don't use those dirty words," Meelya said.

"I neither uttered a dirty word nor permitted a single insult to sully my lips!" he replied.

"Please stop it," she said.

"Fine," he said. "I'll stop. No insults? The young men of Beirut use insults all the time. Every time you talk to one of them he makes fun of you by using insults like 'How are you, you son of a whore?' as though words like that were supposed to endear him to you. I couldn't stand it at first and almost got into fights more than once. Then I got used to it and it was okay. There's no call for you get upset, Meelya, my sweetheart."

He wanted to tell her that in the past all he had felt had been the desire that God has placed in men for them to burn themselves with — the match that ignites and sets the entire body on fire — and that he'd feel the fire consuming his guts and then spreading to all his limbs, so that he couldn't go without that thing. When he saw her, though, he felt an emptiness drop from his heart down to his feet and started to burn in a different way, because he never burned out. He wanted to tell her that when he'd used to "milk" himself (as people call the secret habit) while thinking of her, he would not be quenched; in fact, his hand would burn. But he didn't say these things as he was afraid she'd get upset and the welts would appear on her throat, for the moment she became upset at a word or a comment, three horizontal lines would trace themselves around her neck. When he had asked her about them once, she'd said it was the nun's fault.

She went into the bathroom, washed and returned with a neck gleaming and rippling with the colour white.

"Now that's the colour of love!" he said.

Mansour told no-one how he tasted fire and jealousy at the Hotel America. He'd sensed that there was some mystery about the story of the absent Saleem and felt that Meelya had something to do with the split that had broken the family's back. He didn't hear the whole story, though, until three months after his marriage, when he understood that the red lines that traced themselves on his wife's neck were the wounds left by a man named Najeeb Karam on the woman who had waited so long for him.

"You mean you loved him?"

"No, it wasn't love. Just something like love."

"What's that supposed to mean?"

"It means we were like an engaged couple and then it ended, and I realized that it was my brother Saleem's fault. Saleem was hung up on Angèle, and her dad, the one who made out he was a saint, said to Angèle, 'I won't let you marry until your elder sister's married.' Then I don't know what happened, but suddenly Saleem and Najeeb disappeared and opened a carpentry shop in Aleppo. Saleem didn't dare get in touch with us. My mother said Saleem had got married behind her back, but really she knew all about it. The nun told her about a large wedding in Aleppo, that two sisters had married on the same day, and that Saleem had persuaded Najeeb to leave everything behind and go with him because the family was rich. I don't know the ins and outs. Moussa knows it all."

Moussa returned to the house to find Meelya waiting for him. She had lit a candle in the *dar* and was waiting on the sofa in the corner. Everything was sleeping except for the young girl, who was covered in sorrow and shame. She leant back against the darkness and waited. The fire burned inside her and the emptiness was dropping from her heart down to her womb. Jealousy consumed her. All she wanted to know was why and how things could change like that, and how Najeeb had been able to love two women at the same time. She told Moussa she was certain that Najeeb loved her, but had he also loved that woman who'd become his wife?

Meelya heard the story as it emerged in fragments from her brother's lips and saw everything transformed into shadows. Najeeb was a shadow of Najeeb, and his hand, which had reached out for her body, became the black shadow of a black hand. Even that explosion on her fiancé's face that she'd taken as a reflection of the whiteness of her breasts exploding in his eyes became just a shadow. She said that she remembered only remnants of the story she'd seen in her dreams. What was she to say? Even the encounter in the garden that had left the red lines on her neck she remembered only as a dream. How could she tell Mansour what he wanted to hear that night, and why did he want to hear a story that was dead?

"There's a difference," she told him. "Stories divide into two types: stories that end and stories that die. The story that has ended we restore to life when we tell it, and then it's here with us, but the story that has died is extinguished, and there's no light left in it. How can one read in the dark? You're asking me to read in the dark, but I don't know how."

She tried to tell him the story and it came out in no particular order, so he understood nothing. He thought she was lying. He said she was lying, and she said something like, "Okay, but what do you want me to do? You want me to tell it, but I've forgotten. You want to know, and I don't know. What do you want me to say so that I can say?"

But she did say. She told a dead story. She didn't tell him what happened in the garden or about the welts imprinted on her legs by the nettles she backed into when Najeeb came towards her, but she told him about the betrayal.

Trying to explain the difference between stories that had ended and stories that had died, she said that all families have at least one story that is buried and that no-one dares to dig up, and that her story with Najeeb was one of those; also that she remembered it only as ambiguous fragments of old dreams that she couldn't put together into words. Then she began to realize that she had better stop the kind of talk that unfolded before her eyes like pictures or the man would never understand anything. He'd told her more than once that he couldn't make sense of what she was saying, and at first she'd been amazed at this inability of his to understand. Then she'd realized that he didn't understand because he couldn't slide along with her to where the sliding words themselves went. Words were Meelya's way of skating. She'd skate from one word to another, or from one word to a series of images, and then be unable to recover the end of the string that they call the story's beginning. Her string had no end; she told stories like someone winding string, and would keep going without being able to tie things one to another.

"I can't put your words together properly," said Mansour. "Words are supposed to be spoken as a group, meaning they have to be arranged inside your head first; that way they make sense. Do you always talk like that?"

At the Hotel Massabki, when Mansour had opened his eyes the next morning, he'd moved closer to the woman lying on the bed next to him, pulled her to him and, feeling her cold legs, moved closer still. Turning towards her, he'd reached for her waist. Meelya had closed her eyes and stiffened. Then her body had relaxed and she'd entered the stupour. She said she'd dozed off and didn't remember, but he heard her saying words he couldn't understand because they were more like the indistinct clamour of a crowd than anything else. And when he got up and went to the bathroom, where he hopped about under the water that ran alternately hot and cold, the memory of Najeeb and the red lines on Meelya's neck returned to his mind, but he decided not to ask about them; it would be inappropriate to ask a woman about her relationship with another man on her wedding day. He puffed and blew under the shower, making a noise and calling to her to come and join him, but when he returned to the bed he found her asleep. She was lying on her back as though swimming over the pillow, in which her head and long hair were buried. When he went closer to wake her, she opened her eyes as if rising out of a deep sleep, smiled at him, turned onto her left side, covered herself with the quilt and went back to sleep. Mansour lit a cigarette, sat down beside her and waited. When she didn't get up, he dressed and went down to the lobby to look for the dining room, where the elder Wadeea trotted over and asked if he wanted eggs with his breakfast.

"That won't be necessary," he said.

"Eggs are good for newlyweds, Mr Groom," Wadeea 2 said, appearing as suddenly as if she'd emerged from the wall.

"Okay," he said, and sat down.

The bald chauffeur approached Mansour and patted him on the shoulder as the two servants, Wadeea 1 and Wadeea 2, appeared with coffee, milk and fried eggs. Putting the food on the table, they went and stood by the driver. The driver said he wanted to return to Beirut, and Mansour pulled some money out of his pocket and gave it to him with thanks.

"You're a good man," the driver said. "Every time I think of how you walked through the fog in the snow, I can feel the cold spreading through me from head to toe and I become afraid. Why didn't you feel afraid? A lion, I swear. You're not a bridegroom, you're a lion."

Mansour didn't respond, but he noticed mocking smiles on the lips of the servants, who, he also noted, were replicas of each other. Meelya had said the day before that their resemblance frightened her, and that Wadeea 2 could have been Wadeea 1 if her shoulders weren't stooped and her legs weren't bowed. Mansour had noticed nothing the night before; his entire being had been shivering with cold. He'd felt that his bones had come apart at the joints and that he needed a warm bed and the darkness of his closed eyes.

Wadeea 1 came over and asked after the bride. A few seconds later, Wadeea 2 asked the same question, in the same voice and with the same gestures.

"Where's *Khawaja* Georges?" Mansour asked, not knowing why he sought to use the hotel owner to hide his fear of this female simulacrum that kept reproducing itself before him.

"The *Khawaja*'s asleep," 1 said. "All that waiting yesterday tired him out."

"The *Khawaja*'s tired," 2 said.

They must be mother and daughter, thought Mansour. *Khawaja* Georges Massabki was lucky to have the two women because it meant he had to do nothing himself. The "eternal bachelor", as he called himself, had found the perfect solution in a woman replicated in her daughter. Everything worked fine. The woman was a servant – meaning she made no demands, simply engendered silence and peace and quiet – and a widow –

meaning she had no-one else to turn to. The widow had a daughter just like herself – meaning that he would have raised the young one to suit his own needs. In other words, the two women were like two rings on his finger, and he lived both served and serviced. "Now there's a man!" Mansour wanted to say as he started in on the plate of fried eggs, but he heard Meelya's soft footsteps, looked up and saw her standing between the two Wadeeas. He thought she looked taller as she talked with the two women in a low voice. She sat down across from him and raised her eyebrows, and he understood that he was going to have to stop eating fried eggs.

In the bathroom, he had felt dishonoured. He had locked himself in and called for his mother because he was sure he was going to die. Only death can kill sexual desire. When desire vanishes, it means we are in the presence of death.

"Nothing makes you hang on to life so much as this," said the ageing man of whom all Mansour could remember was the whiteness of the thick hair that covered his head. He had come to the workshop and bought a quantity of iron bars, saying they were for the fighters in the mountains. Looking at Ameen, Mansour's brother, he'd said, "Would that youth might one day return!" He'd also said he knew his time was at hand because "that thing", and he pointed between his thighs, didn't want to any more, and when it didn't want to, it was telling you to follow it to death. These fragments were all Mansour could remember of the incident. He'd reached the shop just as the man was getting ready to leave, so this sentence was all that had stuck in his mind. It came back to him in the bathroom, in the midst of the vomit, while lethargy paralysed his feet and pain punched him in the guts. He thought it was death, and called out for his mother. He saw his mother lying on the ground, her thigh bone broken, screaming for her own dead mother, as though life were a closed circle of mothers and nothing persisted but the tie between the child and its mother, meaning death. When you cry, "Mother!" you are calling, unawares, to the grave, for man lives between two graves, his mother's womb and the dust. In each he is in an inchoate state and on the threshold of mighty transformations, which will take him wherever he is to go.

Who had mentioned the business of the two graves?

Had it been Meelya? It couldn't have been: Meelya was happy with the rounding of her belly. She slept, drank water and behaved as though life were just beginning. It must have been Sister Milaneh, then. But Mansour had only met the saint once in his life, when she had attended the wedding in the church, a day when he had neither seen nor heard anything. Could he have seen the nun in a dream? But he didn't dream, and he didn't remember his dreams.

Mansour had wanted to tell his wife about his adventures with women before he got married, but she didn't want to hear, so why should he tell her? The story that mattered most had begun when he'd seen this woman and been attracted to her without knowing why. He didn't understand what had happened to him, why his groin started aching every time he closed his eyes. Meelya had bewitched him with the sinuousness that extended from her midriff to her hips. He had beheld her whiteness exploding beneath a white dress printed with red cherries and wanted to approach and speak to her but didn't dare to. Three months passed before he talked with her and noticed the dimple in her right cheek and her wide eyes outlined in drowsiness:

> "A woman white, her body covered o'er with beauty,
>   Which another skin did make for her skin.
> Her breasts I thought to camphor trees
>   By incense topped akin."

"What are you saying?"

"Poetry."

"Why? Are you a poet?"

"No, but I love poetry."

"How does it go on?"

"Abla's phantom came to see me in a dream,
*   Kissed three times the scarf that o'er my face was thrown,*
Bade me farewell, and left me with a flame
*   That I now guard and burns inside the bone.*

Did I not into myself withdraw
*   To dowse with tears my passion's pain,*
O perfect moon, whose memory I guard,
*   I'd die of grief but ne'er complain."*

"And did he see her in a dream?"

"Of course. Otherwise how could he have loved her?"

"So you fell in love with me in a dream?"

"I told you, I'm not a poet."

She noticed the likeness between him and her brother Moussa, her heart beat harder, and she smiled. That smile was the beginning that would bring him in the end to the Church of the Angel Mikhail and take him on the foggy journey to Chtaura, where, in the cold bathroom, he screamed for his mother because he could feel the approach of death.

In fact, that's not how it was, but he told it that way to his wife three months after they married, when he wanted to open the file of the buried story.

He doesn't say that he'd felt icy cold in the bathroom but didn't dare to come out in case it made things more complicated. The bathroom's red tiles seemed like pieces of ice that burned his naked feet as he sat on the toilet. Meelya was knocking on the door, saying she was going to call a doctor. "No, Meelya," he said. "I'm fine. Go to sleep, please."

He didn't know how he got the words out from between his trembling lips, but when he heard her move away from the door, his joints gave way and he was swept by the trembling that had been lurking behind his ribs. He returned to the bed shaking and desperate. Tiptoeing to the burning stove, he warmed himself in front of it, then found his way to the bed and curled up like a snail.

Meelya was sleeping. He lay down at a distance from her. He covered his body and head with the quilt and warmth started to course through his veins. He dozed a little, opened his eyes in a panic, then remembered that he was a groom on his wedding night and that the groom couldn't sleep until he had possessed the woman lying beside him.

He told her he hadn't been able to sleep because of the longing that had swept over him. He had seen her waist as she stood beneath the almond tree and imagined penetrating her. With each touch and kiss, the taste of things started to come back to him and he began to reassemble the fragments of his soul that had scattered in the cold and the fear.

And today, he saw her rounding out, telling him she was pregnant, as though she'd been born anew, as though the child in her belly had drawn her final form. He saw the red lines on her neck, remembered the story they hadn't told him and wanted to know it.

She paid no attention. Her constant downward glances, which inspired Mansour with the thought that "modesty was the very mark of Meelya", had taken on a different shape, becoming part of that world of circles in which she lived. She would look down at the ground, the circle would be completed, and she would close in on herself and go to a place where no-one could follow.

He felt jealous. Or rather, not jealous, but distant, as though the woman had traced with her circles a space between them that he could not break through.

Saying she was going to bed, she stood up.

"Sit down," he said.

"Call him what you like," she said. "I don't know why you're like this. I thought you'd be happy like everybody else is when they find out their wife's pregnant."

"It's not about the name," he said. "It's something else." And he asked her about Najeeb.

It was the first time in two years that she'd heard the man's name. The family had stopped mentioning it; when they needed to refer to him, they'd say, "him", as though the pronoun had replaced the man. Najeeb was no longer a man; he'd become a series of letters signifying nothing.

Najeeb had disappeared, his image had disappeared, his name was no more, and now he was to be resurrected at the very moment when Meelya had been freed from her past and her memories of those days. She wanted to say she didn't know, or, "No, it's not that I don't know, but that story's dead and buried and there's no need to dwell on it."

Her grandmother Malakeh was the first to teach her the necessity of distinguishing among stories. She would chide Saada if ever she mentioned the name of her father-in-law and the story of the house he'd bought.

"A story that's turned rotten should be buried. Stories can stink," the grandmother said.

The grandfather had been a source of constant pain to the women of the family, and the story of the house needed to be forgotten. No-one repeated the story of the Egyptian woman and *Khawaja* Afteemous, or the scandal of the grandfather's purchase of the house after his mistress, who was also the mistress of another man, died. Why, then, did Mansour want to dig up this story that Meelya had buried?

Saada had relaxed because the nightmare of Saleem's maybe becoming a monk was over. Where had the boy got his infatuation with Jesuits and Catholicism? He was the only one of his brothers who'd completed his education and he was to become a lawyer. Then suddenly he'd started going on about joining the Jesuits and stirred up a storm in the house.

His brother *Hajj* Niqoula, having listened to the tumultuous discussion between mother and eldest son, said he'd kill him. Going to the *leewan*, Niqoula returned to the *dar* wearing his father's red tarboush and told his brother, his voice broad and low, that he was going to kill him.

"What kind of a brother kills his brother?" Saleem screamed.

"That's exactly how killing started!" Niqoula said. "Brother killed brother. Cain killed Abel. Now Abel wants his revenge. No-one messes with me. Stunts like that have no place in this house. All it'll cost me is the bullet. The coffin's free, from the shop."

From that day on, Niqoula never took the tarboush off, and fear ran in the family's veins. Saada didn't know what to do. She went to Saint Milaneh and consulted her: "I have two sons. The first wants to be a Jesuit and the second wants to be a criminal. What should I do?"

"A Jesuit!" the nun said. "I seek refuge with God from lapidated Satan! Has he forgotten he's the grandson of the Saleem who was the first to ring the bell of Beirut's Church of Mar Jirjis? Now there was a man. And now Saleem Junior, the very same who inherited his grandfather's name, wishes to abandon the true faith and follow the French?" She asked Saada to spit on the Devil. Saada spat and then asked the nun how to escape her dilemma.

"Does his brother really want to kill him?" the nun asked.

Saada nodded.

"There's a real man for you!" the nun said. "He should have been your eldest. If Saleem wants to be a monk, he can go to Mount Athos in Greece. That's where they have proper, Orthodox, monasticism, the kind God likes."

"Now you want to send my son to Greece. Please don't say such things."

"Wouldn't it be better if he died?"

"Why should he die?"

"You're the one who told me his brother Niqoula wants to kill him. Niqoula should give him a scare so that he gives up the idea. Then I'll see what we can do."

"And if he doesn't?" Saada asked.

"He'll die," the nun said.

"Die?"

"What can we do about it?"

"You mean you're for killing him?"

"No, I didn't say I was for killing him. But it would be God's will."

"So it's alright for me to lose my children?"

"You wouldn't be losing more than you already have. What could be worse than blasphemy like that? Let Niqoula say what he wants and don't try to stop him."

"You don't mind if a brother kills his brother?"

"Of course I mind. 'Thou shalt not kill,' says the commandment. But that doesn't mean mortals know how God's will shall come to pass. The commandment says, 'Thou shalt not kill', but people haven't stopped killing one another. All men are brothers, which means, Saada my dear, that the only people people kill are their brothers. But of course I'm against killing."

The nun led Saada by the hand and they prostrated themselves in front of the icon of Mar Elias, the nun mumbling her prayers before the saint, who stood in a chariot of fire, flaming sword in hand.

"He's the one who'll save your children. Don't you worry."

Saada wept that day. The woman who spent most of her time at the Convent of the Angel Mikhail felt she had lost a lot. True, her correct Orthodox faith led her to pray, fast and promote brotherly love, but she hated the Jesuits because they spoke Jesuit and prayed in Latin, which she didn't understand.

"But you're just the same – you pray in Greek and don't understand what the words mean," Saleem said.

"No, we understand even if we don't. Greek passes through the heart, and that's how we understand."

"We don't have to understand the prayers," Saleem said. "The Pope is the only one who understands. That's why you have to know at least seven languages to become Pope."

"Shut up! Don't even talk about him!" the mother said, and made the sign of the cross as though seeking refuge from the Devil.

The storm over Saleem died down. Once Niqoula announced his intention to kill his brother, Saleem never again brought up the subject of becoming a monk. Meelya was convinced that her big brother would disappear and never be heard from again because he'd be swathed in black in some Jesuit monastery outside Lebanon. Thus the crime would never happen and Abel would never take his revenge on Cain, for what would the story mean if it were simply revenge? If it had been an easy matter for Abel to have his revenge, the story would have died and fallen into oblivion.

Nobody knew why Saleem changed – was it his relationship with Frère Eugène, or his failure as a law student, or what?

The relationship with the Jesuit monk began with the Sunday school and the films, and it continued for a long time. Saleem started going to the summer camps that Eugène organized for the neighbourhood boys. Then suddenly Saleem announced that he'd been given a grant to study law at the Jesuit university and that it wouldn't cost his parents a penny. Saleem was incapable, however, of completing his law studies. He stayed in the university for many years and, when asked when he was going to be an *avocato*, would reply that he was working and studying at the same time, and that was what was delaying his graduation. What his work was and where, nobody knew; it appeared he'd failed in his studies or been distracted by other things. And when he dropped his bombshell about the Jesuits, everyone believed that he'd never studied law at all but had been taking courses in Catholic theology. He told Moussa that Frère Eugène had promised to have him sent to Rome to pursue his studies there, but on condition that he entered the monastic ranks.

Ten years were lost. All that time, while Niqoula and Abdallah were working in their father's shop and had shifted to making coffins, and while Moussa was continuing his education and Meelya had to leave school because she'd become a housewife, Saleem was, as the mother put it, "messing about with theology". Then along he came and told them he was going to be a monk! "Thank God *Hajj* Niqoula threatened him," Meelya said, hearing her mother's voice coming out of her mouth, as though she weren't speaking herself. "Frère Eugène must have been the cause of the trouble, but as soon as we escaped from one disaster we found ourselves in a new one."

The new disaster was the story that had been buried and to new fragments of which Mansour was now listening, becoming convinced as he did so that he'd been wrong and ought to rebury it out of fear for Meelya's neck and the red lines encircling it.

"It was nothing to do with me," Meelya said. "They told me, 'A groom.' I said, 'A groom,' and accepted because they told me to, and then he disappeared, and we thought Saleem had taken him away so he could marry Angèle. Nobody knew how it happened. What did I have to do with Saleem's marriage?

I swear I have no idea. All I know is that Angèle had an elder sister called Odette, and that her dad wouldn't let Angèle marry before her elder sister. Thus it was, my dear sir, that Saleem convinced my fiancé, and the two men disappeared and went to live in Aleppo, where they worked in the carpentry workshop owned by the girls' paternal uncle, Jacques Istefan. In other words, instead of the brother killing his brother, he killed his sister. To make a long story very short, it was my brother's fault, or so all of them said. I said no, maybe it was Najeeb's fault, maybe it was he who set up the whole thing. Najeeb is cleverer than Saleem and doesn't have a conscience. My brother was a victim, I'm sure of it, but nobody believed me. All of them kept saying it was Saleem's fault, so I believed them and started saying the same. Then the nun came and said, 'Kill that story. It's two scandals in one, the scandal of the girl and the scandal of the brother. We all know the girl's scandal — she was engaged and the engagement was broken off, but she's as much a virgin as Our Lady, God bless her name, and she's going to stay one.' The nun said all this in a loud voice so the neighbours would hear. Then she lowered her voice and talked about Saleem. She said he'd gone and married a Greek Catholic and become one himself. In other words, out of the frying pan into the fire."

"Keep your voice down!" Saada shrieked.

This was the only time Saada yelled at the nun. No-one had ever heard Saada raise her voice in the nun's presence before. Usually, she grovelled in front of the saint, hunching over as though making obeisance before her, swallowing her words as though her throat was sore, mumbling. That day, however, when disaster struck, Saada feared for her daughter. The business of Saleem and the two women he'd married didn't concern her, she said — she said he'd married two women but then said, "No, what am I saying? It's my heart speaking. It's like he kidnapped my daughter and killed her. I spit on you, you beast."

Meelya told her brother about the two women who looked the same: two girls of middling height, two round white faces, two long noses, thin, barely visible lips, small teeth with exposed gums. Saleem took the thin one and Najeeb took the fat, and that was that.

"Where did you see them?" Moussa asked.

"They were with Saleem in Burj Square. I was on my way to look in on my brothers at the shop in Souq el Najjarin, and I took a detour in the direction of Souq el Tawileh and I saw them. Saleem was hiding behind the women. Or no, I was walking in the street and it was dark and raining and I slipped. My clothes got soaked. I got up and shook myself off and that was when I saw them. Najeeb had his arm through the stout one's and Saleem was walking behind them as though he was trying to catch up but couldn't. Then Saleem fell down. They looked back and left him. He was lying in the road and all wet. I wanted to go over to my brother and help him, but Najeeb came back. I panicked and started running. I saw Najeeb kissing the stout woman, and they were laughing and I started crying."

Moussa closed his eyes and said he didn't understand any more. "As far as I'm concerned, my brother Saleem is dead and that's it. I have to forget him and you have to forget him too."

Tears rolled down Meelya's cheeks. Moussa bent over his sister, reached towards her eyes, saw a little girl, saw himself kissing the eyes wet with tears, drew back and heard his sister telling him not to cry: "It's not worth it, brother, and anyway, it's better like this. It could never have been. If he and my brother were failing at the university and wanted to work as carpenters, why didn't Saleem go to work in the shop with his brothers? And what does the other one know about carpentry? Saleem we can understand. He's the son of a carpenter and became a carpenter. But what does Najeeb have to do with such things? Since when did he have any connection with carpentry, and what sort of father wants to marry his daughters off at any price? And what are they supposed to do in Aleppo? One day they'll be sorry."

Did Meelya tell the story the way it happened? Of course not. Nobody can tell a story with all its events and in the order in which things happened, or one would spend one's whole life telling one story. Meelya left lots of things out. She didn't, for example, say anything about her love for Najeeb, her fondness for his anecdotes, or the obscure feelings that had taken possession of her, body and soul, and which she hadn't felt the like of since, until yesterday, when she'd discovered she was pregnant.

She told him and said it was nothing to do with her.

"But you loved him, right?" Mansour asked.

"I've never been in love," she responded.

"What about me?"

"You're different."

"What do you mean, different?"

"You're my husband."

"I'm asking if you love me."

"Is there a woman who doesn't love her husband? Of course I do."

That day, when she became pregnant and gave her body the freedom to grow as round as it liked, she felt she no longer needed anyone because the life in her belly made her feel as though she were more than one person.

"I didn't deceive anyone. He deceived me, my brother deceived me, and my mother deceived me, and I didn't understand what was going on. What would you have had me do?"

In the third month, when Meelya entered the realm of duality, she rediscovered young Meelya in her dreams and found that it wasn't her longing for her mother or for her brother

Moussa that had been the cause of her loneliness and sadness. Her longing had been for the little brown-skinned girl who had filled Meelya's nights with movement, brought light into her life and allowed her to see the world illuminated by the light shining from her eyes.

Meelya didn't stop sleeping when Mansour moved close to her, but she would start to feel nauseous, and in the nausea her water would overflow. Once he claimed that he had seen her smile, but she didn't believe him: the room was dark and there had been no moonlight to steal through the window facing her bed. She had chosen this bed because of the window, saying she couldn't sleep without it. She had chosen this bed, leaving the one opposite to her husband, and would close her eyes onto the colours of the darkness, refusing to put curtains over the window, as they would destroy its colorations, which she wanted, but for which Mansour cared nothing. Every time they entered the room together, she'd say she was tired. She would put on her long blue nightdress, pull the covers up to her neck and sleep, and the little girl would be waiting for her. He would doze a little, wake up, then get out of bed and tiptoe to hers. Meelya would press herself against the wall, turning her back on her husband's bed. He would lie next to her and his hand would begin its journey to her shoulders, descend to her back, then wrap itself around her breasts. When he heard the first gasp he'd turn her over so that she lay on her back, then lift her nightdress and enter her. Her breathing would become deeper and she would gasp hoarsely. Her hands would lie loose, her head would sink into the long chestnut hair covering the pillow, her eyes would close, and her lips would part just enough to allow Mansour to snatch kisses from them. The gasps and the limpness that allowed the darkness to bear the woman's body incited Mansour to delirium, and his desire would go on burning even after he'd come. He'd withdraw quietly, go to the bathroom, wash himself and feel, as everything within him began again, as though he hadn't slept with her. But when he returned to the room, he'd find that she'd turned her back to him. He'd try to slip in under the bedclothes again, but there'd be no room; he'd shove her, but she wouldn't budge, so he'd return to his bed disappointed.

Not once did Meelya go to the bathroom to wash after love-making. She would get up in the morning shining and giving off a scent of soap. He'd try to remind her of what had happened the night before and she'd look at him with wide-eyed astonishment, as though it hadn't been her, as though what had happened hadn't happened.

When, then, did she wash herself?

Did she wait till he was asleep and then rush to the bathroom, or did she get up early, bathe and go back to sleep?

Mansour got up at 7.00, when his wife was asleep. He would prepare his cup of Turkish coffee in the kitchen, sit down at the wooden table, light the first cigarette of the day and see her coming. The minutes dividing his waking from her coming into the kitchen weren't enough to explain how her hair could give off that scent of soap and bay leaves. She would come, glistening with water, he would ask her when she had bathed, and she wouldn't reply. "I've a mind to watch you having your bath," he said once. She removed the coffee-maker from in front of him, added a little orange-blossom water to it and made breakfast, which consisted of *labaneh*, cheese, thyme, honey and quince jam.

"What do you say to tonight, before we go to sleep?"

"What do I say to what?"

"To having a bath. You have a bath and I watch."

"Watch me?"

He said he wanted to watch her in the bath because of the poem by Abu Nuwas.

"Get along to work now. I've got lots to do today too."

He didn't ask her what all that work could be, for he knew that she walked alone through the streets of the town, and Mansour was convinced that this was his fault because, after two short turns through the streets of Nazareth, he'd stopped going out with her. Even on Sunday he'd leave her to go to Mass at the Church of the Annunciation on her own while he "mooched" around the house. He didn't know what "mooch" meant exactly but considered it an adequate description of how he wasted his time on Sunday mornings while waiting for it to be noon, when he would pour some arak and grill some meat in preparation for a massive drinking session that usually ended in an argument because he'd insist on having sex with Meelya in broad daylight. In the end, Meelya would leave, only to return two hours later, by which time Mansour would be sleeping. She would proceed to do the washing up and tidy the house.

How did she bathe, and when?

Mansour imagined his wife as the bather in Abu Nuwas's poem. She would appear to him as delicate as water, as water falling on water.

He'd put the glass of arak to his lips, sip the white liquid and chant,

> "She faced the air, she whom a gentle breeze lighter than wind
>   Had naked made,
> And reached out a hand that like unto water was
>   To water in a vessel ready laid.
> She saw the watcher's eye as it drew close . . .

No, that's not it.

> Then, when she was done and to take her robe
>   She quickly made,

She saw the watcher's eye as it drew close
   And darkness over light was laid.

That's not right either: at the beginning it's 'disrobed' – note what a beautiful word that is. 'Disrobed' here means 'undressed herself'.

She disrobed that she might water pour
   And modesty her face a rosy hue had made.

Then it's 'She faced the air, she whom a gentle breeze', et cetera, and it ends like this:

Then morn did cede its place to night and she was left,
   While water still on water dripped in shade."

He'd jump around among the verses, going back to the first one, then sliding on to the last, bringing things forward and pushing things back, moving on top of the water and falling into it, as though swimming. He would say that poetry was water, that a woman's body was water, that love was water and that God on His throne was water – "We made every living thing from water." He'd jump up to steal from the woman with the parted lips a kiss that she sought to hide, or a word that she wanted to say, then find he was exhausted and had lost all his strength. "I am the bearer of the wind," he'd say. "Bearing the wind is tiring." Meelya would depart for the kitchen, but he'd catch her up and say, "This is what arak should be, woman. God, what arak does to you! White on white, ten out of ten. Arak is ten out of ten."

Meelya didn't understand why her husband thought only about that thing and couldn't see how much of a stranger she felt, and how alone. Meelya was afraid. Of course, it wasn't something Mansour would do, but fathers do kill their children, that was something she'd believed all her life, or at least it was a story her father had told; or rather, it wasn't her father who'd told it, it was the family story. The story hadn't been buried with her father when he died because the scene was dominated by the image of the grandfather, Saleem, even when, as Saada told her children, the father had become like his own father – for the image of a victim had been ever present in Youssef's face, with its black gaps everywhere, and in its half-closed eye.

"Can a father kill his son?" she asked her grandmother.

"No, my daughter, he didn't mean to kill him. He hit him with the stone because he didn't know who he was."

"How can anyone not know his own son?"

"He thought he was a thief, so he threw the stone at him and hit him. It wasn't the father's fault, or the son's. It was the fault of the way things were. Those were hard times, my daughter, and maybe it was the woman's fault. She created the problem and dragged us into it after she died. Your grandfather Saleem bought the house and the house was the problem. First your father tried to sell the house, but he couldn't. To sell, you have to find someone to buy, and in those days there wasn't any money, and that was how Youssef, and you along with him, got stuck with it. No, your grandfather didn't mean to kill his son. That's just what that nun says, the one your mother's always parroting. No, it's not true, and it couldn't be true, and that's all there is to it."

That night, when she became round with pregnancy and entered the realm of duality, Meelya decided to start her life over again. Where, then, had the ghost of Najeeb come from? Why had Mansour brought him back from the cave of memory?

Mansour had married the girl because he'd fallen in love with her, and he tried to explain the meanings of love to her because he thought she was in love like him but couldn't find the words to express her feelings. Borrowing poetry, he rolled it out at her feet, saying that Bashshar ibn Burd was describing love when he wrote of his body in these two verses:

Take my hand, then lift my robe and you will see
  My body, yes — but decency's preserved:
What from its eye erupts is not its juice,
  But a soul that melts and into droplets is transferred.

He was wolfing down his plate of eggs in the hotel dining room. She came over to him, took the plate and gave it to one of the two Wadeeas, saying they were bad for his health.

"I'm better now," he said.

"No. You haven't recovered," she replied.

"How can you say such a thing? Didn't you see what a tiger I turned into yesterday?"

"Yesterday?"

"I hope you're just pretending not to understand."

"On the contrary. I understand very well that you have to look after your health and we have to go to Beirut. Where's the driver?"

He told her he'd paid the driver, who had eaten his breakfast and left for Beirut.

"What about us?"

"We're going to stay another two nights. Then we'll go to Beirut and from there to Nazareth."

"No, we have to go today. It's cold."

She sat down across from him, ate a little cheese, drank a cup of tea and saw how the man gobbled up everything on the table.

Meelya was hungry but knew that in the presence of her husband's ravenous appetite she'd never eat more than a little. She would content herself with watching him as he sighed over her wonderful cooking, while he would say that he was the first man ever to prefer his wife's cooking to his mother's. Listening to him, she'd be reminded of her three brothers in the old house in Beirut and of how they'd be having to get used to their mother's insipid cuisine all over again. Because of the disturbances in Palestine, though, the road was closed and letters weren't getting through, so she decided to speak to her brother Moussa using her own special means. When Mansour left for work and the house was empty, she'd call to Moussa and he'd appear, she'd question him and he'd answer, and she'd see him standing there before her. She'd complain of her loneliness and fear and of her yearning for the scent of the chinaberries in the garden.

Meelya spent three days with her husband in the empty hotel. All there was were *Khawaja* Massabki and his two maids, the view of the little pond in the garden, which was covered in snow, and Mansour's voice declaiming poetry to her while he held her hand.

"That's the king, and the one standing next to him is the Prince of Poets, Ahmad Shawqi," Mansour said. "The king ran away when the French attacked Damascus and became King of Iraq. What a cock-up! Did you ever hear of a king betraying one kingdom for another? That's the way we are, though, and Ahmad Shawqi's standing there weeping for Damascus, which the French army bombarded with cannon:

> *Greetings exceeding frail from Barada's east wind,*
>   *And tears unceasing, O Damascus!"*

Meelya is between waking and sleeping. She feels fire in her bones. She goes out into the garden, scoops up some snow and devours it. The snow melts on her burning lips and thirst ravishes her. She sleeps beside Mansour and the man takes her in his strong hands. She drowses in the fire and dreams. Little

Meelya will not return for three months, though. Her place has been taken by a 24-year-old woman stretched out above the fog of Dahr el Baydar and departing for a mysterious world, led by a blue woman she doesn't know.

THE SECOND NIGHT

Darkness.

Meelya is in bed, dreaming. Pain squeezes her belly and
climbs upwards. She feels as though she's suffocating, as though
a fist has buried itself in her depths and is gripping her. Her
body is paralysed and her head heavy. She opens her eyes and
can't see. Then the pain recedes, seeming to spread through her
belly before melting away, leaving behind a fading memory.

Nine months have passed, and the time has come.

The pain returns. Her belly contracts and with the pain comes
her grandmother, Umm Youssef. Why had this grandmother
vanished from her memory? Why has she returned today?

The elderly woman sits paralysed and silent on her bed, her
white hair in a bun at her neck. An elderly tomcat hovers, not
daring to climb onto the bed beside her.

Umm Youssef – Haseeba Haddad – died when Meelya was
three and vanished from the girl's memory, which it had never
entered anyway. Why had she come back? And why the cat?

Meelya awoke, opened her eyes onto the rays of morning,
rose from the bed feeling with her feet for her slippers, just
as she usually did, and the cat jumped and landed between
them. The slippers turned into a running cat. She ran after it,

penned it in a corner of the room, got close to it, stamped on it and heard a yowling, rattling sound. Then she saw her grandmother Haseeba, whose name, before she changed it, had been Habeesa.

Saada had no idea why Abu Saeed had given his daughter that name, which means "imprisoned". Perhaps it had been *her* grandmother's name; but then why should her grandmother have been given such a name? What matters is that the woman changed her name and everyone started calling her by her new name except for her daughter-in-law, who went on calling her by her original name even after she was dead. Youssef would become furious and beg his wife in a trembling voice to stop, but Saada was Saada.

"I want to call her Granny Haseeba," Meelya said to her mother.

"Call her what you like, dear, but her name was Habeesa, God rest her soul, and ours, and the cat's."

What was the cat (which Saada was said to have poisoned twenty-four hours after her mother-in-law died) all about? Meelya doesn't remember her father's tears, but Saada told her about them: "He cried more over that cat than he did over his mother."

The cat was called "the Pasha". The grandmother gave him that name because, she said, he was like the Turkish pashas — blonde-haired and brown-eyed, with long whiskers and as fat as a sheep. He was old and had problems with his eyes; he probably had cataracts and was short-sighted. Saada, though, said his stumbling about wasn't due to poor eyesight but to senility. The cat had become senile and could no longer distinguish between things, and instead of behaving in a dignified fashion, like other cats, he started wetting himself and defecating everywhere, filling the house with the smell of his messes. Saada wanted to get rid of him, but Youssef felt sorry for his sick mother and decided to let the cat remain in the house, under his protection.

"I beg of you. Mother will go crazy."

"She already is."

"God grant you a decent end, woman. Don't say such things. I'll clean up after the cat."

"And who's going to clean up after your mother?"

"Keep your voice down or she'll hear you."

The grandmother in her bed heard everything but didn't speak. She had entered "the desert of silence from which there is no return" – Meelya doesn't know where the metaphor came from; it must have been the nun. The sainted nun referred to Haseeba's silence as "the desert", saying that all the saints had chosen the desert in the end. Sister Milaneh was the only person who would bow with veneration and respect before Haseeba. She would enter the house and go directly to the aged woman's bed, wipe her brow with a piece of cotton wool dipped in oil, kiss her head and show no disgust at the smell of the woman's cracked skin.

"You mean Granny's been bedridden ever since I was born?" Meelya asked.

"No, dear. When you were born she was still a great beauty. She used to sleep in the bed here, next to the one in which I gave birth to you, but she wouldn't stay at home. She'd go wandering off, and one day, when you were five months old, they brought her back and said she'd fallen in the road, and that's how she stayed till she died."

"Where was I sleeping when she died?"

"You used to sleep in the same room with her, but we made sure you didn't notice anything, you and your brothers. Or at least, Saleem, yes. Saleem came to our room and said his granny was as cold as ice and I came running. Your father stayed in bed like a lump, but then I shouted at him and he followed me.

We sent you children to my mother's and you didn't come back till everything was over and we'd buried the cat."

Meelya doesn't remember her grandmother. All the images of the aged woman that she can summon up come to her as memories of things she heard from her mother – fragments of stories she pieced together from words like motes in the air that turned into images that came to occupy a certain space in her dreams.

"I have to get out of this dream," thought Meelya. She opens the door of her room, asking the cat to come, but the cat runs away, sits under the bed and starts yowling. She kneels down, saying, "Pussy pussy pussy" to make it come out. The old cat raises its head and pulls back, as though about to pounce. Fear makes little Meelya retreat. The cat is under the grandmother's bed in the *leewan* and she is watching, her head resting on two pillows placed on her thighs, her eyes open. The woman is bent in two and can no longer sit upright.

Why did she sleep that way?

All Meelya saw was her back, her white cheek twisted on the pillow, and white foam around her lips, which she kept tightly sealed over her silence. This was how she spent her last three years.

The story went that Youssef had got up one morning only to find his mother sleeping in this strange position. His mother said she'd decided to sleep doubled up to keep death at bay. "If I sleep on my back," she said, "Azrael will come and steal the soul out of my mouth."

Haseeba believed she might die if she lay on her back and that the only way to avoid death was to make herself into a ball: death couldn't get a grip on a ball because life was round. This is what Youssef said she'd said, but no-one believed him. How could a senile woman, who could no longer distinguish anything from anything else, speak in such philosophical terms?

When she died, she was stiffening and cold – doubled over, her face resting on two plump pillows, feet bent inwards and a thread of blood running down next to her ear. But for Saada's presence of mind in asking her husband to pry the woman's folded body open, she would have hardened up and it would have been impossible to get her into her coffin.

Meelya makes noises at the cat. The cat readies itself to leap and then, without warning, makes a zigzag dash, emerges from beneath the bed and buries itself in the slipper.

"No, no!" yelled Meelya, and saw Mansour standing next to the bed. The hands of the clock pointed to 5.00 in the afternoon. It wasn't dark yet. Meelya had got into bed because she'd felt a heaviness in her belly and had decided to lie down for a little. Then she'd got up to make dinner before her husband came home. The same tingling sensation that took her into sleep swept over her, and the pain, in conjoined waves, came and faded away again. The cat appeared in the shape of a slipper she'd put on, and she heard someone moaning for help.

She opened her eyes and gestured to Mansour to leave her for a little. "Five minutes and I'll get up," she said. Everything vanished and she sank into the dark. Her belly was contracting, she bent double to lessen the pain and sank into the story once more. She saw how the cat died and heard her father sobbing as he picked up the murdered animal, wrapped it in brown paper and went to bury it in the garden. The cat had eaten the poisoned food and then walked meekly, without uttering a sound, to the bed where Haseeba had slept, laid down on the floor and died.

The cat, "the Pasha", was only the last chapter in the life of Haseeba, who had ended up incapacitated on a white iron bed, where she would sit, too frightened to sleep, and wake up panic-stricken by the fear of death.

The aged woman lived out her last days in a tightly sealed

silence disturbed only by obscure ghosts that crept into her room through the window. She heard strange voices and experienced a continual ringing in her ears. The ghosts, which took the form of black smoke, surrounded the woman on her bed and told her stories of a past that hadn't passed but had turned into a series of interlocking images wrapped in the colour grey, and a ringing that wouldn't stop.

"Please, the voices!" she'd scream every now and then, but when Saada ran to her to find out what was wrong, the woman would return to her desert of silence.

Habeesa was the third daughter of Naseef Haddad, who in 1860 had fled the massacres of Mount Lebanon with his wife, four daughters and only son. In those vicious days that saw the spilling of so much blood, he left the house, the silk loom inherited from his father and the small vegetable patch, escaping with nothing but the clothes on his back from the village of Kfar Qatra in the Chouf in order to save his family. Twelve-year-old Saeed, his only son, was lost on the road, and Naseef spent the rest of his life waiting for his son, who never returned. He'd sit in the garden of his house in Beirut's Museitbeh district and never go out because he was waiting. Every morning he'd recount how he'd smelled his son in a dream. The son didn't return, three of the daughters got married, and only Habeesa was left. Having rejected all suitors, she then, to her father's astonishment, agreed to marry Saleem Shaheen, carpenter and thimblerigger, who spent most of his time in the courtyard of the Church of the Angel Mikhail playing the thimble game or drinking arak in a small bar next to the church. The agreement of Habeesa, who never removed her long black dress with its seven fastened buttons, took everyone by surprise. She was twenty years old, and the wondering looks of her father and sisters as she refused all suitors had implied that she was on the verge of spinsterhood.

She had, however, stubbornly refused marriage, taking refuge in a silence that became her veil. It was said she wore black in mourning for her brother, whose mysterious disappearance she could no more accept than she could her father's theory that he must have left the country in disgust, found a French ship to take him to the new world of America, and would return. Having made up the story of his son's migration, her father believed it, and his waiting stirred everyone's pity. The man's wife had died seven months after leaving for Beirut, a victim of homesickness, a malady widespread in nineteenth-century Lebanon and attributable to its migrations, massacres and assorted other woes. She died after three days in bed in the small shack her husband had built on land belonging to the church. The girls were afraid their father would remarry, but the man himself had no interest in a wife when women who had come down from the villages were "there for the asking", as he used to say, in Beirut.

He found employment in the silk shop owned by Abdallah Abd el Nour, working on an old loom the Beirut merchant had set up in an adjacent shed. Naseef returned to his profession, life returned to him, and he erased the village from his memory.

Habeesa stayed on in the house, alone with her father, who would come home drunk late at night, eat the food his daughter had prepared and then bury himself in sleep, leaving Habeesa awake in the black dress she never took off.

No-one knew the story. Saada would say that she had heard the woman, in the early days of her senility, speak French with an imaginary man called Ferdinand. A story of Habeesa's love for a French officer who promised her marriage and then disappeared, as soldiers always do, thus caught fire in Saada's imagination. Did she wear mourning because of her lost love and wasted virginity? Had the youth bewitched her with his white complexion and blue eyes and transported her to the illusory realm of dreams before departing?

Saada consulted the nun, who rebuked her and told her to mind her own business, because God alone knew what was hidden, and He was the keeper of the heart's secrets.

What was it all about?

When Saada asked her husband about the business with Ferdinand, Youssef knit his thick eyebrows and told his wife she was a liar: "Give over, woman, she's my mother. How would you like it if I talked that way about yours?"

That evening, though, Youssef tried to talk with his mother, who went silent, gazing into the distance as though not listening to her son's questions. Then suddenly she began mumbling in a foreign tongue, and the name Ferdinand came out, and he recalled the story of the great secret hidden in the breast of the aged woman who had entered the desert of silence.

The story Youssef knew was of how Haseeba had married his father at night. The girl had insisted on one condition, that she marry Saleem Shaheen at night, and her request was honoured. She emerged from her house in her long black dress, her father, her three sisters and their husbands all around her. Night covered the bride's funereal procession. Saleem was waiting at the church door wearing a silk *abaya* embroidered with metallic thread and a red tarboush. He was alone, as the bride also had requested. They stood before the candlelit altar and Father Andrawus blessed their marriage. Haseeba and Youssef left for his house on foot. The bridegroom had provided a four-horse carriage, but the bride refused to use it. Saying she wanted to walk, she set off arm in arm with her husband. Darkness enveloped them and they disappeared into silence.

Did Saleem find out about the Ferdinand business and then take revenge on his wife? Or was what Youssef thought of as revenge merely Saleem's reaction to his inability to father more than one boy, as a result of his having been stricken with mumps?

"What does it all mean?" Meelya asked her mother. "A man spends his life waiting to get married, and as soon as he does he feels he has to look around for something else?"

"That's the way men are, dear. A man is empty. He has no life to fill him up. Anyone who can't give life feels empty all the time and starts behaving like a monkey, eating shit and pissing around, and then God help us."

Saleem learnt from his wife how to make a veil out of darkness and hide his life. Haseeba only awoke properly at night, when she would do the chores by the light of the oil lamp. Then, when her husband left for the shop, the woman would lean back upon the light and sleep.

Youssef had persuaded her to move into the new house, telling her, "Don't fuss, Mother. It's just a house like any other." But when she discovered that her husband had bought the house that *Khawaja* Sergius Afteemous had built for his Egyptian mistress, who had then become Saleem's semi-public mistress, she had a crazy fit and started screaming.

It was only then, in those days that witnessed the woman's sorrow and sobbing and her sense of failure and shame, that she discovered the truth about the stone that had taken out her son's eye. It all happened when the family moved to the house Saleem had bought from *Khawaja* Afteemous's heirs after his Egyptian mistress's death. Haseeba hadn't been upset by the infidelity, for, as she'd said to her only daughter, she pitied the man and all his sex. But that things had got to the point where she had to live in this overgrown garden surrounded by trees and infested by snakes and scorpions just so her husband could keep faith with his Egyptian mistress was too much.

No-one asked Haseeba how she had found out about her husband's affair with his Egyptian girlfriend. It occurred after the matter had become well known, and well-known stories don't need anyone to tell them: they turn into smells that rise and spread.

The scent of scandal arose, plunging the woman into a new kind of blackness. What bewildered her was the deception. "The jackal, the son of a dog" was what she called her husband. Saleem was a jackal in every sense of the word; a man as fearful of his wife as the carpenter was of Black Haseeba had never been heard of before. Then suddenly the woman discovered that behind all that fear and cringing hid a rat bent on revenge.

With what, though, could he take revenge, given his condition?

The man was in an unenviable position. After the birth of his son Youssef, he'd caught what they called "the lumps", meaning mumps. Usually, it is children who are afflicted by this disease, so called because of the swelling in the lymph nodes. When it afflicts adult males, however, things take on a different complexion, as there is a danger of its causing infertility. If it spreads to the testicles, all you can do is thank God you're not dead.

This is what happened to Saleem. The man suffered long from the accursed disease, and the traditional Arab doctor came more than once, prescribing bitter herbs which Saleem had to infuse and drink. When he was fully recovered, the doctor said, "May God reward you in other ways," for from that day on he would father no more children and have to be content with the one son God had given him. Now, with Saleem no longer able to perform his conjugal duty, things took a new turn; all of a sudden, everything within him went limp. He considered suicide. He visited the doctor, who assured him that, though the disease cut the flow of seed, it didn't affect erectile function. He prescribed tonics and advised Saleem to breakfast on honey and pine nuts. Nothing, however, could restore the man's powers, though the pine nuts became part of the family's heritage. Youssef acquired a taste for them and passed the custom on to his children, and when Meelya took over the kitchen she made pine nuts an essential element of almost every dish, adding them to cracked wheat and stuffed vegetables and decorating desserts with them. She even went so far as to make *qatayif* with pine nuts, which was then, and perhaps remains, something unknown to anyone else in Beirut, made only among the "Meelyaites", a community that expanded as her brothers married and succeeded in persuading their wives to make the same dessert.

"The Pines" is, according to the stories, another name for Beirut, though in fact these trees were an Egyptian introduction, Ibraheem Pasha, the nineteenth-century conqueror of Lebanon and Syria, being the one who planted – or replanted – Beirut's pine forest (though the truth is known to God alone). Saleem ate Ibraheem Pasha's pine nuts dipped in honey morning and evening, but to no avail: no sooner did he approach his wife at night and feel the life force coursing through his body than he'd abruptly deflate. Haseeba wouldn't utter a word. She'd feel his weight on top of her, he'd try, then he'd pull back and turn away, pretending to go to sleep. Saleem "ate the stones off the ground" in his desperate search for a cure, and it took the Egyptian woman to rescue him. That expression – where had Saleem come up with it? And how had he been able to restore himself to himself by using the Egyptian dialect and speaking to his only son in the language of the descendants of the pharaohs? It must have come from her. She said that her name was Maryam, though Saleem, to his dying day, was unable to establish that that was indeed her real name. It seems that she belonged to the secret line that Ibraheem Pasha's expeditionary campaign had established on the Levantine coast – and here the question that puzzled Youssef poses itself again. Who was this woman, and how had she entered the family's life? The question cost him his right eye and led to his lifelong feeling, which he passed on to his children, that fathers kill their sons. When the secret was revealed, Saleem said he'd thought Youssef was a thief making his stealthy way into the old house, so he'd thrown a stone at him; it had never occurred to him that it could be his only son spying on him. The stone hit the boy in the eye, which remained forever after half closed, and Saleem entered the house of his Egyptian mistress puffed up with pride.

Maryam wasn't really Saleem's mistress, however; she was the mistress of another man – a story as tangled as a mass of yarn. Grandfather Saleem told no-one of his long relationship with the Egyptian woman. In his last days, when asked about the matter, he'd smile foolishly and content himself with singing the praises of the beautiful almond tree for which he'd bought the house. Maryam's original lover, *Khawaja* Sergius Afteemous, hadn't been married, but he'd been one of the first Lebanese to abandon the robe and tarboush in favour of European clothing. A confirmed bachelor, he'd studied architecture in Paris and belonged to the generation of Lebanese architects that introduced the Italian style to the spacious Beirut houses built by the city's silk merchants. Why a bachelor should enter into a relationship and guard it so fiercely from discovery is one of the characteristic secrets of those wealthy Beirut families who laid the foundations for their own extinction through their tendency to bachelorhood. They also created a social tradition based on a double life whose public face was all religiosity and regular church attendance but whose private reality was one of illicit relationships with sequestered courtesans belonging to one of two lineages: the Egyptian, which began with Ibraheem Pasha's invasion, and the more ancient Greek, which some said began with the arrival of Alexander the Macedonian and which was embodied by Madame Maryka Spiridon, though that is another story.

Haseeba said, "Enough humbug. I refuse to live a moment in that house. It's the house of sin."

Which of the two sins did she have in mind? The relationship with a woman whose life was not above suspicion? Or the father's attempt to murder his son there, when he threw a stone at him and then, preening, entered his mistress's house?

All Haseeba knew was that she went back to being a virgin, as she had been before bearing her only son, Youssef, and hid herself under her long black dress, whose fastened buttons symbolized her closed body. A tall woman with a body slender and svelte, eyes that bulged a little, a large nose that took up half her face and an impregnable dignity forged out of taciturnity, Haseeba lived in silence and cloaked herself in the colour black. Her son said she could see in the dark, that her shining eyes could penetrate the gloom. He begged his wife to be kind to his mother as she faced her end with a back snapped in two. He enumerated the woman's virtues and recalled the torments she'd endured: "Can't you see the pain engraved on her face? That's how her entire life was. Pain upon pain. I beg you, Saada."

"But the smell. Your mother refuses to sit on the bedpan, and if she does she doesn't do anything, and the moment we go to sleep, you get the smell. What torment! What did I do to You, Lord, to deserve this?"

The smell of which Saada complained was the last thing one would have expected from a woman like Haseeba, who had floated in a cloud of soap, perfume wafting off her. Haseeba made the perfumes herself, steeping damask roses in water and blending them with jasmine and basil, and from this mixture she made the water with which she washed her face. Her perfumed scent spread everywhere – a woman buttoned up in a black dress from which the only thing to escape was perfume, carrying herself like a silent ghost, stirring feelings of admiration and fear among those whom she passed, despite all of which, her husband, Saleem, subjected her to mortifications climaxing in his purchase of the house following the death of Maryam the Egyptian. Meelya knew the story because her mother had told it to her, and her mother knew it from her husband, Youssef, and Youssef knew it from the stone that had struck him in his right eye.

Why did Youssef say nothing when his father bought the house?

When Saleem came bearing the good news that he had bought a new house, Haseeba said nothing. The joy she'd expected to accompany the decision to move out of their two small rooms with a bathroom out in the courtyard never materialized. Her husband invited her to see the house, but she refused. He asked her to suggest suitable new furniture and she said it didn't matter, and instead spent her time getting their existing belongings ready for the move. Everything proceeded normally. The family moved into their new house, the man and his wife took up residence in the *leewan* that opened onto the spacious *dar*, Youssef slept in a corner of the latter, and everything was fine until Haseeba found out. Then she exploded. All the silence that had been stored up inside her buttoned black dress emerged, and she poured her rage onto her son Youssef, whom she never forgave for hiding the secret of the house. As to how she found out and who told her, there is no need to look far. "We have no secrets," Saada told her daughter. "That everyone knew about Saleem except his wife is something I don't believe. I think she knew from the beginning but pretended not to. I don't know what made her go crazy. And when you think about it, what did she have to be afraid of? After all, the man, God grant you health, having had the disease, was finished. But when she found out that the house was the

Egyptian woman's and the bed her bed, she started wailing and said she wanted to die. She doused her dress with paraffin and tried to set herself on fire. Youssef threw himself on top of her, and God shielded her from harm."

What happened to Saleem when he discovered that he was impotent? That's the unanswerable question. He "ate the stones off the ground", as Maryam the Egyptian put it. He visited numerous doctors to no effect, but when his feet led him to her house, the problem was solved, as though it had never existed. *Khawaja* Sergius Afteemous had ordered a walnut bed from him. Having made the bed, he carried it, with the help of his son Youssef, to that place, and there he saw her, and saw the light. The man was living in utter misery, feeling dumb desire sweep over him every night, and then, when he approached his nightdress-enshrouded wife, turning as cold as ice. Before this plump, short, brown-skinned woman in her forties, however, he felt himself a man. He had put the bed in the *leewan*, nodded to the woman and taken his son's hand as if to leave, when he heard her speaking in Egyptian dialect and felt a shiver run down his spine. "We'd better take the bed for a spin, guv. Hang on a mo. Wow!" she said and sat on the bed. Then, propping herself on one elbow as if she were about to lie down, she exclaimed, "Brilliant!" Standing up again, she offered him her hand to thank him. He felt her give his big, coarse hand a squeeze and heard her say, or so he claimed, "Don't be a stranger, guv!" He understood and decided he'd return.

When he told her later that he'd understood the signal of her hand and the hidden meaning of her words, she burst out laughing and said that she hadn't said a thing, that he'd invented the whole story, that she hadn't given him a second thought.

In fact, it was Meelya who made that dialogue up, for nobody, not even Youssef, knew how what happened had happened and how things had come to pass. Meelya said she'd dreamt she saw her grandfather leaping through the grass and that he'd turned into someone different. The bloom of youth had returned, he was full of strength, and his ringing laugh, stifled by repression, had returned. It seems he promised the Egyptian woman marriage, and it is said that he thought of embracing Islam, but the hand of God saved his wife from mortification because the Egyptian woman died unexpectedly, leaving nothing but the house, in which her shadow would linger until Haseeba's death.

When Saleem spoke to Maryam of marriage, she refused him and simpered, her desire shooting skywards. It was the first time she had heard the word. *Khawaja* Afteemous had treated her in a manner befitting a courtesan. He'd taken her in, made a lady of her and built her this beautiful house among the trees, where he would visit her once a month, but he had never proposed marriage, and it had never occurred to her that he would. The *Khawaja* was seventy-five years old. He would come to his mistress on the first Wednesday of every month, pay what had become, by force of custom, her salary, and they would speak of love in the past tense, until he disappeared once more. The man remained loyal to this woman whom he had loved since she was twenty, when he had rescued her from the fate imposed by Ottoman law, whose regulation of prostitution forced fallen women to reside in a closed quarter named after the Arabs' greatest poet, al Mutanabbi. The *Khawaja* had taken Maryam under his protection and treated her as the respected mistress of a Beirut aristocrat.

The story says that Maryam died unexpectedly, that *Khawaja* Afteemous's heirs put the house up for sale and that in the end it went to Saleem Shaheen, who bought it for cash.

A year after moving into the new house, Haseeba worked out that she'd been duped. All she could do, though, once "the dog, the son of a dog" had "burnt" her heart, was to mix her screams with paraffin and burn her body too. Surrendering herself to God, she added to her infatuation with lonely nocturnal walks an infatuation with cats, the garden becoming a refuge for all the city's homeless felines. From among these she would choose a favourite tom, which she would take into the house and force her son and husband to treat as one of the family.

The pain struck Meelya in her belly. Feeling a need to scream, she called for Mansour. She knew her husband wasn't in the house but had no-one else to turn to. She heard the voice of her grandmother, which she had never heard before, and the tomcat came, and she saw her grandfather Saleem standing in the garden, throwing a small stone at the window to let his Egyptian mistress know he was there. He was squatting beneath the eucalyptus tree waiting for the woman, whose silhouette could be made out behind the window through the latticework formed by the leaves of the jasmine bush, to appear. Meelya saw them all, and she felt afraid. No, it wasn't a dream. The dream was the tomcat she'd put her feet into as though it were a slipper and whose yowling had hurt her. The rest was circles surrounding the dream, circles formed from the memories of the dead who visited Meelya in her dreams. She was watching a story that wasn't her own, as though she were reading a book, as though the ancient chest that her grandmother Malakeh had given her had opened, and, instead of books, pages and letters, there had emerged a man, a woman and their only son with, in the distance, the lover standing beneath the window, waiting, *Khawaja* Sergius Afteemous sitting in the corner in his red tarboush and carefully pressed European suit, and the sound of his coughing.

Meelya knew Mansour wasn't there because for three months now he'd been disappearing for days on end, only to return with his face and eyes enveloped in sorrow.

"Where has the poetry gone?" she asked him.

She knew that poetry's greatest enemy is death. It isn't true that poetry vanquishes death, as he had claimed. Poetry's job is to make us accept death and become so familiar with it that we believe it has overcome death, when in reality it is death's own child and secret voice.

When Ameen, Mansour's brother, died, life turned upside down, and Meelya watched another man being born inside her husband. It was incredible. The man she knew, and about whom she knew everything, vanished. He'd been like a palm in which she could read everything. Now, as the pain squeezed her, she would say that she'd fallen in love with him on that night at the hotel. She had fallen in love with the man who had entered her sleep and her waking, filled her silence with speech and bewildered her with poetry. His love of life had showed itself in his passion for the food his wife prepared. Every day he would find an excuse to drink arak. "Good food demands arak," he'd say, "because it'd be a crime for someone to eat such good food without arak." He'd dive into the various stews, then sing the praises of the patties of veal-in-its-mother's-milk, laughing, saying that the Arabs had written poetry about halvah, and recalling Ibn al Rumi and his affair with fried doughnuts. "Dessert is gold," he'd say. "Listen, woman:

He casts the dough like silver from his fingertips
  Turning it into nets of gold

– though no-one's written in praise of watermelon, which is a pity. Anyway, tell me, what's this fantastic dish, patties of veal-in-its-mother's-milk with rice?"

"That's not its real name. They call it that in Beirut, but it's a Damascus dish. In Damascus they call it *shakiriyyeh*," Meelya said.

"It doesn't matter. What matters is that its name – this is

amazing! – its name is like a challenge. Do you know what it says in the Torah? 'Thou shalt not seethe a kid in his mother's milk,' which is why our cousins the Jews won't eat meat cooked with butter."

"You're right," Meelya said, and then announced that she would stop cooking the calf in its mother's milk because it was cruel.

"Fiddlesticks to cruel! Patties of veal-in-its-mother's-milk is the king of dishes, and we shall go on eating it till kingdom come."

He drank arak and ate *labaneh* and said he was the first to do so. Milk and milk: "lion's milk" – another name for arak – and cow's milk: "We mix milk with milk, as though men were babes suckling at the breasts of heaven."

Then he'd start reciting poetry. How had he been able to memorize that unstoppable gush of verse? How had he been able to come up with a new verse each day to add to his gargle of words?

She had loved him and loved his words and loved his love for her, and she'd begun to get used to the triangular life she lived in Nazareth, between the house and the street and the dream. Then came the news that shook her life to its foundations, that forced her to make the acquaintance of a new person and attempt to love him again when she was no longer equipped to do so.

Her husband suggested that she go to Beirut so her mother could be with her when she gave birth but withdrew the proposal before hearing his wife's answer. He said that life was ever a hostage to the times, but that in those days the security situation was particularly unsettled, and he didn't want to expose her or the unborn child to danger. Instead, he suggested that they invite her mother to Nazareth. Meelya rejected both suggestions. She didn't want to go to Beirut because she had come to Nazareth so that she could give birth there, and she didn't want to invite her mother because she was a chronic invalid and Meelya would have to look after her.

Since the beginning, which is to say as far back as the girl's memory went, she had seen herself as a mother to her mother, and felt that she was an orphan. No, she didn't want Beirut or her mother. She wanted to give birth here, because that was what the child wanted, while all she wanted herself was to meet this child, his wide-open eyes seemingly lash-less, whom she saw gazing at her in her dreams through the water in which he swam and telling her the story that no-one had ever heard.

Then the news came, everything changed, and she realized that Mansour had taken refuge with her in order to escape his brother but that Ameen had succeeded in getting his brother back, and that she was powerless, and that in the end she wouldn't be able to avoid Jaffa.

Jaffa isn't Beirut, el Manshiyyeh isn't Burj Square, and the dampness that would caress her cheek there wasn't the dampness of rotting leaves that she could smell in Beirut. She went to Jaffa to attend the brother's funeral, and there she saw the land called Palestine. In Beirut, she hadn't seen the land; despite the joy she'd felt at independence from the French Mandate, she hadn't given the matter much thought. She hadn't heard of Faisal I, or not until she heard the story of the kingdom he'd founded, stretching from Damascus to Beirut, from her husband Mansour, at the Hotel Massabki, where he'd made her stand beneath the photo of a drowsy-eyed man said to be King of the Syrian Lands.

In Nazareth, she lived outside of time. The city was in ferment, but she didn't notice. The only person she saw much of was Mansour's aunt, Mrs Malvina Surouji, whose sole topic of conversation was the man who'd married her daughter. "'He's instead of Mansour', people told me. My poor daughter, you should have married your Uncle Mansour, but it's all fate." The bride from Beirut was supposed to feel solidarity with this woman who still dreamt of Mansour as a husband for her daughter.

Then appeared the elderly man who claimed he was a descendant of Prince Fakhr el Din II of Maan. He frightened Meelya at first, before she got used to him. She asked Aunt Malvina about him, and was told that he was Crazy Tanyous, and that he'd left Nazareth long ago. He wasn't crazy, though. Meelya didn't know how to describe this strange man who dressed in a monk's habit, a felt cap like those worn by the peasants of Mount Lebanon and, tied around his waist, the black-and-white chequered headscarf of the Palestinians. "I'm alone," he told Meelya in his Palestinian accent, some of whose letters he tried to twist into sounding Lebanese. He would appear at her window at night, then disappear again, only for her to find him walking behind her through the city's streets in the mornings.

The woman experienced Nazareth by walking its narrow streets and exploring. The place was itself the awe that it inspired; that was how the woman understood her relationship with the city of Christ. She would see Tanyous in her wanderings. She would give him a few piastres because she thought he was a beggar, and he would take them without a word of thanks, as though she were only doing her duty. Then she started taking him bread and other food. Indeed, she invited him to the house a number of times to eat but didn't dare to let him in. She'd feed him in the garden and look on as he ate, which he did as though he weren't eating, not looking at the food but bolting it as though he despised it, then wiping his moustache and beard with his red palm and leaving. She hadn't told Mansour that she'd invited him; she'd just said he'd come, and told a story that hadn't happened but that she was certain had in fact happened somehow.

"And where was I?" Mansour asked.

"You were sleeping indoors," Meelya replied. "I tried to wake you but couldn't. I found him at the window. He said he was hungry. That's how he started coming."

Meelya wasn't telling the truth. She'd heard a rapping on the window. It was night and Mansour wasn't there. Everything had changed: in the aftermath of his brother's murder, Mansour had started travelling to Jaffa and had made the decision to take over the workshop. Mansour wasn't there and Meelya was sleeping alone in the house. She wasn't afraid, but she felt awe in the face of the night, awe in the face of the solitude, awe in the face of the unborn child in her belly. She heard an unceasing rapping on the window, got up and saw the silhouette of a man, who quickly disappeared among the trees. She went back to bed, covered herself with the quilt and waited. The next night the scene repeated itself, but on the third night it was different. It was 10.00. Everything in Greeks Alley, where Mansour had bought their marital abode, was quiet. She heard a violent rapping on the glass, went to the window and saw the man's silhouette.

"Who is it?" she asked, quaking with fear.

"Me," the silhouette on the other side of the window replied. "Open the window. I've brought you a present."

Meelya doesn't know where she found the strength to open the window. It was as though it weren't her, as though she were sleeping, as though someone were giving her orders and she was obeying. She opened it and saw that the man was holding a glass of wine. This he gave her, saying that he would return.

"This is the water of life," he said before he disappeared.

She didn't see him leave, didn't see his back. He was there; then the darkness descended and covered him.

The little girl with the swollen belly finds herself standing at the window holding a wine glass overflowing with red liquid. She brings it to her nose and smells aged wine. She touches her lips to the glass but doesn't drink. Going to close the window, she finds that it is shut. She cries out for Mansour, but no-one answers. She sees Moussa approaching and wants to ask him what has brought him there; Moussa takes the glass from her hand and drains it, then he holds it out to his sister, and the dark falls upon him and erases him. The girl sees herself standing alone, holding an empty glass. She draws back and drowns in the dimness, which is pierced by a single light. She is holding the light in her hand and the glass is shining. Suddenly, without her understanding what has happened, the glass falls and shatters. She bends down to pick up the pieces, which are mixed with the light. Whenever she touches a small piece of the light, it is extinguished and blood flows from her fingers, as though she were exchanging light for blood. All the same, she is compelled to pick up the scattered glass, for she is waiting for Mansour, and Mansour hasn't come, and she is afraid he'll tread on the glass and cut himself. She picks up the beads of glass, whose light goes out between her fingers, and sees the black blood cover them. She holds the pieces of glass in her wounded hands, slides to the ground and sees the blood.

Opening her eyes, she found herself in her bed, her heart-beats reverberating throughout her body. She made the sign of the cross, decided that she would forget that dream and closed her eyes once more.

In the morning, when Mansour came by the house on his return from Jaffa and woke her with that dark face he'd acquired since the murder of his brother Ameen, she leapt bare-foot out of bed to make him his coffee and breakfast. Recalling the glass, she felt something cut her heels. She looked for her slippers under the bed and found them full of blonde feathers from she knew not where. Brushing off the feathers, she put on her slippers and went to the kitchen. She put the coffee brewer on the fire, reached towards the small wooden cupboard to get the coffee cups and saw it. The glass shone in the midst of the cupboard among the coffee cups. Where had the wine glass come from? There were no wine glasses in her house. Mansour drank arak, and she drank with him.

She asked him where the wine glass had come from. He was in the bathroom and didn't hear her question. Picking up the glass with trembling hands and setting it on the table, she saw flashes of light and slivers of glass. The coffee boiled over and she didn't notice. She saw Mansour hurry into the kitchen. He put out the fire, placed the coffee brewer on the table and asked her why she was standing there as though paralysed.

"The wine glass?" she asked.

"What wine glass?" he asked.

"The one on the table," she replied.

"This tumbler?" he asked. He picked up the tumbler, which slipped out of his hand and fell, covering the floor in broken pieces.

"You've broken it!" she screamed.

"It doesn't matter," he said. "It means nothing else will go wrong. We've got lots like it."

"Oh dear, what am I going to do?" she said, kneeling on the floor and picking up the pieces. The shards buried themselves in her palms and the blood began to flow.

"What are you doing?" he yelled. "Fetch the broom."

The kneeling woman picked up all the pieces of glass, placed them on a tray and washed her hands at the sink, making the water run crimson.

"There's blood," she said, staggering as though she were about to faint. "Let me lean on you, please."

He took hold of her, led her to her bed, fetched cotton wool and antiseptic, cleaned her fingers with it and told her to get some sleep.

"Don't worry, I'll be back at noon. And don't make any food; I'll bring something from the market."

When she got up again, she found no trace of the bits of glass on the tray. Feeling that she had committed a great sin, she shed bitter tears.

Everything in Meelya's world had been turned upside down, suddenly and without warning. The news came and she found herself in Jaffa. She said she didn't want to live in that seaside city. She said she hated the house, which was in el Ajami, where Ameen's widow lived with her two boys and her mother-in-law. She said she was frightened of the roaring of the sea. She said that she'd left Beirut and left the sea and didn't want to go back to them. She said and she said, but it made no difference.

There, in the church, Ameen's coffin was draped in a flag of four colours, and there was weeping and rage. Meelya had never before seen the like – a city clamorous with rage that drew shadows of fear and hatred on its people's faces. She saw faces covered in sorrow and a city slipping towards death, and she feared for the unborn child in her belly. She feared he might fall into the foaming, thundering waves and disappear. On the face of her mother-in-law Najeeba, she saw deeply etched lines of despair.

"You killed him," Najeeba told her son Mansour. His mother didn't mean what she said, but she said it anyway, as though borrowing the voice of the young widow, who held Mansour responsible for his brother's death, or believed that his brother had died in his place. Not only had she lost everything, but now she would have to live with the two children and the elderly woman at the mercy of this Mansour who had fled Jaffa, leaving his brother to die.

There, on the bare mound overlooking the sea, Meelya saw Mansour change. Mansour stood with the others in the Sea Cemetery, where the Hourani family had buried its dead for a thousand years. When the coffin was lowered into the earth, a single ululation rang out, launched from the mother's hoarse throat as a salute to the martyr. At that instant, Mansour changed before Meelya's eyes, seeming to grow shorter, his limbs retracting. Meelya can't describe what happened, but at the time she felt that her husband's joints had cohered as though he'd turned into a single block. In Nazareth, Mansour had wept. A sort of wail had emerged from inside him, as though the man had exploded, and all the tears of the world had flowed from his eyes. But Mansour hadn't wept when he entered the house and saw the women gathered around his brother's bullet-ridden body. A slight frown had traced itself on his face, he'd bent over his brother's body to kiss the dead man's brow and felt himself falling. His head struck the pillow hard, and he laid his cheek next to his dead brother's. The women's keening grew louder. The mother said she had seen tears running over the dead man's cheeks. "Woe is me, he weeps for himself," she said, but the dead man's widow said that the tears were Mansour's. "He shouldn't let his tears fall on his brother's cheeks. It's a sin," she said. Meelya recalled how the poet Dik al Jinn al Himsi had killed his mistress Ward and how his tears had started pouring down her cheeks, causing him to recite:

> "How dear the countenance on which death's day has dawned
>> Harvesting with her hands destruction's fruit!
> With her blood I wet the ground, and how many a time
>> Love wet my lips with hers.
> My sword found its target in the orbit of her sash
>> My tears running o'er her cheeks.

By the sandals on which she walked and with which she
                                                    trod the earth,
        Naught is dearer to me than her foot."

Meelya couldn't see the point of this story. What kind of
love was that? A poet from Hims had fallen in love with two
people: a Christian woman called Ward and a boy called Bakr.
Mansour's explanation of the customs of the Abbasid period and
of how there had been no shame in one male loving another
so long as the beloved was too young to have a beard and had
a pretty face didn't impress her. He'd married Ward and
brought Bakr to live with them in the same house. When the
poet was told that Bakr had fallen in love with Ward and that
he'd courted her and slept with her while the poet was on one
of his journeys, Dik al Jinn went mad and killed the two of
them. "But that's not where the story begins," Mansour said.
"The story begins when Dik al Jinn finds out that the whole
thing was a pack of lies and that Ward hadn't betrayed him.
That's when he went to the grave, removed two handfuls of
clay, one from Ward's side and the other from Bakr's, made
them into two wine cups, and started drinking from the two
cups while weeping for his two beloveds and composing poems.
That's how he came to say, 'My tears running o'er her cheeks',
meaning that as he was killing her he was weeping for love of
her. That's what I call true passion, my dear."

"That's what you call passion?" she said.

"Of course."

"Meaning you'd kill someone?"

"Of course I would. There isn't a lover who isn't ready to
kill his beloved if she betrays him, or at least to wish she were
dead."

"So you'd kill me?"

"It's a story, my dear. It's what the story of Dik al Jinn says.

Every mortal is compelled to relive his own story. Dik al Jinn killed Ward because that's what the story demanded. Every mortal is a story. What is life, my darling? We live a story written by someone else, we don't know who. That's why I'm afraid to read novels. Whenever I read one, I feel the writer must be a monster, putting people into tragic situations just to entertain his readers. I feel as though I'm being stuffed with stories that never end, as though at any moment I might fall out of life and find myself inside a book. No, poetry's better. For the Arabs, poetry was the highest art because it described without telling a story. When they wanted to make a story readable they put poetry into it, so the poetry's the story and the story's the structure, and so on."

"So you'd kill because of a story?"

It was then that your story began, Mansour. You told me that every story has to begin with killing and death: "We think that a person's life begins when they're born. That's not true, my dear. The story begins when we die or when we kill."

It was then that Mansour entered his story, standing by the bed of death, when a brother's tears ran down his brother's cheeks.

Mansour hadn't wept. Meelya doesn't know where the story of the tears on the brother's cheeks came from. She was there and didn't see any tears. All the same, the story must have had a beginning. She told him she was starting to be afraid of his story; she said she'd seen everything about him change. Mansour had come to resemble his brother. It wasn't just the man who had changed; he'd taken off his old self and dressed himself in a new shape. The poetry had disappeared. Gone was the look of infatuation that had traced itself on his eyes, which had never tired of looking at the white, angelic face rounded by shyness and fermenting with desire. Everything had gone dry. Even that thing that Meelya never spoke of, even that became empty of water. He would sleep with her as she drowsed and she wouldn't feel the water that emerged from deep down in the sleeping land inside her, as if it wasn't him.

When they returned from Jaffa, she discovered that the man who had come to her in Beirut in flight from his story had fallen into the story that fate had written for him. The hunter of stories had caught him. The brother had died and there were no choices left to the cloth merchant who had dreamt of transforming himself into a silk merchant because, as the proverb says, "If you would love, trade in silk". The Eternal Lover, as Mansour used to call himself, who drank daily from the water of his beloved's eyes, had fled to fabrics and to Beirut because he knew there was no future for that other, prophet-afflicted land, that his brother had gone far but that Jaffa couldn't win and was doomed: "I know them. I told Ameen we couldn't win, but he replied that it was the motherland that was at stake and that we had to commit ourselves." Mansour had known that Ameen had right on his side and that the metal shop left them by their father had to be placed at the service of the beleaguered city.

"How can we not?" Ameen had asked him. "At least we can make cartridge cases and repair rifles. Do you want us to let the Jews take the land and throw us off it?"

That was what had made Mansour leave. "No. I'm not a coward, but I don't like weapons. You and Mother are right, but I don't have what it takes," Mansour had said.

"So how are we supposed to fight the British and the Jews? With words, or should we do something?"

Mansour had told his brother that he didn't have what it took and left for Beirut, where he fell in love with a Lebanese woman and the idea occurred to him that he might stay there for ever and find rest, though he discovered that that was impossible. He opened his small shop in Nazareth, travel to

Beirut to fetch the new European fabrics became a necessity, and that was how it was. And, looking over into the Shaheens' garden, he fell in love and said it was the beginning.

The beginning, though, was awaiting him in Nazareth. There, as he contemplated the apple of life, which is what he called his wife's swollen belly, came the news that turned everything upside down, proclaiming the end of their stay and the necessity of moving the small family to Jaffa.

"It's the dream," Meelya said, but instead of smiling at her dream, as he had always done before, a frown traced itself on his face and he said he didn't understand.

She said it was the dream and reminded him of the wine glass she'd broken. He said it wasn't a wine glass: "You talked about a wine glass, but all I saw was a tumbler, and the tumbler fell and broke. For heaven's sake, let's pack our bag and go. That's enough stories."

She said Moussa had drunk the wine, and that the shards of the glass scattered across the floor had shone with light, and that when she'd knelt down . . .

He didn't let her finish her sentence, screaming at her to have done. She froze where she was and felt that the words *have done* had done for her and struck her dumb. She realized that from now on she would be dealing with a new man.

Haseeba had said that a woman doesn't marry one man in her lifetime; that was a lie. The Saleem whom she'd married wasn't the Saleem who'd got sick with "the lumps", and the Saleem who'd got sick wasn't the Saleem who'd recovered and become obsessed with the problems of his little member, problems that lent his eyes a vacant stare. The Saleem of the vacant eyes was different from Saleem the lover of Maryam, and the lover of the Egyptian prostitute wasn't the same man who'd bought the house and taken Haseeba there after the late lamented whore's demise. The Saleem of the house wasn't the man who'd tried to kill his son with a stone, and the would-be killer of his son wasn't the man prostrate on the floor whom a coma had carried off to a place unknown. "I married a series of men, and each time I had to get used to things all over again. I'm tired, my son. Let me die here."

This is what she said to Youssef when he found her sitting alone on the earthen path beneath the carob tree. Haseeba had left the house, as was her habit every evening. She had put on her long black dress and walked the night streets but hadn't come back, so Youssef had gone looking for her. He had walked all the roads around the house and, after he'd exhausted himself, had found himself face to face with his mother beneath the carob tree. At first, he reproached her, but then he heard how faint her voice was and saw that she could no longer stand up properly. She said she couldn't get up and when he took hold of her hand he discovered how slack her muscles had become.

"What's the matter, Mother? Come on, up with you."

Her speech about the husband she'd married so many times were the last rational thing to pass the woman's lips. He pulled on her arm to get her up, but she collapsed.

"What's wrong, Mother? Tell me."

Youssef saw tears on the white face, where now black wrinkles spread. He bent over the woman, folded her in two and hoisted her over his shoulder. She was as light as a feather. Beautiful, tall Haseeba had turned into a clump of bones, as though her body had come apart and the woman been transformed into a little flightless bird.

He picked her up and went, knowing that he was taking her to her death. He'd heard her screaming in his father's face and watched her wrap her rage about her and say she wouldn't stay a moment longer in that house and that he had to find her another one. Turning to her son, she'd asked him why he hadn't told her the truth about his eye. The boy had placed his hand over his half-split lid and looked at his mother with eyes that pleaded with her to stop talking. But she talked: "I dare you to say who put my son's eye out. Be a man for once in your life and speak. I dare you to."

"Shut your mouth, woman, for your own sake. Anyway, the boy's eye wasn't put out. He was playing with the other boys and, praise God, it was fate."

"Never in my life did I hear of a father trying to kill his own son. You wanted to kill the boy so you could keep the Egyptian whore under wraps and I don't know what. You're half a man. You've been weighed and found wanting. But I'm not going to spend another minute in that house."

Youssef said – Youssef tried to say – but his father ordered him to keep quiet: "Keep your mouth shut, you. Get out of here and let me try to make the stupid woman understand what happened. You want to know what happened? Everyone knows what happened. It's all about that French officer, the one you've worn black for all your life. I'm the one who's kept your honour and your family's honour clean, and you'd better not make me say any more."

Saleem smashed her words with his. He said what couldn't be said. He undid the buttons on the long black dress and laid bare the soul of the woman standing before him. Haseeba staggered. Her knees gave way, and her young son sat down next to her like a dog. Youssef had made up his mind that he would humiliate his father that day. He had long endured the wound sliced through his eyelid by the stone, and his mother's cry marked the moment for him to take his revenge and tell the truth; he felt he might even strike this man who had created out of his impotence a celebrated story of passion for an Egyptian prostitute. But his mother's staggering and her naked-ness before the words made him sit down at her side like a dog denied the right to bark.

Youssef had believed that his father was a fool, and that Maryam didn't belong to him. *Khawaja* Afteemous had given her the house to make a living from. He'd got what he wanted from her and had gone to the expense of buying her the house to get her to leave him alone. Even then, he hadn't put the house in her name; he'd just given her the right to use it during her lifetime. Which was why Saleem was able to buy it from his heirs after her death. The man had bought the house – situated on Daaboul Street, off Saint Mikhail Street, in the midst of an overgrown garden fenced in by trees – and had permitted his concubine to live in it and off it, and the woman had turned the house into a brothel.

"You're an idiot, Dad," Youssef said. "She's just a cheap prostitute."

"Shut up, you bastard," Saleem yelled. Then he turned to his wife and shamed her with the story that Haseeba had thought buried in her heart, where she had dug a grave and buried the blonde young man with sky-blue eyes. But it was love, not a story. He'd seen her twice and spoken to her once, or at least he hadn't said anything but had smiled at her. And then he had disappeared. That was all, but it was love. She felt as though she'd gone blind. All she could see was the blonde youth, and all she could smell was the scent of whiteness emanating from the body of a snow-white man. Haseeba didn't know how her sisters got to find out about the story. She'd covered herself with the black dress so as to erase all trace of the white angel and then married Saleem Shaheen, the part-time carpenter, to silence the throbbing of her heart. Her heart was extinguished and her body was extinguished. Now Saleem, whose impotence and infidelities she'd borne, had come along, opened the wound and dragged from her depths the corpse of the boy with the blue eyes.

Haseeba was devastated. Her closed lips trembled and she

sat in a corner of the *dar* weeping dry tears. Youssef felt that he was suffocating and wanted to understand. He imagined himself as the son of a Frenchman whose name he didn't know and about whom he could ask no-one.

After her son's marriage, Haseeba had agreed to have the concrete wing added to the house, and it was she who'd encouraged Saleem to abandon his *abaya* and wear European clothes. This was another of the stories that took its place in the annals of the Shaheen family, where it was told and retold daily. Youssef would act out the story in front of his children in exactly the same way each time, and Saada would ask him to stop, because the girl was growing up and it wasn't right to talk about such things. However, the man – who on his return home from the shop would take off his trousers and put on a long gown because he didn't want to constrict his testicles at night too – would pay no attention. He'd describe how, when he first put on trousers, he'd felt as though he were suffocating and hadn't known where he was supposed to put his limbs; he'd felt a heaviness down below and hadn't known how to walk. He said that when he arrived at the door of the church, the bride on his arm, he'd felt as if he were going to fall over. The bigger difficulty, though, was on leaving the church, when he'd felt his trousers were going to rip under the pressure.

Youssef never tired of telling the story, which was the preoccupation of Beirut in the twenties. Suddenly, following the fall of the Ottoman Empire and at the beginning of the French occupation of Syria and Lebanon, people started adopting the ways of their new masters, and trouser-wearing became customary among the middle classes. The upper classes, on the other hand, to which *Khawaja* Afteemous belonged, had been wearing trousers since the beginning of the century, under the influence of the Ottoman reformers who believed that Europeanization held the answer to everything. Trouser-wearers, though, were the butt of jokes among the common people. Even Maryam the Egyptian couldn't keep herself from laughing with Saleem over *Khawaja* Afteemous's goods, which looked taut inside his trousers but appeared as they really were the moment the seventy-year-old took those off.

Anyway, the transition to European clothing was experienced by Beirut as a festival of comedy. Men walked about with their legs wide apart, as though every man in the city had gone lame. The jokes never ended, and the traditional tailors who couldn't adapt to this new style of dress were devastated.

After this, Youssef said, he had realized that the importance of trousers lay in their sanctification of a male's manhood and its presentation to the eye. "But I still don't like them," he'd say. "At first I found I could see myself with everything God had given me, which is shameful, and I used to be stiff all the time when I was wearing them. I'd feel as though I couldn't sit down. Then I got used to them. Now, God forbid, they say that women have started wearing trousers. It can't be right for men and women to go around stark naked – what are we coming to? I swear to God, the Last Day began when we put on trousers. Or that's what we thought then, but later on we discovered it was all meaningless."

"So why don't you shave off your moustache and stop wearing a tarboush?" Saleem asked.

"You think you're a Frenchman, boy. I don't know who you get it from."

"What's that got to do with it?"

"Men without moustaches? What would be left? And the tarboush, God forbid – ask your mother, I can't take my tarboush off for an instant except when I'm sleeping, and even when I'm asleep I dream I'm wearing it. A naked head is uglier than a naked body. No-one exposes his head; I don't know how you can do it, Saleem. All I know is that the world changed and everything keeps on changing, but not me. When I die, bury me with my tarboush on."

And when Youssef died, Saada dressed him in his robe and tarboush. But then the saintly nun said it wouldn't do: a man had to face his Lord with his head uncovered. They removed the tarboush and put it next to him on the bed, and when they carried the coffin to the graveyard, the tarboush was placed on top of the casket, the black tassel swaying as it bobbed up and down on the hands that bore it, as though the man were delivering his last words in black. Then the tarboush disappeared. Meelya thought they'd buried it next to the man himself, but three days after his death she discovered that Niqoula had placed his father's tarboush on his own head. It was a sign that the new man of the family had been born.

Meelya stands with the others before Ameen's coffin. There is no tarboush on top of it. Instead, there is a four-coloured flag – green, white, red and black – which she will later discover is the flag of Palestine, the flag created by the Great Arab Revolt against the Ottomans that was led by King Faisal, whom Meelya called the King of the Massabki Hotel. Mansour explained that the four colours referred to the ancient Arab states that had succeeded one another on this land, and that they embodied a line by Safi al Din al Hilli that explains how these colours became the symbol of the awakening of the Arabs:

White are our arts, black our doughty deeds,
  Green our vernal pastures, red our cutting blades.
No vaunt the Arabs make
  The world gainsays.
To every prayer the Arabs make
  "Amen" exclaim the days.

There in the church she saw a group of men with blue eyes and white skin standing at the front and receiving condolences along with the family members. She was told that they were members of the Husseini family, relatives of *Hajj* Ameen el Husseini, Mufti of Jerusalem and leader of Palestine. Also that Ameen Hourani, who had put the workshop he'd inherited from his father at the service of the revolution and of resistance to the British occupation and Zionism, had died a martyr for the homeland. She became aware that the smell of death was coming closer. For the entire week she spent at the family's house in Jaffa, she never lifted her hand from her belly, as though seeking to protect the unborn child from dangers that threatened it. The short blonde man said to be the uncle of *Hajj* Ameen stood next to Mansour in the church and never left his side at the house. She had wanted to ask why they looked like that – like Europeans, or the way she imagined Europeans – but she didn't. She felt the irony of it and said nothing. How could it make sense for the descendants of Crusaders to resist the new Crusaders who were occupying Palestine and endeavouring to hand it over to the Jews? Later, though, she discovered that the Husseinis were an ancient Arab family and that white skin and blue eyes weren't the exclusive preserve of Europeans. She recalled the verses of the ancient Arabs, who used to compose love poems dedicated to white-skinned women, and smiled at her own naïvety.

When Meelya got married, she had given no thought to what might await her in a land descending into the abyss. "I didn't think because I don't know about those things, but why didn't my brothers think about it? Or maybe they did but saw this as the only way to marry me off and get rid of me," she thought.

After Najeeb and his birds, Meelya's life had become oppressive. She'd felt as though she were taking up too much space in the house. The storm over Saleem and his "two wives" (as Saada called his wife and her sister) had died down completely; Saleem was no longer mentioned in the house, as though he'd never existed, and Niqoula had taken on all the men's responsibilities, ruling with a hand as hard as the tarboush he'd donned following his father's death and which he would never again remove until his own. Meelya, though – the sister-mother, as they used to call her – had to leave. Her mother's looks said as much, as did her brothers'. Even Moussa started to avoid his big sister and didn't know what to talk about with her. Such is life: it changes and contracts. Meelya experienced the greatest anguish. Her dreams turned into moments of suffocation when she experienced darkness and birds and desertion. Anguish was always with her, constrained by her ribcage, along with a feeling that there wasn't enough air any more – a lost girl falling into the valley. She would walk and see herself tumbling, as though the little Meelya who appeared in her dreams had forgotten how to walk. Her dreams seemed to turn into a series of falls, one after another. Indeed, the feeling was so acute that one morning she couldn't get out of bed for the pain in her back and legs from falling as she walked on the bare, dusty road. It occurred to her that she ought to take a stick along with her to her dreams, and she laughed.

"I wish life were like that," she told her husband.

"What do you mean, like that?" he asked.

"I mean like when I'm dreaming. I get an idea to take something with me to the dream and then it happens," she said. Then she told him about the dream of the stick that saved her from falling on the roads of night and allowed her to put up with her oppressive life, a life whose doors had reopened only with the appearance of Mansour and the blue woman.

"I wish we could go back to the Hotel Massabki," she said.

"Why?" he asked.

"Because then your brother wouldn't have died and we wouldn't have to go to Jaffa."

Mansour made it very clear to her that there would be no going back on the Jaffa decision, that he couldn't. He said he'd been running from the truth all his life, that his brother had faced up to it on his own, and now he'd died, "so I have to do what has to be done."

"What about afterwards?" she asked.

"There won't be an afterwards," he said. "The Jews want to throw us out of our country. Are we supposed to just sit there and take it?"

"It's unbelievable," she said. "But what can we do?"

"We can fight," he said.

"And if we fight, can we change anything? Because . . ."

"Because what?" he asked. "Don't tell me you had a dream that the Jews took our land and threw us out!"

"No, I didn't have a dream," she said, and fell silent.

Meelya didn't want to leave Nazareth. She tried to persuade Mansour, but there was no longer any point in talking to him; the man had put an end to talk when he'd taken on the persona of his brother, and when talk ends, everything ends. Logically, it was impossible for him to abandon the workshop, and his mother wouldn't be able to run it on her own. According to another type of logic, though, Mansour hadn't been able to work with his mother before because she was a tyrant and because his brother had kept everything to himself and hadn't told Mansour the truth. Meelya couldn't say that Mansour had been a coward, or that he'd said he'd left Jaffa because he was afraid. He'd said he'd preferred to escape that atmosphere to avoid the headaches, but the headaches had followed him all the way. Ameen's story remained obscure to Meelya. Or, at least, she'd dreamt something that night but hadn't told her dream. She'd been afraid, believing it was Moussa.

She'd awakened from sleep with swollen eyes and said she'd dreamt of herself weeping. She didn't get out of bed that morning to make the coffee, telling Mansour she was tired and pretending to go back to sleep until he'd left. Then she got up and rinsed her swollen eyes with rosewater, but she didn't leave the house. She was afraid she'd meet the old man and drown in tears once more. She'd wept because she'd seen Tanyous stretched out on the ground, his belly swollen and flies hovering around him. She'd tried to stop people on the road leading down to the Church of Our Lady of the Fright to tell them the man was dead and had to be taken to the graveyard, but no-one paid attention to the little girl standing there with her wide-open eyes, as though waiting for her mother. Men filled the narrow street, walking shoulder to shoulder, and wouldn't stop. Then a hand holding a pair of scissors reached out and grabbed her by her short hair, and the black started pouring into her eyes and she couldn't see any more and started crying.

Mansour returned at noon to say they had to go to Jaffa immediately and that there was bad news. She didn't ask what the news was but got dressed and said that she was ready. Then he asked her to pack their suitcase as they were going to stay about a week. He said that his brother . . . and started crying. Mansour's gushing tears stained his face black, and from then on this new colour never left it. Moussa disappeared from view – Meelya didn't know what had become of the resemblance between the two men traced on her memory. Mansour had become a true dark-skinned man of Jaffa, looking at her with his brother's shining eyes and yawning loudly to cover his weeping.

She smelled oranges. No, this wasn't Beirut. Beirut was a mixture of swaying pines and sweet acacia blossom, but Jaffa was quite different. It was the scent of lemon blossom, of spacious houses spread out before one's eyes, and of fear. The first time she'd visited Jaffa had been a month after her wedding. She'd told Mansour she'd never go back because she'd seen the fear carried on the scent of oranges. She'd said she didn't like oranges any more; their scent evoked an obscure apprehension that crept into her limbs and made her unable to walk. She'd said she couldn't abide the scent of oranges and had had to cover her face.

"It's because you're pregnant," her mother-in-law said. "Be patient."

But it wasn't because she was pregnant. It was a feeling that crept into her bones and couldn't be kept out. She just wanted to cover her face and wear the veil that she saw the women of Jaffa wearing.

Meelya is there now, in the Scented City, as people call Jaffa. People said it was "aromatic" because the scent of Seville orange blossom wafted through it. They did not know that the scent that blanketed the sky would become the city's shroud, the token of its death.

The woman from Nazareth, an unborn child of seventh months in her belly, was to be stricken with a sorrow that bore no relationship to the sorrow that was everywhere in el Ajami, and particularly, due to the calamity that had struck their eldest son, in the house of the Hourani clan. Her sorrow grew because she'd seen what no-one else had seen. She had smelled in Jaffa's scent a token of the end. It wasn't the fault of Ameen, whom she'd seen only as a dead man. The fault was that of the scent that turned yellow on people's faces, changing the mourners into ghosts. Multitudes made their way to the house to bid farewell to the martyr who had left behind two children, one seven, the other five, and his young wife, who came from the district of Beit Sahour, and there was a hoarse cry for vengeance in their throats that rendered Mansour speechless. The killing of Ameen had been connected to a wave of explosions that shook Jaffa in 1947. It seemed that the man's chattering had led to his demise – Mansour was convinced that his brother had died from talking too much. Someone who manufactures bullets for British rifles and plans to make armour plating for cars so that the Palestinians will have some heavy weaponry with which to face the Zionists' superior war machine shouldn't talk about it. Ameen was a chatterbox and loved to show off. That had been the main reason behind the dispute between the two brothers which had led to Mansour's move to Nazareth. Or if not that, it had been the mother. The mother favoured her eldest son, indeed was infatuated with him. Since the father had died, she'd treated him as if he were her husband, asking him to move into the departed's bed in her room because she was afraid of sleeping alone. Ameen was active in the ranks of the city's Orthodox Association and a member of the Local Action Committee formed by the Arab Higher Executive. He saw Palestine's Chief Mufti as its saviour and dreamt of travelling to Iraq to support Rasheed Ali el Kinani's uprising against the British. He was even said to have taken weapons training and to have an English rifle in his house.

Mansour said his mother didn't love him, though he didn't know why – perhaps because he was too like her. From childhood he'd heard the story of a mother waiting for God to give her a daughter and being blessed instead with a second son whom the mother had treated as though he were a little girl, letting the boy's hair grow long and plaiting it and addressing him using the forms one uses when speaking to a female. Ameen had played the same game with his brother and even tried to carry it over into school, where Mansour would hear his fellow pupils calling him "Mansoura". This made him react violently and behave like the bad boys, thus exposing himself to almost daily beatings from his peers, so he'd return home covered in blood. He told Meelya he knew the taste of blood, and that he'd spent his adolescence drinking the blood from his own nose. And when he grew up, he found himself in a strange family ruled by a merciless woman of iron.

"I'm not like her," Mansour said. "She's a tyrant and all she thinks about is making money. That's why I left her everything. I don't want to go back to Jaffa, to the smell of blood that fills the city. Resistance is a duty, but . . ." Meelya recalls fragments of this story about his family as she watches Mansour changing before her eyes, saying, as he takes on his brother's shape, that he will return to Jaffa. He told her he would be going back the day they returned home after the funeral. She said that she herself couldn't go yet, that she had to give birth first, because she couldn't have the child in that city.

"But my mother's there," he said, "and she'll help you."

"No, I don't want your mother," she replied. "And my mother doesn't want to come. I'm going to stay here. You go if you want to."

He said he'd thought of sending her to Lebanon, but it wasn't easy because the roads weren't safe. He said he was willing to agree to her decision on condition that they moved a week after the child was born. He said that he had to sell his shop in Nazareth now and spend a lot of time in Jaffa, renovating the workshop and reverting to his original profession.

Meelya's night filled with oranges that resembled bombs, the reddish colour covering every face and object. Mansour started staying away three days a week, and Meelya started living her nights alone. The man was no longer capable of breaching the veil of solitude behind which the woman lived. He no longer went to her at night, the poetry disappeared, and the words they spoke became repetitions of words they had spoken. Mansour became another man and Meelya became another woman, her dreams taking new forms. She sees everything drowning.

Meelya's nights are long and sad. There, in the hollows of the dark, she sees short, blue-eyed men surrounding the coffin, lifting it onto their shoulders and taking it to the Sea Cemetery where, on a mound facing the high waves, the casket bobs and dances above their hands. Then the waves rise higher, the sea moves towards them, and, like a blue animal with an endless body, it leaps at the mound and sweeps over it, carrying off the casket. The water swallows the men. The little girl stands next to Mansour, shivering, not knowing how to escape. She holds his hand, but the hand slips. She runs and the waves run after her. She climbs and the waves pursue her. She falls and finds herself in the water. Everyone is gone; the waves have swallowed them up and taken them she knows not where. The waves devour the people. The little girl is alone. Her hands cannot get a purchase. The water has almost swallowed her. She weeps. The water finds its way into her lungs. Her chest swells and the air vanishes. Water and salt. Water in her throat, lips cracked, her hand waving in space. The lid of the casket comes off and a blonde man rises and holds out his hands to her. Where had the French officer come from? He is standing alone in the street. Night and an autumn breeze bearing fine rain. The woman wearing the black dress is waiting for him in the garden, but the man doesn't move. He stands at a distance, as though spying on the woman, then moves forward, stumbling as though he were dizzy. His torso moves forward and he falls, blood gushing from holes in his upper back. Blood fills the place, the street drowns in blood, and the casket floats on the red fluid.

Meelya was aware that she was the only one who knew the story, because she'd seen the blonde officer whom her grandmother had buried in her breast – seen him more than once, walking, stumbling, falling, then enfolding in his arms a pillow that lay on the ground. He had become what Haseeba became in her last days – a mass of skin and bones broken in two at the middle, incapable of moving, the coughing depriving her of breath, dry orange and lemon peel hanging on the iron window grill facing her. The woman used to set orange and lemon peel aside, hanging it out on the washing lines in the garden to dry. Then she would use it for its scent, burning it on the brazier so that the house filled with its odour, setting light to it with the firewood in the boiler so that the bathroom took on the flavour of oranges, and placing it next to her pillow so she could breathe in the scent of life. When she took sick, she made do with a little peel as medicine, asking for it to be hung on the window grill facing her bed, and when she lost the power of speech and the peel disappeared, she moaned and sighed, refusing to taste her food for three days until her son discovered the secret of her sorrow and put the peel back.

Saada came to hate the smell of the dried peel, especially in the last days, when it mingled with that of urine and faeces, but had no choice but to obey her husband's wishes and her mother-in-law's moaning. When it was all over, though, it wasn't enough for her just to burn all the lemon peel; the entry into the house of any citrus fruits became a problem, which is what made Meelya cook *kibbeh arnabiyyeh* when she was ten. Later Meelya had become the queen of cooking and mistress of flavours and had taken all that with her to Nazareth, only to find herself, after ten months of marriage, obliged to leave once more. Meelya hadn't been allowed enough time to become attached to Nazareth. The White City, the Rose of Galilee, with its three quarters (Greek Orthodox, Maronite and Latin) that looked out over the plain of Marj Ibn Amir, was made larger by the smell of incense and poetry. Anyway, she had never known any city other than Beirut, and of Beirut she had known only the quarter in which she lived, the street on which her grandmother Malakeh lived, the bakery from which had emerged an ephemeral love story, and the sea that had frightened her before entering her dreams as a door opening onto distant worlds. Had it not been for her fear for the unborn child in her belly, Meelya wouldn't have objected to making the journey to Jaffa. True, she had imagined an intimate relationship between her pregnancy and Nazareth because of its sanctity, the apparition of the blue woman in her dreams and the whiff of discovery of secret places that hung over her encounters with Tanyous. She knew that in the end a woman has to follow her husband and go with him wherever he wants her to go – but still there were the fear, the undertones of death, the faces of the blonde men at the church and the scent of oranges filled with morbid promise. She wanted to tell Mansour the dream of the casket to stop him from moving there, but the man no longer believed her dreams. She therefore wrapped herself in her sorrow, took his anger on herself and lived the last two months of her pregnancy in virtual solitude.

She had seen her grandmother Haseeba in the dream, in Nazareth, the French officer at her side. The officer was reaching out to the black-swathed woman, and the woman was standing at a distance, not coming any closer. Meelya went over to the officer to tell him that Haseeba had got married and forgotten about him, and that she couldn't come any closer because she was bedridden and couldn't speak, but the officer couldn't hear her, as though he were deaf or couldn't understand. Before, in Beirut, Meelya had never dreamt of her grandmother or the officer. What had brought them to Nazareth? Meelya had been certain the officer didn't exist, was just a story invented by Haseeba to justify her tardiness in getting married, her refusal of earlier suitors and her self-absorption, but now she dreamt of herself as a little girl in her room in Nazareth with her grandmother sleeping on Meelya's bed while she looked through the window, where she could see Ferdinand in the distance, holding out his hands, bending over and falling. And Meelya was afraid. Mansour was no longer there to protect her from the creatures of the night.

When he'd married her, he'd told her that Palestine was a land governed by the Curse and the Fault.

"It's God's fault," he'd said.

"Don't misunderstand me — God forbid I should utter blasphemy. But humanity was incapable of comprehending the meaning of God's announcement that one city among the thousands of cities in the world should be His alone, and that a little country, no larger than a grain of wheat, should become a land for His only son. All wars, in the past and to come, have happened here. When Egypt's Akhenaton discovered the One God, all eyes turned to the Land of Canaan because it was God's land, and the endless wars began. The war will not end until God decides to abandon His city, or to come to it, though He never will. Don't be afraid — I'm with you and will never let anything harm you. Although this country is moving towards many wars, we shall live far from war. No-one will dare to come and light the fires of war in Nazareth. We shall be you and I and over us shall be peace."

Meelya didn't believe this talk of peace, but the man had enfolded her in his words. Listening to him, she felt as though he were taking her, that the verses he was reciting were flutter-ing around her eyes and gathering her into a magic world fashioned by his voice. She said she loved his voice, its slight huskiness a result of the combination of tobacco and coffee, a tender inflection imbued with the lilt of Arabic verse and a soft-ness seemingly lined with velvet. She would find herself carried away on the voice, swimming in his worlds, which took her far away. Then suddenly she discovered that the man had been hiding a great secret and had come to her seeking sanctuary. He had promised her protection, but what he really wanted was to join her worlds and escape the danger hovering over Jaffa.

"I don't mind us going to Jaffa or wherever you want to go, but I'm pregnant and I can't do it just now."

Meelya was prepared to look sympathetically on the idea of placing the workshop at the disposal of the defenders of Jaffa, out of the shoulder of which the new city called Tel Aviv had grown, attempting to engulf it so that the Jews could thereafter occupy the whole country with ease. But she hated violence, she hated blood, and she feared for her son.

Had not her grandfather killed her father?

Why did she say this, when she knew that he hadn't killed him?

"But he meant to kill him," Saada told her daughter, "and but for God's mercy and his mother's purity of heart the boy would have been lost."

Had the man tried to kill his son, or had he, as he claimed, thrown a stone at him because he didn't know who he was? Anyway, it didn't matter. What business of Meelya's was her grandmother and this legend that had been transformed into a memory wrapped in obscure dreams?

The story returned after Ameen's death, when, in the last two months of her pregnancy, the ghosts of Jaffa took over Meelya's life.

"It doesn't matter," she told Mansour.

Instead of returning from Jaffa the following day, as he'd promised, Mansour had returned after three days. He said he'd been forced to stay on and hadn't found a means to get a message to her. He read doubt in her eyes and stammered as he told her he'd had no choice.

"Enough. It doesn't matter. Just stop talking, please," she said.

She'd overheard fragments of what her mother-in-law had said about Mansour's getting married. She'd said it would be better not to rush into it – "What are we supposed to do with the woman and the children?" – and Meelya had realized that she would have liked Mansour to marry his brother's widow, as was the custom when a brother died, though that wasn't possible now.

"What's done's done and what's gone's gone,' said Meelya in her Lebanese accent.

"What's that you're saying?" Mansour asked.

"I said it makes no difference to me. Be where you want, but don't make me worry. I'm not my grandmother and I'm not going to make a fuss and I'm not going to say anything. The child is enough for me."

Though in fact, that's not what Meelya said, and her mother-in-law hadn't wanted her second son to remain a bachelor so he could marry his brother's widow; Meelya had imagined these things while she was waiting for her husband. He'd kissed her and said he was tired and wanted to sleep. "I wish I could go to sleep and never wake up," he'd said. "May evil stay far from your heart," Meelya replied, biting her lower lip and tasting blood.

Meelya tossed and turned in her bed. She heard Mansour calling to her from far away. She tried to open her eyes and wanted to say, "Enough," but at that instant the glass cut her lips. She was sitting on the swing, the air swooping around her, and she was flying. The oblong wooden swing was attached to two long ropes. She looked up and couldn't see the fig tree. Where was she? There was a swing and no tree and the garden looked like the garden of her new house in Nazareth. How had the swing got there? She decided to stop and grasped the ropes, pulling herself up on her thin legs and bending her knees to launch herself. Then she stood up, pulling herself forward, and flew. She rose into the heights and in the heights were only heights. The sky was grey and there was fear. Her heart dropped. She gazed, saw nothing but a grey sky blotched with clouds and suddenly lost her grip on the ropes, as though something had propelled her higher still. Arms outstretched, hands grasping nothingness, she was as though crucified. Then she started to fall and heard a scream, and the taste of blood spread over her tongue.

She opened her eyes and found no-one in the room. Her heart was beating fast and a ringing filled her ears. She decided to get out of bed and discovered the pain, which spread to her belly, coming and going in little continuous waves. She bit her lips and wanted to drink, but couldn't find the glass of water next to the bed. She closed her eyes and saw him. Najeeb was standing there covered in dust. He came over, sat down beside her on the bed and wept.

"Why are you crying? What have you come here to do? Go on, get up and go off to your wife. It's over now. I'm here and you're there."

He reached for her and she felt the man's heart beating in his fingertips. She wanted to weep, but didn't ask him why he'd done it and didn't tell him her heart had been broken. How could she explain to him that a heart could be broken and that mending it was harder than mending glass? She said she'd left her broken heart there, in Beirut, and that she'd found a new one here: "No, you shan't break more than one heart of mine. Shame on you!" She withdrew her hand from his, opened her eyes and found Mansour covering her with the blanket.

"When did you get back?" she asked.

"Just now," he replied.

"I'll get you your dinner," she said.

"No. You rest. I'll go and call Nadra," Mansour said.

"But Nadra's dead," Meelya said.

"Now there's what I call a woman!" Youssef said.

Whenever Youssef saw Nadra in that short skirt of hers that revealed her full brown thighs, he'd be frozen to the spot and stare at her ravenously with goggle eyes. Meelya learned from her father how eyes can turn into balls of fire and how a man's whole body can become an extension of a mysterious lust that falls upon him. And, in the end, Youssef died at the hands of the plump brown midwife after whom he had lusted his whole life.

The man had fallen to the ground and lain there. Nurse Nadra described how he'd fallen and died, even though she hadn't been there, and her story of his death became *the* story. She said he'd gone home feeling tired and found no-one there. The children were at school and Saada at church. The man had gone home because he had a pounding headache, and when he got there he drank a cup of orange-blossom essence with hot water and sugar, what Beirutis call "white coffee". Then he walked sluggishly to the *leewan*, where he fell and lost consciousness.

The children returned to find their father lying on the ground. Saleem ran to Nadra's house, and Niqoula ran to fetch Saada. Nadra arrived before Saada, helped Saleem and Niqoula to pick the man up and put him to bed, and said, "No hope for a stroke, as the saying goes. There's nothing to be done." When Saada arrived, Nadra informed her how the man had gone home feeling tired, drunk a white coffee and fainted. Saada asked her eldest son to call the doctor. Saleem ran to the doctor's and Niqoula ran to the church. The doctor and the nun arrived together. The doctor examined Youssef, felt his pulse, took his blood pressure, tried in vain to revive him. Then he looked at Saada and the nun, said, 'Stroke. God willing, he'll go quickly and not suffer or make you suffer," and left without taking his fee. The nun said she'd fetch the priest to administer the last rites, and the house filled with the smell of incense. But the man didn't die. He lasted four days laid out on the bed. Nadra would come every morning, wet her fingers with water and moisten his lips. On the fourth day when Nadra came, she said, "It's over," and that was how he died.

"He died at your fingertips," Saada said.

"God have mercy on him and on us," the nurse said, choking on her tears.

"She loved him," Saada said.

"No, that type doesn't know what love means. All they know about is you-know-what," the nun said.

What brought Nadra here?

Meelya told Moussa that she'd started to fear the midwife. "She came and brought death with her," she said.

Nadra was carrying a bowl of steaming water. She rolled up her sleeves and started coughing. The cigarette fell from her mouth into the bowl, Meelya heard the hiss as it went out, and the place filled with smoke.

"I don't want to," she screamed, and opened her eyes.

She saw Mansour standing next to the bed with his aunt. "Come along, my dear. We have to get you to the hospital," he said. The aunt took her hand and helped her to get out of bed.

"It's not today," Meelya said. "Let me go back to sleep."

"It's definitely today," the aunt said.

"What day of the month is it?" Meelya asked.

"The twenty-first," Mansour said.

"No, not today. I'm not going to have the baby today. The doctor told me the birth would be on the night of 24 December," Meelya said.

Mansour fetched a small bag and asked his aunt to help him get Meelya's things together. Meelya looked at her face in the mirror. It was puffy, her white cheeks were turning yellow, and she could see black circles under her eyes. The contractions returned, she gasped with pain, and Mansour made her sit down on the end of the bed. "Come along. We have to go," he said, turning towards his aunt who was dithering over the cupboard. "Come on, Auntie. We're not getting her trousseau ready. A nightdress and two changes of underwear are enough, then I can see what's needed later."

Meelya found herself in the car. Mansour was sitting next to the driver and she was in the back seat next to the aunt. The car passed a small, crowded street, then turned right and climbed the hill leading to the Italian hospital. The sky flashed and the ropes of rain descended. Meelya shivered and said she was cold. The aunt took off her coat and covered Meelya with it. The car seemed to be having difficulty making it up the street; it roared as though pleading for help and the wheels slipped, proclaiming their inability to gain purchase on the asphalt.

"The wheels," the driver said. "The wheels can't get a grip."

The driver pulled the handbrake upward and pressed his foot on the accelerator. The car made a strange noise, like the moaning of an injured animal, and started climbing again, shuddering as it went.

"What's the matter?" Meelya asked.

"Nothing," the driver said.

But when the car reached the top and started moving over the puddles, the engine died and all that could be heard was the sloosh of the rain.

"What are we going to do?" Mansour asked.

"There's nothing we can do," the driver replied.

When Mansour opened the door to get out, he heard Meelya crying, "Please don't get out." Mansour closed the door again and started pleading with the driver to do something: "She'll have her baby here! Let's get a move on." The two front doors opened and Mansour and the driver got out. Meelya watched as the two men disappeared behind the open bonnet. She turned towards the aunt but didn't find her. Then she closed her eyes onto the first inklings of the dark, which had begun to steal in through the downpour, and heard her father saying, "Snow! It's snowing!"

"Where are you, Mansour?" she cried.

Mansour isn't there. She's alone in the car, covered with a brown coat and shivering with cold.

The men got back into the car. The aunt reached out to touch her forehead, as though taking her temperature. Mansour turned to her and asked her to be patient. She said she couldn't feel the contractions any more but that she was afraid because the fog was so thick. "There isn't any fog," he told her, but she saw fog, she saw heavy snow falling, and in the distance she saw a man carrying a small girl and running with her beneath the falling snow. What had brought her father out in this storm, and why was he carrying her through the heavy snow? Youssef was carrying his daughter and running with her to Dr Naqfour's clinic. He had pulled her out of bed while the nun was reciting prayers over her head, censing her and asking her to open her mouth to swallow the piece of cotton wool dipped in oil. Youssef had snatched his daughter from the nun, wrapped her in a brown woollen blanket and run with her to the doctor's. The snow fell heavily in Beirut that year. Meelya doesn't remember the snow, but she remembers the woollen blanket and her father's panting. The girl was four years old. She remembers the weeping around her bed and herself floating above her burning body. Did she hear the word *death*? She doesn't know. Or rather, sometime later, when her grandmother told her the story, she felt how death had come close in the shape of a fever that tore at her small body for ten whole days. Malakeh said that she'd only felt easy in her mind when she'd woken the girl up in the midst of her fever and asked her what she was dreaming. The girl's fiery eyes had cracked open and she'd replied that she wasn't. Malakeh said that was when she'd stopped worrying, because death needs a long dream. She'd told her daughter Saada that she wasn't afraid and had gone back to her house.

"No, Daddy, I don't want to," Meelya screamed, trying to

twist out of her father's hands. She moved her hands and the woollen blanket was pushed aside and flakes of snow wet her. "Ay!" she screamed, as though the snow were hurting her. Then she screamed, "Let's go home, Daddy." But Youssef paid no attention. He ran, the tears streaming from his eyes, repeating, "You're my darling, my darling." He ran through the heavy falling snow, then stopped in front of a large black door and knocked. The door opened, the snow stopped falling, and darkness covered the girl's eyes. The memories were extinguished.

The driver lit a cigarette and started smoking tensely. "Please don't smoke!" Mansour said. "Can't you see the woman's pregnant to her back teeth?" The driver opened the window to throw out the cigarette and a cold wind blew in, lifting the coat that covered Meelya. Gasping, she felt the unborn child shivering in her belly. "O Virgin!" she cried, and heard the engine start again and found herself standing at the entrance to the hospital.

"Not today. Maybe tomorrow," said the Italian doctor who examined her. He told Mansour to take his wife home and keep an eye on her. "When the contractions are continuous and the pain mounts, bring her back. There's no need for her to be here now."

"Right," she said, and stood up. "Let's go home," she said to her husband, who couldn't believe his eyes as he watched how the thread of pain slipped from her eyes, as though the doctor's words were a magic medicine that had wiped the spasms from the white face, erasing the black threads that had closed her eyes and restoring the milk-like clarity with which the curves of her cheeks were fashioned.

"Let's go home," she said, and set off. The rain stopped and the sun's rays broke through the grey veil covering the city sky.

"Where are you going? Wait till I call the driver!"

"No, I want to walk," she said, and walked.

"Is it alright for her to walk, doctor?" Mansour asked.

But the doctor had disappeared and the only people left in the room were two nurses who looked just like one another – one young, the other old, the first blonde, the second brunette. Mansour thought that the first must be Italian and tried to speak to her in English. The nurse smiled and indicated that she didn't understand what he'd said. He turned to the brunette and asked her in Arabic. She too smiled as though she didn't understand and raised her eyebrows. Mansour left the hospital and couldn't see Meelya. He stood like a lost soul on the steps leading up to the Italian hospital. The city was full of alleys and slopes, and he had no idea which direction to go in to catch up with his wife. He saw his aunt standing next to the driver in front of the American car and got into the passenger seat, asking his aunt to get in the back.

"We want to go back to the house," he said to the driver.

"What about Meelya?" the aunt asked.

"Later," Mansour answered.

Meelya walked. The pain, and the sight of her father carrying her in his arms while she asked him to put her down because she wanted to walk, seemed to have aroused in her a desire to meet Tanyous so she could tell him that she'd reached the end and was getting ready to leave for a distant city.

Meelya said she could remember the first time she walked: her father had been carrying her and she'd cried: "I started fussing to get down, but Daddy didn't understand. I heard my mother asking him to put me down. I couldn't speak yet but I could understand, and I found myself going down from high up. He put me down on the ground on my tummy because he thought I wanted to crawl. I pulled myself upright and heard my mother saying over and over, 'The girl's walking,' and she started ululating. From then on I never stopped walking. I kept going round and round the house, as though I'd discovered the world. When you look at the world from above, it's different."

"You really remember those things?" Mansour said.

"Of course."

"But nobody remembers what happens before they're three."

"Well, I remember."

"Right, right," he said, and didn't go on. Since the incident with the broken glass, the words *right, right* had become his polite way of saying she was lying. He'd be listening to her stories and suddenly the idea that she was lying would light up in his mind. "You're lying to me, Meelya," he'd say, and the ghosts of her words would vanish before his eyes and he'd smile. She would say nothing. Meelya had grown accustomed to the phrase, which her mother had used, and the nun had used, and her brothers had used. Only Moussa had believed her and believed in her. Once, he'd told her that he believed in her and she'd said, "No, you mustn't believe in people. You can only believe in God."

"But Mother believes in the nun."

"I don't like nuns."

"But she's a saint."

When was that conversation? Had Moussa said he believed in her or was she confusing her dreams with the truth?

She'd told Moussa that he didn't know her. Or, she hadn't actually said that. She used to think that Moussa had never ever seen her. How could he have when he hadn't entered her dreams and seen the brown girl who ran through the thorns and felt no pain? On that day, though, when he brought back the photograph and hung it on the wall, she'd felt afraid of the light radiating from its eyes. He'd seen her then, but had paid no attention to the truth that had been shown him without his asking.

"What's the picture for?" she asked, backing away. "Take it out of here."

"So you'll still be with us," Moussa said. "This way I won't miss you when I miss you."

Meelya walks alone. The child is ready to come out of her belly, and she is cloaked in sorrow and fear. "Nine months of fear," Meelya told Tanyous. Where had he come from, this mysterious old man who looked like an Old Testament prophet?

Meelya remembers the glass. He gave her a glass full of yellowish white wine. Or rather, he didn't give her the glass, he left it at the window. Meelya was alone in the house, Mansour was in Jaffa; she'd heard a knocking on the window, covered herself with the quilt, told herself not to open her eyes. Her fear of the dream mixed with her fear of night. She closed her closed eyes even tighter, turned on her side and heard a ringing in her ears. She surrendered to the ringing and the drowsiness, let herself go limp and heard the sound. The unborn child moved spasmodically in her belly, kicking against the roof of her womb for the first time.

She opened the window and saw him stealing away among the trees. "Uncle Tanyous!" she cried. She took the glass that had been placed on the window ledge. The liquid was like gold. Meelya brought it to her lips and drank a single drop, and it filled her with ecstasy. Putting the glass on the bedside table, she sank into a deep sleep.

How, by morning, had the white wine turned to red? Why hadn't Mansour seen the wine? And why the bloody colour that stained her fingertips and wouldn't come off with soap and water?

Tanyous was the sign. A man so old his years were uncountable, wearing a black habit like a monk's, with a white beard, long and matted, eyes like two dying points of light set deep in their sockets, and a voice like a death rattle that rose from the depths of his belly.

Mansour said he'd never seen the man in his life.

"You must have. He's a monk," Meelya said.

"Monks don't wander the streets," Mansour said. "I've never seen him, and my aunt, who's lived here twenty years, has never heard of him. And anyway there's no-one from Beirut in this town. The Beirutis work in Tiberias and Haifa. Give over, woman. Soon, God willing, you'll give birth and stop dreaming."

Mansour was convinced that the strange things his wife saw in her dreams were the result of her pregnancy and her solitude. His mother had told him that women started behaving oddly when they became pregnant. Some slept all day and some ate earth and some . . . well, she didn't want to say. When she'd been pregnant with him she hadn't been able to stop eating bitter lemons, even though her stomach hurt: "There's nothing to be afraid of, son. It's just a symptom of pregnancy." Even though he was convinced that his mother was right and hoped that after she gave birth Meelya's strange behaviour and daily wanderings through the city's alleys and streets would stop, Mansour was persuaded that the problem was Nazareth. "This is a mad city," he'd told his wife, saying he'd realized this truth the moment they'd entered the house; it was as though something had flipped over in Meelya's eyes so that he could no longer read her feelings from the shadows in them. Before, Mansour had known everything about this woman by looking into her eyes. "That's what love is," he'd told her. "I read your eyes and I know. The lover is the one who can read eyes. It's the sign of love. It means I love you."

"But I don't now how to read that way," she replied. "Does that mean you love me more than I love you?"

"Absolutely," he told her. "Look into my eyes and I'll teach you how to read them."

They were in the garden of the old house. Mansour reached for her hand, but she gave him only her fingertips. Her cheeks flushed and she lowered her lashes to hide her eyes and said she was reading him.

"But you've got your eyes closed," he said.

"That's how I read," she replied.

Meelya wasn't lying to Mansour, for she did read others when she closed her eyes. What puzzled her, though, was that she hadn't seen Mansour once in her dreams. This worried her at first: she felt she was being disloyal to the man whom she had married, and felt guilty. Could the wife tell her husband that she was unfaithful to him? For sure he'd be furious at first; then, when he learnt the details of this strange infidelity, he'd laugh and say that he knew everything and didn't need her confessions.

Meelya was aware that the time for her to dream of Mansour had not yet come. When Tanyous told her that he was waiting for her child to be born so that he could depart, and that he loved her greatly and wanted to take her with him, she felt the soles of her feet go icy cold.

She said no. She said she didn't want to go with him, that she would like to stay in Nazareth, and that she was the daughter of a carpenter and would open a workshop there for her son, so that he could learn Christ's trade. The old man smiled and told her that her son would live in a distant place, that she had been chosen by God to see things that no-one before her had seen, and that she would come to know Mansour all at once because time had meaning only for people who had not been given the grace of vision.

"But I already know him – he's my husband," she said.

"No, no. You're going to find out things he doesn't know," he said.

"But what's it to do with me?" she asked.

"All in good time," the elderly monk said.

When she had first come to the town, her first question had

been, "Where was the house of the Messiah?" Mansour watched everything about the woman change. Her eyes clouded over; nimbuses unlike the shadows he'd seen in Beirut formed around them, and he cursed the hour he'd decided to live in Nazareth.

Mansour felt that Meelya was slipping away from him to unknown places, but didn't know how to follow or catch hold of her, and her wanderings around the churches and insistence on searching for the house in which Christ had lived frightened him.

"No-one knows the house. Anyway, maybe it's a myth. Maybe the Messiah didn't live here, maybe Nazareth was in a different place."

Since their marriage, Mansour had discovered that he hated the town in which he lived. "How can anyone live in a town full of myths, superstitions and prophets? The town drives everyone who lives in it mad. The town is just a town. No-one should walk in the footsteps of the saints because if he does he'll become terrified, frightened of his own shadow. The woman has made me afraid. We people don't have any truck with such goings-on. They're for tourists and religious maniacs. We live here as though it isn't anything special."

"But there are lots of special things," said Tanyous, when Meelya told him what her husband had said.

Who was Tanyous?

What was this story that she heard from him about the Lebanese?

When she told her husband that modern Nazareth had been founded by Lebanese sent by Emir Fakhr el Din in the sixteenth century to work as sharecroppers at the Franciscan monastery, and that it was the Franciscan monks who had first built there in what had been a wilderness, he laughed.

"What do you mean, Lebanese? This is Bilad el Sham, the Syrian Lands. God rest your poor soul, Faisal I!" Reminding her of the photo of the lean king at the Hotel Massabki, he started telling her the story of the Battle of Maysaloun, of how Youssef el Azmeh, Syria's defence minister, had died hugging his rifle as he tried to stop the French army's advance on Damascus, and so on and so forth.

"I'm not talking about politics!" she said. "I'm telling you that half the natives of Nazareth are Lebanese, Maronites and Latins, whom Fakhr el Din sent to work for the monks. Then the Greek Orthodox came from Houran and the area around Ramallah, and everyone looked for the house of the Messiah and they found nothing. The only one who knows where it was is the monk Tanyous."

"Who told you those old wives' tales?" he asked.

"The monk Tanyous," she said.

"Where does this monk come from? I've never seen him, not once, and no-one else in town has seen him."

"I've seen him," she said.

When Mansour Hourani took up residence in Nazareth, it had never crossed his mind that he was coming to the city of the Messiah. From the beginning, the people of Nazareth had proclaimed their distance from the holy story by calling themselves Nazarites rather than Nazarenes, which is the name chosen by the Koran to refer to followers of Eesa of Nazareth. Where did the woman get these religious stories that were making his life hell?

Mansour was aware of the religious atmosphere that prevailed in the Shaheen household in Beirut, but it didn't irk him greatly. He attributed it to Saada's hysteria, about which Meelya had spoken. He considered the mother's religiosity and her attachment to the nun just one aspect of the "age of despair" when women go crazy because they have stopped menstruating and are battered by hot gusts from the depths of their dry wombs. He told Meelya that Saada was less of a problem than his own mother. Saada may have worked off her rancour by kissing icons and swallowing cotton wool dipped in oil, but his mother's obsession was maintaining her dominance over the workshop and her two sons; she thought she was more important than *Hajj* Ameen el Husseini because she'd repaired a few rusty rifles. What was happening now, though? Why did he feel the phantom presence of the sainted nun dwelling with him in the house? And why did he feel that this man called Tanyous, who claimed to be of Lebanese ancestry and said that his forefathers had come from Beit el Deen in the Chouf to work as farm labourers for the Franciscan monks, had turned into a ghost hovering over his life and that of his wife?

"You want to get out of Nazareth," Meelya said, "but I want to stay here, and I don't know why you're making such a fuss about it. Your business is doing well, praise God, and your mother can look after herself. Didn't you tell me your mother prefers to run the workshop on her own? I feel as though you're running away from something I don't know about. Maybe you're right. Maybe it's a vision. It's what Youssef did – flee from here to Egypt – and he was right."

"Who's Youssef?"

"Youssef the Carpenter," she said.

"And where did you come across this one?"

"He's the father of the Messiah."

"You talk about Saint Youssef as if he were a friend of ours! I never liked Youssef the Carpenter – he was a cuckold. All the prophets liked women, from Abraham to Noah to David and the rest. Take Adam. Tell me, why was Adam expelled from the Garden of Eden? Not because of the Tree of Knowledge. What do you think that 'knowledge' was? That 'knowledge' was Eve, meaning *fuck . . . ing*."

"Please don't say that word."

"And you stop being an idiot."

"But Saint Youssef wasn't the way you say. Saint Youssef saw the angel in a dream and the dream told him everything."

"Back to dreams again. My dear, sweet Meelya, I don't have anything against Saint Youssef. What do I care? But explain to me one thing: how could he say yes?"

"Yes to what?"

"Yes to being the boy's daddy when he wasn't his father and no-one knew who the real father was."

"Because he was a saint."

"God grant us all sainthood!"

"You mean you wouldn't have agreed?"

"Certainly not. I mean, the boy's either my son or he isn't. Please, that's enough of this stuff. I mean, it really makes you want to spit."

How could the elderly man have accepted the story told him by his young wife? Was it she who told him, or did the angel really come to him in a dream, as is written in the Gospels? What kind of a person believes his own dreams?

"All the prophets were like that," the sainted nun said, "but it could still have been the Devil." She muttered prayers while Saada wiped little Meelya's brow with a handkerchief dipped in holy water. Meelya doesn't remember the story, but she hasn't forgotten the dream; whenever the mother tells it to her daughter, Meelya feels a sense of estrangement from herself. She was ten when she got the fever for the second time, and everyone, including the sainted nun, was certain the girl was going to die. The doctor came and said there was no hope but in God. To Saada, God meant one thing – the nun. She ran to the Convent of the Archangel Mikhail and clung to the hem of the nun's robe, but the nun paid no attention because she was praying.

Whenever Milaneh stood before the *Book of the Triodion* and began reciting its prayers and invocations, and especially at

Evensong when she would pray to the Evening Light, melancholy would descend upon all those standing in the church, and a reverence not unlike drowsiness would fall upon them. In the worshippers' ears, the nun's voice would be transformed into a swing that swooped them into the twists and turns of the divine. They would hear strange sounds and watch as the bodies of the saints depicted in the Byzantine icons cloaked themselves in feathers. Sister Milaneh didn't allow the electric light to be turned on in the church, which was the reason for her chronic conflict with Bishop Gerasimous, who compelled the nuns to light the electric chandeliers whenever he joined them in prayer. The saint saw this as blasphemy because she believed that the angels didn't like electric light, that their own light was light enough. His Grace the Bishop, though, insisted on having his way. He mocked the nun's superstitions and pretensions to sainthood and humiliated her before the other nuns and her faithful followers.

Though in truth it wasn't the electric light that was behind the conflict. Milaneh had solved that issue by asking the nuns to close their eyes when the light was turned on: "We shall close our eyes and the angels will close theirs and nothing will have changed for us." No, the real problem lay in that woman of satanic beauty known as Maryka Spiridon.

The Maryka affair generated much noise and gossip at the time in Beirut. Was she the bishop's mistress, as was rumoured, or just a new version of Saint Maryam the Egyptian, who had begun her life as a whore but repented at the hands of Saint Antonious the Great? Maryam the Egyptian abandoned her old profession, but the woman Maryka did not. She'd come to the church every Sunday morning accompanied by three Greek women, they'd attend Mass and take Communion, and then they'd return to the street of sin known as al Mutanabbi Street to ply their trade.

What made the nun angry wasn't this fact, which was known to everybody. "God alone knows what is in men's hearts and He alone shall judge," she would respond when asked about "the prostitute who's got her hands on His Grace and keeps making donations to the church and bought the biggest chandelier in Beirut and donated it to the Church of Mar Jirjis". The saint wouldn't allow anyone to use the word *prostitute* in her hearing; she preferred the term "fallen woman", and after using it she would adjure God to preserve the decency of all His servants. But the situation had reached breaking point. What is said to have happened (though God alone knows if this is true) is that word went out that His Grace had issued a special permit allowing Maryka and her girls to walk the streets of Beirut on Sundays, a practice that had been prohibited ever since the law forbidding whores to leave the public market area had been issued in Ottoman times. It seems that the governor of Beirut, a member of the Greek Orthodox Bastiris family appointed by the French Mandate authorities, had agreed, either as a favour to the bishop or because he was himself among the lady's customers. Anyway, with this permit, Maryka was able to go to whatever church the bishop was praying at on a Sunday. It is true that His Grace Gerasimous held Mass most Sundays in the Cathedral of Saint George, which Maryka was allowed to go to because it was close to the public market, but he would also say Mass, for pastoral reasons, in Beirut's other, more remote parishes, such as el Museitbeh, el Ashrafiyeh, el Mazraa and Ras Beirut. Under the new arrangement, Maryka was no longer compelled to leave the bishop's side on Sundays, and thus it happened that the sainted nun came to lay eyes on this satanic woman – an event which caused Milaneh to lose her composure in front of everybody and use the very word she'd told everyone else not to use.

"His Grace is coming and bringing that prostitute with him.

I will not go to Mass today," she told the other nuns, and she withdrew from the church to her cell.

What transpired in the cell when the bishop entered and ordered Milaneh to go to the church? No-one knows, but everyone saw how Maryka prostrated herself before the nun and how the nun repaid the Greek woman prostration for prostration, and everyone heard the nun's weeping, which continued throughout the Mass.

Forty years later, the story would come out, but no-one dared publish it in the press. Iskandar Shaheen, eldest son of Moussa Shaheen, would one day catch the shameful sickness of literature and go to work on *al Ahrar*, the newspaper founded by Saeed el Sabbagheh and others. The paper's guiding concept was to spread the ideas of the Masonic movement, then active in Syria and Lebanon, to promote secularism and to mock the clergy.

Iskandar stumbled upon an unparalleled scoop. By accident, he had come to know an elderly woman living in Furn el Shubbak, near the Church of Saint Elias, who was an object of special care of the priest Sameer Abu Hanna. The young Iskandar, then in his twenties, used to visit the priest's house because he was in love with the latter's only daughter, Fouteen, who would later break his heart by deciding to become a nun, though that's another story. He discovered that the elderly woman was Maryka Spiridon, sometime *grande dame* of the public market, who was passing her last days in prayer and repentance.

When the youth visited the elderly woman armed with information about her relationship with the Thrice-Blessed Bishop Gerasimous provided him by *Khawaja* Saeed el Sabbagheh, he found himself confronted with the story of his paternal aunt Meelya, and with unbelievable details of the miracle performed by the nun to save Meelya from the fever when she was ten.

Maryka wasn't stingy with information. She gave him every-thing he wanted, telling him that her relationship with the bishop had been unlike her relationship with any other man.

"I'm Greek," she said. "We're a people you'll come across everywhere. The Spiridon family is Greek, father and son. We're originally from Istanbul, and I didn't just stumble into the trade. It's been a family profession for ages. My mother did it, and my grandmother and my great grandmother, but in those days it wasn't a problem. My mother married like any other woman in the world. I don't know what's wrong with people these days and how prostitutes came to be untouchables. If you knew, sonny, the things I've seen! Without us, how would the kids stay decent? You know, men are dogs. It's not their fault; it's the way God made them. Adam, God rest his soul, betrayed his wife Eve when she was the only woman in the world; don't ask me how he managed it or what he did, you can ask His Grace the bishop about that. He told me. Who sent you to me, sonny?"

He told her about *Khawaja* Saeed, and she fell about laughing. "*That* Saeed? Naama's boy? God grant him success, what a generous man he was, but a coward. I was around forty-five when I opened him up. You think only girls have to be opened up? Not so, sweetie. Boys too. Heavens, what can I say? He was in ecstasy. When it's a boy's first time and he's full of juice, one touch and he's finished. I loved that boy. I touched him and before he could get it in, it was over. Then he wanted to scarper, but I told him no, the first one's for the Devil, come on back here. But the second was the same. What a waste – he still hadn't opened up and the minute he put it in, he came. Stay, I told him. I felt really sorry for him – a boy fresh as a sprig of basil and he looked like he was from a good family. The third time, I felt how he opened up and became a man. God, how beautiful he was! I said to him, 'Now you know, so you come back and see me.' I swear I came myself that time, maybe because he was young and intact. What are you laughing at, sonny? You can say that of a man too. I don't usually come with anyone, though of course with His Grace, naturally. God rest his soul and treat him kindly, he used to tire me out. He was an old man, around sixty-five. His beard was white and long. Anyway, you know how it is – maybe because he was shy, I don't know, but he refused to take off his clothes. I said to him, 'That's fine, Your Grace,' but I took off everything myself and then went over to him. He was soft, poor thing. I mean he couldn't get it in. He turned as red as a tomato – even his white beard turned red. He said, 'Let's forget it, my daughter. It's because of the medicine.' 'Medicine, my foot!' I said. 'You're talking to Maryka, Your Grace,' and I went for him and stripped off his clothes and got down to work. Don't ask me what I did because I went through the whole bag of tricks, and it began to move. Things started going okay and I heard him yelling, 'Halleluiah! Halleluiah!' I told him to keep his voice down. 'It's not right, Your Grace,' I said. 'We're in your cell and there are people outside.' But it didn't make a bit of difference to him. He took to calling me Miraculous Maryka. No, I didn't love him, though maybe I felt sorry for him. Pity is a gateway to love too. Love, sonny, is the secret, and it has a million gateways, and if someone tells you they know what love is, tell him he's a liar. No-one can comprehend the miracle that happens between a man and a woman, and perhaps between a man and a man and a woman and a woman – when Sister Milaneh prostrated herself before me in the church and I prostrated back, I felt something strange. God curse the Devil, sonny, I wouldn't want to say anything and have it on my conscience, because the woman was a real saint, and I know – the miracle she worked with your mother, Meelya, when she was little was enough."

"Meelya was my aunt, not my mother."

"You aunt, your mother, it doesn't matter. Where were we? We were with the bishop. When His Grace after all the hard work I'd put in became a man and attacked me with his halleluiahs, I got frightened. He used to call me 'the Last Supper' and he'd eat me like food. What can I say? The smell of incense and honey rose off him and he'd become like some god. He told me that this was how man became divine, and I'd melt in his hands. God keep him, he was well built and I'm thin, as you can see, but when I took off my clothes he'd go into shock. He'd back away and say, 'Where did you get those things?' My thighs are wide and full, but you can't really tell under the dress. Maybe because I was afraid of him – no, the truth is, I was afraid *for* him, and maybe that's why he used to make me feel good. I'd gone to him to make my confession. I knelt on the ground, he covered my head with his stole, and I started talking. I'd never been to confession before – or at least, of course, on the eve of Easter I'd go to church and stand with the people in front of the altar, and the priest would raise his hand and bless us and that was fine. I don't know what I was thinking that day. I set off for the church early and they were doing Matins. I got close to the bishop's throne and His Grace stretched out his hand to me. Maybe he thought I wanted to kiss it the way everyone does. Taking his hand, I kissed it, then I went closer and whispered that I wanted to confess. He looked at me strangely, and I understood. I heard his voice tremble when he said, "You?" He made me kneel to the left of the altar and that was that."

Iskandar Shaheen wrote down every word Maryka said about the bishop and about Saeed el Sabbagheh (changing his name, of course) and about Maryka's passion for the nun and about how the bishop had become furious and ordered Milaneh exiled to an abandoned convent in the Koura district, and about how, in that near-desolate place, the nun was transformed into the saint of the village of Bkeftine. At first she lived alone. Then three nuns from the Convent of the Angel Mikhail joined her to serve her. It was there that the nun lost her sight and her miraculous powers started to make themselves manifest: when she prayed, incense would come out of her mouth, and she no longer needed the cotton wool dipped in holy oil to cure the sick – a simple touch of her hand was enough to make a smell of oil arise and force the devils to leave the afflicted, wailing as they went. The miracles multiplied in her last days. Though crippled, she began moving around the convent without help. And three days before her death, she was pleased to accept the repentance of Bishop Gerasimous, who came to her weeping, seeking forgiveness and asking her for absolution.

Maryka told the young man that until the day she died, his grandmother Saada had made regular visits to the nun at the Convent of Saint John the Baptist in Bkeftine, these visits being her sole consolation in the face of the catastrophe that had befallen her family.

Iskandar was surprised when *Khawaja* Saeed el Sabbagheh put the article in his drawer, telling the young journalist that while he appreciated the enormous effort he'd put into this most interesting piece, he wouldn't be able to publish it because it defamed the reputation of the bishop, which in a country like Lebanon might well lead to communal strife. When Iskandar asked for his manuscript back, he found that *Khawaja* Saeed had lost it, or at least he claimed to have done so. Thus all that remained in people's minds of Maryka's story was a name to stir desires and memories, especially with regard to the magic interrelationship between the *kaf* and the *alif* at the end – as though these two letters, with their dovetailed shapes, limned repressed desires.

When the young man asked his father, Moussa, about his aunt, Meelya, and the stories of the nun and the bishop, tears poured from the old man's eyes. The brown-skinned father, his head crowned with white hair, said not a word. Perhaps he hadn't heard his son's question, and it was just hearing his sister's name that caused his silent tears to flow and his voice to choke.

Saada clung to the hem of the robe of the nun, who was praying to the Evening Light, and screamed, "Mother of God, save us! It's Meelya, O Mother of Light! I beg of you, Meelya's dying."

The nun turned towards the source of the voice, pulled her hem from Saada's hands and asked her to go back to her house. "Meelya's hour is not yet come," she said, "and an evil hour it will be for you, Saada, when it does. Go home. I'll be along soon, and, God willing, all will be well."

The nun spoke truly, and Meelya crossed over the valley of death borne on that strange dream which had engraved itself on her heart. Meelya forgot the days of the disease that had afflicted her. She forgot how her mother and the women of the quarter had hovered around her bed weeping for the dying girl. She forgot the raving and the body that grew thinner and thinner until it was no more than a shadow. That dream, though, on which she had crossed over the valley of death, remained fixed in her memory as clearly as though she had dreamt it yesterday or seen it times without number. Now the dream manifested itself again as she listened to Mansour talking about Youssef the Carpenter. Perhaps Mansour was right; certainly this saint, who had given the Messiah his royal descent from David, was completely marginalized by the Church. He had no feast day and no miracles were attributed to him. Not even his date of death was known. Did he die before Christ was crucified and, if so, when? If he died afterwards, why wasn't he with Maryam at the foot of the cross? It's as though he were a mere vessel, of marginal importance, for the divine will, not a prophet or a saint. All the same, Meelya loved him because he had fled with his son to Egypt when he sensed danger, and he refused to sacrifice his son as Abraham, peace be upon him, had done. Probably if he'd been alive, he would have stopped Christ from entering Jerusalem riding on the foal of an ass and proclaiming himself king, in the adventure that led him to the cross.

She was in a strange place, lying in a field of green plants. As she relived that odd dream, the woman couldn't find her own image in it. Probably she just didn't see herself in the shape of that little girl. Usually, Meelya would see the girl and blend into her, believing that they were one. In this strange dream, though, she saw everything without seeing herself, which may have been the reason for her fear and for the incoherent cries that made the hovering women think she was in her death throes and gazing on the dust-covered phantoms of the world of the dead. Meelya cried out that all was dust; she didn't remember the screaming and the fear, she remembered only the boy child covered in dust lying at her side. Her lips were cracked with thirst, and the plants, yellowish in colour, were climbing over her eyes. The plants were climbing over her and she was screaming that the child needed water. And then suddenly the man came. Who was that man wearing a coat who leapt over Meelya to pick the child up and throw it into the fire?

"Why did you kill it?" she wanted to scream, but her voice had disappeared, and the fire devoured first the mother and then the body of the boy.

She saw herself flying without wings. She was at the summit of a stony slope that led down to a deep valley full of dry plants and thistles. She saw the man picking up the child and throwing it into the valley and the boy spreading out his arms so that he became like a bird with wings, though no feathers sprouted on them. "Where are the feathers?" Meelya screamed.

She is standing in the high place, the heat is suffocating, and the smell of the fires is all around her. She wants to grab onto something. She wants a rope she can hang on to, but the plants are dry and crumble in her fingers and she sees herself falling towards the bottom of the valley and sees the child opening its shattered arms as though waiting for her, and she screams.

At that instant, Meelya opened her eyes and found the nun hugging her, rubbing her dry hair and asking the mother to bring her daughter a glass of water.

"The girl's cured, praise be to God," the nun said. "Bring her a glass of water and make her some lemonade. Keep her on liquids for three days and she will be back to normal."

The miracle performed by the nun when she reached out and saved Meelya from falling into the valley was the last thing she did for the girl: "I saw her falling, and I stopped praying and ran to the house, and if God hadn't been merciful I might not have got there in time. I reached out and caught her, and at that instant she opened her eyes and was saved from death. That was the second time. The first was when she was born. I came and pulled her from the womb, which is the symbol of the grave. When a person is born, they're practising for the Resurrection, and when they're baptized and we plunge their whole body into water, from head to toe, we're burying them in the water so that the old Adam may die and a new person be born. I heard the voice of Saint Elias the Living. I was standing there and praying, and suddenly I heard a voice coming from the icon. Saint Elias, who was riding, swooping through the sky, on a chariot of fire, told me, 'Run, Milaneh, to Saada's house, and catch the girl before she falls into the valley, and tell her mother this is the last time, because the third time you won't be there and she won't be there, and the girl will have no-one to intercede for her but the Son.'"

Did the nun tell this story after hearing Saada recount her daughter's dream?

"The nun's a liar," Meelya said, "and I don't believe a word. She sat down beside me and heard me saying that I'd fallen. I became conscious because my heart had fallen. When you fall, your heart falls first. I told her that my heart had fallen because I was falling into the valley, and she made up the whole story. And anyway, who says the womb's a grave? That's blasphemy. Your friend the nun hates me. Didn't she say, Mother, that my dreams came from the Devil and I ought to go to church with you and pray so I'd forget them?"

Meelya didn't forget her dreams, but she did forget the nun's assertion that she would have no intercessor but the Son. Now this man who had become her husband stood there insulting the monk who told her the stories of Nazareth and had taken her to the ruin near the Church of the Annunciation, where he told her to make a full obeisance before entering, because the Lord had lived with his mother and father in that secret place untrodden by human feet. It was there that he had learnt to walk and there that the vision had come to him telling him that he was God's only son.

He had led her to a dry olive tree and told her that it had withered following the arrest of Youssef the Carpenter by the Romans. It seems the man had disappeared and been killed ten years before the crucifixion of his son. He would never have let anyone crucify his boy if he'd still been alive.

Here, beneath this tree, when the Messiah was twelve years old, had come the vision telling him that he was God's only son. How could a child understand the meaning of an angel's words heard in a dream? Lying beneath this tree, he heard the rustle of feathers and saw a six-winged angel hovering above him, its incandescent whiteness blinding him. Then he heard a voice telling him that he was the awaited *mashiach*, that God had

233

chosen him to be a son to Him since before the beginning of time, and that He would give him the throne of his grandsire David and make him king forever.

The child awoke, frightened and thirsty, and for three days was dumb, unable to utter a word. He was like someone in shock, drinking and not quenching his thirst. His mother intuited that her son had beheld a vision and recalled how Zacharias had been struck dumb when the angel had told him the news of his wife's pregnancy. She said nothing to her husband, however. Since her journey to Egypt, and even since her pregnancy and her attempts to tell her husband the truth, she had lived with the man in silence. Whenever she tried to open her mouth to speak, he would silence her with a wave of his hand and shake his head, as though to say there was no call for words, as though he knew everything. And when he came back from the olive tree with his son and she tried to speak with him, he averted his face. Going over to her son, she asked him what had happened, and he said, "Woman, what have I to do with thee?" The Gospel is wrong when it states that he rebuked his mother at the wedding in Cana of Galilee, where the first miracle, which turned the water into wine, took place. That's not how it was. In Cana, he kissed his mother's hand and embraced her before performing the miracle, because he knew that the hour for him to proclaim himself had come. But there, before, he was full of fear and didn't want to speak with this woman who had hidden his secret from him.

He had gone with Youssef the Carpenter to the olive tree and informed him of the vision that had come to him in his dream, and the elderly man had wept before his son like a child and taken him in his arms and kissed him and told him that now, for the first time, he could walk with his head held high. That day, for the first time, he was sure that his dreams were not illusions and that God had tested him as He had no other prophet. He said that God had tested his sense of self-worth and that he had waited twelve years for this blessed moment. Then he knelt, asked his son to kneel next to him and said, "Blessed is the ram that Thou hast sent, O God, for Thou hast spared me the trial of Abraham, who wished to kill his son for the sake of Thy holy name. Blessed art Thou, O God of Abraham, Isaac and Jacob, for this is my son who will become a king in Thine eyes and bear Thy name and be holy for ever. Blessed art Thou, O God of All, because Thou hast made me a partner to Thee in the fathering of this child. From now on I shall be the brother of the Lord and I shall sit in Abraham's bosom as Thy friend and Thy companion."

The elderly monk recounted how his grandfather the priest had possessed a secret manuscript that he'd stolen from Abbot Bucci, the Italian head of the Franciscan monastery, and that in it was the whole story of Youssef the Carpenter. He also said that there was a secret sect that venerated the man, whom they regarded as a twin of the prophet Elias the Living, and that God had raised him unto Him ten years before the crucifixion.

He said that Youssef the Carpenter had been written out of the story because Paul, who had set it down, hadn't understood the relationship between the son and the father and hadn't understood why Youssef had wept, as he was taken up into Heaven, at having seen what would befall his only son.

Tanyous took Meelya to all the quarters of Nazareth. He drew a line between the Nazareth of Christ and the Nazareth of the Franciscans, who had founded the city in the sixteenth century, and he told her the story of his grandfather, who had been the owner of the wondrous manuscript that revealed the secret of Youssef the Carpenter.

"Have you read the manuscript?" Meelya asked.

"No. The manuscript is written in Syriac, and I don't know

Syriac, but my grandfather could speak and read the language of Christ and he told me," the monk replied.

"And why did your grandfather drop the Latins and go Greek Orthodox?" she asked.

"Because he fell in love with that woman from Houran. He discovered that God manifests Himself only through love, and when he went to the abbot and told him that, the man went berserk and started cursing women and sent my grandfather to the monastery lock-up to cleanse himself of his sin. But my grandfather had done nothing wrong. All that had happened was that he'd seen the girl at the spring next to the monastery and she'd stolen his heart, and he couldn't think of anything else. He'd gone to the abbot to seek advice, and the answer he got was imprisonment, torture and beating. It was there that he heard the voice of the angel and Saint Youssef appeared to him. At first he thought he was Youssef son of Jacob, the beautiful youth whose brothers tried to kill him and whom all the women fell in love with. He said, 'God has sent me guidance' and knelt before Saint Youssef to ask his forgiveness for the sin he had committed in his mind, but then he heard the saint whisper that the manuscript was in the abbot's safe. He told him to read the manuscript and then he'd understand everything.

"After a month, my grandfather left the lock-up and found a way to steal the manuscript. The truth was revealed to him and he decided to abandon the cassock, marry and become a Greek Orthodox."

"But Saint Youssef wasn't . . ."

"What are you trying to say? I hope you don't believe the lies invented by certain repressed men of religion that Saint Youssef, God forbid, was impotent, that he had an accident when he was doing his carpentry and lost his manhood? That's a lie. There's no such thing as an impotent saint, and above all the Lord Christ, glory be to him. Take care, my daughter, that you do not believe such things. The fellow was a widower with five children, and the story of his marriage to Our Lady Maryam is entrancing. Listen, my daughter. Listen."

He started reciting as though reading from a text lying open before him: "And Maryam, daughter of Joachim and Hanneh, had been promised from birth to the Temple, where she lived a life of piety and sewed the porphyry tent and prayed, and grew in stature and in grace. And when she reached womanhood, the elders of the Temple took counsel amongst themselves and it was decided that the girl should leave the Temple and wed. And there was among the men of the Temple a pious old man called Youssef, known as the Carpenter. Youssef asked the elders gathered in the Temple to pray to God and ask Him for a sign. And when they came to leave in the evening and while they were taking their sticks, that they had placed by the door, they beheld the violet flowers that had grown out of Youssef's stick, and they cried out with one voice, 'It is he!' 'I?' said Youssef. 'How may it be that I should take this virgin girl, and how may it be that I should marry her when she is of the age of my daughters and I am an old man and a widower who counts the days remaining to him?' For wise is the man who knows that life fades like the flowers of the field and his body grows thin in the dust, and that life is losses that follow one another while awaiting the great loss. But the wise men of the Temple, having seen the miracle performed by Youssef's stick, had decided, and their decision brooked no refusal. So Youssef took the woman and performed the marriage covenant with her, and before he went in unto her he discovered that she was with child and he wept greatly and . . . I've told you the rest of the story."

"What does 'porphyry' mean?" Meelya asked.

"It means 'red'," the monk said.

"But why do you talk as though you were reading. You told

me yourself that the book's in Syriac. How could you memorize it in classical Arabic?"

Instead of tugging on his beard and closing his eyes before replying, he looked at her for a long time and then said, "Blessed are they that believe and have not seen. I fear for you, Meelya. Come with me. I have been counting the days because I have been waiting for you. I am going to take your hand so that you may cross the valley without harm. What do you say?"

But before she could say anything, the man disappeared as though swept up in a cloud of dust that took him far away.

Meelya told the Italian doctor that she was afraid. The elderly man in a white smock bent to look between Meelya's legs, which were raised above the half-bed upon which the nurse had asked her to lie. The doctor left the room and the woman was left on her own. The pain had diminished to the point of non-existence and she took a deep breath, as though she were no longer pregnant. Her lightness of soul returned and the blackness cleared from her eyes. She closed them in order to rest and it was then that she saw him.

How had the monk got into the hospital room?

He was covered in dust, as though coming from far away, and he drew close to Meelya bearing a tall censer from which poured blinding white smoke. Through the smoke she saw a little girl climbing the air and dissolving. "No, that's not my daughter. I'm going to have a boy, not a girl," she said. Then she discovered that the girl she'd seen was Meelya. "Dear God, how hard it is to give birth! Mother of Light, now I understand how much you suffered. You forget your own self." The girl vanished into the smoke and the white incense grew thicker. All that was left was the elderly monk.

"Leave me be, I beg of you! I want to give birth now. Please, you're not supposed to come here."

And she heard a voice issuing from the smoke.

"Please, Virgin, tell him to stop!"

But the words continue. The Virgin refuses to intervene, leaving Meelya to her fate. And she hears the story. It's not the first time she has heard it. Who first told her the story of Eve? She remembers saying, "What nonsense!" but no longer remembers where or when. Or rather – yes, it was the nun Milaneh. What brought her here, and why had the beggar-monk appeared, seemingly disguised as her?

Could it be? No, it was impossible. Though he *was* a beggar. When she'd seen him the first time, he'd left the glass on the windowsill and disappeared, but on many later occasions she'd given him food and money. He was just a beggar who'd claimed to be Lebanese to curry favour with her.

"Please go now. Afterwards, after I've had the baby, I'll make you the best food I can. Now I want to be on my own."

Her husband was convinced that a conman was making a fool of his wife and that no-one in Nazareth knew anything about a monk of Lebanese origin called Tanyous who lived alone in the town. "Pay no attention, woman. There isn't a Greek Orthodox monastery in the country. There's the Moskobiya, but the monks there are Russians. How could he be a monk and live on his own and know where Christ's house is? Show me the house and I'll make our fortune. I mean, it'd be the biggest tourist attraction in the entire world. Come on, get up and show me where the house is," Mansour said.

She wanted to tell him that the location of the house was a secret confided to her by the monk and that she couldn't tell it to anyone else, but she found herself walking through the narrow alleys searching for the olive tree and the ruin next to it and not finding them. Where was Mansour? They'd left the house together but he'd disappeared and she was walking alone, stumbling at every step, looking for the dry olive tree so she could lay her tired head upon it and rest. But she could not find the place.

Milaneh said that Youssef the Carpenter had been overcome by astonishment when he saw how fast the midwife performed her work in that little cave they stumbled across in Bethlehem. The nun said the woman whom Youssef found at the entrance to the cave had been waiting there for him. She'd knelt down beside Maryam, reached out her hand, and the boy had come out in seconds. The Virgin had felt pain, according to Milaneh, because no woman could give birth without pain, which was because of the original sin. But the pain was slight and hardly worth mentioning, because the newborn wasn't a child of sin like his mother; indeed, he was the New Adam who had not been driven from the Garden. Therefore, the Old Eve had to come and kneel before the New Eve, Our Lady Maryam being the New Eve before whom the whole universe made prostration. And when the boy spoke in the cradle, he thanked the midwife who had pulled him from his mother's belly and named her Eve. Maryam heard the name but didn't dare tell her husband, whom she was afraid would think she was raving or wouldn't believe her. She had told him of her vision, but the man had knit his brows and forbidden her to finish the story, implying that he knew everything already. In fact, though, he had known nothing and wouldn't until such time as the boy told him his dream. Then the elderly man would prostrate himself before his virgin wife, whom he had not allowed close to him because he had doubted her fidelity, and to whom he would eventually become as close as a man should to his wife, by which time it was too late and life had erased all desires, transforming them instead into kindness and sympathy.

The nun didn't tell the story that way. She said that when she'd come running to the Shaheen family's house and seen the yellow colour covering Saada, she'd ordered the midwife to pull the girl-child from her mother's body, and that at that instant she'd seen two women, the first bending over and pulling a boy-child from his mother's belly, the second standing beside her, cloaked in purple and blue. She said that this was the Old Eve, who from that blessed moment had become the midwives' intercessor – nay, the midwife herself, sent by the Holy Ghost to save women from death in childbirth. She said that when she saw the two women together, she knew for sure that God wanted this little girl to live so that she could bear witness to Him.

Tanyous, however, mocked Meelya when she told him that Eve had attended her birth. "That makes no sense, my daughter," he said. "God sent Eve to Maryam so she could see that it's possible for the pains of childbirth to vanish with the vanishing of sin. Don't misunderstand me. Maybe the nun's a saint and maybe she had a vision, but in the cave in Bethlehem it wasn't like that. Eve herself came and knelt and pulled Eesa out. The other thing was a decision Eesa's father made personally and that decision forced Youssef to keep silent for twelve years and not say a thing, because Eve only uttered a single sentence. He asked, 'Who are you?' and tried to give her money, but she waved the money away, said 'I am Eve' and vanished. But that's not the important story. The important story is the story of the Messiah and the fish. When the Messiah, peace be upon him, walked on the face of the water, a fish came to where he was standing, bringing a message from Saint Elias. People call the fish of the Sea of Tiberias *musht*, or Peter's Fish, but that isn't its real name. The real name of this particular fish was Saint Youssef, though nobody knows that except for the fish, Saint Youssef and God. The fish stopped next to him and said, 'Don't go to Jerusalem because they will kill you there.' The Messiah blessed the fish and told it not to be afraid.

He said it wasn't about fish any more and that his daddy was going to send him the lamb."

"And the fish?" Meelya asked. "The fish knew how to say all that in Syriac?"

"Of course. After all, fish can talk, but man forgot the language of the animals after that business with Our Master Abraham, peace be upon him."

"What business?" Meelya asked.

. . .

"You mean the business with the ram, don't you?"

. . .

"You mean when he sacrificed his son. Who could kill his son?"

. . .

"Of course he'd taken his son to kill him. God had ordered him to kill him, so he didn't have a choice. No, the ram had no right to feel upset, or at least, it did, of course – I mean, no-one dies without feeling upset about it – but what was he to do? I mean, either he ate his son or he ate the ram."

. . .

"Are you trying to tell me Isaac sat down with his father and they ate the ram together? No, that's not a story I'm prepared to believe."

. . .

"Now you've really got it coming from God. Why do you say things like that?"

. . .

"Of course he had two boys. The elder he raised in the desert with his mother, Hagar, and the other he took to offer as a sacrifice."

. . .

"Oh dear, I don't know what I'm saying, Lord forgive me. Maybe the story now hasn't got anything to do with the past, you're right, but why was Ameen murdered in Jaffa, and what am I supposed to go and do there? Please tell Mansour that Meelya's sad and wants to live here, next to the olive tree, and that she can't take any more."

. . .

"I don't like these stories. Let's go back to the story of the fish. Tell me, when the fish passed Youssef's message on to the Messiah, what did He reply?"

. . .

"Please, I want to go home. I've forgotten the way back to our house and Mansour will be worrying. Take me home."

Hearing her cry that she wanted to go home, Mansour was overcome by an unbearable feeling of impotence. This cry had come to dominate Meelya's sleep since his brother's murder in Jaffa, as though the woman had broken with the traditions that had governed her sleep and entered into an obscure struggle with the world. The first time it happened he woke her to tell her that the road was full of dangers but he was prepared to contact the Red Cross to guarantee safe passage to Beirut, and she could give birth there – "But I won't be able to go with you. Things are difficult and I can't leave my mother on her own. What do you say, my dear?"

She regarded him with drowsy eyes, tossed in her bed, turned onto her side and sank into sleep once more.

Mansour no longer knew how to deal with the woman. Since the murder of his brother, she'd changed her ways. She no longer got up early in the morning. He'd set off for work and she'd still be sleeping; he'd return and not find her in the house. He had learnt not to search for her in the byways of the town because she'd become angry and accuse him of treating her like a little girl. So he took to coming home from work and waiting for her, consumed by anxiety. Entering the house, she'd behave as though nothing were wrong. She'd go to the kitchen, heat up his food and sit quietly, neither eating nor speaking.

243

If he asked her anything, she would burst into tears and say she was tired and wanted to go to bed.

"But where do you go every day? God bless you, Meelya, it won't do, for the boy's sake. You're in your last month and the doctor says you have to rest."

"But it's for the boy's sake that I go out."

"What do you mean?"

"You wouldn't understand. Anyway, there's nothing you can do about it. I don't want to go to Jaffa. I want to stay here."

"But you know why we have to go."

"I know and I don't know, but I'm frightened for my son."

"You're talking like a madwoman. You have to see a doctor."

Raising his glass, he gazed into her eyes and said,

> *"Thus she is as one who drowses as she gazes*
> > *Or as one sick and not yet cured,*
> *Her eyelashes free of any rheum,*
> > *For it is her eyes themselves that have the cure ensured.*

You're right. It's my fault, damn it. It is me who's changed, and what fault is that of yours? But 'We walked steps that were written for us, And he whose steps are written must walk them.' Let's go back to the way we were at the beginning. What's happened to 'mother's milk'? I long for the taste of cooked milk. Make some for me tomorrow. We'll have a glass and recite poetry like in the old days." He reached out to caress the unborn child in her belly and she jumped back.

"No, please," she said.

"I just want to feel his voice with my hand," Mansour said.

Mansour couldn't understand her fear. When at night he'd heard her screaming that she wanted to go home, he'd promised to find a way to send her to Beirut, but she'd fussed and said no, she didn't want to go to Beirut, she'd come to Nazareth for good, and she'd begun to fear him because he was listening to her dreams, and when someone learns how to listen to your dreams it means he's become your master.

Since his brother's death, his mother had become a different person. Suddenly and without warning, she'd come to depend entirely on Mansour. She told him she saw his brother in him, that she'd never noticed that they were as alike as two teardrops. Did she really use that expression? Probably not. That was how Meelya spoke; when she arose from sleep, her words would be full of softness. She'd told him that speech was like dew, it came at the moment that divided night from day, and that she could taste the flavour of that moment in her mouth when she got up. He said that he loved to kiss her in the morning because her lips tasted like fresh basil. When she spoke in the morning, she would use soft words that oscillated with drowsiness in a way Mansour had previously heard only in ancient Arabic poetry.

Why did Mansour confuse his mother's words with those of his wife?

Could it be because a man loves only one woman in his life, which is to say his mother, and spends his life looking for her? But Mansour wasn't like that. He'd told Meelya he hated his mother's infatuation with his brother; he couldn't understand how his mother had managed to organize life around her in such a way as to make herself the axis of both house and workshop. Asma, Ameen's wife, was like a visitor in her own home, not allowed to take on any chores, and if God hadn't made women's breasts a wellspring of nourishment for children, she would have found herself with nothing to do.

Then her son died and the woman became as one lost. The strength disappeared from her piercing eyes, and a timidity she had never known took possession of them. The wife, though, was a different story. This woman, who had seemed wrapped up in herself, as though hiding from notice and veiled in modesty, became a new person. The beauty of her black eyes shone forth, and, in an instantaneous reversal of roles, she became mistress of the place. Mansour told Meelya that he was amazed at Asma's beauty: "Where was she hiding those good looks? I mean, how can a woman become lovelier when her husband dies? In the old days they used to bury a woman with her husband because the death of the man meant that her life was over. Now just see how lovely she's become."

"I can't leave my mother on her own," Mansour said.

"Suddenly you love your mother? What do you want me to say? It's going to be the way you want, but I'm afraid for you and I'm afraid for my son. I mean, we don't have to die the way your brother did."

Where did Mansour get this new language of his? Standing in the kitchen, he spoke to her about the poet-cavalier Abd el Rahim Mahmoud:

"I shall bear my soul on the palms of my hands
    And cast it in the chasm of woe.
Let me live a life to bring joy to my friend
    Or die a death to bring chagrin to my foe!"

"That's not poetry," Meelya said. "I mean, you're not going to tell me that it's to be compared to these verses of al Mutanabbi, are you?

Should'st thou venture all for an honour desired,
    Accept naught but the stars.
Death tastes the same however it comes,
    Be the venture small or large."

"No, no. This is prettier," he said.

> *"You stood, and death is the certain fate of him who stands*
> > *As though on ruin's sleeping eye.*
> *Your face shone bright, your mouth alight with smiles,*
> > *While wounded and downcast, the champions passed by."*

"But I like these two verses," she said.

> *"A single parting has come between us,*
> > *And, after this parting, in death shall be parting too.*
> *Is not night's body also now frail and wasted,*
> > *Having had, like me, your eyes in view?"*

"This is no time for love songs," he said. "Listen:

> *Think not that glory is a wineskin and a singing girl,*
> > *For glory is the sword and sudden killing,*
> *And the striking of the necks of kings, your place in battle marked*
> > *By black dust rising and soldiers milling."*

"Give me verse like that, give me a poet like al Mutanabbi, and I'll go with you to the ends of the earth. Then the taste of war will come from the taste of poetry and the taste of poetry will come from the taste of love. But that stuff by the fellow who wants to bare his soul . . ."

"He was a great poet. It wasn't enough for him just to write. He took up his weapon and went to war and died, and he named his son 'the Goodly One' so that people would address him as 'Father of the Goodly One'."

"I'm all for martyrs, but this country's poet has yet to be born, and when he comes, you Palestinians will discover that your country can be fashioned only out of poetry. This country isn't soil; it's words bound together with stories. Ever since the Messiah walked its earth, its dust has been made of letters and words. 'In the beginning was the word and the word was with God, and the word was God.' In other words, He is the word, and poetry is the highest order of words, and one day soon, my dear, some fifty years from now, when a great poet is born in this land, you will find that the only way you can win the war is with the word, which is mightier than the sword."

"First of all, don't say 'you'. Aren't you one of us?"

"You're right, my dear. I apologize. I've become us, and when I speak about you I'm speaking about us."

"And second, we're not going to wait fifty years for that poet of yours to appear. We're going to go into battle with the poetry we know how to write and we're going to win."

"I don't know about that," she said.

"What do I care whether you know or not, because, third, what I know is that my brother's dead and I can't leave my mother on her own."

"Have you noticed how you're starting to do things just like your mother? You yawn like her, you suck your lips like her when you get angry, you punch a dent for your head in the pillow before going to sleep just like her. Lord, how you've changed."

"I've done those things all my life."

"Maybe, but I didn't notice. It's as though you were her son. I don't know why I didn't notice from the beginning."

"I *am* her son! But I'm not like her the way you're saying I am. I'm just doing my duty to my mother and my brother's children and wife."

"Thank God you're not a Muslim. You might have married your brother's wife and got me a co-wife, now that you've worked out just how beautiful she is."

. . .

"Don't get angry. I was just joking. But how should I know?"

She said, "But how should I know" so that she didn't have to say that she'd seen him in the dream with that very woman, with Mansour looking like Najeeb.

Her husband had never before blended with the image of that man who'd exited her life as though he'd never been. Usually, it was Moussa Mansour got confused with. She'd see Moussa in her dreams and understand that the message was being channelled through someone else. Mansour would appear only in the last dream, when the woman would discover that the end of things resembles their beginning.

The place resembles the garden of the old house, but it's not Beirut, it's Jaffa. The smell of the sea mixes with the scent of oranges. Najeeb is peeling an orange and standing next to a woman of medium height, full of figure but not fat. "Are you Najeeb?" the girl wants to ask the man. And who is the woman? What has brought Asma here?

Meelya hides behind a jasmine bush whose tendrils branch out and curl around each another, but she can't smell the jasmine; the oranges, the sea salt and the humidity fill her pores. The man who looks like Najeeb tosses the orange from hand to hand, then reaches over to the woman's chest, extracting from it a second orange. The woman moans.

Holding the knife in his right hand, Najeeb extends his left hand to the woman's chest, pulls out another orange and starts peeling it. The woman weeps as though in pain. The man, having devoured the orange, throws the knife aside, goes over to Asma – or whoever this person is who resembles Asma – puts his lips to her chest, which has been transformed into half an orange, and starts kissing it.

"What are you doing here, Najeeb?" asks the little girl, who has come out from behind the jasmine bush carrying the knife. "Didn't I tell you I didn't want to see you again?"

"Who are you?" the man asks, his features changing suddenly.

. . .

"No, you can't be Meelya. Where are your green eyes?"

How had this man who looked like Najeeb come to know the colour of her eyes?

"Go back to your country, girl, and keep out of my way."

The man bends over the woman's chest once more and the colour orange starts dripping from his mouth.

In that instant they disappear. Meelya has no memory of where the man took the woman.

She lies down among the plants, and there is the man who resembles Mansour.

The woman is weeping as though the man, who has a knife in his hand, were stabbing her. Meelya hears her pleading with him but can't understand what she's saying, as though she were speaking a language Meelya doesn't know.

"Or perhaps she's speaking German, but German's not like that – I know German. They taught us French in Lebanon, and, no, that isn't German. It's like Arabic, but I can't understand a word, so it's Incomprehensible Arabic. Yesterday you were speaking Hebrew. How come you know Hebrew?"

"Me?"

"You, who else?"

"Where?"

"It's not important. But I'd like to know."

"No, I don't know Hebrew. Okay, I know two or three words, but my brother knew it."

"Maybe the man is your brother."

"What's this about my brother, God rest his soul?"

"Nothing. Forget it."

"The important thing is for you to get better and start

packing our things. We're supposed to move to Jaffa as soon as you've given birth."

"No, we'll have the boy baptized here. Then we can move if you want to."

"That's wonderful! You mean we have to wait forty days. That's why we have to get ourselves ready starting now."

"It doesn't matter," she says.

The woman weeps. She disappears from in front of Najeeb, or whoever it is that looks like Najeeb, and drowns in her tears. Meelya, hidden behind the jasmine bush, sees and doesn't see. When she tries to recall this dream, all she can come up with is a mysterious image of a man with dishevelled hair carrying an orange and a knife and a woman covered in fear and tears. Then the second woman appears: Mansour's mother has a pair of scissors and starts pruning the jasmine bush. As the scissors approach her hair, little Meelya trembles where she's hiding beneath the bush.

She didn't recount the dream to Mansour because she couldn't find the words. What had brought Asma to the old house in Beirut? What did Najeeb want after all this time? That story was over and done with, and the emptiness that had struck her following Najeeb's flight and his marriage was gone now; time had filled in the gap that had opened inside her. Mansour had been the messenger who'd brought the tidings that it was over, so why was he now opening a new gap deep within her and making her confuse the move to Jaffa with the ghost of that fear of loss that Najeeb had planted in her heart? What did her mother-in-law want with the scissors? "They want to kill me," Meelya screamed, and she jumped out of bed, only to find Mansour sitting by her side lighting a cigarette, his face full of pain.

She'd said no to Mansour's suggestion that they live in the family house in el Ajami:

"It's your father's and your grandfather's house and we're

two women with two children – where else would you go?"
his mother had asked him. "You and your wife will come and
live here. It's a large house and it won't be a problem, and that
way you can look after your brother's children. You're the man
of the family now."

When he told Meelya that he was the man of the family and
had to behave as such, the woman looked at him askance.
Mansour would become embarrassed when he saw that look
and understand that he had to shut up. The lids would come
down and then the look would rise, passing through the two
small corners formed by the honey-coloured pupils before
coming to rest on Mansour's eyes. It was this look that, in the
beginning, had enchanted him – a mixture of a diffidence that
manifested itself in the flush on the girl's cheeks and a desire
that could express itself only indirectly. As time went by,
however, the meanings of things started to change and that
look began to carve fear into the man's heart.

He listened to her look and corrected himself, saying it
would be just a temporary arrangement: "Don't even think,
my dear, that I could live all my life with three women. One's
more than I can handle."

. . .

"Of course, of course, my dear, but we need a little time.
Then, when work's going well and we're making some money,
we'll move. The plan is for me to buy a house for my mother
and the children. That way they can live on their own and we
can live in the family house."

. . .

"No, I don't like the family house. After all, I ran away from
it to Nazareth. We'll buy a house in the nicest quarter – you
choose and I'll do the necessary. We just have to get ourselves
to Jaffa soon. It's the easiest thing in the world. You decide and
I'll take care of everything."

. . .

"No, we'll need a bit of time. Say a couple of years."

. . .

"Give me nine months. Let's say the house will take as long as the boy did. Then we'll have our own independent life, don't worry. Just devote yourself to the boy. My mother and Asma will cook and clean, and you can live like a queen. Then we'll go to our own house. Houses are hard to come by in Jaffa. Jaffa's a city and it's not easy to find a decent house. So it needs a bit of patience, and then, God willing, everything will work out."

Her meeting with the Lebanese monk had changed everything. Before, when she'd lost her temper and yelled, she'd felt as though the voice coming from her throat was her mother's, and she'd hated herself. A little girl had found herself responsible for a whole family, consisting of four men and a nun. The mother was the sick nun, in civvies, whom everyone had constantly to placate. And when Meelya had yelled at her big brother Saleem that she wasn't a maid and heard her mother's voice coming out of her mouth, the words had stuck in her throat, as though she were choking. Meelya can't remember exactly what happened. She doesn't even remember the cause of the disagreement with her brother and what she was saying when she choked on her voice and could say no more. She decided – she tells herself now that she had decided – never to imitate her mother's voice or gestures again, and she became calm, accepting everything. During the first days of her stay in Nazareth, however, she started hearing her mother's voice coming to her out of her memory. To remember voices is frightening. It's different in dreams: you don't hear the voice of the person speaking to you; the words come without a voice – that is the secret of dreams and their magic. But when the voice of someone far away, or dead, bursts out of your memory and you hear it with your own ears, you are taken aback. Meelya's astonishment when her mother spoke and she heard her was transformed into fear by her discovery that this woman, who for her only daughter embodied absence and abandonment, could manifest an unexpected presence. In Nazareth, her mother's presence didn't make Meelya hate herself but she did discover that the mother is a necessity imposed by language, even in her absence. You cry "Mother" not because you're thinking of the woman who bore you but because your lips need to form the letters that make up that word. Meelya, who, in the Italian hospital in Nazareth, at the moment of pain, would cry out that magic word just before Mansour heard the cry of the baby emerging from its mother's womb, wasn't seeing her mother, or sensing her presence; she was seeing the world clothed in a whiteness like light.

Meelya sensed that Mansour's voice had lost itself in that of his mother, and told him so. He pretended indifference, it's true, and said it had always been like that, but he started noticing his own habits and avoided imitating his mother. He no longer opened his mouth wide with a loud noise when he yawned, as his mother would do, exclaiming at the same time, "O God!"

What he didn't notice, though, was that his wife had also lost her voice and had taken on the Lebanese monk's way of speaking. When she spoke, she'd feel that she was adopting the voice of that strange man whom Mansour had tried to persuade her didn't exist and was a figment of her imagination.

One day, Meelya returned to the house exhausted, the pains of pregnancy traced upon her face. Mansour was sitting alone in the house with a handful of roasted yellow chick-peas in front of him.

"You must be hungry," she said and hurried to the kitchen to prepare some food.

"No, I'm not hungry. Come and sit beside me. I want to talk to you."

She sat down beside him and he told her about Tanyous. He said he owed her an apology and was amazed that she'd run into the monk. The man had been expelled from the Franciscan monastery twenty years before and was living in the country-side. He was to be seen from time to time at Marj Ibn Amir and only rarely came to Nazareth, where he would pray in a cave in which he believed the Holy Family had lived. When the monks caught sight of him, they'd chase him away, pelting him with stones.

He said he'd been afraid for her and had gone to look for her at the monastery, where he'd knocked at length before the door was opened by an elderly monk who spoke Arabic with difficulty: "I asked him about you and he replied in amazement that women never entered the place and tried to shut the door in my face. I begged him to hear me out and asked about the Lebanese monk. He hesitated before answering, made the sign of the cross several times, and asked me if I was a relative. I lied and said yes. He said he'd thought so because of my Lebanese accent. I don't know why he thought my accent was Lebanese – maybe it's your influence, Madame Meelya. Now you can't keep telling me I talk like my mother. Is it true my accent sounds Lebanese?"

"I really don't know."

"It's the same with you – your accent's become Palestinian, so now we speak the same. Anyway, the man told me the whole story. The monk was thrown out of the monastery because he claimed he'd found a Gospel written by one of the disciples of Youssef the Carpenter. He said it was written in Syriac, told the story of the Messiah in a different way from the four Greek Gospels, and claimed that Youssef had refused to accept the idea of the Messiah being crucified, saying that he wanted to do the same as Abraham did when God told him to offer his only son as a sacrifice . . . this along with countless other heresies that put Youssef the Carpenter on the same level as the prophet Elias. The elderly monk said Tanyous was mad and probably possessed by devils, which is why he'd been expelled from the monastery, after which he'd returned to his home in Lebanon. It was said that he'd tried to propagate his claim in the holy valley where the Maronite monks live, believing that the Maronites would still be faithful to the covenant because in their prayers they use Syriac, which was the only language spoken by the Messiah. However, the monks in the Valley of Qadisha mocked him; in fact, they lured him to the Madmen's Valley, where they put him in chains and threw him into a dark cave without food or water. He claims that God sent him food by means of a huge eagle whose wings hid the sky and sent him an angel in the form of a leopard that loosed his chains, though that was all lies, the man was insane. The abbot explained that this kind of madness was widespread in this country which has fathered all the prophets and that the land witnesses a continual struggle between God and the devils. Things got confused in people's minds and they ended up unable to distinguish between God's voice and the devils'. The Lebanese monk was a victim of this inability to distinguish and had become the devils' plaything."

"And you believed him?"

"It doesn't matter. What matters is that I became convinced that what you'd said was the truth. At first I thought the monk was a meaningless hallucination. But you mustn't believe him, my dear. He's a devil, not the saint you imagine."

"You may be right," Meelya said.

The woman didn't know how to tell her husband when she first saw the Lebanese monk. Had she dreamt of him before they met or only afterwards? The world of dreams only opens all of its doors at that terrifying moment when the real world comes to a stop and everything merges with everything else – when, as her grandmother used to scream, recalling the words of Solomon the Wise, "Vanity of vanities, all is vanity." "At that moment," the grandmother had said, "everything enters into the light, and we see what the eye cannot and become acquainted with all the people we know and know not."

Was the glass the man put on the windowsill dream or reality? How had she recognized him when she ran into him in the street in front of the Virgin's Spring? She remembers that he approached her and told her to follow him – "The goal is the same, Marta. Arise and follow me" – and she'd followed him.

She told Mansour she wanted to go to sleep because things were getting mixed up in her memory. Mansour had changed and she had changed. One year had been enough for life to unroll itself before her. She felt herself growing old, tired of life and of time's upheavals – "For a thousand years in Thy sight are but as yesterday when it is past, and as a watch in the night."

When she sees a picture of her mother-in-law, or of Asma, she is afflicted with grief. How could it have happened? How could the house have become so full of pictures? When they got married, the photographer stood in front of the bride and groom taking pictures, in the house and then in the church, and asked Meelya, who had tears in her eyes, to smile. The camera's eye and the black cloth behind which the photographer hid had remained fixed in Meelya's memory. The woman had been afraid the photographer would steal the colour of her eyes, like the photographer from Zahleh whom Moussa had brought to the house, so she closed them, causing the photographer to beg her, first gently and then angrily, to open her eyes so that light could enter the picture. When they passed through Beirut, though, on their way to Nazareth, Mansour had refused to wait "just two more days, while they get the photos ready". He'd asked Moussa to send them on to Nazareth. Then the road was cut and Meelya never saw her wedding pictures.

In fact, no-one saw the pictures because the photographer tore them up in a fit of rage. He told Moussa when he went to his shop that he'd torn the pictures up because they wouldn't help his reputation: "The bride never once opened her eyes. It's as though she were sleeping."

Saada lost her temper. Then she asked her son to write to his sister and tell her to bring her wedding dress with her when she visited Beirut with her husband: "Then they can take the pictures again. What's wrong with that? It's not right for someone not to have photos of their wedding."

Meelya wasn't aware of what had happened to the wedding photos, and Mansour didn't ask about them. He put several mirrors in the house: a large one in the parlour, one in the dining room and one in the bedroom. Meelya made no objection until he tried to put one in the kitchen. "No," she said. "That's too much. Who on earth puts a mirror in the kitchen?" He said he wanted the house to be filled with one picture that he could see everywhere. "I want to see nothing but you, my darling," he said. Obsessively, each morning, he placed Meelya before a mirror to show her how nothing ignited a woman's beauty like love. "See how beautiful you've become? It's love. When you were asleep you were as hot as fresh-baked white bread. I turned you over onto your back and it was wonderful. It was the best time."

"Don't say that."

"You mean you wouldn't agree with me that it was the best time?"

Substituting mirrors for photos, Mansour kept the walls of the house bare of anything else. He told his mother, who had reproached him for not putting a picture of his late father in the main room like everyone else, that he hated photographs:

"A photo freezes a person and makes him look dead. I prefer to preserve the image of my father as it is in my memory."

"But your father *is* dead," his mother replied.

He gestured his refusal, as if to say that a person never dies; we kill him when we hang him on the wall. His father was alive in his memory, and he didn't want to kill him.

"Why did you kill her, Moussa?"

Now suddenly the whole house was filled with photos. First he put up a large photo of his brother, draped in black. Then he brought his father's photo and the photos of his brother's children. Next came the photo of his mother, along with a photo of the widow standing next to her husband in her wedding dress. He started cramming photos, large and small, into the corners of the mirrors that were scattered around the house. One day he returned from Jaffa bearing a creased, almost indecipherable photo he said he'd try and find a photographer to fix because it was a rare picture of the departed with the freedom fighters.

"Why did you kill her, Moussa?"

Meelya didn't feel jealous: "Jealousy has never entered my heart, ever. Even with Najeeb, I didn't feel jealous."

"You're right to feel jealous. Tomorrow the photographer will come and take your picture and I'll put it up on the wall."

"I don't want to have my picture taken."

"I want a picture like the one in your family's house."

"Why did you kill her, Moussa?"

Little Meelya was standing alone among the mirrors looking at herself in the early evening darkness, watching the images of the narrow street reflected in the large mirror that had been placed in the *dar*, when she saw Moussa come in via the mirror carrying a large picture of a woman traced in black and white on a cream background. When the girl saw him, she ran and hid beneath the sofa, waiting for him to come and look for her as he always did. The dark-skinned young man, who was wearing a white shirt, did not, however, turn towards his sister. He took a hammer and some nails from a small box and began nailing the picture to the large mirror through which he had entered. Meelya put her hands over her ears so that she wouldn't hear the splintering of the mirror beneath the large nails, which turned the mirror's light into shards.

Meelya wanted to come out from beneath the sofa to stop the man destroying the mirror. She knew that broken mirrors in a dream are a bad omen. She crawled along under the sofa and suddenly found herself in the open. It was dark and she sensed danger. She didn't know where she was, but she knew that the valley lay before her and she didn't dare move for fear of being swallowed up by the darkness. The sound of hammering was giving her a terrible headache. She wanted to cry out, "Moussa!" but heard herself crying "Mansour!" and covered her mouth lest her husband, sleeping wrapped up in himself next to her, should wake.

"Where are you, brother?"

The girl's voice was lost in the darkness and she decided to open her eyes. She wasn't going to let this dream go on and she wasn't going to see the mirror in her house smashed: "Oh dear, maybe it means that Mansour is going to follow his brother and die and that we'll be two widows in the house with the old woman. Then what will I do with myself? And the boy – maybe once they've killed his father they'll kill him. Didn't they do that to the Messiah? First they killed his father, Youssef the Carpenter – or they kidnapped him, how should I know? – and then they crucified him.

"Please stop hammering in the nails, brother!"

She saw herself get up from the bed and walk barefoot towards the *dar*.

Darkness floods the place, a pale nocturnal light creeps into the house through the window, and little Meelya walks over the shards of glass, butterflies of blood tracing themselves on the tiles.

The mirror is in its place on the wall. She wants to thank God because the dream has failed to break the mirror, but her heart sinks and she feels she's going to faint: she sees her picture hanging in a shimmer of light coming from the mirror. The picture that Moussa has hung on the wall of the *leewan* in the big house, over the bed in which she'd been born, now appears, its whiteness mixed with black. Only the wide-open eyes are free of the black spots that cover the nose, lips, chin and forehead. She can't see the long hair that covers the background like a black and brown river.

"Where's her hair?" she asks in a low voice.

Looking around her, she finds Moussa sitting on the sofa beneath which the girl had hidden. He is wearing his father's tarboush and holding a string of black prayer beads.

"Where's the rosary from, Daddy?"

Although she calls him Daddy and doesn't wait for an answer, she knows that the man sitting on the sofa and looking in the mirror is not her father but her younger brother, whose fear of the dark she used to dispel with a touch of her fingers.

"What brings you to Nazareth?" she asks.

"I've come to take the boy," he replies.

"No, he's my son. No, I won't let you do to him what your father did to you when you followed him to the Egyptian woman's house and he threw a stone at you to kill you."

Why does she get people mixed up like this? She knows he isn't her father because his olive darkness isn't the pale white that coloured Youssef's skin. But why had he come to take the boy who hadn't yet been born? And why was he hammering nails into the mirror? She hears the rhythmic strokes of the crucifixion. The Lebanese monk told her that the worst pain suffered by the Messiah in his final moments was the noise: "When they hammered the nails into his hands and feet, the noise grew louder and louder and his whole body felt as though it had been transformed into two huge ears reverberating to the sound. Everything was banging. Can you imagine the sound of blood pulsing as it escapes through the rib cage? The crucifixion, my daughter, was the sound of violent banging echoing through an entire body. Cry out before the valley and listen. Imagine that your body is the valley and that hundreds of nails are crying out inside it."

Moussa has once more become a small child over whom she has to bend, whose tears she has to wipe away with her fingers and whom she has to raise to manhood.

When she bends over, though, and reaches for him, he pushes her hand away violently and stands in front of the picture.

Looking where he is looking, she sees the image of Mansour reflected next to the image of Meelya that has been nailed onto the mirror. Instead of calling her husband by his own name, she cries, "Moussa, why did you kill her?"

Leaving her husband with the Italian doctor at the hospital that day and setting off for wherever her feet might carry her, Meelya searched the streets and alleyways for the Lebanese monk, but could find no trace of him. She sat on a low stone wall in front of the Virgin's Spring, closed her eyes and saw.

Don't ask her what she saw because she cannot say. This was the miracle for which she had been waiting since the mysterious vision-like dream that had led her to her fate in Nazareth. Had not Tanyous told her that the carpenter had lost the power of speech when he went in to his virgin wife and found that she was pregnant? He had tried to question her, but his tongue had become like a piece of wood in his mouth. Instead of expressing his anger or pain, he had entered a state resembling the stupor that had brought him the angel, which was when he heard the beginning of the story he would only understand fully when the boy told it to him beneath the olive tree.

Tanyous said that they called Youssef the Carpenter "the silent saint". True, he spoke when his son told him the story, but he lived out what remained of his life on this earth half dumb, speaking only when absolutely necessary, as though understanding that his words would not be spoken until the end, when he would go to look for the boy before being snatched upwards.

Is it true that Meelya saw the sainted nun?

Tired, doubled over with pain, she sits down and tries to speak but cannot. The Italian doctor, not knowing what to do with the woman, turns to the nurse and says something in Italian. The patient, who doesn't understand, begins the journey into the world of birth, with all its secrets.

The words vanished and the nun appeared, speaking in the voice of Tanyous and telling the woman that she must stop Mansour from taking the boy to Jaffa.

Meelya tried to say, "Please, *Hajjeh* Milaneh," and heard her mother's voice, full of fear. The woman sitting on the low wall encircling the spring had no choice but to continue with her plea. "Please, *Hajjeh*," she said seeming to hear herself using her mother's voice, "I don't want to become like my mother."

"Please, *Ma Soeur*, why does your voice sound like his? Where is Father Tanyous? He said he wanted to tell me the secret. Then he disappeared. Now you've come instead of him and I'm frightened of you. I've been frightened of you ever since I was a little girl. I don't want all this. I'm not my mother. My mother's half a nun, but I'm different. I'm just frightened for the boy. All I want God to do is leave me alone. Please leave me alone, all of you. I'll go to Jaffa. It's enough, I'm tired.

Just tell Tanyous I want to see his face before I have the baby. I want him to bless me and have done. Then it'll be over, and what will be will be. Where is Tanyous?"

"I am Tanyous."

Meelya heard Tanyous's voice coming from the nun's body. Was it all an illusion? Why had Mansour told her that he'd gone to the monastery, and why had he made up a story about the Lebanese monk? Who had told her about Youssef the Carpenter? Had it all just been just a dream?

She stood up slowly and walked towards the house, keeping her head bent so that no-one would see her. Entering the *dar*, she found her picture hung over the mirror. She wanted to ask Mansour why, and where he had got the picture, but discovered that she'd lost her voice. She walked over to her bed, laid her head on the pillow and fell into a deep sleep.

Moussa came because she had wanted him to come.

She had been alone in the house, the December darkness spreading throughout the cold room. She'd put on a blue nightdress, entered the whiteness of the sheets, closed her eyes and told Moussa to come.

She had told him that she needed him and that she wanted to tell him a story. She didn't dare to say that she'd heard the story from the Lebanese monk. She was no longer sure of anything. The monk had disappeared into Milaneh's long black robe, and she neither loved the nun nor wanted her there.

Mansour sat alone in the *dar* waiting for the first of the signs about which the doctor had told him, and Meelya lay on her side on her bed. She told Moussa that her belly had grown as large as the world. Moussa wasn't there, but she wanted him. She wanted to tell the story but couldn't find ears to listen. It was no longer important to prove that what she'd seen was real. She had felt tired and asked her little brother to come. He used to believe everything she told him, looking at her with a mixture of grief and love and drinking in her words. During those difficult moments when Najeeb had disappeared and the family had broken apart, he alone had seen the sorrow in his sister's eyes and believed every word she'd said and not said. Meelya had told no-one the story of her mysterious love. The mother had said it was the girl's fault: "Why did you let him fly away when you had him in your hand? That makes the second time, my girl. Wadee we could understand, he was a miser, but what was there to complain of in the other one? How am I supposed to find you a husband now?"

During this period Meelya had fallen sick, stricken with a strange headache that couldn't be explained, and no-one knew what to do for her. She would tie a wet handkerchief around her temples to reduce the pain. Then she'd peel raw potatoes, cut them up and bind them to her forehead with the wet handkerchief. Why had she forgotten the story of the sounds that nested in her ears and left her incapable of speech? And why had she erased from her memory that brief swoon from which God had rescued her she knew not how?

The story goes that Meelya was alone in the house when she fell. She'd been standing in the kitchen stirring the milk in a large saucepan on a paraffin stove. Moussa, the first to arrive home, found his sister lying on her back, the aroma of hot milk, coriander and boiled *kibbeh* filling the place. He had tried to revive her by sprinkling orange-blossom water on her face, but the girl appeared sunk in a deep sleep. Having carried her to the bed, he ran to call the doctor, but when he returned with Dr Naqfour he found his sister had recovered consciousness. The nun was walking around the bed in circles muttering prayers, brass censer in hand.

The doctor did nothing, contenting himself with kissing the hand of the nun, who told him that all was well. The nun bent over Meelya and whispered something in her ear. Mansour appeared two days later, and the love story that led Meelya to marriage began.

The story says that that night Meelya saw the dream that would determine her future. Had she seen the blue woman when she fell in the kitchen or in the cloud of incense? Or had the whole thing been engineered by the nun?

"It was love at first sight," Mansour would write to his mother and brother; the story about Sonya Rahhal having something to do with it was of no importance. After spending a long day in Souq el Tawileh choosing fabric for the new shop in Nazareth, Mansour had accepted a dinner invitation from his friend the merchant Sameer Rahhal. The merchant's wife, Mrs Sonya Rahhal, would talk to him at length of the advisability of marriage and suggest that he go out into the garden, where he would behold the most beautiful girl in Beirut.

That is how the story began. Meelya was standing among the branches of the flowering almond tree, her milky whiteness blending with the whiteness of the almond blossoms, and the heart of the man from Nazareth burst into flame with love: "It doesn't matter that Sonya was a friend of the nun's. It had nothing to do with the nun; I only saw her at the wedding. No, it had nothing to do with the nun. I fell in love with you at first sight, and that was that."

Meelya closed her eyes and only opened them again when she felt herself to be drowning. She turned towards Mansour, but he wasn't in bed with her.

Crying out that it was the water, she watched Mansour lift her up, help her into her clothes and take her to the hospital.

THE THIRD NIGHT

Meelya closed her eyes and saw.

Everything was white, and the doctor's voice came to her wrapped in cotton wool.

Two nurses. One holds Meelya's right hand and the other stands at the pregnant woman's feet, which are placed far apart; the first is an elderly woman, the second a young girl. Two women as alike as two drops of water.

The first is short and the second is short. The first is hunchbacked and pigeon-toed, and the second is hunchbacked and pigeon-toed.

What brings Wadeea here?

The mother and daughter are like twins. They encircle Meelya and issue orders. Even the voice comes sometimes from the right and sometimes from below. The pregnant woman listens to a sound like the sound of waves coming from the depths of her belly. It is as though the child, who has pointed his head downwards and is ready to fall into the world, were using for the last time the language of the womb, which he will forget. Meelya listens and wants to tell him not to be afraid.

The nurses' voice sounds decisive; behind it she sees a ghost enveloped in fog. It's the doctor. No, it's *Khawaja* Massabki.

What has brought him here with his two Wadeeas?

Khawaja Massabki stands by the stove rubbing his hands before the blazing fire. He narrows his eyes as though he were the groom, and the two women, the mother and the daughter, stand waiting for his sign.

She remembers that she was sleeping. She remembers that she cried out, saying it was the water; then fog enveloped her: "Mansour, I don't want to go to Chtaura, my darling. I want to go home."

Mansour carries a lit candle in his hand and walks in front of the car: "Where did you come up with that story about the candle? Yes, I got out so I could walk in front of the car, but who could carry a candle in all that wind and snow and cold? If I hadn't walked in front of the car, we would never have got to the hotel."

Meelya doesn't want to argue with the man. She has grown sick of correcting memories: "Memories can't be corrected. You remember one way and I remember another, and in the end it doesn't matter. You mean I'm supposed to remember the way you do? Thanks very much! Enough. Please tell the driver to hurry up. I'm tired."

She was sleeping, the car was swaying to the sound of the ice storm that battered Dahr el Baydar, and the driver was asking her to help him persuade the madman to let them return to Beirut.

"Why are you talking like that?"

"The groom is mad, Madame. Please help me. What a mess. I don't want to go on. Who said everyone who gets married has to go to Chtaura? Help me, please."

What is the man saying?

"O God, where am I? I want to go home. Where's Mansour?"

She knelt at the bathroom door and heard him gagging. She knocked. She begged him to open the door. She said she'd ask *Khawaja* Massabki to call a doctor.

But Mansour refused. His voice emerged from the coughing to tell her to wait for him in bed. He said it was the cheese: "Don't eat the cheese. It's gone off. Go to sleep, I'll join you. Don't be frightened."

She hadn't said she was frightened, but she was. She'd dreamt that her dream would be different. "Marriage," said Najeeb, "makes a woman like dough. I want to knead you and bake you. Come closer."

They were in the garden. The shadows of evening tangled with the blossom of the two sweet acacia trees bent over the entrance.

"I love sweet acacia blossom. Do you know why these trees are called sweet acacia? Because they're like women. They're sweet and drive men wild."

. . .

"Because they're white on the outside and yellow on the inside and have two scents, one for each colour, and when they mix they become sweet. What do you think of my explanation?"

. . .

"Come closer and I'll tell you what I think."

She pressed herself against the tree, her back against the sloping trunk, one arm raised, caressing a blossom-laden branch.

"That's what drives me wild," he said, pointing to her arm. "But I want to put my lips here."

"Don't come any closer, please. Any moment they'll see us."

"I said you're like the sweet acacia. Just one kiss."

And with a single bound, he grabbed her by the waist and pulled her to him.

"Aaakh!" she screamed.

"Scream if you like," the nurse said.

Meelya opened her eyes, saw the screen of whiteness and said the smell was suffocating her. "Why has the sweet acacia scent changed like that?" she asked.

"Close your eyes and breathe deeply. It's chloroform, to reduce the pain," said a voice coming from she knew not where.

The whiteness disappeared. Little Meelya ran through the streets of the dark, the voice that had penetrated her night breaking up, its octave a low moan that emerged from the woman's throat, then disappeared. She heard the doctor order the two nurses to step away.

"Let her rest."

Where was the sound of the bells coming from? "This is a *labaneh* bridegroom, Uncle. Take your hand away and let me eat."

Meelya knows that the story of her uncle Mitri is not to be told. The young man, an only brother between two sisters, died hung from the church bells, and no-one dared take down the body, which swung there, tied to the long bell rope, until Nakhleh came running from the house. Seeing his son's suspended body, he cried that they'd killed him and asked the young men of the quarter to help him untie the rope from the young man's neck, which had become as thin as a piece of string.

Mitri had stepped out of the large photo that hung on the white wall in Nakhleh Shalhoub's house. Meelya sees him stepping down from it, as though the photo, which was surrounded by a gilded wooden frame, has become a window. Her uncle, wearing his red tarboush and white silk *abaya* that hid his round belly and leaning on his cane, passes through the wooden frame and steps down into the *dar*. He approaches Meelya and embraces her, and the aroma of *labaneh* and onions rises. The little girl feels that the man is taking her far away. Mitri picks her up and enters the picture frame. Extending his right leg, he jumps as though crossing a river.

"Take care, girl. Be careful not to fall into the river or you'll drown."

"But it doesn't have any water, Uncle."

The roaring of the water rises to her small ears. "Why is the river green?" she asks.

"The river isn't green, your eyes are green. That's why everything looks green to you."

"Please put me down," she screams.

She calls out to her brother Moussa, but Moussa is standing on the other bank, waving to her with both hands.

"I don't want to go with him."

And the girl starts kicking the man, but it makes no difference. Mitri holds her by her waist, sits her on his big belly and walks on the water without drowning.

"See how I walk on the face of the waters? If Zureiq's boys had known who I am, they wouldn't have done what they did to me."

"What did they do?"

"They killed me," he answers. "Five youths attacked me in the church square. The bell was ringing. They all had kitchen knives. They tried to stab me with the knives, and all I could hear was the ringing of the bell. The bell started reverberating in my belly and my eyes and my hands and my feet. Then I understood what death means. Death consists of sounds. You never know what you're going to get. I got the church bell."

"How did they kill you?"

"The bell killed me. I grabbed hold of the rope and I flew. The rope got wound around my neck and I flew upward. They were standing down below like dervishes, waving their knives over their heads to frighten me, but what did I have to be afraid of? I was flying."

"So why did you die?"

"I died because I died. I hear the ringing of the bell even now. That's why I pull my tarboush down over my ears, even though Mother kept saying, 'Pull it up!' How did she know what I was hearing? And anyway she's not my mother. I used to call

271

her Mother because that's what she wanted. When my daddy married her and she came to the house, I said, 'Welcome, Aunt Malakeh!' She said, 'Don't say "Aunt". As the proverb says, "When stepchildren call their stepmother 'Aunt', the home's foundations go aslant." Call me Mother.' But how could she be my mother when she was almost the same age as me? Or not the same – perhaps ten years older – but she looked like a little girl. She married and had children and instead of getting older, she got younger. She had my sister Saada, and five years later my sister Salma came. Her belly barely got any bigger and she didn't look like she was pregnant. Slender, short and pretty. I was fifteen when my daddy got married. I asked him, 'Your wife's very young and pretty so how can you . . . her, Dad?' He looked askance at me and said, 'Get out.' He threw me out of the house. Well, he didn't really throw me out, but he let me understand I should make myself scarce. So I took off. I built a tree house in the big eucalyptus tree in the garden and slept there. When winter came, Mother Malakeh would stand beneath the tree and beg me to come down and into the house. I'd do as she said, and when my dad saw me he'd look askance at me and I'd feel like a stranger. I lived my whole life in my dad's house as a stranger, and if Malakeh hadn't taken pity on me and fed me, I'd have died of hunger. God, how pretty she was! To tell you the truth, I'd been very upset. My mother hadn't been dead two months before I started hearing the gossip. They said the man ought to marry to preserve his decency. Poor Nisma. Her name was Nisma, she was as delicate as the breeze she was named after, and she died, I don't know why. She woke up one morning and couldn't open her eyes. I heard her telling my dad she couldn't. She couldn't see and her temperature went up. She stayed like that for two days and then she died. She asked for me. They all told me my mother wanted to see me. I went and sat next to her. She took my hand

and squeezed it and I felt as though I was holding a block of ice. But I didn't move. Then I heard the women wailing and they said she was dead. I tried to pull my hand out of hers but I couldn't. It was like cold wood and I couldn't do anything. I heard the women saying, 'See how the boy loves his mother, he won't let go of her hand!' Then my dad came and told me, 'Come on now, old chap. Get up.' My dad took me by the shoulder and pulled me away, and started yelling. I don't know how, but Mother got pulled along with me.

"'Let go of her hand!' yelled my dad.

"I was crying too hard to say anything. The worst thing is when you cry through your nostrils. The tears go down your throat and collect there and the words won't come out any more.

"My dad took hold of my hand and jerked, Mother was jerked towards me, and the wailing grew louder. Suddenly my voice came out, I don't know where from. I said, 'Aakh, my hand!' and saw him trying to force the fingers open, sobbing like a child and saying, 'Forgive me, wife.' Then Malakeh came and became my mother."

"What about your hand? How did they get it out of hers?"

"The sound of the bells is still ringing in my ears. Tell them, Meelya my dear, to stop ringing them. I want to rest."

"Alright. Put me down."

"I can't put you down. If I put you down, you'll die."

"I want to die," Meelya screamed.

Mansour, standing next to the bed, heard her say, "I want to die," and rushed to get the two nurses, who were chatting in the corridor, waiting for the Italian doctor.

"Please, Meelya's dying."

The first nurse looked at her twin and smiled before turning to Mansour and telling him not to be afraid: "That's what they all say and then everything's fine."

Mansour saw the sweat covering his wife's neck, took her hand and asked her to open her eyes. The woman turned towards the source of the voice, opened her eyes a crack and gestured to Mansour to go. Her lips parted and uttered the single word *thirsty*. Mansour ran to the nurses and told them his wife was thirsty and he wanted to give her water.

"No, that's not allowed," the second nurse said. "Give the anaesthetic a little time to work so the doctor can get started."

He said he was thirsty – "Death makes you thirsty." He said the bell rope had suddenly lifted him up and that death had come like a long swoon and that he'd seen Saint Elias in his fiery chariot and been afraid of him, and that he wanted to go back to Zureiq's boys and tell them, "Drop it, lads. We've taken it. You want us to take it, we'll take it. Let's be friends again."

Nakhleh Shalhoub was alone in the church courtyard. He told his wife Malakeh that he hadn't seen anyone. "They'd all vanished," he said. On the third day after his only son was buried, he made peace with Abdallah Zureiq and his sons. Some say he collected the blood money for the murdered man, but he told his wife he got nothing.

The story goes that Mitri's death by hanging from the bell rope was the first such tragedy since Bishop Masarra had obtained a *firman* from the Sublime Porte permitting him to put bells in the church squares. Before, people had beaten wooden boards; the bells came only with the intervention of the Russian consul, who persuaded Beirut's Ottoman governor to allow the Greek Orthodox to hang bells in their churches. At the time, many protested, thinking that this Frankish habit would distract people from prayer and open the door for the transformation of church courtyards into squares where young men would hold jumping competitions using the bell ropes. It never occurred to anyone that a bell rope could become a gallows and that Mitri Shalhoub would face his Lord hanging from a rope along which the ringing of bells was carried to his ears.

The young man from Beirut's quarrel with the Zureiq boys came about for a comical reason. The joke started at the port of Beirut, where they were all working as stevedores. Nakhleh worked with his only son unloading goods at the depot belonging to *Khawaja* Jirji el Jahil, who imported broadcloth, and Abdallah Zureiq worked with his four sons at that of Mr Muhy el Deen el Daouq, who was a timber importer. The joke started with an insult. As everyone knows, Beirutis are aficionados of the insult; indeed, insults are a part of every conversation they hold. They love with insults, hate with insults, make friends and work together with insults. Thus, the insult has no meaning in and of itself; it's up to the person who hears it to deduce its meaning from the tone of the insulter's voice and the rhythm of his cursing.

The insult that cost Mitri his life was both novel and obscure. It was uttered by Samih, Abdallah Zureiq's oldest son, who was carrying a heavy plank on his back. Mitri passed him, saw that he was tired and reached over to help him, saying, "Too heavy for you?" But the Zureiq boy screamed, "Get your hand off the timber!" When Mitri insisted on helping him, an insult that nobody had ever heard before escaped Samih's lips, to wit, "Take your hand off before I push you back up your mother's cunt!" It seems the boy was greatly taken with his turn of phrase, for he repeated it more than once in a sing-song voice. This was how the problem started. Mitri fell on Samih and started beating him. Samih set down the plank and, instead of defending himself, started yelling his insult even louder. Workers gathered around to separate the two young men, but Samih wouldn't stop saying it, which maddened Mitri and made him say the following, which no-one on the dockside had ever dared to say before: "Get out of here, you son of Laure, and God protect your mother's Pharaonic cunt!"

Mitri told his father he hadn't meant anything by it, he'd just wanted to repay Samih in the same coin, and what came out was what couldn't be said. The Zureiq boys, despite their miserable circumstances and those of their father, who was known for his large, upward-curling moustaches, were called "sons of Laure" because it was Madame Laure who wore the trousers in the family and who was said, though only God knows if it were true, to be a "customer" of *Khawaja* Naji Pharaon, the port's director. It was also said that her husband knew but turned a blind eye. The reference to Pharaon, coupled with that to the "sons of Laure", turned the quarrel into a massacre, with Zureiq's five sons gathering as quickly as if they'd popped out of a hole in the ground and beating up everyone in sight. This provided Mitri with his chance to escape, leaving the field of battle to the others, who quickly discovered that he'd disappeared. The melee broke up and the youths of the quarter heard the Zureiq boys say that they were going to send Mitri back up his mother's cunt.

Mitri was terrified. Mrs Malakeh said the boy slept three nights in a row at the house, abandoning the tree house and not going to work at the port, and that his father came on the morning of the fourth day and reassured him, saying he'd talked with Abdallah Zureiq and it wasn't worth making a fuss over; everything was forgiven and forgotten. Mitri wasn't convinced. He told Malakeh he'd seen his mother in a dream and that the thin woman had clasped him to her breast, and that he'd seen the dark and was afraid.

"Did he dream of the bell that hanged him?" Meelya asked.

"No. He dreamt of his mother, and she, Lord save us, was . . . And you know what? He asked me if I could smell his mother's cologne and told me his father hadn't bought new bedclothes when he married me. He'd put one over on me and said he'd bought a new bed, but in fact he'd painted the old bed and hadn't changed the bedding. From that day on, I couldn't get to sleep. I'd get up at night and walk around the house like a ghost. Nakhleh thought I couldn't sleep any more because I was sad. A week after the boy died, I yelled at my husband, saying, 'Either you buy a new bed and bedclothes or I go back to my parents' house!'"

Saada talked of her dead brother constantly, saying her mother Malakeh had suffered greatly for him, had worn mourning for four years, and had made up her mind to do as other bereaved mothers did and wear black until her dying day. Her husband had forbidden this, saying, "What's he to you? He's not your son, he's his mother's son," and had forced her to stop wearing black.

"His mother's son" died by hanging. Sameeh Zureiq said that he'd gone with his brothers to the church square to take part in the bell-ringing, having forgotten the incident following the apology offered by Nakhleh Shalhoub on his son's behalf. But as soon as Mitri, who was holding onto the bell rope, had seen them, he'd flown up into the sky. They couldn't understand how the boy had been able to climb the rope: the higher he went, the louder sounded the bell, its ringing like nothing any of them had ever heard before. Sameeh said they'd seen the boy flying and hadn't taken in what was happening until the sound of the bell started to die away, which is when they saw Mitri hanging by his neck, flapping about like a bird with its throat cut. They'd climbed the rope to try to save him, but by the time they got to him it was too late. His neck had become thinner than the rope and his face had turned pale blue. Nakhleh wasn't convinced, but he had no choice. War with the Zureiq boys meant certain death, and a feud wouldn't restore to life the boy who'd gone back into his mother's womb, just as they'd predicted.

"You mean, when someone dies, he goes back into his mother's belly?" Meelya asked her grandmother Malakeh.

"There's no call for that kind of talk, dearie. Like I said, death is a dream. You stay where you are and you travel, and you don't come back until you see the light."

"But why did they kill him, Granny?"

"No-one killed him, dearie. Don't believe your grandfather. His old man's foolishness comes out in his crying, and in his tears he's made up the story that the Zureiq boys hung Mitri with the bell rope. The poor kid died of fright. The only thing that can cause death is fear of death. Your grandfather's old. He was twenty years older than me when I married him and you can see how he is now – now he's forty years older than me, maybe more. God grant me the patience to put up with him. I told him not to tell that story in front of the children, but when people get old, they become like children themselves and can talk only to children. Forget the story, dearie. It's not Mitri's story that matters, it's mine. I'm the one who went through hell. I don't know how I agreed to marry a widower."

Malakeh's marriage had been the big surprise. A girl aged twenty marrying a widower of over forty! Was it the man's wealth? True, the incident that had stuck in Meelya's memory had happened when Nakhleh and his only son were working as stevedores at the port of Beirut, but Nakhleh wasn't a stevedore and he didn't die poor. Those had been "the days of dearth", as he called them, when the silkworms went bad, as though they were just any old worms, and there began in Lebanon – this was the late nineteenth century – the famine that was to ravage the country during the First World War and destroy one third of its population. After that, emigration took the rest, leaving only those who had no means of escape.

Nakhleh was one of the latter. He found himself with nothing to do in life. At this point – this was around 1890 – the man decided to close the silk shop he owned on Abd el Malik Street, roll up the sleeves of his robe and go, with his son, to work. The fact is, it was Mitri who was the stevedore; his father was his manager. Things improved, however: Nakhleh said that *Khawaja* Afteemous paid off his debts and his problems were solved. But by the time he returned to work in the small shop it was too late.

It was too late because Mitri had died by hanging and what was left of Nakhleh's life was worthless because he hadn't had the courage to demand vengeance for his murdered son. From that moment on – from the moment of Mitri's death – the household was turned on its head and Malakeh took charge of everything.

Why did Meelya tell Mansour this story? Was she trying to convince him not to go to Jaffa, or to find a link between her grandfather Saleem and his Egyptian mistress and the dream about her aunt, which had changed her life? Meelya had heard the name Afteemous once before from her grandmother Malakeh. Malakeh had been talking with her daughter Saada and had said something about the moment of relief when Afteemous paid, and Saada had said, "Afteemous again! I can't seem to turn around without finding *Khawaja* Sergius in my face." The phrase had stuck in the girl's mind, and here it was again, mixed with the sound of the bell.

She wanted to say, "What's it to me?" She wanted to say that she was who she was: "I'm me. I'm not my grandmother or my grandmother's grandmother. God, how other people get mixed up with me! I don't even know who I am any more."

"That's how it is," the monk Tanyous said. "On his way to the cross, he felt he wasn't he. He felt all people had become a part of him. He tried to remember things, so he saw everything. He became the mother and the father, the master and the mistress, and the lamb, which is why he could no longer speak.

If he spoke, what was he to say? And if he said, who would understand? And if someone understood, who would believe?"

Meelya was walking up the slope to the spring when she heard these words. She felt that the sky had opened up in front of her and realized she'd gone there to protect Mitri from death – in her mind, she'd named the boy Mitri; or at least, the first name that had occurred to her was Eesa, the Arabic name for the Messiah, and she'd wanted people to address her as "Mother of Light" so that she could draw grace from Our Lady the Virgin. However, she didn't dare announce this even to her husband, so she called the boy Mitri, out of fear for him. She wanted to protect him from the bell and stop the Zureiq boys from killing him, but there was fear in her heart because his father was going to take him to Jaffa, where all that would be waiting for him would be war and death. She wasn't, as her husband thought, afraid of having the child; she was certain she could just rest her back against the trunk of a palm tree and give birth, and wouldn't need the nun Milaneh to raise her son and trace his outline on the hospital's white wall the way she had raised her into the sky of the old house in Beirut.

Mansour said his name was Ameen. The boy's name suddenly changed, and Meelya felt bereft. She'd become used to calling him by both his names: his public name, which, it had been decided after long discussion, would be Elias, to draw grace from Elias the Living, whose secret Meelya had guarded since she'd visited him at Maaret Seidnaya close to Damascus, where she'd slept in his cave and tasted the taste of eternity mixed with that of the Damascene fig honey she'd eaten; and his secret name, which was Mitri, after her sole maternal uncle, whom she'd met only in her dreams. Both names died at one go when Ameen was killed in Jaffa and it became her task, in her seventh month, to get used to a new name and a new child.

When Mansour brought her the news of the new name, she

said it was impossible: "No-one changes their son's name. It's a bad omen to change a name."

She said his name was Elias, and wept. Mansour, however, paid no attention.

What had happened, and how? Usually, Mansour would become distraught when he saw her cry. He'd plead with her not to, saying, "Whatever you like", and bending over and brushing her tears away with his fingertips. He'd calm her with poetry, which flowed from his lips like water, soothing her wounds. But Mansour had changed. He'd turned into another man, one she didn't know. She wanted to tell him that she didn't know him any more, but didn't. Or rather, she did, but regretted it.

This was the only time she'd regretted a dream. Usually, she took her dreams as they came, for dreams are like fate. She'd never discussed her dreaming before, for dreaming was her window onto her own soul and those of others. When he expressed his wonder at her way of speaking in the language of dreams, she told him that she "dreamt and lived".

"Don't believe your dreams," he told her.

"Who am I to believe if not them?"

"Believe me."

"You, of course. But dreams tell me what's happening."

"Dreams are illusions," he told her.

"And the poetry you keep chanting at me isn't?"

"Poetry is a kind of truth – the music of words and figures of speech, that's what gives meaning to things. Do you remember how I used to spend my time travelling back and forth for your sake? I used to think of a verse by Ibn Abd Rabbih and say, 'That's me.' Listen:

In one land my body, in another my soul.
How lonely the soul! How homesick too the body!"

"Poetry's a dream," she said. "The only way I can picture a poet is as someone who had a dream and wrote it down."

She told him that poetry descended on the poet like divine inspiration because it belonged to the same order as dreams, and invited him to contemplate the lives of the prophets and saints, because God speaks to His people through dreams.

"That's how He spoke to Youssef the Carpenter. He told him, 'Your wife is pregnant' while the man was asleep."

"But no-one spoke to me like that. You told me you were pregnant, and that was that."

"But I saw that I was pregnant in the dream . . ." Meelya didn't finish the sentence, fearing Mansour would think she was mad. How could she tell him about the dream of the child, and how could she tell him that she was certain that she wouldn't give birth in Nazareth, that in fact her husband would be compelled to take her to Bethlehem, as Youssef had his wife?

That night she stopped her dream in the middle. Mansour was standing in the kitchen, looking at the window. She saw him from behind and his bald patch frightened her. Mansour's hair was thick – he'd told her that the men in his family didn't suffer from baldness – but here he looked like the driver. At first she thought that the person she was seeing was the driver of the car that had taken them to Chtaura. She found herself standing on tiptoe to look at his bald patch and asking herself what had brought him there. Only then did she hear the voice, and it was the voice of Mansour. He told her that she too had changed greatly: "It's as though I don't know you. Why have you become like this, as though you'd covered your face with a veil?"

She didn't reply. Shivering, she decided to stop the dream. The disappearance of her husband's hair could mean only death. "If someone dreams that his hair has fallen out, he has to say, 'Lord save us!' because it means someone's died," her grandmother Malakeh said. "The night Mitri died, I dreamt a lock of my hair was coming out and suddenly I found I'd gone bald. I cried out, and that was the boy's death cry."

She opened her eyes and found she was uncovered, so she covered herself with the woollen blanket, told the dream to stop and went back to sleep. But again she saw the dream. She was in the same place. His bald patch was covered with white flecks of dandruff and she heard a voice saying, "It's as though I don't know you." She opened her eyes again. She knew she couldn't go back to sleep, for a dream thrice repeated comes true. She decided to get out of bed, go to the kitchen and make a cup of aniseed infusion. Ever since childhood, she'd loved aniseed. Her father, Youssef, used to make aniseed sweetened with sugar every Sunday and leave it to cool; then, at noon, when the family gathered around the table to eat *kibbeh nayyeh*, he'd pour himself a glass of arak and pour what he called "kids' arak" – small glasses of cold aniseed. They'd clink their yellow glasses with his white one, and he'd drink and they'd drink. Then the children discovered that arak tasted like aniseed and they'd started drinking arak, which is made from grape alcohol flavoured with aniseed, in memory of their father. In the early days, Meelya had tried drinking glasses of cold aniseed with her husband, but he'd refused to play the game. "You want me to drink while you watch? Never!" he'd said. He only became convinced of the benefits of aniseed after Meelya became pregnant, when the Italian doctor explained to him that alcohol was bad for the unborn child and Meelya went back to drinking "kids' arak".

That night she went into the kitchen to drink hot aniseed; only hot aniseed can revive your soul. True, she'd learnt to drink tea there, instead of coffee, but tea remained for her a medicine for runny colds and fevers.

"Who'd swop Arabic coffee for tea? But that's the way we are." Mansour explained to her that tea drinking had spread as a direct result of British colonialism and marked the beginning of the Arabs' defeat. "We gave up our coffee for their tea. Did you know that the Arabs used to call wine *qahwa*, the same word as for coffee? And when coffee arrived and became established in their lands, they called it *khamr*, the same word as for wine, become it was a spiritous liquor. But now we drink tea and we've got used to it and it's become a sort of Palestinian national drink. History is a big lie. And arak – did you know that arak is Turkish, not Arabic? You thought arak was our national drink; here in the Levant we all think that. But arak isn't Arabic. In all that poetry about *khamr*, there isn't a single mention of arak; *khamr* means 'wine', but we're so ignorant we've forgotten and talk about arak as though we'd invented it."

She didn't turn on the light when she went into the kitchen; the night was full of light. She placed the little pot on the flame and stood waiting, but the water refused to heat. Everything in the kitchen was strange – the moonlight that came through the window and wrapped the sink in its haughty silvery rays, the deafening chirruping of the cicadas, the marbled tiling of the floor, which gleamed as though itself emitting light, and the aniseed, which had taken on a bluish tinge. When she saw him, Meelya put her hands over her ears to stop the sounds. The man had appeared suddenly, out of nowhere – Mansour, standing next to the window with his back to her.

"I'm making aniseed. Shall I make you a cup?" she asked.

Then she saw the man's bald patch and felt her knees giving way.

"And you've changed too," Mansour said.

"In the name of the Cross, the High, the Mighty!" Meelya shrieked, and found herself in bed, wrapped in the quilt. Everywhere was dark.

But the sound of the bells – where were the bells coming

from? And why didn't they fetch the dead boy down from the bell rope?

Mitri picked her up and took her into his photograph, which hung on the wall. He was tall and dark-skinned, and his arms were well muscled. That was how she imagined him and that was how she saw him in the dream of the bamboo cane and the *labaneh* bridegroom, though really he wasn't like that.

Describing her son to whom she hadn't given birth, Malakeh said he was slender and white-skinned and his red tarboush tipped forwards and the cane never left his hand. Here, though, he was tall and dark-skinned, his brown *abaya* covering his white robe, and his hands were extended, the right one holding the cane while the left one grasped the little girl's waist.

"Put me down, please! I'll get you the *labaneh* bridegroom now. I don't want to go into the picture. One picture's enough for me."

She cried, "No!", opened her eyes, smelled the hospital smell and saw Mansour standing at her side, trying to take her hand.

"You're perspiring a lot," he said. "Please calm down. Everything's going to be alright." Taking a small handkerchief, he wiped away the beads of sweat that glistened on his wife's brow and hands.

Meelya smiled, and she saw him. He was drinking arak and reciting poetry, and it was the heat of July.

"Who drinks arak in this heat?" she asked.

"Listen," he said. "This is the King Errant's most beautiful verse:

You have sliced my heart in two. Half now
Lies murdered, the other in irons shackled."

"That's not beautiful," Meelya said. "I don't like to hear death talked about that way, as though it were like any other word. Death isn't like that. Words kill, and they can't be spoken like

285

that, any old how. And I don't like similes and metaphors any more. Poets imagine and then they forget, and you recite and then you go off to bed and sleep like a dead man . . ."

"No. You're forgetting something important. Before I sleep, I get hot and . . ."

"That's all you think about. I'm being serious. I was saying that you and the poet forget what you've said and go off and sleep, but I see these things in my dreams and get frightened. What is this nonsense? Imagine if that stuff were real, if people lived the way they do in novels and poems – everyone would go mad. So what's it for? No, it isn't beautiful."

"You're the beautiful one, you beauty," Mansour said. With a paper hankie he wiped away the shining drops of sweat running down from her bare armpit.

"Do you remember?" he asked.

She said she remembered so as to make him shut up and stop the endless flow of memories of the days of his Beirut passion, which she knew only through his words. She was in an odd position regarding this memory of love for which Mansour was so insistently laying the foundations. She had told him that she believed his memories "in the same way as – how can I put it? – when my mother tells stories about when I was two and keeps on telling them; it's what she likes doing most, telling the same stories over and over. And each time she tells the same story as though she were telling it for the first time, so in the end we've ended up believing them and made them our own. You're the same, my dear. You're going to make me believe everything. When I listen to you, I feel as though I'm remembering, not just listening."

She'd been sitting in the shade of the huge fig tree, the autumn sun filtering through the green leaves, scattering spots of light on her bare wrists, when suddenly Mansour had appeared. Meelya was experiencing that moment of panic that precedes marriage. During her relationship with Najeeb, she had decided that marriage would be the moment at which she would come face to face with the truth. She would leave the house of pain that her mother had created, leave behind the shadows cast by the nun and by her family, and start a new story that had nothing to do with the world of saints. Now, though, she found herself with a man about whom she knew nothing except that he loved her. Is it enough to sense the vibrations of another's love to fall in love oneself? She'd loved Mansour's love and been convinced that he valued her. Then had come the dream that decided the matter. Mansour would be her great dream and she would live her story with him as she had lived all of her earlier stories.

Appearing suddenly, Mansour stood watching her. He didn't say a word. He was looking at a drop of sweat oozing from her armpit.

"When did you come?" she asked.

. . .

"What's the matter? Why won't you reply?"

. . .

She got up to go into the house and heard him begging her to remain seated on the small cane chair she had placed under the fig tree: "Please don't get up."

"What's wrong?" she asked.

"Stay where you are. I want to see where that drop's going," and he pointed at the pearl moving slowly towards the underside of her arm.

She looked with irritation at the sweat forming in her armpit, started to wipe it away and heard him yelling at her not to do so.

She stood up, wiped the sweat off her arm and went into the house. He followed, telling her she didn't understand the meaning of love.

"What is love?" she asked.

"Love is me loving everything about you, even the pearls of your sweat."

"Don't call them pearls. Only tears can be called pearls."

She doesn't know how the rest of the conversation went, but there he stands, ready to wipe the sweat oozing from her wrist, swollen by pregnancy, and repeating a story she has forgotten, or that never happened.

She wanted (goes the story) to go into the house, but he grabbed her wrist. Slipping out of his grip, she fell into his arms, and when he bent over to kiss her wrist, he could feel her trembling: "You were like a little bird."

"Don't say 'like a little bird'. I told you, I don't like similes, because a simile isn't true. Nothing's like anything else, and that's why I don't understand you."

She remembered he'd asked her what she was thinking about and she'd replied, "Nothing," but he'd insisted so she found herself obliged to tell him something. Whenever he found her looking pensive, he'd ask her what she was thinking about. When she didn't reply he'd get angry, obliging her to tell him anything that might cross her mind so he'd stop fussing.

On that occasion, she told him about her visit to the cave of Saint Elias. There, she said, when the priest unlocked the cave's iron door and she entered to prostrate herself in the place where the prophet Elias had slept when fleeing from Jezebel and her husband King Ahab, she had found peace. There, in a cave too small to take more than one person at a time, Meelya had lain down while the nun Milaneh stood outside, burning incense and praying.

Mansour listened to the story and said he didn't understand a word: "I talk to you of love and you think about saints? It's too much."

Why had she gone to Maaret Seidnaya and descended that

infinitely long stairway ending at a cavity in the rock extending from hill to valley, like some awesome scouring made by God?

The nun had said they had to go to Seidnaya: "I made a vow to take the girl and I must take her. Come with us, Saada."

Saada, though, was sick and incapable of undertaking the long journey to Damascus, so the nun decided she would just take Meelya.

And there, on the road to Damascus, Meelya beheld Dahr el Baydar for the first time. The nun had wanted to take Meelya to the cave of Saint Elias on 19 July, the eve of the feast of that prophet who had ascended to Heaven in a fiery chariot, when people lit joyful fires, ate date paste and spent the night singing songs to this most popular of saints throughout the Syrian Lands.

Meelya was eleven, emaciated from her long fever and fearful of the prophet whom she was to visit. The nun had told her that Saint Elias had saved her life and that her future depended on the visit: "Listen well, my girl. When you get to him, you have to talk to him. Your whole life depends on this visit. Saint Elias saved you from death because he's the only saint who didn't die, and he doesn't like death. God sent him a car made of fire and took him up to Heaven. He's up there, living with them. He's the only one who's still alive."

"Isn't he frightened?" Meelya asked.

"What's there for him to be frightened of, girl?"

"The dead. You said he was living with the dead."

The nun laughed at the naïvety of this girl who couldn't grasp the meaning of things. She would have liked to explain that the prophet was living with the cherubim and seraphim, but how could she explain that those two complicated words meant the angels, or that God had kept His prophet alive for the Messiah's sake, so that the Lord would find someone there to receive him at his Second Coming?

"Don't talk like that, my girl," the nun said. "These are things

we can't understand. Faith is more important than understanding. Just go to him and put your heart in his hands."

Meelya saw fog for the first time on Dahr el Baydar. It was
a light, white cloud that spread over the hills and touched the
earth. She would tell her brother Moussa that the soul of the
prophet had been transformed into a cloud that had caressed
her as she ascended towards him. When she reached Damascus,
encountered the magic of the city's smells and listened to the
nun tell her the story of the apostle Paul, who had found
guidance there on the road, she had wanted to stay. The seven
rivers known as the Barada traversed the city from every
direction, making of it a ship floating on the scent of jasmine.
The little girl walked in the nun's shadow, went with her to
Seidnaya, entered the emptiness, and in the candle-lit chamber
saw the icons bending over one another, the saints' images
blending with the shadows of the throngs kneeling in silence
and darkness. The nun ordered her to prostrate herself, so she
did. She ordered her to kiss the ancient wooden icon of the
Virgin, so she kissed it. She ordered her to whisper the Lord's
Prayer, so she whispered it. Then the nun helped her up and
took her out into the monastery's courtyard, where she asked
her if she had seen God.

The girl didn't know what she was supposed to have seen.
Entering the low-ceilinged chamber filled with icons, she'd
believed that she'd arrived at the cave of Saint Elias, had fulfilled
her vow and could now go home. But the nun wouldn't let go
of the girl's hand and gave her to understand that the journey
had just begun.

She stood before the rocky slope that led down to the
bottom of the valley and saw God. The sky was adorned with
something like birds' feathers, and there was the endless
horizon and there was the cave. Meelya remembers how she
descended the two hundred stone steps, remembers how she

panted as she plunged, remembers that she felt dizzy, remembers how the long-bearded saint took her by the hand and asked her to sleep and not be afraid. But she doesn't remember how she climbed that same distance on her return to Beirut. According to the nun, she'd been forced to carry her because the girl had started panting and coughing, but Meelya doesn't remember.

She saw a man opening the iron door to the cave and telling Milaneh that he had only agreed to do so in her honour, because the lord bishop had given orders that none were to enter.

"Go in," the nun said.

Stepping hesitantly, the girl found herself bending over and then crawling, and she saw him. A long white beard covered his face and chest. He stood facing her, and around him was fire. Afraid of the flames, she tried to back away, but heard the nun telling her to stay where she was.

"Lie down where he used to."

Meelya turns over onto her back and sees him turn around, strike the rock with his cloak and depart. The rock splits in two and water gushes forth. The water extinguishes the flames; Meelya is in the water, a cool, gentle breeze envelops her, and the elderly man ascends, disappearing. She reaches out to grab the edge of his cloak, but it flaps in the wind and slips from her fingers.

The elderly man disappeared and the girl felt afraid. Looking at the door through which she'd entered, she saw that it was closed and that the nun wasn't there: "Why did you go to sleep inside? You were supposed to pray. Saint Elias was meant to have heard you thanking him. That's why we put you inside, in the place where he slept when he was fleeing from the king. It was there that the birds came down from Heaven and brought him food. And instead of praying, you go to sleep. Dear God!"

Meelya wanted to tell the nun that she hadn't slept. She

wanted to tell her how she'd seen the water spurt from the rock and that hundreds of birds, permeated with the smell of incense, had spread their wings to bear the old man upwards, and that she had sensed herself to be part of another world. True, she had covered her eyes, but not so that she could sleep, so that she could see. And she had seen. She had wanted to tell the Prophet of the Fire one thing. She had said that she wanted to be a boy, and she had heard him grumble with annoyance and say that all the girls wanted the same thing because they didn't know, and that if people knew, everyone would want to be a woman. He told her about the two Maryams, Magdalene and the Virgin, and said that every woman had it in her to become one or the other, and that only a woman could possess the two complete feelings, love and motherhood: "Fear not! You, Meelya, will have both."

When she asked the nun about Maryam Magdalene, Milaneh averted her face as though she hadn't heard and carried Meelya up the long stone stairway, huffing and puffing.

Mansour had asked her what she was thinking about, so she told him about her visit to the cave of Saint Elias at Maaret Seidnaya and asked him what the words she'd heard could have meant.

"Saint Elias told you you were going to be both Marys?"

"That's what I heard him say."

"God save us!" he said.

"From what?" she asked.

"From women," he replied.

"I don't understand," she said.

"Neither do I," he said.

She hadn't understood a thing, but now found herself suspended above half a bed with Mansour standing by her side.

She'd said that she'd seen the birds on the roof of the church and that the bell, the bell that carried away Mitri's long, thin neck, was surrounded by the birds of Saint Elias. She told Saada that the birds had carried Saint Elias away and that the nun was wrong. She said she'd seen them: "Look at the icon, Mother. Those aren't horses of fire, they're birds."

Where had the birds come from, to fill the place with the sound of bells?

She wanted to say she didn't like the sound of bells and didn't like birds and that she longed to hear poetry. Why had Mansour stopped reciting poetry? She wanted to tell him she'd changed her mind, that she loved similes and metaphors and that it was better for a person to listen to words than to become words.

No, it wasn't her fault. He'd told her he was tired and couldn't take it any longer. She'd wanted to understand but couldn't. It was the fault of Asma, the wife of his late brother Ameen. Or rather, it was Ameen's fault. Or, really, it was his mother's. She'd never liked Meeyla. She thought Mansour had changed because of his wife, but the opposite was true. Mansour had gone to Meelya because he had changed, but how could the mother be persuaded that it was her son's fault? The mother was blind, she couldn't see. Mansour had told Meelya that his mother was blind: "It's nothing to do with you. She doesn't want to see that I'm running away from her and Ameen." But Meelya saw; since Ameen's murder she had seen how everything had changed.

The poetry vanished, along with the story of how al Mutanabbi had died on his way home because his servant had told him, as he fled from Dabba's uncle lying in wait for him in the desert, that he shouldn't be running away when he was the one who'd said,

Horses, night, and the desert know me,
    The sword and the lance, paper and pen.

"You mean he was killed by poetry," Meelya said.

"What else could he have done?" Mansour asked.

"He was an idiot. Who believes himself? He was an idiot because he believed his own words."

"At the end, you have to believe. That's what death is: the only moment in a person's life when he speaks the truth," he replied.

She wanted to ask him why he had disappeared from her nights. She didn't, but the words escaped through her eyes. All of a sudden the poetry had disappeared and, along with it, Mansour's desire. He drank his coffee quickly and told her he was leaving the house, but stayed where he was. Then he went over to her, placed his hand on her cheek and said it was the doctor's orders.

"The doctor said I had to stop, starting in the seventh month."

"I don't understand," she said.

"Forget it. I'm off."

Tanyous had told her that the death of the infants was the sign. The wild-haired monk had been standing in the distance, beckoning to her.

"Please go away! I'm going to Jaffa with my husband, and that's that."

"What's in Jaffa?" he asked.

She turned, opened her eyes and found Mansour telling her to calm down: "Pull yourself together, my dear. The doctor said we have to wait a little. Everything will be fine."

Meelya asked him about the child.

"Not yet, my dear. We have to wait."

She understood. She said she wanted her mother. She spoke about the pain. She said that everything hurt, and she started trembling, her teeth chattering.

Mansour went to get the two nurses.

The tall one looked at the woman stretched out on the bed and said she was going to call the doctor. "It's time," she said.

The short one took Meelya's hand. Then she took a paper hankie, wiped the sweat from her forehead and told her not to be afraid.

"Outside, you!" she said to Mansour. "And you, my dear, help me and help yourself."

And the waves of pain began. She felt that her insides were bursting open, that she wanted to scream, that she was alone.

"Come to me, Mother! Look what they're doing to me!" she screamed. Everything was spinning and the dark swept over her.

He stood there, hanging his head. "I can see the boy," said Tanyous.

"No, please don't mention him!"

"I like children," he said. "I like pregnant women. Pregnancy is the yardstick of feminine beauty. Don't you believe those women's tales that say that a woman carrying a boy turns ugly and a woman carrying a girl becomes prettier. It's not true. Look at you. You're carrying a boy and you've grown more beautiful. The pretty woman grows prettier when she gets pregnant. Don't tell me the Virgin Maryam became ugly when she was carrying the Messiah! I told Sister Mary something wasn't right. It's better for men not to marry, because the Messiah died unmarried. All his women had the same name – he called them all Maryam so he wouldn't get their names wrong. He would speak with any of them as though he were speaking to all of them. God forgive me, no . . . I don't mean to imply anything, but when I saw you standing there on your own, I said to myself, 'It's Maryam, to whom God has sent me. I have to go to Jerusalem.' I thought I'd take you with me, but no, your name isn't Maryam. I have to change your name for you."

She saw him drawing closer: "I don't want to change my name. Please!"

He had told the nun that it was alright for men to remain unmarried because the Messiah, peace be upon him, had had no children. It was different for women, though. A woman who hadn't been through what Maryam had would never understand the secret of life.

Meelya wanted to ask the man, when he'd come a bit closer, about the secret of life. She wanted to tell him that she was married and that this wouldn't do and that she was pregnant, but he appeared at her side on the bed.

Why had the monk approached her? Why indeed had this man entered her nights at all? She wanted to tell him that Mansour was right, that he was a madman, and that the nuns didn't recognize him as a monk. Once, she had found herself falling asleep on a narrow bed in an old stone house on a towering hill and felt the monk drawing close to her, his drowsiness mixing with hers, his hot breath climbing her neck. She saw herself in the open air, tasted the world's saltiness, felt him and told him it wouldn't do: "The doctor said, Mansour – you said, my dear, that the doctor said." But he silenced her with his black sleeve, and she felt the waters gush.

She opened her eyes to find the bed was wet, turned towards Mansour's bed and saw him lying there borne along on his deep breathing. She wanted to get up and wake him, but then she realized that the water was still gushing and felt embarrassed. Closing her eyes to go back to sleep, she found him approaching her, resting his entire weight on her chest. She screamed at him to move or he would kill her child, and heard Mansour panting by her bed and asking what was the matter.

"The water," she said. "I'm covered in water."

"The sac has burst. We have to go to the hospital."

"No, not today," she said. "I'm going to have the baby tomorrow."

Getting her out of bed, he said he was going to fetch a car.

"Not today," she said. "I'm not going to have the baby today, and it's raining too."

"Make yourself ready. I'm going to get a car."

But Meelya was right. Though the rain kept pouring down, she knew that she would give birth to her son on the night of 24 December, and that the sign that had come to her signified the breaking of other waters.

That was what the doctor at the Italian Hospital had said. He'd sent her home and told her to wait for the water.

"But the water, Doctor. There was a lot of water."

The doctor smiled, told Mansour not to worry and warned him off sleeping with his wife during the last days of her pregnancy.

"I swear I didn't do a thing," Mansour said.

Surprised, the doctor said that his examination had revealed sexual activity the previous night: "But it may just have been a dream. Pregnant women have dreams. There's no reason to be afraid."

She'd been in bed asleep when he had approached her, kissing her brow before going to his own bed. Then he saw her sit up, light radiating from her hair and oil oozing from her neck.

"Come here," she said.

He found himself getting up and going over to her.

"Get some cotton wool," she said.

He got up, went to the wooden cupboard and got out a roll of cotton wool.

"Wipe the oil off my neck with the cotton wool and put it aside for the boy," she said.

He wiped away the oil, but it wouldn't stop pouring out.

The whole roll of cotton wool became sodden with it.

"Shall I bring a towel?" he asked.

"There's no need for a towel," she said. "But know that the oil is for the boy. Rub him down with it to protect him from sickness."

She had seen his ghost in the shadows of the house in Jaffa. Her mother-in-law had said that they'd live in the family house for ever – "It's his father's house. Who leaves his father's house?" – and explained that Asma, Ameen's wife, would remain in her room with the children, who would move from Mansour's room to their father's, that Meelya and her husband and daughter would live in Mansour's room, and that there was no need to build another house.

Meelya replied, "As God wishes." Then, regarding her mother-in-law, she said, "A boy, my dear mother-in-law. The child in my belly is a boy, not a girl."

Meelya had been certain from before her pregnancy began that the child would be a boy. It was for his sake that she'd undertaken the long journey and tried by many means to make Mansour understand that her love for him was love for the child in her belly, that in the end a woman lives only one love story, which is her love for her child, because the secret relationship that develops between the woman and her womb is unlike any other.

But she sees him. He's standing in the shade, in the dark passageway between the dining room and the kitchen in the house in Jaffa. He's standing there and Asma is clinging to him, as though they were embracing. The short, brown-skinned woman with her plump, curvaceous body is clinging to Mansour's neck as though climbing up it, and Mansour is bending over and sinking his face into hers. Meelya moves closer and coughs to signal that she is there. Mansour has to stop, but he doesn't hear her. Now she is right behind him and sees how Asma's small, wide-open eyes have changed, as though they've gone to some faraway place. She finds herself passing between them, as though she were a ghost that can penetrate doors and bodies, turning and looking at her life as she returns once more to nothingness, just as she had in the dream of Najeeb, when she saw him embracing the other woman. And she understands that the man will leave her.

"Shame on you!" she told them. "The man's only been dead a month. Aren't you ashamed of yourselves?"

They don't hear and they don't see, as though they have sunk into a sea of pleasures and secrets. Retracing her steps to Mansour, she seizes his shoulders from behind and shakes them. In the distance three boys appear, two as alike as facing mirrors, the third brown-skinned with curly hair and green eyes. The three youths approach the man embracing the woman and disappear among the four intertwined legs. Meelya runs towards the brown-skinned child, who is lying on the ground, blood running from his eyes. "Woe unto you!" she screams at Mansour. "Can't you see the boy?" Bending over, she picks up her son to flee with him. Everything turns black and she finds herself swimming in sticky water, the small brown child flapping about as though suffocating – a little fish, its dark-grey skin gleaming with water and salt, gasping for air, opening and closing its eyes as though asking for help. Meelya takes the little fish in her hands, swims through high waves, and sees Mansour swimming and carrying the fish as she stands on the rocky shore trying to cover her small breasts with her hands. She yells to her brother to come: "Don't leave him, brother. He is my son and I have named him Eesa and I am alone, brother. Hurry, before the boy suffocates." Moussa disappears, and the fish reaches Meelya. The white of the fish becomes suffused with shades of purple. It rises, then floats on the surface of the water.

Mansour approaches, picks up the dead fish and throws it

into the sea. Turning to Meelya, he orders her to go with him to the house in Jaffa.

"But our home is in Nazareth," she says.

"Our home is in Jaffa now. Take up your things and follow me."

Opening her eyes to the voice of the short nurse standing across from her, Meelya heard the second nurse, behind her, saying that it was a difficult delivery and that the doctor had to do something.

"Move away," the doctor said, and she heard a guttural voice say, "Don't be afraid, my daughter. I'm here with you."

The nun had come. *Hajjeh* Milaneh was old and blind, her body almost bursting through her black robe, and before her knelt a woman of shining whiteness wearing a long white robe, her fair hair gleaming in the candlelight. The nun is wiping the woman's head and the woman is weeping. Then, what seem to be pearls scatter from her eyes and form a carpet covering the stone-paved courtyard of the Church of Our Lady of the Fright.

Little Meelya approaches and stands behind the kneeling woman, bends over to pick up the pearls, and the shining white beads slip from her fingers.

The nun's voice is abrasive: "Meelya, my daughter, where's the boy? You should be at the hospital. What are you doing here, girl?"

"I am at the hospital. Can't you see how I'm hurting? What are you doing here, and who is that woman who is prostrating herself?"

"That woman was a sinner who prostrated herself and cleansed the Messiah's feet with ointment. She is waiting for you and your son."

"Waiting for me?"

The fair-haired woman stands up and approaches Saleem the grandfather. She takes him in her arms. The nun fades, as though her image had been obliterated by the water.

The grandfather, whom Meelya has never seen in her life, slips out of his mistress's embrace, approaches the little girl and picks her up.

The nun Milaneh stands up and opens her arms as though plunging through the air. The fair-haired woman dons a black habit; she approaches Meelya and starts hitting her. She grabs the girl's short, curly hair and the hair grows longer, its tresses scattering over the ground. The girl feels as if the woman wants to pull out all of her hair.

"Please, *Hajjeh*, I don't want to die!"

The nun stands watching, and little Meelya, rolling on the ground, hears her laughing loudly and screams, "Mother, I beg of you!"

"Open your eyes," the doctor said.

Meelya opened her eyes to find Tanyous holding her hand and leading her to the spring.

"This is the Lady's spring," he says. "Drink."

Meelya bends over and drinks. She drinks much, but her thirst is not quenched. Raising her head from her cupped hands that hold the water as it drips through her fingers, she says she's still thirsty.

"Drink as much as you like and you'll still be thirsty. Maryam came here after they crucified her son. She stood where you are standing and wept, and from her tears arose the spring. Bending over it, she drank of her tears, but her thirst was not quenched. What thirst can be quenched with tears?"

The short nurse said that the woman was weeping, that her tears had covered her face.

She told Tanyous she wasn't weeping: "Why should I weep? I'm thirsty and I'm drinking. But what thirst is this, Father?"

"It is the thirst of love. Love makes you thirsty. The woman feels thirst because she will never again quench her thirst before her son. Before the cross, the Virgin Maryam discovered thirst, and she drank and drank for the rest of her life. Her thirst was endless, because she felt regret."

"Regret for what?" Meelya asked.

"She felt regret because when Youssef the Carpenter died she'd thought the difficult days were over, that he was no longer in peril. Youssef had been living in dreams and visions. He had told her that he was like Abraham, peace be upon him, and that he was going to lay the foundation for a new people. That's what's written in the Syriac Gospel that I inherited. The truth isn't in me, it's in the book. Now I have to show you the book. Come to me tomorrow at the cave and I'll read to you."

"But I don't know Syriac," she said.

"It doesn't matter," Tanyous replied. "What matters is that the book reads itself. That's how I was able to read everything. When Youssef died, she was at peace, but the poor woman didn't know. She only knew at the end, when what was going to happen happened."

Meelya hadn't believed Mansour when he'd told her that the nuns had thrown the Lebanese monk out of the convent and the church.

"Is it likely, woman, that a monk could live among nuns, when the only men nuns see are outside the convent?"

"But he's a saint," Meelya said.

"Like the nun you told me about, the one who ruined your mother's life? She's no saint."

"She is, it's just that I don't like her. No-one's obliged to like all the saints. God has granted us the freedom to choose."

The monk stands next to the half-bed where the white woman has raised her feet, the two nurses and a grey-haired doctor arranged around her. Little Meelya stands next to the nun and asks her who the woman is and what is happening to her.

"That is you, Meelya, when you get bigger and have gone to Nazareth and have your only son in the Italian Hospital."

"But they want to take me to Jaffa. I don't want to go."

"You won't go, never fear."

"And my son will stay with me?"

"God protect your son."

She saw him. He was walking beside his father in the alley-ways of Nazareth, a boy of twelve, his eyes devoured by the vision. He was trembling with fear, listening to his father telling him the story of Abraham, peace be upon him, and his son Isaac.

Youssef the Carpenter said that God had wanted to test his servant Abraham, and when the servant obeyed, God had rescued the son from death: "And God wanted to test me too, through you. I heard a voice telling me to kill you. You weren't my son, so whose son were you? I wanted to take you to the mountain and offer you as a sacrifice to God, but then the dream came and told me that the angel had breathed into your mother a spirit from God."

On that day, Eesa of Nazareth felt that he'd had been saved from having to relive Isaac's suffering. Whenever he reached the story of Abraham and his son the sacrifice, he would feel faint; he couldn't believe the story as it appeared in the Torah. In fact, he sensed in the depths of his soul that the father had taken his son to the mountain, tied him up and then indeed slaughtered him to make a burnt offering for his god, and that the Jewish prophets had rewritten the story to save the boy from his father.

Mansour said he didn't like stories about the Messiah: "I get bored when I hear the same story. See the difference from poetry: you can repeat a line of verse till kingdom come and feel the same ecstasy each time, but you can only listen to a story two or three times and then you get bored. The stories of the Messiah bore me, but what can I do? I was born a Christian, and here I am. Honestly, when I came to live in Nazareth I never gave it a second thought, but I've had enough. No-one can live in God's own city. We're going to Jaffa, the city visited by the Prince of Poets, Ahmed Shawqi, who lived there in el Manshiya, the town's leading citizens arrayed around him, and recited poetry."

She replied that the ancient Arab poets had their stories as well as their poems, and that the stories were one of the reasons for their immortality. She said that the poetry wasn't complete without the poets' stories: "Take Imru'l Qays, for example. We'd never know from the poetry that he was a king and son of a king, and that he died for the emperor's daughter, with whom he'd fallen in love, and that they called him 'the man with the sores', and all the rest of it."

"Where do you get all these stories?"

She said she'd studied Moussa's book so that she could teach him. He'd been their only hope: he had to pass the baccalaureate so that they could eat. "Niqoula and Abdallah had married two sisters and pretended they were princes of the Abu el Lama family – those shits – so only Moussa was left. I was at his side the whole time, memorizing and studying with him, till God sent him a stroke of luck. He found a year's work at a hotel in Tiberias, then a job with Shell in Beirut."

When she'd told him that Moussa had worked in Tiberias for a year, he'd fumed with anger, saying he realized that he'd been deceived and asking why Moussa had never told him that he'd lived in Palestine.

"How should I know?" Meelya said. "All I know is that the boy changed a lot after the year he spent there. He came back and he was . . . I don't know. I couldn't talk to him. And he became furious with my brother Saleem and said he'd never speak to him again for the rest of his life."

Meelya doesn't know what happened to her brother. All she knows is that he worked as an accountant at the Shati, near the Sea of Galilee, a hotel owned by a Lebanese member of the

Salhab family, and that Sister Milaneh had come to the house after he'd returned to ask him if he'd eaten the *musht* that Christ and his disciples had fished for.

The nun spoke of the taste of a fish she'd never eaten and of the torment experienced by an eighteen-year-old away from home. Then suddenly she paused, saying she could smell the stink of sin. "Come to the convent, my son, and make your confession!" she told Moussa.

How had the nun found out about the American girl with whom Moussa had fallen in love? Moussa said the whole story was made up by the nun: "I never fell in love or anything. I'm just like any other young man, and that's all there is to it."

The story everyone believed wasn't true. Only Meelya knows that. Entrusting her with his secret, Moussa told her she had to keep it and never tell it to anyone. Listening to him tell the story of Suzanne, the daughter of the priest Yacoub Jamous, she realized how words can turn into living things, quivering with desire, consumed by passion.

When Moussa spoke to her of his love, she told him that it wasn't love but a combination of erotic passion and spiritual ardour, and recounted the story of the poet Jamil ibn Mu ammar. The poet had changed his name to make his beloved's name part of his own, calling himself Jamil Buthayna because he believed that then his love wouldn't die with him, that its echo would follow his beloved's ghost after they both were dead.

"But I'm not like that," Moussa said. "I'm not crazy like your poet. There's a kind of fire in my heart. I left Tiberias and forgot all about it – I don't even remember what the girl looked like – but since then that burning sensation has been there. It rises from my heart into my throat, and I feel like I'm going to suffocate."

He told her about the seventeen-year-old girl with the huge eyes who had come to the Shati Hotel every lunchtime to eat fried fish with her father the priest. The minister wore a red tarboush and a black collar to indicate his religious calling. He would drink chilled white wine and talk at length to his daughter, his gaze never leaving her brown eyes.

When Moussa saw her for the first time, he was enchanted. All her dresses were brown or brownish, she had a slender figure, a narrow waist, a small, finely turned nose and thin lips, and she kept turning around as though looking for someone for whom she was waiting.

The Reverend Yacoub Jamous had been guided to Christianity in America. He belonged to a Jewish family that had lived in Safad since the middle of the nineteenth century, had fallen in love with an American tourist fifteen years his senior and followed her to the city of Portland, where he'd married her in a church of the Seventh-Day Adventists. He embraced his new religion, studied theology and worked in commerce and as a missionary with his wife's brother. After his wife Dorothy died, the man returned to his country, bringing his only child Suzanne with him. There they lived on handouts sent to him by the American Adventist Missionary Society, for he had become a minister with neither flock nor church. His relatives would have nothing to do with him, and the Arabs weren't attracted to a form of Christianity that held Saturday to be holy, like the Jews. The Orthodox congregation in Tiberias that had converted to Protestantism followed the American missionaries and their Presbyterian church. The head of the latter in Tiberias was a minister of Syrian origin called Abdallah Sayigh who was known for his strong pro-Arab sympathies and his hatred of Jewish immigration. The Reverend Abdallah led a devastating campaign against the Reverend Yacoub Jamous, whom he accused of charlatanry, and he forbade members of his flock to speak with Jamous because he wasn't a Christian; in fact, Abdallah claimed, Jamous must be a

Zionist spy working to split the Palestinian Christian community.

The only member of the man's flock was his beautiful daughter, who spoke only English.

Moussa never had an opportunity to speak to Suzanne and discover that she didn't speak Arabic. He would see her every Sunday when he'd select a table that allowed him to see her. He would gaze at her brown eyes and, when her glance rose to meet his, begin a silent, secret dialogue with her. The girl's charm lay in her fugitive smile, which seemed to escape from her lips without her intending it to; calling it back, she would frown and stop eating.

Her father was different. Though repudiated by both his old and his new environments, he didn't care one bit. He would stuff his mouth with fish from the Sea of Galilee and chat away to anyone, and when people didn't respond, he'd continue his one-sided conversation with them in his strange Palestinian accent.

Moussa wasn't concerned about the man's ambiguous reputation or the accusation of espionage that clung to him. He was taken with the girl's delicacy, and his heart would start pounding as soon as he heard the whisper of her feet on the restaurant floor. He looked forward to Sunday because of her, counting the days and, when he got to Saturday night, counting the hours. He'd stay awake waiting for her and then go to sleep to make the morning come sooner, but when she arrived with her father he'd be at a loss as to how to attract her attention. He'd sit watching her, order fried *musht* with fresh thyme crostini, slowly sip a glass of arak and swim in the girl's eyes instead of eating. Time went by and Moussa found no opportunity to speak to his beloved until one day the Reverend Yacoub himself provided the solution.

Having devoured the plate of *musht* in front of him and had some carob treacle mixed with sesame paste for dessert, the minister turned to the Lebanese youth and asked him why he wasn't eating. Then, before he could hear the reply, he got up, went over to Moussa's table, took one of the fish from his plate, blessed it and ordered him to eat: "Now, my son, you can eat as much as you like. This food will never run out because Adonai, peace be upon him, blessed this sea which is called the Sea of Galilee with his holy feet. Did you know that Adonai walked here on the face of the water and didn't drown? He walked and the fish walked around him. Christ would walk on the water bending over and blessing the fish, which is why the Sea of Galilee will never become empty of fish until the end of time."

The minister talked and ate and told his daughter to sit with them at Moussa's table. The girl sat down and looked at the ceiling, as though she weren't of this world, and Moussa discovered her secret: he told his sister that the girl wasn't of this world. He said he'd met her three times after the brief encounter in the restaurant. He'd waited in front of her house for her. When she'd left the house, he'd walked behind her before moving closer and walking beside her. The girl responded to his greeting with a nod. He told her how beautiful she was and asked if she would go and live with him in Lebanon. He said he'd fallen in love with her at first sight and that he could always tell she was coming from the whisper of her feet on the floor. Raising her hand in farewell, she disappeared into the little entryway to the women's baths. Two days later, when the girl was sitting at her father's table at the Shati Hotel, Moussa plucked up the courage to approach their table, offering the minister his hand. Then he offered it to the girl, blushing as he asked her opinion of the Turkish bath. Although Suzanne didn't respond, the minister delivered a lecture on the importance of the Arabs' bathhouses in forging Andalusian culture, saying that Jews and Muslim Arabs had bathed together in

Cordova and Granada, and that water signified tolerance, which was why the essence of Christianity was baptism – something not understood by the Catholic Church, which explained why the Castilians, after occupying Andalusia, had destroyed the bathhouses and burned the books: "That's true barbarism, my son. Why don't you come and worship at our church?"

Each time Moussa met his strange beloved was like all the others, so there wasn't much to tell his sister. He followed her, he walked beside her, he talked and didn't listen to her replies, and then she would disappear into the alleyway leading to the bathhouse.

Then Suzanne disappeared.

The Reverend Yacoub started coming to the restaurant on his own and began drinking arak instead of white wine. His ringing laugh disappeared, and lines of grief traced themselves on his face. Moussa would get up and go over to the minister's table to say hello, but the minister wouldn't raise his eyes from the fried fish on his plate. He would munch the fish and drink the arak, and his eyes would pucker as though he were on the verge of tears.

Moussa didn't dare to ask after his beloved. The girl had disappeared. There was no longer any point in waiting in front of the house. Instead of Sunday being a joyous day for meeting, the sight of fried fish stirred feelings of fear and disgust within him. He stopped eating the Messiah's fish, contenting himself with sitting in the Shati Hotel's café, watching the quiet waters of the Sea of Galilee and feeling lonely.

Then the minister told him what had happened.

Coming over to Moussa's table, the minister wondered if he might sit down. He asked Moussa why he hadn't enquired after Suzanne, whom he loved. Moussa stammered and didn't know what to say. Then the minister said that the girl had gone back to America and that she hadn't been able to adapt to life in the Holy Land. She'd refused to learn Arabic and forgotten the few words of Hebrew she'd learned in America. She'd told her father that from the moment she had set foot in that land she'd been afraid. The only dreams she'd had were nightmares of death. She hated the country and wanted to return to Portland. The minister said he'd tried to convince her to stay, and that he'd talked to her of Moussa: "I told her that you loved her and that love was the gateway to life." But the girl was insistent, "and I don't know what I shall do with my life here. The Arabs regard me as a Jew and the Jews say I've betrayed the religion of my fathers. I'm going to follow my daughter back to America."

Moussa was dumbstruck when he heard the minister's proposal, which was that he should go with him to Portland: "There's plenty of work in America. You'll join our church and become one of the brothers and I'll marry you to Suzanne. What do you say?"

Moussa was at a loss. Should he say that he now realized that the girl had understood nothing of what he'd said to her and that she'd left without knowing how much he loved her? Or that he'd didn't like these new religions and that the pills of cotton wool soaked in oil that his mother had made him swallow when he was young were enough religion for him? Or that he didn't like *musht* and never had, and had only eaten it for the minister and his daughter's sake, because the only real fish was Sultan Ibraheem – a fish with the colours of coral, the sun and salt – and there was nothing to beat the fish of the proper salt sea, and that this lake that had witnessed the story of Christ had started to bore him, and that he wanted to go back to Beirut where he could sleep soundly because the dampness of the sea and the smell of salt there made that possible?

Moussa said he'd felt he'd been tricked and saw himself as a dupe whom an American girl had bewitched with the scent of whiteness that wafted from her arms. He said that he'd looked into the minister's closed eyes – the minister would close his eyes when speaking, as though to summon the devils that whispered in his ears – and felt that he'd been tricked, as though the beautiful girl who'd seduced him with the scent of the bathhouse had been nothing but an illusion.

The minister asked him why he'd tried to take his daughter's virginity.

He said the girl had been in shock after her encounter with Moussa, and that she loved him. She'd told her father that she had fallen in love with the Lebanese youth who had stood all day on the corner waiting for her, but that he'd never spoken to her. "It was as though he raped me," the girl told her father. "He came to the house. I invited him. I met him three times. He'd walk with me to the bathhouse and sit at the side of the road waiting for me, and when I came out he'd bring his face close to my hair and sniff the scent of the bathhouse, as though he were breathing me in. Then he'd leave. The third time, after he'd smelled my hair and seemed about to return to the hotel where he worked, I took his hand and dragged him to the house. He seemed frightened and almost fell over more than once, but as soon as he entered the house and saw that you weren't there, he attacked me and tried to rip my clothes off. I wanted him, so why did he do it that way? I felt I'd been wounded and wanted to cry. He hugged me and then ran off. I don't understand. I felt as though I hated him and didn't want to stay here a moment longer."

"No, I didn't," Moussa said. "She made the story up. The minister started yelling at me in the restaurant to make me look bad."

Moussa only told his sister fragments of his story. It was as though he'd lost his memory and all he could remember of the business was that he hadn't known that the girl didn't speak

Arabic. "It was her father's fault," he said. "He'd sit with me at the table along with his daughter and we'd talk in Arabic. It's true she didn't say anything, but she seemed to understand, nodding her head and laughing when her father laughed as though everything was fine. When I walked with her she'd nod as though she understood what I was saying, but she wouldn't say anything herself. I thought maybe that was the way she was, that maybe the women of those revivalists and Adventists and all those sects that have come to us from America don't talk to a man until they are married, who can say? But he was crazy. It was him she ran away from, not me.

"The Lebanese manager of the hotel, *Khawaja* Salhab, told me that he'd decided to ban the minister from the restaurant because he'd started getting drunk every Sunday and quarrelling with the customers, and 'besides, it isn't very nice, a man of religion getting drunk like that. No, I don't want him in my place. Now, just between you and me, what are American girls like?'"

Moussa said no-one had believed him. They'd all pretended to, but he'd read the jealousy in their eyes, as though he really had slept with the girl, so he'd ended up believing the story himself. He even told it to his son Iskandar, a reporter with Beirut's *al Ahrar*, when Moussa was seventy. When his son asked about Maryka's relationship with the bishop, Moussa could only tell him the story of his stay in Tiberias when he'd been eighteen. He explained that he'd embraced the American girl, who hadn't said a word, and then he'd become aware that he was running away. He said he hadn't taken a conscious decision to leave the place but had found himself running away because he wasn't ready for what was happening: "It was the last thing I expected. I found myself inside her without realizing, and I felt terrified. All I remember is my fear and feeling alone and hearing her calling for help."

"So it's true," the son said.

"I don't know. What the minister said can't have been true, or at least not that way. Later I found out how it's done. I refused to go with the boys to Tel Aviv. They said there were bars and women there. I never went even once. Later on in Beirut I learnt how to do it with a woman from Aleppo, I don't remember her name, but that's how things were in our day, the only place you could do anything was the prostitutes' quarter. That was where we learnt. But the American girl in Tiberias was a love story, and she was the one who ruined it. Maybe it had nothing to do with her. Her father was mad, and he invented the rape and all of that, but the real problem was the nun. The nun said she could smell sin on me, and my mother, God rest her soul, decided I had to go to church and confess. But I didn't have anything to confess. What was I supposed to say? The important thing is that the only one who stood by me and told my mother to leave me alone was my sister Meelya."

Moussa looked at the picture on the wall and the tears started pouring down his cheeks.

"Why are you crying, Moussa, my darling," Meelya cried.

The woman stretched out on the thing like a bed was moaning. The two nurses were standing either side of her, and the doctor was grumbling.

"This isn't going to work," the doctor said.

The first nurse said there was a problem.

The second nurse said the woman's face was turning blue.

The Italian doctor went over to the window, opened it a crack and took a deep breath. The older nurse asked what she was supposed to do, but instead of replying he turned to the second nurse and murmured that he didn't understand what was going on. The younger nurse came over and asked him what he'd said. "Nothing," he replied.

The doctor wasn't, as Mansour imagined, Italian. The

nickname "the Italian" had stuck because he'd studied in Italy, whence he'd returned with a beautiful Italian wife who had stolen the hearts of everyone in Nazareth, in which small town, stuffed with monasteries and churches, monks and nuns, Rita had come to be regarded as a paragon of loveliness. Thus Ghassan el Hilw had become known as "the Italian" by virtue of being married to his eccentric wife, who carried a white parasol in summer and winter alike and who walked through the alleys of Nazareth seeking the miracle of pregnancy. Four years she went without conceiving. In the fifth she left for her home country, never to return. The doctor, however, never acknowledged that his wife wasn't coming back. He'd speak of her as though she'd gone on a short visit to her family and would return the following week. He waited for her, or so everyone thought, as the months and the years went by, always repeating, when asked about his Italian wife, that she was making a short visit to her sick mother. The doctor ended up wandering through the town carrying his wife's white parasol, speaking a mixture of Arabic and Italian, and practising his profession as Nazareth's first gynaecologist.

The doctor bent over to speak to the younger nurse, whom Meelya called Wadeea 2, the smell of cigarettes carried on his breath. The nurse averted her face, then turned back to the doctor and raised a finger in his face, as though to tell him that he should stop smoking. Hearing the pregnant woman moan, she bent over her and heard her saying something about weeping.

"What's going on, Doctor?" she asked.

"I really don't know," he replied. "It's strange. Everything's normal. She seems to be afraid."

"Hang on, dear," the nurse said. "The worst is over. Not much more to go."

Meelya's lids parted, a tear ran from the corner of her left eye, and she told Moussa not to weep: "Don't cry, my dear. It's a dream. All you have to do is open your eyes and everything will be back the way it was, and you'll see that there's nothing to be afraid of."

But Moussa didn't open his eyes. The little boy twitched amid the bedclothes at his sister's side, dreams fluttering about his eyes. She had seen him coming in the dark, little Moussa dragging his bare feet over the tiles of the *leewan* as he made his way towards his sister's bed, his torso thrust forward, his green-striped pyjamas reeling under the silver shadows of the moonlight that stole through the shutters. Meelya made room for him next to her, extending her arm so he could rest his head on it and go back to sleep. But the boy threw himself down on his sister's bed, curled up and fell into a deep slumber. Meelya withdrew her arm. Turning over and closing her eyes, she found herself stealing into her brother's dream.

Moussa was sitting in the garden exhaling cigarette smoke and thinking about the story he couldn't see how to tell anyone. After he'd returned from Tiberias, he'd felt he no longer knew what he wanted from life. His mother, Saada, complained of being in pain, but with her daughter's marriage and departure for Nazareth she had been obliged to look after the house and family. Saleem had gone to Aleppo, taking Najeeb with him, to enjoy the hospitality of the Aleppine carpenter, who'd thus rid himself of his two daughters at one go. Niqoula and Abdallah had turned their father's carpentry shop into a workshop for making coffins, married two sisters from the Abu el Lama family, and behaved like foolish princes because they'd married into a family that had inherited the title of 'Emir' from Ottoman times but now lived in genteel poverty. He realized that, with his brothers out of the house, responsibility for the sick mother would fall to him. Moussa was convinced that the family's disintegration was due to Saleem's stupidity and his mother's malice. He'd never believed that his mother had had no hand in Saleem's manoeuvre, which, by persuading Najeeb that marriage to the two rich sisters from Aleppo was the solution to their inescapable poverty, had cost his sister hers. When Niqoula had jumped up and said that he'd kill his dog of a brother, Moussa had looked at his mother as though to accuse her. The mother had said she hadn't known, but Moussa was certain her eldest son had had her blessing when he had taken the step he had. In the end, after Moussa's marriage to Adèle Naama, whom he brought to live in the old house, his mother decided to move out and live on her own, because Adèle couldn't put up with the never-ending game of sickness and because Saada didn't want to end up like Haseeba, surrounded by hatred, fear and memory loss. Moussa rented a flat for his mother close to the convent, and there she lived with the saint – whose eyes were starting to be devoured by cataracts – for company, and began swimming in the world of blue incense, which made her feel as though she were surrounded by saints on all sides.

Saada had wanted to take Meelya's photograph with her to her new home, but Moussa had refused. Or rather, he didn't refuse but said, "Whatever you say, Mother," took the photo down from its place and gave it to Saada. Saada wrapped the photo in old newspapers while Moussa stared at the empty space on the wall and wept. His mother looked at him in surprise: "Just say you can't do without the picture. No, my dear, I don't want to make you cry. I don't want it if it's going to upset you that much." The mother unwrapped the photograph. Then she climbed onto the bed to put it back in its place.

"Get down! Get down!" Moussa cried. "Leave it on the bed."

Leaving the photo on the bed, Saada went to her new home.

Moussa didn't tell his mother that it wasn't the taking down of the photo and its wrapping in newspaper that had made him weep. He'd already promised his two daughters that the *leewan* would be theirs and was well aware that the teenagers would cover its walls with pictures of Abd el Haleem Hafez, Dalida and the other artists who had seized the imagination of a city that had so abruptly adopted modernity and its new ways. It seemed natural to him that Meelya's picture should come down, which was why, when his mother had asked for it, he'd felt relieved and given it to her. However, when he looked at the white space left by the photo, he had been afraid: he'd seen a simulacrum of his sister's image imprinted there, the almond-shaped eyes limned by shadows cast by the light shining from within them, the features transformed into small grey flakes scattered across its peeling surface.

"The picture's stuck to the wall," he'd wanted to tell his mother, but she couldn't see and didn't want to see, so why should he say?

"It's all your brother Saleem's fault," Saada said.

Moussa had wanted to explode and scream in the face of this woman who'd made a hell of his life and of his wife's with her unbearable daily rituals. But he didn't. Nor did he tell her that it was all her fault, and that if it hadn't been for her conniving with Saleem, what had happened would never have happened: the eldest son wasn't so brave that he could have taken the decision to move to Aleppo and abandon his studies at the Jesuit university without his mother's encouragement. Such was Moussa's conviction, and it never changed.

Saleem came to visit his mother ten years later. She said let bygones be bygones and invited her children to a great feast in honour of Saleem and his fat wife. Everyone wept as they embraced their elder brother, who had reverted to his father's trade instead of becoming a lawyer. All of them forgave him except Niqoula. Only Niqoula, with his red tarboush, his huge body and his bulging eyes, refused to kiss his brother.

The mother said it was the return of the prodigal son: "Slaughter the fatted calf, children, and come to the table of love!"

Saleem, though, had come to Beirut to discuss the possibility of his returning and working with his brothers Niqoula and Abdallah. He said things weren't going well in Aleppo and he wanted to come back and work in his father's shop.

"So after all these years you've come back to claim your inheritance?" Niqoula yelled. "The shame of it! You messed up our lives and messed up your sister's, and now you come asking for your share! Get out!"

Saleem didn't go. Niqoula got up and left, saying to his mother, "Since Meelya left we haven't been given anything to eat in your house that anyone could stomach."

Moussa paid no attention to the talk of the shop and religion. He was looking uncomprehendingly at this elder brother. Saleem's face had lengthened, and grey hairs had invaded his head. His lips had become thin, his eyes sunken. He had turned into a copy of his father – anyone seeing him would think Youssef had come back to life. Niqoula had put an end to the discussion by rejecting the idea that his brother return to work with them in the shop, Abdallah was embarrassed and behaving as though he couldn't grasp what was going on, and Moussa was contemplating how his eldest brother had become an identical copy of his father, when they all heard Saleem's rasping voice say, "It's all your fault, Mother. You told me, 'Go and don't worry about a thing. God will fix things for Meelya.'"

Silence reigned, as though Saleem's words, which had come out almost in a whisper, had exploded in their midst.

"You? You said that to Saleem?" Moussa said.

"Certainly not. I don't remember," the mother said.

"You? You're the one who made the girl's life hell and sent her off to a country that was going up in flames?" Moussa said.

Saada wept and the quarrel grew more heated. Abdallah cursed his mother and his elder brother and said they'd destroyed his sister's life for nothing.

Then the symptoms began. Saada's face turned red and she couldn't breathe. Abdallah ran to summon the doctor and Moussa went to his room, locked the door and decided never to speak to his mother again.

Such decisions within a family don't last long, though. Saleem returned to his home in Aleppo and they lost contact with him once more. And now here was Moussa helping his mother get ready for the move to the flat in which she would die. The photo of Meelya would continue to hang where it had done because the wall had refused to give it up.

"Come here, Moussa, my darling. Come sleep by me. Don't cry."

She sees him. Moussa tosses and turns in his bed, and the shadows of the dream hover around his eyes. He is sitting at the edge of the Sea of Galilee. Suddenly, the waves leap towards his eyes. The Sea of Galilee rises up, white foam covers the horizon, the waves grow higher, and the restaurant starts to totter beneath their implacable blows. Moussa is in a small boat tossed by waves and wind, and in the distance stands Meelya. The little girl walks on the water. She walks across the water and reaches out her arms, looking from a distance like a small bird spreading its wings to fly but flailing in the waves, rising and falling, appearing and disappearing, approaching and retreating. Little Meelya stumbles as she chokes on the waves, little white drops of water covering her. Mansour seizes the oars in both hands and tries to row towards her. The girl begins to retreat into the distance, the water swallowing her up, and Moussa's voice cannot command the waves to be still. Moussa sits on his own on the west side of the Shati Hotel's restaurant. He is alone on this wooden deck that extends like a spit into the lake, making those sitting in the restaurant feel like passengers on a sailing ship. The place is empty, silent but for the faint roar of the waves striking the wooden piles on which the restaurant stands. Moussa takes a mouthful of *musht* seasoned with salt and lemon, starts eating, feels dizzy and becomes aware that his teeth have fallen out, though he doesn't notice until they're all gone. At first, he thinks his mouth has filled with fish bones, so he bows his head over the plate and spits, but it feels as if his cheeks have stuck to one another and his mouth has become an open hole. Then he sees. Moussa gazes at the plate and sees that all his teeth have fallen out. He reaches out, picks up the teeth, starts trying to put them back in his mouth and feels pain. His mouth has turned into a mass of pain. He wants to scream. He looks for the lake so he can tell Meelya of the terrible pain, but he can't find the lake. The waves have disappeared and he finds himself in darkness. Everything is drowning in the shadows of night, and the night clings to his body. He tries to open his eyes, but he can't. They seem to be fastened shut with some kind of wax, and he smells incense. The man shakes himself, makes the sign of the cross over his forehead, rises from his bed and tiptoes, just as he did when he was little, to sleep next to his sister.

"Don't be afraid, my dearest. I'm here beside you."

She wanted to tell her brother that Father Tanyous had disappeared. Was it true that the Lebanese monk's body had been found close to the Virgin's spring? When she asked Mansour for the details, the man denied knowing anything about it.

"But it was you that told me, my dear!"

"Me?"

"Yesterday you told me that they'd found the body and didn't know what to do. The monk seemed to have been crucified. Someone had shot him in the mouth and spread his arms out on the ground, and the French nun who's in charge of the convent decided to cover the whole thing up. She wrapped the monk in a white sheet and said he was going to be buried in Lebanon and that nobody was to mention the matter."

"Me?"

"You, of course you. Why, who else do I see in this town?"

"I told you," Mansour replied. "Let's leave and go to Jaffa. We have family there. You said you wouldn't move from here until you'd had the baby, and here I am, still waiting. Don't tell me you don't see anyone. This is the way you wanted it."

"But that's not the point," she said.

She wanted to be back with Moussa so she could put his teeth back in his mouth. Meelya knew, because her grandmother Malakeh had told her, that there are two dreams that portend death: the cutting of hair and the falling out of teeth. Malakeh said all other dreams were journeys one made to distant worlds because the human soul couldn't bear to remain in the body but would leave it where it slept. When the soul returned, made light by the things it had seen, the body would rain blows down upon it, making of sleep a kind of wrestling ring for soul and body. The grandmother said a person wasn't aware of his soul when he was awake. When the angel of sleep came to him, though, and his soul floated above times and places, then and only then was he assured that he was composed of two separate things joined through the will of the Creator, great and glorious. And here was the miracle, for how could water and fire meet? Man was a meeting of two elements, namely earth and air, which had nothing in common. The body was of the earth and the soul of the air. People became aware of the sublimity of their souls only in dreams: only when they journeyed, leaving the earth to wait for them, did they understand the hidden meaning of life, while the soul practised separation from the body and discovered that it possessed its own life.

"You mean I'm two things, Granny?" Meelya asked, fearfully.

"Of course you are, dear. Didn't you dream of your Aunt Salma before she died and see how she dreamt she was flying?"

"Me?"

"That's why your aunt didn't really die. Her soul had understood there was no need for the body, but the body can't take these things in, so it keeps making problems and feeling pain until the soul feels pain too and doesn't dare to leave it any more. How Salma suffered, the poor dear! Do you remember, Meelya, how your aunt suffered?"

"I don't know," the girl said, trembling with fear. She felt as though her soul were about to leave her body and was terrified. She looked into own her eyes in the mirror of the small garden pool where she spent most of her time playing and wanted to ask her grandmother whether the eyes belonged to the body or the soul.

"The eyes are part of a person's soul," the nun said. "Look into the eyes of Mar Elias and you'll see how they flash with fire. Why did you go to sleep, my daughter? I brought you to the cave of Mar Elias so that you could see him and he you. That way, he'll remember you. I, my daughter, am going to die, and I won't be able to keep asking him to do you favours. Look into his eyes and tell him that you love him."

The eyes of the prophet who hadn't died emerged from their sockets and hung themselves on the wall enclosing the cave. Meelya saw the lights from the eyes everywhere in the round cave, which was too small to contain a human body stretched out at full length. The prophet would not have been able to stand upright in his low-ceilinged cavern; he would have had to crawl on all fours to reach the place where he laid his head. His eyes emerged from the red and blue icon that had been placed near the stone he had made his pillow and could be seen everywhere. Meelya feared his scattered eyes. She wanted to thank him for saving her from sickness and tell him not to forget her, and then she saw the eagle. How could an eagle have got through that small opening in the roof of the cave? Meelya saw it, as though her eyes had acquired the ability to see through the intersecting walls to the open space beyond, where the eagle hovered, its great wings extended, encompassing the thin clouds that covered the sky. It circled and circled, its piercing eyes searching for the opening to the cave, and then, suddenly, it folded its wings and plunged. Meelya screamed at it to spread its wings: "You'll die. Please don't die. Who will bring Mar Elias his food?" But the eagle didn't hear her; it continued its fall as though resolved on death. Then, right before the opening to the cave, it spread its wings once more, retracted its limbs and shrank into itself, eventually turning into a little bird no larger than a fist. It then entered the cave, spread its great wings again and began beating them against the walls as though it wanted to make the place wider. Meelya was sitting, unable to move, in the hollow belonging to Mar Elias and found herself being dragged by an irresistible force towards the bird's claws. The eagle seized her and flew off with her into space. Meelya is high up; there is dizziness and fear, and she sees the face of her aunt Salma looming in the distance. Salma asks her about Ibraheem Hananiya. She is weeping.

"Why are you weeping, Auntie? The dead do not, must not, weep."

Meelya didn't hear her aunt's reply. She disappeared, and the little girl found herself lying on the broad pavement in front of the Church of the Annunciation in Nazareth, her belly distended, her arms outstretched to form a cross.

And she saw the two of them. They were standing right in front of her and she couldn't make out which was which. The sainted nun was holding Tanyous's hand and they were like two old men, their faces consumed by wrinkles. She heard a voice coming from far away telling her to push.

She felt a hand shaking her shoulder hard: "Open your eyes, girl, and push. Come on, let's get it over with. The worst is behind you. Not much longer now."

Meelya opened her eyes slowly and everything was light. Brilliant sunshine flooded the place. The rain had stopped, the sun had come out, and behind that light stood the elderly Italian doctor, who told the woman lying on the bed to help him: "Everything's alright, my dear, and, God willing, we'll get through it fine, but you have to help us a little."

Meelya smiled. She felt a towel belonging to one of the nurses wipe away the cold sweat running into her eyes, and she asked for Mansour.

Mansour was next to her. They were in the lobby of the Hotel Massabki, and the photographs were everywhere. He wanted her to stand beneath the ones showing Sheikh Bishara el Khoury, Lebanon's first president after independence, and Jameel Mardam Beik, the President of Syria. He explained that this wall of photographs summarized the histories of Syria, Lebanon and Palestine.

"Strange," he said, "as though our history could find no better place to write the story of the Arabs' defeats than on this wall in a small town on the Beirut–Damascus highway."

"Please, I don't like politics. From the moment we arrived at this hotel you haven't stopped talking about King Faisal and Maysaloun and all that, and it's given me a headache."

Letting go of his hand, she looked at another part of the wall, where she found two poems side by side in separate frames.

Mansour went over to her and read:

"At Massabki's we tasted all one might desire
Of music's pleasures and the pleasures of the glass.

So handsome the place, so restful for the soul,
   Methought the drinking-master there was Abu Nuwas.

That's by the Prince of Poets. Shawqi always used to come to
the hotel and Mohammed Abd el Wahhab with him, carrying
his oud. Abd el Wahhab would collect Shawqi's words and
set them to music. And here's Khaleel Mutran, the Poet of the
Two Lands."

"But what's Christ got to do with it?" Meelya asked. "I don't
like that kind of poetry."

Mansour went over to the second frame and read:

"Petrified, Maryam searched for her son
   Eesa in that broad spot.
'Maryam,' called I to her, 'do not grieve.
   Eesa's at Massabki's, fear not.'"

"What would Christ be doing here? No, that's not poetry,
my dear."

That day, the second of their married life, Mansour realized
that he would never own this woman who had become his
wife. He had told his mother that he'd fallen in love with her
because she was a woman – a tall, full body, full thighs, a slim
waist; a woman whose whiteness seemingly derived from that
of the Daad of *The Pendant Pearl*. Her full, svelte body had been
limned in his imagination by dozens of odes that sang of love,
making of the desired woman's body twisting lines and columns
beyond numbering.

Where had the desire gone? And why did Mansour feel a
murderous loneliness? Since his brother's death he'd been
living in a maelstrom of anxiety and fear. He wasn't afraid
of Jaffa, or of the war. He'd made his decision to return to
his city because he had to. Asma, the young widow, was now

his responsibility. Once he'd even dreamt that he was husband to two women, Asma and Meelya – why not? – and he'd had felt an irresistible surge of desire. Meelya had rounded out with eight months of pregnancy. While she slept, her long hair spread over the pillow, he would sit on his own in the living room sipping a glass of tea and smoking. He saw himself between the two women, felt a throbbing in his veins and became aware of how desire had taken hold of him, as though a strong hand had grabbed his testicles and squeezed them.

He found himself undressing and slipping into the bed next to Meelya. Sliding over to her, he grasped her waist. The woman squirmed, turning away from him, her face disappearing behind her hair where it spread over the pillow. He turned to face her so that he could take her, took her breasts in his hands, and climbed her neck with his lips, but at the very instant he decided to enter her, everything dissipated. Desire vanished as though cold water had been poured over him and put out the fire. He felt as though his soul had been extinguished, and a sense of suffocation constrained him. Pulling away, he lay on his back, overcome by embarrassment. Mansour was convinced that Meelya wasn't asleep and was observing his discomfiture. From the beginning, meaning from the first night at the Massabki, he hadn't been unable to accept the idea that he was having sex with a sleeping woman, but he'd enjoyed the pretence nonetheless; it was as though Meelya had liberated him and made him king of the bed, as though she was giving him unstintingly whatever he wanted whenever he wanted it. He'd come to love the game, which set his bones afire with an unquenchable urge, and the uneasy sleep of the woman next to him became the great pleasure for whose sake he recalled the poetry. Now he didn't know what to do, or how to withdraw from the arena of failure into which he'd fallen.

He got up, hastily put on his underclothes and pyjamas, and heard her voice.

"What's the matter, my dear?"

Instead of replying, he went into the bathroom and shut the door.

Meelya got out of bed, knocked on the bathroom door and asked if he was sick. She heard his voice rasp, "It's nothing, my dear," and tell her to wait for him in bed.

"Where are you, Mother?" screamed the woman on her bed of pain in the Italian Hospital in Nazareth.

Tanyous the monk stood before her, his hands stretching towards her, as though waiting to take the child.

"I don't want to go to Jaffa. I want to take the boy and go to Beirut. Please, Father Tanyous, tell my mother to come and take me away from here. No, tell my brother Moussa to come so we can run away."

Tanyous said that the Lord, peace be upon Him, had gone to His death of His own free will. He opened the book and started reading. Meelya couldn't understand the Syriac words mouthed by the Lebanese monk, but she saw Him walking the streets of Jerusalem on the road to Golgotha, carrying a large wooden cross, surrounded by soldiers – walking as the scourge ripped His back, looking and seeing nothing but the face of Maryam Magdalene, which had taken on the features of His mother, resting His weight on the pain of His lash-scored body, looking into the distance and seeing Abraham, the Friend of God, marching behind his son Isaac, who, bent in submission, carried on his back the firewood his father had prepared for the sacrificial victim.

"Did he know what his father meant to do, or did the father hide the truth from his son?"

This was the question that Eesa of Nazareth put to his father Youssef the Carpenter when they sat together and made peace, after the father had confessed to his son that he had wanted to kill him, though now he understood that it was all God's will.

"So you were like Abraham," said Eesa. "You meant to kill me just as he was going to kill his son and offer him as a sacrifice to his god."

"A father doesn't kill his son, my son," Youssef said, grief tracing itself in his eyes. "I was confused. It was as though there were a black cloud over my eyes. It's all over now. You are my only son, and who would kill his only son?"

"And him?"

"I don't know. I don't think Abraham knew there was a ram. He heard God's command in his dream, and there was nothing he could do."

"I'm talking about Isaac."

But no, that's not how the story goes. Where had the story about the father running away come from? Father Tanyous had told the story differently. But why did she see the son standing before the fire, knife in hand? Where had the fire come from? Maryam had trembled before the Mount of the Leap in Nazareth and not seen the fire. She'd seen him at the moment when they wanted to throw him into the valley. She'd stood before the valley and started to tremble. And there, before the courtyard of the so-called Church of Our Lady of the Fright, the pregnant woman from Beirut became cloaked in darkness and trembled with the cold. Tanyous the monk asked her why she had come to the church in her nightdress, and she said she hadn't realized: "I'm asleep, Father, and dreaming. This is a dream, not the truth. What brings you into my dreams? In a moment I shall open my eyes and find myself at home, and you will disappear."

"No, don't open your eyes," Tanyous said. "I have something important to tell you."

The monk read out the story of Abraham, "the *Khaleel*, or

Friend, of the Merciful God", and his son. "Do you know why that city in southern Palestine is called 'The City of the Khaleel'? Because that is where his tomb is, and that was his real name, because he was the *khaleel* of Eesa's father, Abu Eesa."

"Who's Abu Eesa?" Meelya asked.

"It seems you're no reader, my daughter. You may be right not to know. This is something written in a book that will be written in Beirut in fifty years' time. How can you read it, if it hasn't yet been written?"

"And you as well, how can you have read something that hasn't been written yet?"

"Because I read people's eyes. You, Meelya, will also read things before they are written. You will read them at that moment when an old man stands before your bed at the Italian Hospital and says, 'Lord, now lettest Thou Thy servant depart in peace.'"

"You mean you're going to die when I have my son?"

"Not just me."

"No, I don't want my son to die," she screamed. "How can it happen like that? How can a father kill his son?"

The monk opened the book and started to read:

"Abraham tied his son with the ropes, placed him before the heap of firewood, and sat waiting, and suddenly the sky shone with light and Abraham saw three angels bearing a white ram from which came the smell of water, and they placed it on the pyre.

Then the prophet went down on his knees and his tears began to flow. He went up to his son, undid his bonds, and pushed him to one side. Isaac stood up and went up to the white ram. He put his hand on its head and heard a moaning coming from the belly of the small trembling animal. He ran and cut green plants from the meadow and approached again, the plants in his hands, to feed them to the ram. The ram rubbed its head in the plants and its tears flowed. Isaac's hands filled with tears. He turned around and saw his father approaching, the knife in his hand.

'No, Father!' cried the youth.

Abraham shoved his son side, took hold of the ram by its neck and slaughtered it, uttering halleluiahs as he did so, and the blood spurted, filling the valley, and the boy heard the sound of the blood, and it rang in his ears. The blood gushed out before him, twisting and turning, seeking a gap in the earth, and the screaming grew louder.

When Abraham slaughtered the ram, and the man and his son smelled the smell of death, a lust for blood erupted in them both. Abraham moved back and looked at the sky, asking God to get him through this test. He looked at his son and saw the youth bent over the slaughtered ram as it lay kicking in its pool of blood, trying to grasp the last pulses of life that quivered over the white wool, which was stained with the red of the sacrificial victim.

He ordered his son to pick up the ram and place it on the pyre.

The youth obeyed, picked up the ram and, as he approached the pyre, sensed the blade behind his back. The boy smelled his father, a smell blending blood and dung, and felt fear. He threw the ram down, turned around and saw the blade glinting in his father's hand, and he fled running. The father ran after his son, beseeching him to return, but the son was well aware that to do so would be to fall beneath the flensing knife.

The father tried to catch up with his son but could not. Returning to the pyre, he lit it and offered up the sacrifice. Then he sat in the open, the knife in his hand.

And the father remained seated where he was, unmoving, waiting for the coming of the true ram."

"You mean the Messiah knew that He was going to be
sacrificed?" Meelya said.

"Certainly," the monk replied.

"So why did He come back?"

"Because the story had to end."

"But I don't want the story to end," she said.

"Every story has an end," he replied.

"That's not true. No story ever ends, and I don't believe
that the father sat waiting for a thousand years for his son to
come back so that he could kill him."

Meelya said that she was tired and wanted to open her eyes.

"Don't open your eyes," the monk screamed. "There's
another story I want to tell you."

"I'm tired of you and your stories. That's not how the story
goes. The Messiah knew there was a ram. Abraham took his
son against his own will, because he couldn't refuse God's
command. He took him to the hilltop, and he was torn apart
inside, but there was nothing he could do about it. There he
tied him up, raised his eyes, and screamed and wept, and it was
then that the sheep came. Abraham saw the sheep and understood that God was testing him so that He could be sure of
his loyalty. Abraham knelt and sought God's forgiveness, and
he hugged his son and they wept together, and then they
slaughtered the sheep and went home as though nothing had
happened. The Messiah knew this story by heart. He'd read it at
least a thousand times, and that was why, when they sentenced
him to be crucified, he wasn't afraid. He knew that his father,
who had sent the sheep to save Isaac from death, couldn't
possibly abandon His own son."

"So why did He abandon him, then?" the monk asked.

"I don't know. You're asking me? You're the one with all the answers."

"Because it was as I told you. Because he was still waiting for him from those days."

"But he didn't know — no, don't say he knew. He thought there would be a sheep or he wouldn't have gone."

"I don't know," the monk said.

Meelya said she didn't want to hear the story again. Her body was wracked with pain. She tried to moan but felt as though a hand had been clamped over her mouth and nose and was stifling her. "I'm dying," she wanted to say, but she couldn't. This was death; you're dying when you can't say you're dying. "No, I don't want to die. To whom am I to leave my son? They might take him to Jaffa." She wanted to open her eyes so she could return to her bed. She told the Lebanese monk that she could open her eyes whenever she wanted and that then he'd find himself outside her world, because she'd be alone in her bed.

Her lids parted, the light ground into them, and she found herself on a bed that wasn't her bed, laid out on top of a pile of firewood, the smell of blood all around. Reaching down to her belly, she felt congealing blood, and water. "This is marriage," she said, closing her eyes again.

When she saw him, she realized that the yellow sunlight that flooded her eyes and made her close them was coming from the halo encircling his head. This was why they called him the Sun of Justice. He was the sun, and justice, going together to their death. Eesa walked towards Golgotha alone and thought of his father, and how fear of his father's story had consumed him until he was reassured that the true story was that of the sheep that comes from the direction of the sun to save the son from death. The scourges struck him everywhere and he walked with a smile of triumph on his lips. He saw his face tracing itself in the eyes of his Maryams and felt the pain of ecstasy. He walked, the sheep hovering about him. No-one saw the sheep but his mother, and when she went over to the friendly animal and reached out to take hold of its head, she felt she was grasping emptiness. She looked at her son to be sure that what she was seeing wasn't an illusion, and he turned his face from her and said, "Go, woman, mine hour is not yet come."

Blood in the streets. The city garbed itself in blood and decked itself in ruin. Where had the scent of oranges gone that once had extended the length of the white shore?

Meelya had agreed to go to Jaffa just once with Mansour. He'd told her, "Come just once and see." She said she'd been and seen and there was no need to go again. He replied that she'd gone for Ameen's funeral, and no-one sees anything at a funeral. She said she hated the city. He replied that Jaffa was the Bride of the Mediterranean: "To speak of Jaffa is to speak of horse-drawn carriages, the sea and the white shore, the Prophet Reuben and Daadaa's." He said the best grilled meat and houmous were to be found at Moallem Daadaa's restaurant on the Youth Beach in el Jbeileh. He said he'd take her to see the mosque of Hasan Bey and the Red Hill and the Rasheed quarter and would feed her slow-cooked broad beans at Fathallah's restaurant. He said and he said and she listened and wanted to tell him that she was ready to move from Nazareth but didn't want to go to Jaffa; she wanted to go to Bethlehem.

"I know," she said. "They want to take you and then take my son, and then I don't know what will happen. I smell war and death. Yesterday I dreamt . . ."

"Please, no more of your dreams!"

He said, "No more of your dreams" to force her to go with him. What had happened to the man? She had wanted to explain that death wasn't a problem, that the dead slept and dreamt, their dreams having no end, but he no longer understood anything she said. Had he understood anything before, or had he just wanted to swim with her in bed? When he used the word *swim*, he would chant the verses of Imru'l Qays and tell her how the King Errant had had sex with a woman while she was suckling her child: "One day soon I want to do the same as the poet. It must be amazing." When she didn't reply, he said that when he slept with her he felt as though he were swimming.

She went with him and smelled the smell of the oranges. Everyone, everyone in the world, loves the smell of oranges, finds the scent of bitter orange blossom intoxicating. Meelya too loved that scent like velvet, but in Jaffa she smelled blood. She told him that his city was like Tripoli, in northern Lebanon.

"Jaffa is sister to Levantine Tripoli," he replied.

She said she'd been to Tripoli once. Her big brother Saleem had taken her there. She'd been seven. She said she remembered nothing but had smelled the scent of bitter oranges.

"It's as though I was in Tripoli," she told him. "The square with the clock here is like el Tall Square there." She said she didn't like the place because she could smell a strange smell. She saw too how Tel Aviv had turned its back on the sea and opened its mouth to devour Jaffa.

She told Mansour that Jaffa would sink into the sea. They were sitting together on the shore, eating grilled meat. Mansour was drinking arak, and Meelya was looking out into the blue space that extended as far as the eye could see. She told him that the night before last she'd dreamt that the sea had swept over the city. She said that the Ajami quarter had filled with people speaking in Iraqi dialect and that boats were sailing in King Faisal Square and that everyone had thronged together into Rasheed, whose streets had filled with saltwater.

Meelya is lying full-length on the seat of a car that has come to a halt in the middle of the street, and the crowds are fighting like animals to make their way to the shore.

"Dear God, he told me he wouldn't take me to Jaffa before I gave birth. What are you doing, Mansour, on the roof of the house in el Ajami?"

The sound of exploding shells is everywhere. Asma is carrying a tiny baby and Ameen's mother is dragging two small children behind her. Waves of humanity are rushing towards the port. Everyone is pushing. They look around them without seeing. Thick dust covers everything. A group of men finds itself caught up among the women. They hurriedly take off their military uniforms and race away. Mansour is sitting on the roof of the house holding an English rifle.

"Why are they running away?" Meelya asks.

"They're Iraqi volunteers. They threw down their arms because their commander was dismissed; they said they'd only take orders from *Hajj* Murad the Yugoslav."

"I'm talking about the children," she says.

Mansour, in his long coat, bends with the gusting wind that batters the city. She sees him walking along the edge of the roof, in his hand a lit candle veiled by the fog. Meelya feels cold. The two Wadeeas are sitting in the back seat of the American car. Meelya wants to open her eyes, but the sun burns everything and she is burning and Mansour is burning. She hears the ship's horn. The Greek ship has been waiting in the port of Jaffa ready to sail. Mansour stands next to an old man. The old man says that the Jaffa–Lydda Brigade has scattered, that the remaining fighters have fled to the port.

"Where's Michel Eesa?" Mansour asks.

Round white face, black moustache covering his lower lip, clothes soaking wet, Michel Eesa stood among the shells that rained down on the city from all sides and felt that he'd lost his voice; when they ran into one another on the Greek ship, he told Mansour that he'd understood that he was no longer the commander of the Jaffa garrison when even his voice ceased

335

to obey him. He'd understood that the battle was over and that the two hundred men of the Army of Salvation had fled with the others.

Mansour is on the deck. Covering himself with his coat, he listens to the ship's final hoot before it sets off for Beirut.

Asma stands in the garden of the house in Jaffa in her black dress and screams at Mansour, "Reuben or divorce!"

"When did you marry her, Mansour?"

Mansour had never before taken anyone to the annual celebrations for the Prophet Reuben. He remembered them from his childhood, remembered the tents that were set up and the circles for the *dhikr* and the white flag on which was written, "There is no god but God and Reuben is His Prophet". He remembered the procession that would set off from the Great Mosque in the centre of the city and make its way to el Ajami. He remembered how the women would visit the celebrations on 25 April. But he didn't know who this prophet, after whom a small river to the south of Jaffa had been named, was. He didn't understand why the people of Jaffa spent an entire month in Reuben's tents, preparing for the coming of autumn.

Mansour told her that there was a war on and that he'd take her the following year, but the short, plump woman didn't understand. She wanted to make her visit to Reuben then and there.

"You mustn't cry," said the Italian doctor. "Just keep pushing and we'll be done and everything will be fine."

The ship's horn sounded. The Gargour & Fils-line ships left the port. The city was empty. The sea had taken the people. Where were the people?

There was a tall man they called "the Beiruti". Atallah the Beiruti stands before the British military commander and an officer of the Haganah and declares Jaffa an open city.

The ship blows its horn, the Jews are preparing to enter the city. The mosque of Hasan Bey is in their hands, el Ajami is in their hands, the quarters of the city lean in on one another. No sound but that of wind beating on the houses.

"Don't forget the key to the house!" Meelya cries.

Mansour throws his rifle aside, descends quickly from the roof and sets off at a run in the direction of the Greek steamer in the port. Smoke rises, the engine roars, Mansour runs waving his hands and shouting at the captain to wait. He stumbles and falls, stands up again, takes off his coat, which is getting in his way, throws it to the ground and runs.

The ship is in the middle of the sea. Mansour sits on the deck. Jaffa recedes.

"Why did you abandon the city?" a young Greek sailor asks him.

The tents are everywhere.

"What's that?" Meelya asks. "Why have you put tents up here?"

They told her that it was the season of the Prophet Reuben. They said that Jaffa put up tents on the river's south bank and that everyone in the city went there.

"Where is the Prophet Reuben?"

They said that the Prophet Reuben was sitting alone, waiting for the people. They had taken the tents and left. All that remained was the smell of blood.

Blood in the streets. Mansour stood before the ruins of his workshop, the machinery kneaded together with blood and body parts, and a savage silence shook him. "Where are you, Meelya?" Mansour yelled. "I'm dying."

"Don't weep, my dear. I'm here," muttered the woman lying on the hospital bed.

And he walked, bent over. Eesa of Nazareth stoops beneath the weight of the cross. He walks the town's narrow streets, and fatigue saps his body. This man in his thirties has never before felt such fatigue. Working in his father's shop, he would carry huge tree trunks and not feel tired. The lean young man with the green eyes, curly black hair and broad forehead would walk as though his feet weren't touching the ground, work as though he weren't working. It was as though a strange power were lodged behind his ribs, and whenever he tried to tell his father his story, Youssef wouldn't let him finish; as soon as he started to speak of his strange dream, his father would take the words away from him.

It was the same with the fishermen on the Sea of Galilee. As soon as he walked on the face of the water and commanded the storm to be still and wanted to speak, the fishermen began to talk, saying they'd understood the message.

And when he stood on the Mount of Olives and addressed them, they didn't listen. They were bewitched by the light that shone from his eyes, transforming the earth into a field of olive trees.

When he told the people to let the woman cleanse his feet with the ointment and dry them with her long black hair down to her buttocks, they bent over his feet and wouldn't let him tell them that it was love, and that a woman's outspread hair was a pillow for the whole world.

And when he told his mother he was going to Jerusalem and that she mustn't go with him, she didn't let him finish his sentence. Placing her hand on his head, she said that she was coming because she knew he was the king.

And when they passed judgement upon him and he found himself alone before his executioners and wanted to explain his story, they slapped his face with questions that were more like answers.

He smiled at the Magdalene when she asked why he didn't speak and said that he was the word. She asked him to answer her question.

"Verily, verily, I say unto you that speech is like ears of corn. Speech belongs to none for speech is naught but the echo of a word that is traced on the cross."

He felt the weight of the cross they had made him carry and was afraid. Or rather, it wasn't fear; he was taken by surprise, as though the strength that had been within him had left him, and he felt weak and depleted.

He fasted for forty days, and when he invited his disciples to dine and gave them the best wines of Palestine to drink, all he ate was one crust of bread. His soul no longer required food, and he was filled with longing for his father.

In the midst of the weakness and depletion, amid the scourges and the insults, he remembered the sheep and smiled.

"Why is there so much light? Please turn off the light."

The ache in the eyes, and pain. What is Habeesa doing here, and why has the clock stopped? The locks of white hair are strewn over the pillow; the elderly woman tries to raise her head and cannot. Little Meelya stands beside her grandmother. Her grandmother says that the clocks in the house have stopped. She tries to raise her hand from the pillow, but the hand falls back before it has risen. Meelya is at her side, not knowing what to do.

The girl runs through the house. The house becomes like a circle, the girl runs around and around, and all the clocks stop at 3.00 in the morning.

"Wind the clock, Moussa my dear."

Moussa comes quickly, his clothes covered in mud, his chapped knees bleeding.

"Why the blood, my darling? I told you that dreams of blood aren't nice. Why do you let me dream of you covered in blood? I came all the way from here to Beirut. Yes, I made the journey despite the fix I'm in. I told my son to wait in my belly. I told him, what did it matter, it was just a few hours – I have to go to Beirut, Uncle Moussa is having an ugly dream, I have to go to him. And I came to you and now here you are covered in blood. Enough blood. 'Save us from the blood, O God!' Isn't that what the nun always used to pray? She would stand us in front of the icon of the Virgin with her Son in her arms and cry out, 'Save us from the blood, O God, O Lord of My Salvation, that my mouth may glorify Your justice!' She would tell us to say it after her and we would say it. Where is *Hajjeh* Milaneh? Why is she sitting there on her own, and why does no-one answer her? She said that she saw everything as blackness and, in the midst of the blackness, incense. She said that she could no longer see people's bodies and lived with their souls instead. Why is the nun alone? Why can't she get up from the bed, and where does that smell come from? How can we leave the saint in that condition? No-one is taking care of her, no-one is keeping her clean. Where are you Saada, my mother?"

Saada stands next to the iron bed in a darkened room. When she turns on the light, the saint orders her to turn it off. "It hurts my eyes and stops me from seeing," she says. Saada doesn't turn off the light, saying that she has come to this distant convent in order to bathe the nun, and she can't do so without light. The steam rises from the copper of hot water, and the nun screams that she doesn't want to be bathed. "You've come to kill me like you killed your daughter," Milaneh screams. "Get out! Turn off the light and get out!"

"But *Hajjeh*, I've come to give you a bath. Why have they left you like this? Why don't you perform a miracle and rise? What's this smell? Come on, let me take off your clothes. I'll give you a bath, rub you down with cologne. Just wait and see how good you'll feel."

Saada approached the nun to help her take off her clothes. Covering her eyes, the nun started to moan. Then suddenly she sat up in bed and screamed that she could smell the Devil: "You've been sent by the Devil, Saada. Why did the smell of incense disappear the moment you arrived? Where's the incense? Incense flees from light, and you turned on the light. What do you want with me? I know you've come to kill me. You killed your daughter. I saw her. I saw her, poor thing. I saw how her body had turned green as if grass was growing on it. Holy Holy Holy. She was sleeping and dreaming, the doctor yelled at her and told her to open her eyes, she tried to open them, but the light . . . She asked them to turn off the light, but nobody heard her, and her body started to shake like mine is shaking now. She saw everything. She saw you, Saada, and she saw the Devil sitting on your right shoulder. Get out! I don't want to die!"

Meelya tried to open her eyes, and then she saw him. He was sitting beneath the picture of her in the *leewan* gazing at the half-obliterated face and filling in the spaces between the lines in a small hand – a brown-skinnned boy with short, curly hair, sitting in the orange sunlight that filtered through the shutters, holding a pen and writing. She wanted to ask him who he was and why he was sitting beneath her photo. She went over to him. She was wearing the long brown dress and looking up at the high brass bed. The little girl looks at this boy who isn't more than fourteen as he approaches the photo hung on the wall and scrutinizes the black-framed quotation below it. The quotation, written in *nashkh* script, consists of two parallel lines between which is a space that the boy is trying to fill in with his pen: *The maiden is not dead, but sleepeth*. The maiden in the picture closes her eyes, and the boy sitting beneath it hears his father's voice calling him to lunch. Moussa comes into the room, his head overflowing with white hairs, his eyes overhung by thick white brows. Moussa sits beside the boy, who looks like him, raises a finger towards the quotation beneath the picture, and reads in a low voice. Meelya approaches. She tries to make out the words but cannot. She tries to read the story the boy is writing between the two parallel lines of curving *nashkh* but cannot. She decides to open her eyes so that she may leave this dream and return to the bed at the Italian Hospital where her son is waiting for her. She reaches down and her hand collides with another, dripping with water, an unknown hand that grips Meelya's and lifts it, while a voice resembling the nurse's says something she cannot hear.

She sees the sheep, a sheep rising from the sun, a little sheep that approaches her, clambers onto her chest and puts out its tongue. The little sheep stands on top of her as though hugging her to itself. She sees tears in its half-closed eyes. She tries to push it a little, and it opens its eyes. Why are they screaming? Tanyous is standing in the orange light that bathes the place. Wearing a muddy black *abaya*, he approaches the bed, raises his hands as though in prayer and opens his mouth, and something resembling incense emerges from it: "Lord, now lettest thou thy servant depart in peace, according to thy word: For mine eyes have seen thy salvation, Which thou hast prepared before the face of all people; A light to lighten the Gentiles, and the glory of thy people."

The orange light fades to nothing, and white covers the place. Tanyous blends with the white, retreats and then disappears.

Meelya screams that she knows the story now.

There, where they hung him on the cross and gave him vinegar to drink, where they pierced him with a lance, where his mother and his Maryams stood, the fog covering their faces – there he looked up in expectation of the sheep, but the sheep didn't come. His eyes searched for his father, but his father didn't come. He closed his eyes so that he could remember, but his memory failed him and he saw only white.

Moussa removes the photograph of Meelya from the wall, wraps it in white paper and puts it in a drawer. On the wall, black dots trace an image formed by the spaces among the flecks of dust. The boy with green eyes and short curly hair takes a brush and paints the wall white.

Everything is drawn in white, white upon white. Meelya squirms on her bed, thirst assaults her, she reaches for the water and finds no water. Lifting her head to rest it against the wall behind her, she finds no wall. The little sheep crawls over her chest, she closes her eyes and sees little Meelya bending over Meelya the white maiden stretched out on the hospital bed moaning with pain. Little Meelya bends over the pregnant woman and kisses her cold forehead, takes her hand and whispers to her to come with her.

"Push!" the doctor screams.

"Keep pushing!" the first nurse screams.

"Push harder!" the second nurse screams.

Meelya raises her hand to push aside the little sheep and hears a sort of ululation. Sounds of weeping, and the word *congratulations*. Doors opening and doors slamming. Where is the air? She wants to tell them to open the window. She tells little Meelya to help her wake from this long dream.

She hears their voices. What is Mansour doing here; why is he calling to her in a husky voice? Where has little Meelya disappeared to, and why when she tries to open her eyes can she not see?

I must wake from this dream.

"Enough," she whispered.

She tried to open her eyes.

The little sheep is on her chest, and the picture has turned black.

She tried to open her eyes.

She tried harder.

The little sheep is on her chest, and the sound of a child crying comes to her from a distance.

She tried to open her eyes, but the dream does not stop.

She tried to open her eyes, could not and knew that she had died.